THE CURSE OF SAINTS

THE CURSE OF SAINTS

KATE DRAMIS

Cover design by Amanda Hudson/Faceout Studio
Cover images by Nallapol Sritongcom / EyeEm/Getty Images,
yingzphakatorn/Shutterstock, Marti Bug Catcher/Shutterstock
Map illustration © Sally Taylor represented by Artist Partners Ltd.

Published by Sourcebooks Casablanca, an imprint of Sourcebooks
P.O. Box 4410, Naperville, Illinois 60567-4410
(630) 961-3900
sourcebooks.com

Originally published in 2023 in the United Kingdom by
Michael Joseph, an imprint of Penguin UK.

Cataloging-in-Publication Data is on file with the Library of Congress.

Printed and bound in Canada.
MBP 10 9 8 7 6 5 4 3 2 1

For Cassie and Mollie, who have read
every version of this story to ever exist.
I love you both to the moon and back.

The Realm
ETYERIUM
DUNMEADEN
LORAINE RIVER
TALA
MILSAIO
TRAHIR
MIDLANDS
N
W
E
S
RINNIA
ANATH SEA
KAKOS
CHAMEN

Excerpt from the Conoscenza, Book of Exousia 23: 14–23

But after the War the gods were merciful. Rather than banishing the Visya—those blessed with kernels of raw, godlike power—they bound the affinities, so that no Visya may grow powerful enough to challenge the Nine Divine again. Thus was the creation of the three orders:

The Order of the Corpsoma: Physical Affinities

Zeluus: Strength Affinity
Anima: Life and Death Affinity

The Order of the Dultra: Elemental Affinities

Incend: Fire Affinity
Caeli: Air Affinity
Terra: Earth Affinity
Auqin: Water Affinity

The Order of the Espri: Mind, Emotion, and Sensation Affinities

Sensainos: Sensation and Emotion Affinity
Persi: Persuasion Affinity
Saj: Knowledge Affinity

Let us never forget the grace of the gods or Saint Evie, who selflessly sacrificed her life for the salvation of the realm.

We cherish the balance the Divine have commanded.

We rebuke darkness in accordance with the wrath of the gods.

We honor the sacrifice that kept life in our realm so that we may one day find true life in the Beyond.

PART ONE

Predators and Prey

1

BETWEEN THE BLOOD ON HER HANDS AND THE BEER ON HER cloak, it was shaping up to be a horrible evening.

"Bitch," the man snarled as he clutched his nose. The blood seeping between his fingers added to the steady drip of beer that flowed off the bar, left there by his shattered mug.

Aya merely dragged her palms down the leather of her pants, a frown creasing her brow as she took in the stains of red on her hands.

Tova would never let her hear the end of this. Her friend was always commenting on Aya's ability to come back to the Quarter covered in someone else's bodily fluids and smelling like she'd bathed in a pig's trough. But she was never truly surprised. Aya, as the Queen's Third, had certainly seen her fair share of blood. The Queen's Eyes, they called her. Gianna's spymaster.

"Touch me again, and I'll break something you hold far more dear," Aya crooned to the man. She was no stranger to the mess of the Squal, having tracked the men there three times in the last two weeks alone. But the drunk, handsy patron had snapped the ever-shortening leash she kept on her temper.

No one had even batted an eye when she struck him. The Squal attracted the worst of Dunmeaden and its visitors—gamblers and brawlers and thieves. Apparently, Aya fit right in.

The man stormed off, still swearing, and Aya shot the barkeep a coy smile. He'd been eyeing her all night—*every* night she'd been here, actually. He ambled over now, his broad frame gobbling up what little light flickered behind the bar.

"Nice form," he said with a smirk. He rubbed a hand over his hairless head, his biceps rippling with the movement. All Zeluus—those blessed with superior strength—were practically walking giants. This one had the ego to match. "I'll have to charge you for the glass, though."

Aya unfastened her cloak and tossed it onto the stool next to her as she leaned a hip against the bar. "Perhaps I could find another way to make it up to you."

His eyes lit at the suggestion, his thick forearms bracing on the counter. "I know how to throw a punch too, you know. Have I told you about the time I took on two Anima with my bare hands?" She'd heard the story twice. He loved to brag about his days as a ring fighter. The first time he'd shared it, Aya had hardly been able to keep from rolling her eyes. While the Anima used their life and death affinity to serve mostly as healers, they could be lethal. A simple touch of their hand, and one's pulse could be lowered in seconds. Even a Zeluus like the keep couldn't stand against them.

She was fairly certain Anima were banned from ring fights, anyway.

Aya leaned in closer, willing her face into rapt interest as he launched into the tale again. She smiled blandly and twirled her dark brown hair around her finger as the keep droned on, his arms gesturing wildly.

Carefully, she let her affinity flow from her.

No shield. Excellent.

"How *did* a strong fighter like you end up in a place like this anyway?" she asked as she took a sip of her beer. His gaze followed the path of her tongue as she licked the foam from her lips.

He shrugged. "It's not all bad. I'm management, you know."

Aya forced her eyes wide. "Are you *really*? So is that your office you keep sneaking back to then?" She nodded toward the guarded back hall to the left of the bar. She knew full well a shithole like this didn't have an office. But she let her hand dance across the sliver of space between them, her fingers tracing the Corpsoma tattoo on his wrist—a circle with a line through the middle. "Perhaps we could go there. Seems more…private."

The keep shook his head. "Not my office." He paused and looked around. "I really shouldn't say, but…"

She pushed her affinity harder, and the man continued, oblivious to how she persuaded the information from his mind and mouth.

"Two men have been making visits here for weeks. From Trahir, I reckon, given their accents. They don't bother to filter their talk around me. But I listen." He glanced around them again before leaning in closer, his voice dropping to a whisper. "They're buying weapons outside the Council. I'm thinking I can get a cut of it in exchange for not turning them in."

"Really," Aya breathed. As the primary weapons provider for the realm, the Tala Merchant Council had always been mindful of regulating their weapons trade and how much they sold to the other kingdoms.

Apparently, Trahir had had enough.

The keep grinned. "Dealing under the table is no joke. I have leverage." He dragged his eyes down her body, his stare lingering at the deep neckline of her black sweater. "Maybe I'll buy some of your time. You're too pretty to be working the Squal."

Aya kept a coy smile fixed on her face as he reached forward and cupped her chin, his thumb stroking her jaw.

Disgusting. And disgustingly easy.

Persis couldn't manipulate. They could only persuade someone to do whatever they were willing to do. But that willingness didn't have to be strong—especially for a Persi like Aya.

She leaned closer, enough for her breath to brush across his lips. "You can't afford me."

Her hand snatched her mug and cracked it against his head, the glass shattering as the keep dropped like a stone.

Aya whirled and rammed her shoulder into the patron next to her, sending him stumbling face-first into the woman he'd been well on his way to charming. The woman gasped and grabbed a fistful of his white hair as she threw him into the burly gentleman playing billiards behind her, and then…

Pandemonium.

Aya snatched one of the abandoned drinks on the counter and downed it in a single gulp before aiming for the back hall. She had to move quickly. The keep's information had been useful in confirming what she'd long suspected: the queen was right. Trahir was stocking up on weapons—perhaps even preparing for war.

And with the chaos in the bar, she only had moments before the tradesmen slipped away.

Aya felt that cool, calm feeling rise in her—the one that found her when the next step of a mission was clear. She let it spread until everything was muted, until her very veins were ice as she slipped through the brawling patrons, her small form easily dodging blows. She ducked under a chair aimed for her head, her steps never faltering.

Fifteen paces toward the back hall.

Ten.

Five.

The guards finally noticed her amidst the fighting. They made to raise their swords, their warnings primed on their lips. But they weren't fast enough for the Queen's Eyes. Her knife was already free from where it was strapped at her thigh.

"The Dyminara sends its regards."

She lunged for the first guard, her knife sliding under his sword arm and into his chest. He was dead before he hit the ground. Aya whirled, her blade slashing across the other guard's throat. Blood splattered across her face, but she didn't stop. She leapt over their fallen bodies and dashed to the door on the left, her shoulder ramming it open.

The room was cramped and dark. The small wooden table and chairs had been upturned in a rush to the exit, which sat open to the side alley. Aya pushed through crates and boxes as she raced out the door, her boots sliding when she hit the icy cobblestones. The two men were halfway down the street already, heading away from the docks.

As if the backstreets were safer.

Fools.

These streets were a maze, filled with twists and dead ends. She fixed her eyes on the billowing brown coat of the closest tradesman as she adjusted her grip on her knife, her arm drawing back, her inhale deep and steady. The blade flew from her hand and embedded in the man's shoulder with a soft thud. He fell with a scream.

His companion glanced back, his feet catching beneath him as he took in the blood on her face.

Aya sent a knife sailing toward his head, close enough to graze his ear.

"The next one goes in your skull," she called after him. "I only need one of you alive." He drew to a stop, his hands rising slowly in surrender as he lowered to his knees. "Wise choice."

Aya strolled toward the tradesman on the ground, his shouts of pain echoing off the brick buildings that lined the street. "Quiet," she ordered as she hauled him off the ground. "Like I said, I only need one of you."

The man whimpered, but he pressed his lips together, his

body trembling in her grip. Aya glanced toward the docks. No sign of Ronan, the Royal Guard who had been assigned to the alley.

The supplier was missing, too.

"There's supposed to be three of you," she said lightly, glancing between the tradesmen. "Where's your supplier?"

The man on the ground shook his head. "There's no one else."

Aya sighed as she drew a rope from where she'd fastened it to her side. She dragged the tradesman she'd stabbed forward as she approached his companion, letting go only when she crouched to tie the man's hands together. He wasn't going anywhere—not with that knife sticking out of his shoulder.

"Lie to me all you want," she breathed. "But I'll warn you…the Enforcer doesn't take kindly to it."

The man's throat bobbed as he swallowed. Oh yes, the Queen's Second had a reputation that far preceded him; even the foreign councillors knew he wasn't to be trifled with.

Aya stood, her joints stiff and aching in the cold. She pulled out another piece of rope and knotted it around the second man's wrists as she glanced toward the docks again. Still no Ronan. Perhaps he had pursued the supplier.

She pushed against the unease that fluttered in her gut and instead reached for her power.

"I take it you two want to live?" she asked, her head cocked as she studied the men. They glanced at each other warily before giving her a small nod. She let her affinity flow, let it wrap around that will to survive.

"Then start walking."

2

Twenty godsdamn minutes. That's how long it took to get the trembling tradesmen to the abandoned warehouse on the outskirts of the Rouline, the entertainment district that lined Dunmeaden's port. Aya had hoped to see Ronan there with the supplier, but all she found was Liam, another Persi in the Dyminara, waiting inside as planned.

"No Ronan?" he muttered as they shut the heavy wooden door behind them, leaving the tradesmen bound to two chairs inside.

"No," Aya said, her voice curt. She rubbed her hands together, longing for the gloves she hadn't been able to find in her room.

On my oath, if this godsdamn night doesn't end soon…

"I thought he pursued the supplier, but if he still isn't here…"

Liam sighed, the bright light of the moon casting shadows on his dark brown skin and black hair, cut into a high-top fade. He dragged a hand over his square jaw and grimaced against the cold. "It wouldn't be the first time a Royal Guard botched a job," he said darkly.

The queen insisted the Dyminara work with the Guard,

who were tasked with her daily protection and the policing of the city. But substantial threats fell to the Dyminara alone, the queen's elite Visya force of warriors, scholars, and spies blessed with kernels of godlike power from the Nine Divine. There was no one better suited to the task. The stark divide between the Guard and the Dyminara caused a good deal of tension. Though even the Guard wouldn't be foolish enough to act on it. The Dyminara were lethal.

Distantly, the bells from the town's center chimed once. An hour after midnight. Aya straightened from where she'd leaned against the door. "They claim there wasn't anyone with them, that there was no supplier there. Press them on it until he gets here," she instructed, jerking her head toward the warehouse. Liam would begin the questioning, using his persuasion affinity to garner what information he could until the Enforcer arrived to see the hard work through. If anyone could break a source, it was the Queen's Second.

"May Saudra guide me," Liam muttered, half in parting, half in prayer to their patron goddess. Aya nodded her agreement.

They could certainly use the help.

The wind howled as Aya started down the dirt path that would lead her into town, her head bent against the cold. When the Ventaleh wind unleashed its wrath upon the Mala mountain range, its bite was cold enough to freeze the very granite itself. Legend said the Ventaleh was a warning from the gods: though the Visya still held kernels of power, the Divine held the ability to cleanse the world. They'd nearly done it before, and they would do it again should the Visya forget their place.

But the only warning ringing in Aya's mind was of frostbite. There was a reason the Council was hell-bent on keeping their sheep farmers happy. If one wanted to thrive in Dunmeaden, all one needed were wool and weapons, their merchants often crowed. And while her sweater had been effective in enticing the barkeep, it did little against the freezing temperature.

She should've grabbed her cloak.

Aya hurried through the heart of the Rouline, her pace quickening as she grew closer to the cobblestone path that marked the end of the entertainment district and the beginning of the Merchant Borough. The further away she could get from the docks of the river, the better. The Loraine, which flowed from the mountains through the heart of the city and out to the Anath Sea, carried the wind down from the Malas, making the cold unforgivable.

Aya finally reached the Merchant Borough, the high-pitched keening of the wind the only sound aside from the creak of the hanging wooden signs above the shops and restaurants. She ducked into a side street next to Eden, the finest dining establishment in the city. Light flickered in its stained-glass windows, splashing low flashes of color across the blacks and grays and browns of the alleyway. If she closed her eyes and settled her breath, she could pretend to feel the warmth of the main hearth leaking into the street.

Every so often, bursts of laughter and music filled the street as the mahogany door swung open and revelers stumbled into the main thoroughfare. Not one so much as glanced in her direction. She doubted anyone noticed she was there at all. Aya knew how to melt into shadows. Invisibility had long suited her.

Just as the bells in the main square chimed two hours after midnight, a large boisterous group spilled out of the restaurant, shouting promises of lasting partnership and peace for all their days.

Aya rolled her eyes, knowing they'd be back to arguing with each other tomorrow over tariffs and trade routes and whatever else would keep more money in their pockets than they deserved.

Assholes. All of them.

The group bid their good nights, the bulk of them heading back to their estates and the gilded hotels at the edge of the borough. A few made their way toward the Rouline, likely to continue their evening of debauchery. And then just one remained: a young man who set off at a leisurely pace toward the heart of the city.

Aya kept to the shadows as she followed him, staying several paces behind to ensure no one else was tracking them. He was tall, his heavy wool jacket unable to hide his firm build. His hair was tousled from the wind, the back just barely grazing the collar of his coat.

Aya could see the ease radiating off him as he made his way down the main thoroughfare, his pace steady and loose, as if he hadn't a care in the world.

Dangerous for a late-night stroll alone.

Aya closed the distance between them, waiting until he turned onto the winding alley, a cut-through that started the steep climb to the Quarter, before soundlessly falling into step beside him.

In one swift movement, he had her pinned against the stone wall with one arm while the other pressed a knife to the column of her throat.

"Good to know you're actually paying attention," she wheezed.

"Dammit, Aya!" Will dropped the knife, his gray eyes flashing with anger. His cheeks were flushed as he growled, "You're lucky I didn't kill you."

"And you're lucky I didn't do us all a favor and stab you as you strutted home," she mused.

Will's arm pressed her further against the wall as his broad jaw tightened, but he paused as the wind whipped through the alley, his nose scrunching.

"You smell like you took a bath in beer and piss."

"Is *that* how you get into so many ladies' beds?"

"You want to find out?" he drawled, his lips twisting into

a mischievous grin as he stepped even closer, his eyes fixed on her beneath his thick lashes.

Aya shoved him away, hard. "I'd rather impale myself on my own dagger."

Will caught her hand, his eyes tracing the blood caked on her knuckles and face. "I see you've made a mess. Again."

In the span of a breath, she'd wrenched herself out of his grip. He hit the ground with a soft thud as she swiped his feet out from beneath him.

"Touch me again, and we'll see if your face bleeds as richly as his."

Will's laugh was low and dark, but it bounced off the rough stone walls of the alleyway. "As always, you astound me with your charm. Gods help anyone who sees you and assumes you're as meek as you look," he purred as he pushed himself up. "Do you have anything useful to share? If so, get on with it. I'm freezing and do, in fact, have one of those warm beds waiting for me. And you're in desperate need of a bath."

Aya bit back the bitter retort threatening to break free from her lips. She could walk through a bar brawl without even a hitch in her breathing, but Will…

Will had always been able to get under her skin; to poke and prod until that leash she kept on her temper didn't just loosen, but snapped entirely.

His father, Gale, was the first Visya in the history of Dunmeaden to sit on Tala's Merchant Council. He'd helped reinforce Tala's place in trade, even though kingdoms like Trahir had more to offer with their rich delicacies.

It didn't change the fact that he and his son were two of the biggest bastards she'd ever met. She'd resented them from the moment Will arrived on her doorstep thirteen years ago with news of her mother's death on one of Gale's voyages.

And that said nothing of the time he'd almost cost Aya her place in the Dyminara.

But he wasn't wrong about the cold. Or the bath. As

for whoever was warming his bed…that was their own misfortune.

"Given you're needed at the warehouse, your pleasure will have to wait. It's weapons they're after. The buyers are at the warehouse, but the supplier slipped out before I made it to the room. Ronan didn't show."

Will paused as he brushed himself off, one hand tugging through the strands of his hair as he growled, "What do you mean he 'didn't show'?"

Despite the hells Ronan had put her through tonight, Aya's frustration cooled at the dangerous tone of Will's voice. It didn't bode well for anyone at the receiving end of Will's wrath.

When they were younger and nothing more than peers in school, it had been easy to forget that Will's Sensainos affinity—his ability to feel and manipulate others' emotions and sensations—extended to fear and despair, even pain. His handsomeness hid it well. His black hair was thick and wavy, his pale skin tinged with olive, giving him an ever-present sun-kissed look. And with his sharp features and perfectly cut clothes he wore, he looked every part a young noble. Everyone had expected him to take over his father's merchant empire.

But then Will joined the Dyminara instead, where it became evident that his true talent wasn't just as the queen's overseer on Tala Merchant Council, but as her Enforcer.

Dunmeaden's Dark Prince.

Those who had seen him dole out punishment told enough tales to inspire an edge of fear that followed him everywhere.

"Ronan's probably drunk at some bar," Aya finally muttered.

"So you failed," Will replied slowly. "The supplier is lost."

Aya ignored the urge to reach for her knife as she stared him down. "Perhaps I could've caught up with them if you hadn't insisted on me playing messenger to you," she hissed.

Reporting her findings to him like some sort of lapdog made her want to hit something.

Will merely turned toward the winding path that led to the Quarter, looking at her expectantly. Her feet dragged as she fell in step beside him and let the keening of the wind fill the silence. She'd hoped he'd go straight to the warehouse and leave her to head home in peace.

Home. For a moment, the waiting warmth of the Quarter—the small palace-like home of the Dyminara—was enough to almost draw a moan from her lips. Her body was sore from the cold and the brawl at the bar. Hopefully Elara had kept some chaucholda out in the dining hall. It was tradition that the warm honeyed drink be served when the Ventaleh started to howl. *To keep the spirits at bay and your flesh intact*, the head cook of the royal kitchens would say, her eyes set on the neighboring peaks of the Malas. *The Ventaleh bows for no one, not even the Dyminara.*

"Maybe our friends from the west will be generous with their information on the supplier, and I can save you the effort of tracking them down," Will finally muttered, his eyes fixed on the path ahead. Aya didn't miss the threat beneath his words. "How did you manage to confirm they're buying weapons?"

She shot him a look, but his gaze, still fixed ahead, was calculating, not condescending.

"The barkeep was the only one they'd allowed in the back room. All it took was getting him in the right frame of mind and causing a diversion."

Will barked a laugh. "So you beguiled him with your beauty, persuaded him to spill all his secrets, then destroyed his bar." He glanced at her beer and bloodstained clothes. "Incredible."

"You're insufferable."

"So I've been told. The feeling is mutual, Aya love."

Because three years of working side by side in the

Queen's Tría—the rank reserved for the Crown's three most trusted Dyminara—wasn't enough to thaw the bitterness between them.

She ignored him, choosing instead to focus on the approaching palace. The Quarter sat at the back of the Queen's royal grounds, which were nestled in the woodlands higher in the mountains, above the town.

"I suppose I'll have to pay Ronan a visit after I finish with the tradesmen." Will sighed.

Aya raised a brow as they passed through the iron palace gates and kept to the rocky path lined with towering pines that would bring them to the Quarter. "Why *aren't* you on your way to the warehouse?"

Will smirked. "I told you, I have a bed to warm." He laughed at the disgust on her face. "Gods, that *look*. Relax, would you? I want to get changed." He waved a hand at his double-breasted coat and black pants. "I hate this noble garb."

She considered telling him that of all the things for him to detest about himself, his clothes surely had to be the least important. But she refrained as they trudged past the stables, following the bend until the path opened into a large clearing, the Quarter nestled in its center.

It was far smaller than the queen's palace but still magnificent, with its gray stone facade, its stained-glass windows winking from the light inside.

They hurried through the arch that divided the Dyminara's grounds from the queen's and made their way up the winding path to the outer halls that rimmed the intricate gardens. The white winter roses were just visible in the light from the torches that continued to burn in their sconces, no doubt in thanks to the Incends, whose flame could battle the Ventaleh.

They pushed through the large oak doors and stepped into the main hall. Though the space was large, its stone walls stretching high toward the arched wooden ceiling, it still felt warm. Welcoming. A rich crimson rug covered the center of the stone floor, a long wooden table atop it. To the right sat the worn wooden doors that led to the dining room, and to the left was a massive stone fireplace, its hearth still flickering with dying flames.

It was to the fireplace that Aya rushed, thrusting her hands toward the embers for warmth. A glance back at the table had her frowning. The chaucholda had been thoroughly drained.

"Any bystanders from the Squal we need to be wary of?" Will asked as he came to stand next to her.

Aya repressed a snort, thinking of the chaos the bar had dissolved into. "No. If anyone *was* paying attention, they likely would have thought it was Mathias's guild wreaking havoc."

Mathias kept an iron grip on the underbelly of Dunmeaden. His thieves and assassins were notorious. It was a blessing the queen hadn't removed them from the city. They made it easier to deflect a certain type of attention from the Crown.

"And I took care of their guards," she added.

The words brought a wave of exhaustion with them.

Aya was no stranger to violence. Visya were called by the gods to protect and serve the realm and the humans that occupied it, and the Dyminara were the truest manifestation of that will. Not all Visya served in this way, but Aya… she was made to be this, in more ways than just one. But she didn't delight in those moments that required her to end a life. Perhaps she simply didn't care for the memories they evoked.

Will's eyes stayed fixed on her hands, tracing the blood just as he had in the alley. "You were acting in the name of our kingdom," he finally said quietly.

She felt it then, his affinity whispering against her, sensing the heaviness beneath the surface. "I don't need your grace," she muttered. "So stay out of my head."

He raised a brow. "Simply wondering what has such a frown marring that lovely face. Besides…your guilt makes you vulnerable. It's when your shield is weakest. I learned that a long time ago."

"My guilt means I haven't turned into a monster."

Another lie in an ever-growing list.

Will bristled, a muscle flickering in his broad jaw. "Like me," he finished coolly. "If you're going to insult me, Aya, at least have the courtesy to see it through."

She was too spent to argue with him, her exhaustion pressing even more heavily as the warmth from the fire seeped into her bones. She needed sleep, especially before meeting with the queen.

"We meet just after dawn," Aya murmured. "Try to find out something useful between now and then. And watch your back. You're going to get yourself killed strutting down the street like that."

Will's eyes danced in the firelight, the flames illuminating the flecks of green scattered through the gray of his irises. He tilted his head as he considered her, strands of his hair sweeping across his forehead with the movement. "If I didn't know any better, Aya love, I'd say you actually care."

"Don't flatter yourself," she retorted. If anything, his existence was a constant reminder of the merchant entitlement she loathed. But even Aya couldn't deny Will's power and cunning would be useful if conflict was unfolding with Trahir. Both in Council meetings and, gods forbid, on the battlefield. "It's Tala I'm thinking of. If this situation worsens, we won't have time to replace you."

He put a mocking hand on his chest. "I'm *honored* you hold me in such high regard."

The scowl on her face was evident as she made her way toward the staircase on the far side of the hall.

"Don't forget to bathe," he called after her. "I can smell you from here."

She flipped him her middle finger over her shoulder, his laughter chasing her up the stairs as she left him standing there. Her footsteps were slow as she trudged to her room, the blood on her hands and face feeling thicker the longer it coated her skin.

To serve her gods and her kingdom was an honor, she reminded herself.

And for someone like Aya, perhaps it was a penance, too.

3

AYA WAS SCREAMING.

The sound ripped from her throat as she stared over the edge of the Wall. His broken body lay at its base, his shouts of pain piercing the air as he clutched his shattered arm, the white of his bone showing through his skin.

She hadn't meant it.

She hadn't meant it.

She hadn't meant it.

It didn't matter. Because that was blood seeping from Will, soaking the grass at an alarming rate.

Aya dashed down the path, her body trembling as she raced toward the base of the Wall. A pair of arms caught her around the waist, the grip so tight it stole the air from her lungs as she was hauled backwards. A raven-haired healer with pale skin and cobalt-blue eyes dragged Aya away from Will's body, her face grim.

Will's head lolled to the side, his gray eyes going blank as they met Aya's.

She was screaming again.

Aya thrashed against the healer's grip, fighting to reach

him, to prove he wasn't dead, to prove she wasn't the monster she was terrified that she was.

A blinding flash streaked across the sky, and suddenly she was free from the healer's grip. Aya whirled in time to see the woman's body fall to the ground with a sickening, permanent thud. And then…

Darkness.

Aya jolted awake, her fingers instantly finding the small blade on her iron bedside table.

A dream. It was a *dream*.

But her heart hammered anyway, cold sweat soaking the soft cotton of the nightshirt she'd stolen from her last rendezvous with Elias, the handsome young noble in town. She scanned the four corners of her bedroom, unable to shake the feeling that something lingered in the shadows.

The Phanmata, her father would say in the Old Language—the language of the gods. *The lingering ghosts of your nightmares can do you no harm, mi couera.*

My heart. A term he had once reserved for her mother, until she passed.

Slowly, Aya's shoulders began to relax. She released the blade as she settled back against her pillows, forcing her breathing to slow.

It had been a year since she'd been visited by the healer in her sleep. The nightmare always began the same, with a memory that made her stomach roil. Then it would warp into something else entirely.

The queen refusing her a place in the Dyminara.

Will killing her for persuading him to jump.

Saudra, the goddess of persuasion, stripping her of her affinity.

But worst of all were the nightmares like tonight's, where

he never rose from the ground, and Aya would take two lives in the span of minutes.

She closed her eyes and took another steadying breath, prying those invisible fingers of fear loose. Aya had worked extensively with Galda, the trainer for the Dyminara, on controlling her state. She began at eight years old—the very day she learned her mother died.

Her mother, like most Caeli, was born hearing the whispers of the wind. Aya's father used to say it was why she needed to travel for the merchants—she had to follow where the wind called her, or else she would be betraying her very soul. But Aya had heard her parents arguing before her mother left for that fateful trip. Had heard Pa begging her not to go with the volatile autumn weather, had heard her mother confess that Gale wouldn't simply withhold her wages, but would seek repayment for lost labor, and it was payment they couldn't afford.

And she could still hear the way Gale's messenger read Eliza's name off the list of people and goods lost in the shipwreck…as if objects held the same value as human lives.

Gale, the coward, had sent his son, too, to share the news. A child to do a grown man's job. And Will, a scrawny ten-year-old at the time, had simply stared at Aya as her father crumbled, his head cocked to the side, his brow furrowed. As if…

As if he could sense those wretched things she'd said to her mother before Eliza had left. As if he were wondering why, with so much guilt burning inside of her, she wasn't falling apart, too.

Will lost his own mother years later, and Aya wondered if he'd been given the decency to grieve in peace. If perhaps the rich were afforded such things.

It was Galda who found Aya that night in the woods, when Aya's grief called her power forward so strongly it'd driven her to unconsciousness. And it was Galda who offered her the one thing Aya, even at eight, so desperately needed: control.

But if the incident at the Wall had taught Aya anything, it was that control wasn't constant.

It took discipline.

Focus.

Vigilance.

The exact qualities that had been drilled into her over the last thirteen years.

Because she hadn't meant to do it. Hadn't thought twice about the words she hurled at Will that day on the Wall when he taunted her.

You hate me, that much is obvious. But I think there's something else there, isn't there, Aya love? Something you'd rather not explore.

Her mother had always claimed that while Hepha, patron goddess of the Incends, hadn't blessed Aya with her flame, she had certainly given Aya her pride.

Will had gotten under her skin, had pushed her just far enough that she snapped. And when she did…it shattered anything that wasn't a deep bitterness and loathing between them.

She's too dangerous.

Aya had dragged herself to his father's town house that night to check on him; had waited in the hallway, listening to Will argue with Galda inside his room, urging her to remove Aya from the Dyminara qualifications before she could hurt anyone else.

He'd told her that Aya could've killed him, that there was no room in the Dyminara for someone with such a lack of control.

Her one dream. Her one opportunity to ensure her father could rest easy in the cold winters and no longer struggle to provide for himself. The one place she could do some good.

Will had been content to destroy it all.

She never forgave him.

For the way he'd tried to take her future from her, yes. But also for the way he'd affected her. For the way he'd unleashed the crawling beneath her skin that she'd learned to keep locked so tightly; the lack of control she'd spent years shoving deeper and deeper until she could convince herself her affinity was hers to wield alone.

It was as if his darkness had called to hers, and she hadn't been able to resist responding.

And for that, she hated him.

Aya frowned at the pale-gray light that marked the coming dawn as it whispered through her arched window. It would be impossible to find sleep again. Her gaze fell to the Conoscenza—the Book of the Gods—on her bedside table. Its worn leather binding sat open, the Prayer of Certainty to Sage, the goddess of wisdom, staring up at her from its onionskin pages. She had found solace in its verses last night. Her mind had been restless, turning over every piece of information she'd uncovered about Trahir ordering weapons outside of the Council.

Before Aya could reach for the Conoscenza again, her door creaked open, a head of white-blond hair peering in.

Tova grinned. "You look like shit," she said as she stepped into the room, two steaming mugs of chaucholda in her hand.

"So I keep hearing." Aya glanced at the mirror across from her bed. Her dark brown hair had fallen loose from its long braid, the whips covering the angles of her face. She looked paler than usual, any hint of warmth that crept into her skin in the summer from her father's olive complexion long gone from the colder months and worsened by her restless night. The dark circles under her brought her irises closer to the icy blue Will once said matched her disposition perfectly.

She could've done with a few more hours of sleep. But at least she'd washed the blood off.

Tova handed her a mug and flopped onto the edge of the bed, striking a fire in the iron grate across the room with a flick of her wrist. Aya loved her friend fiercely for more reasons than she could count. They'd been inseparable since they could walk. And during their training for the Dyminara, it was clear that Tova was someone you wanted to fight alongside you, not against you. She was the Queen's General for a reason.

And while her loyalty and ferocity were some of Aya's favorite traits, Tova's ability to warm a room in the winter was a close second.

"I hear you had an interesting evening." Tova raised a perfectly arched eyebrow as she took a sip of her drink. The firelight danced across her pale face, a constant of pink beneath—as if the warmth of her fire as an Incend was always just below the surface. "Nice to see you got the gore off you."

"Our suspicions of Trahir breaking our trade treaties are confirmed, and all he shares is gossip about a bar fight. Pathetic. When did he tell you, anyway?"

"This morning," she said, sweeping her long hair over her shoulder. Aya could just make out the inverted triangle tattoo peeking out from behind Tova's ear, its three horizontal lines dividing it into four sections. While some Visya tattooed their order on themselves, others honored theirs in simpler ways—like Aya's mother, who had worn that same inverted triangle, marking the Order of the Dultra, the Elemental Wielders, on a silver necklace that she never took off. It was somewhere at the bottom of the Anath Sea now.

When Tova had pulled Aya into the tattoo parlor three years ago, Aya had considered getting two concentric circles on her wrist for the Espri, the manipulators of mind, emotion, and sensation. But the scar on her left palm from her blood oath to the Dyminara still stung, and she felt a surge of pride every time she saw it.

The Dyminara was her new order. Her home. A way for her to honor what Saudra had given her by doing exactly what the gods had decreed of the Visya: protect the realm.

She needed no other marker than that.

"He was up rather early waiting for Elara to put out the chaucholda," Tova was saying. "He looked as tired as you do. As if he'd spent all night with someone *special*."

"Probably paid a victory visit to Marie after a productive evening," Aya muttered, picturing the sweet-faced brunette she'd seen Will dining with the other week. "Gods help her."

Tova snorted into her clay mug. "I suppose there are worse people for her to spend the night with."

"Are there?"

Tova shrugged. "His arrogance doesn't hide his looks. Not that it makes him any more tolerable whenever he opens his mouth. If only he weren't so good at his job. We wouldn't be forced to suffer him." Her wide hazel eyes sparkled with mischief as she nudged Aya, who watched the sloshing contents of Tova's mug warily. "So did *you* reward yourself with a victory romp?"

Aya rolled her eyes. Tova knew that Elias was far too proper to come back to the Quarter at such a late hour. Or cowardly. Why he'd agreed to get twisted up with Aya was beyond her, especially when they both knew a match between them was impossible. Elias would need a noblewoman. And Aya...

She'd long ago learned she couldn't afford such distractions anyway.

Tova set her mug on the bedside table and picked up the Conoscenza, flipping idly through the pages before tossing it onto the white duvet. Aya bit the inside of her cheek. Tova was constant chaos, always picking up things and leaving them in places they didn't belong. Her friend loved to upset the precious balance Aya kept in her life.

Aya loved order. Structure. Control. There was something soothing about knowing things were exactly as she left them; about the predictability of setting something one way and keeping it that way, regardless of what was going on around her.

"Do you ever read anything *good*?" Tova complained.

"By 'good,' you're referring to those horrible romance novels you can't get enough of?"

"You say horrible, I say passionate."

Aya grinned. "Tala's bloodthirsty general by day, hopeless romantic by night."

Tova lifted a shoulder. "We can't all be serious and stoic all the time."

"I have fun."

Her friend leveled her a look. "Your idea of fun is carving a block of wood. I swear, blades are melded to your hands. Maybe try a hobby that doesn't involve weapons or worship?"

Aya settled back against her pillows, arms crossed. "I went out with you two nights ago."

"Yes," Tova sighed dramatically as she picked at the duvet. "And you hated it."

She hadn't *hated* it. They'd met up with a few Anima who served in the queen's general forces. Tova laughed easily with them. She knew them on a level Aya never would and never truly cared to. For Aya, it was enough to just be near. She'd never been the vibrant one; not like Tova, whose fiery passion drew everyone to her. Tova was a natural-born leader, and the warriors she commanded loved and respected her deeply. Aya preferred to stay on the edges, going unseen and unnoticed. Silence suited her just fine.

"So," Tova mused, pulling her from her thoughts, "aside from discussing Trahir's impending doom with Gianna, what's on the agenda for today?"

"Preparations for the Dawning."

Tova groaned as she flopped back onto the pillows. "Hepha help me. My mother is probably already losing her mind. Remember how much garland we had to hang last year? My fingers still have sap on them."

The winter festival honored Saint Evie. Her sacrifice hundreds of years ago in the War tore open the veil between the realm and the Beyond, and called in the gods to abolish the Decachiré: the dangerous affinity work that had power-hungry Visya reaching to be gods by making their power limitless.

Though Visya power before the War was raw—able to be molded into any of the nine affinities instead of bound to one—it was still contained; set in what was known as someone's "well," which limited the depth of how far the Visya could go before burning out entirely.

But the Decachiré practitioners experimented with the limits of their wells, pushing further and further to gain *more.* They knew no bounds.

It wasn't enough to be blessed by the gods. They wanted to *be* gods. Some tried bestowing powers onto humans, believing there was no greater indication of godlike power than creating a Visya themselves. And using them to further their cause in the War.

It was a dangerous practice that few survived.

The Decachiré nearly destroyed their realm as the practitioners expanded their dark-affinity with one goal in sight: to become powerful enough to kill the gods.

But Evie...she had saved them all.

The Dawning celebration was in three days, and the city was in a frenzy. Garland was hung, candles were lit, and even the Athatis, the sacred wolves that guarded the Dyminara, feasted with a celebratory hunt.

"Come with me instead. Leave the decorating to Caleigh." Tova's younger sister was far better at it. As a Terra, her earth affinity made her a natural grower of things with a patience Tova didn't possess.

"I'll be making pies with Pa."

Tova hummed in agreement before resting her head on Aya's shoulder. Aya let herself settle into her friend, finding a moment of rare peace as Tova's cinnamon scent wrapped around her.

“Do you wear that every night?” Tova finally muttered, her brow scrunched as she eyed Elias’s shirt. A screech escaped her as she tried to dodge Aya’s blow. “By the way, I have your gloves,” she added. “They’re so much prettier than mine.”

“You’re the worst,” Aya muttered half-heartedly, the cold pebbling the skin of her bare legs as she swung out of bed.

Tova grinned. “I know.”

4

WILL WAS FAIRLY CERTAIN HE MIGHT NOT MAKE IT through the day without murdering someone.

The early morning sun streamed through the arches that ran along one side of the cavernous Grand Palace entrance hall, turning the cobblestone floor a blinding shade of bright gray. He pinched the bridge of his nose. The chaucholda had done nothing to ease the steady headache building behind his eyes.

All night. It had taken all night to break the tradesmen, and they hadn't had a lick of power. It was supposedly a crime and sin to use an affinity to harm a human, but he'd always been given leeway when in defense of the kingdom. Gianna made sure of that.

He'd long stopped praying for forgiveness from the gods for it. He doubted they'd listen to someone like him anyway.

Will sucked in a breath, blinking his eyes hard as Aya and Tova approached, as if that would be enough to rid the stabbing in his head. The general gave a muttered greeting, and Aya remained silent, her icy stare sweeping him from head to toe. He hated when she looked at him like that, as if she could see right through to the core of him.

He returned the favor, his gaze dragging across her.

Black leather pants that hugged the curve of her hips, sturdy black boots, another black sweater with a neckline that scooped just low enough to show the swell of her small breasts. Her thick dark brown hair was pulled back into a ponytail with a white ribbon—a touch of innocence.

A laughable notion, if Elias was to be believed. The young noble hadn't been able to keep his mouth shut at the tavern last week. Will had considered sending a sliver of his power to stop his droning, if only so he could enjoy his own company in peace.

He wouldn't have needed more. Not with a sap like Elias.

Aya glared at the brazenness in his stare, and he shot her a smirk he knew would make her see red as they made their way down the hall.

He loved getting under her skin.

Gianna's private chambers sat in the east wing of the palace. The gray rough stone walls made it appear as if the castle was born of the mountain itself. It might as well have been, given the way it was nestled in the pass that overlooked the city. Its many windows and arches gave those inside an unobstructed view of Dunmeaden as it sprawled toward the port basin. One could almost see where the waters of the Loraine eventually became the Anath Sea.

The palace was decorated with subtle richness. Paintings depicting various Conoscenza passages hung on the walls, and hints of silver and gold wove through iron railings and fixtures.

"You're awfully quiet, William. Didn't get enough sleep?" Tova goaded from Aya's right, finally breaking the silence.

"Some of us, Tova, don't have the privilege of getting beauty rest. We actually have to work."

He didn't wholly detest the general. They certainly weren't *friends*, and he supposed he had Aya to thank for that. Though their mutual stubbornness was probably to blame as well. It had certainly led to enough arguments that involved pummeling each other every now and again.

Indeed, it was fire that snaked through Tova's fingertips now as she smirked at him, readying for a challenge.

"Quit it," Aya murmured. They'd reached Gianna's chambers. She gave the guards a shallow nod.

"Buzzkill," her friend hissed under her breath. The fire disappeared just as the double oak doors swung open.

Gianna sat at a low oval glass table in the middle of her circular sitting room, her long white dress just a shade lighter than her cream-colored skin. Gauzy white curtains framed the large windows to the left, which flooded the room with early sunlight. They each dropped to a knee, but Gianna was already beckoning them inside. "Come and sit." She motioned to the table, which was covered with pastries. "Help yourselves."

Aya settled into her usual green velvet love seat across from the queen, Will falling into the space next to her. Tova sat in a sturdy maroon armchair to their right. Gianna poured tea as they helped themselves to food as if they were equals.

Will hadn't known what to make of it at first—Gianna's insistence on informalities. But he'd adapted. Just as the kingdom had when the young queen took the throne seven years ago after the king succumbed to his illness. Quite ideal timing, really, gods rest his soul. Because two years later, Will was training for the Dyminara, and Gianna was announcing she would form a new Tría of her own.

It was exactly where he'd needed to be: in close proximity to his queen.

And it was exactly where she kept him.

She was thirty-five—twelve years older than Will. And yet it didn't stop the rumors that had followed him for years now. The ones that hinted that his relationship with Gianna wasn't merely as her Second, but as something more.

It wasn't as though the queen had a shortage of lovers. She was beautiful. Her golden-brown hair looked like it was lit from within, especially when the sunlight caught it as it did now. And with her rosebud cheeks and soft brown eyes, one might almost mistake her as gentle.

But she was the ruler of the oldest kingdom of the realm—and such a position required cunning and ambition and power.

"What news?" Gianna asked, her gaze landing on Aya expectantly.

"It's as you suspected. They're placing orders for weapons outside of the Council. Both tradesmen were apprehended, but there was no sign of the supplier. Ronan wasn't at his post."

Will watched as Aya's jaw shifted. He didn't need his affinity to know a fresh surge of irritation was rising in her. He'd learned to read her face long ago. It was a challenge, of sorts. The Queen's Eyes: cool, unemotional, unaffected.

Stubborn as all hells, too.

He knew Aya well enough to know she loathed failing Gianna.

"I stopped by his apartment, but no sign of him," Will cut in. "When I find him, I'll be sure we receive an acceptable answer for his absence."

Gianna nodded, her face thoughtful. "And the tradesmen?" she asked him.

"They gave no name for the supplier. But they shared they were buying on behalf of Kakos."

Silence, tense and deadly, followed his words, the only sound being Gianna's fork clattering to her plate.

Even though Kakos occupied the entire lower third of their continent, it had been over a decade since anyone traded with the ostracized Southern Kingdom. Not since the rumors started. They were said to be searching for a way to attain the raw power that the Visya had before the War. "Diaforaté" is what the kingdoms had named them.

The discovery of Kakos's attempted heresy sent fear pulsing through the realm, and the late king created an embargo that banned Kakos from all trade. It was perhaps the only time the lands had agreed on a course of action.

It destroyed the Southern Kingdom.

Will supposed the hope was that they'd end up like Chamen, the kingdom to the far south whose icy climate and remote location made trade difficult and had impacted their economy severely.

But if Kakos was buying weapons…they were planning something. Vengeance, if Will had to take a guess, for the years the realm had left them to wither away.

And they weren't as weak as the realm had thought.

Tova swore softly.

"Were the merchants buying on Trahir's orders?" Gianna asked sharply.

"They claim to be working alone, and I sensed it to be true." Pain echoed through Will, a mere whisper of the night before but noticeable nonetheless. His face remained smooth. "We'll want confirmation from the supplier of the weapons, of course, but…"

He didn't need to finish. Everyone knew he had a particular way of wringing the truth from those who dared to lie in his presence.

"They didn't share much more. It took all night for that information alone."

And he still hadn't gotten what he wanted.

He'd pushed until they'd almost broken entirely, and even then he considered ending them for good. But Gianna had expressly forbade it, and her trust in him depended on his obedience.

Trust he couldn't lose; not now that Kakos had begun to move.

Tova cleared her throat. "What of the other Trahir merchants who are in Dunmeaden? It's not just the two of them. There's a whole host here for the end of the trade season."

Gianna tore her gaze away from where she'd been looking

out the window, her lips pressed into a thin line. "We cannot attack their party. Especially if those two were operating alone. If they were, and we make a move against the others, Trahir could take that as an invitation for war."

"So we go to war." Tova's hazel eyes were bright, as if her flames danced within them. "Our army is strong enough to withstand this battle, especially if we strike first."

"And what would you say to the citizens of Tala?" Gianna retorted. "A war with Trahir impacts our food source. With no time to prepare and no allies behind us, we won't survive the winter."

The Ventaleh howled outside the window as if in agreement.

Relations with Trahir had long been tenuous. They were allies, Will supposed, but in name only. The Western Kingdom was by far the richest and most powerful, and had long lorded their position of power over Tala, whether it be the depths of their coffers, their seemingly endless food supply, or the size of their armies—all bargaining chips leveraged by the Trahir Merchant Council to get better trade deals that deepened their pockets.

An impulse attack on their visiting merchants could truly mean war...and it would be one they'd fight alone. Will doubted Milsaio, the kingdom of four islands that sat between Trahir and Tala, would want to go through the winter without the aid of the most prosperous kingdom in their realm. And the Midlands certainly wouldn't be behind it—not when they already played buffer between Tala and Kakos. Their proximity to the ostracized kingdom had damaged them enough.

Tala and its residents would be dead before spring. Winter was a harsh season in the north, and trade with Trahir was the only thing that kept them from falling behind.

Tova tossed the scone she'd been holding onto her plate with a heavy plunk. "It's the citizens of Tala I'm thinking of. We let Trahir buy weapons for Kakos, and there will be no citizens to feed. If you think—"

"Enough," Gianna interjected. "We will not move without confirmation that the party acted alone. Trahir is our ally. I will not make assumptions and risk the peace the gods have blessed us with for centuries. Besides, they were in *my* kingdom for weapons. A supplier in Tala is sympathetic to Kakos. Let us not be rash, Tova."

Will watched as Tova's jaw tightened, but she nodded. Bold she might be, but Tova would not rebuke her queen.

"For now," Gianna continued, her voice curt as she turned her attention to Will, "notify the Trahir Court that we have apprehended two of their tradesmen and they will be charged for their crimes. And take the rest of their visiting merchants to dinner. Surely they'll be shaken to hear the news. Assure them we mean them no harm."

Will almost scoffed. As if fine dining could alleviate what Gianna planned to do to their two comrades.

"Dominic will seek retribution through the pending agreements, Majesty," Will murmured. Will was due in Rinnia, the Trahir capital, in a matter of weeks to finesse trade terms with the Trahir Council. He had no doubt the months he'd spent planning would go to waste as soon as the king received his missive. Dominic was proud and arrogant, and would certainly see this incident as a blow to his fragile ego and a perfect way to deepen Trahir's pockets by changing the terms to benefit his kingdom.

Will knew the greed of the merchants intimately. He'd been raised by one, after all. It was exactly the move his father would make. Look for a weakness and exploit it.

"I have no doubt this incident with the tradesmen will cause tension with Dominic." Gianna sighed heavily. "But I would be a fool to let them go free. I trust you to smooth it over on behalf of our Council."

Will dipped his head in assent. He was used to soothing tempers and bolstering egos.

Gianna's eyes moved to her Third.

Aya had remained silent throughout the exchange, but Will knew better than to think she wasn't turning each piece of information over in her head. Aya was an expert at lying in wait—at observing and calculating and acting when the time was right.

"I want to know who in Dunmeaden is selling weapons to the one kingdom that threatens this realm's peace," Gianna ordered.

Aya's lips quirked into a small cold smile. Will recognized that light in her blue eyes.

A predator unleashed on its prey.

"Consider it done," was all she said.

5

AYA KEPT A QUICK PACE AS SHE CUT THROUGH TOWN, HER hands shoved into the pockets of her dark gray coat. Tova was silent at her side as they wove through the hordes of townspeople decorating for the Dawning. The crisp scent of evergreen carried on the wind, and Aya inhaled it deeply, tucking it away as they continued toward the docks.

Aya knew being told to stand down didn't sit well with her friend. She hadn't said a word since they'd left Gianna's chambers.

The queen had asked Will to stay behind, and Aya hadn't missed the self-satisfied smirk on his face, nor the way Gianna's own stare had lingered on her Second. Aya loathed to think the rumors surrounding them were true; to think Gianna would stoop so low. But…

It's none of your business. Leave it alone.

"Do you want to talk about it?" she asked as she cut a glance at her friend.

Tova stared resolutely ahead. "No."

"You sure?"

Tova's gaze was burning as it flicked to Aya. "Not so fun being kept out of people's heads, is it?"

"You don't want to be in my head," Aya muttered. "Trust me. It's not a pleasant place."

Tova scoffed, irritation rolling off her in waves. But Aya knew better than to back down from her friend's anger; knew better than to think it was directed at her. She could see the words steadily building in Tova, her round jaw shifting as she worked through her frustration. "We shouldn't be so dependent on Trahir," she finally bit out. "Every year it's the same damn thing: more groveling to the foreign councils so we don't fall behind."

Aya wasn't sure she'd call those meetings groveling. Tala did have weapons and wool to offer for leverage in negotiations. But she didn't disagree with Tova either.

The air clouded in front of Aya as she blew out a steady breath. "The queen is right. Attacking the Trahir merchants could be catastrophic." Tova frowned, but Aya continued before her friend could object. "The fight is here, Tova. We stop the supplier; we stop any of this before it gets out of hand."

She didn't want to think about what might happen if Kakos did get its hands on weapons.

Tova didn't say a word as they stepped onto the wooden planks of the docks of the Rouline.

"Don't expect a friendly welcome," Aya muttered, her eyes set on the faded brick of the Squal.

Tova snorted. "I rarely do with you."

It was exactly why she had chosen Tova to accompany her. A formidable general she may be, but Tova was also naturally alluring. She knew how to be magnetic and how to put people at ease. And while Aya had been trained to meld into any setting, this particular one didn't need her feigned charm. It needed the Queen's Eyes. Tova's presence could soften the fear just enough to get them what they needed.

Aya shouldered the rotted wooden door open, her gaze sweeping the dark seedy tavern once. She had done her job thoroughly. Shards of glass littered the floor, sparkling like diamonds in the soft glow of the sconces that lined the walls. Most of the tables were upturned, and it looked as though a few of the chair legs had been wielded as weapons.

"We're closed," a rough voice growled from the bar. An older man stood with his back to them, his body stooped as he cleaned up broken liquor bottles. He ran a hand through his gray hair as he stood upright, releasing a heavy sigh as he surveyed the damage in front of him.

Aya stepped over a brown puddle, her nose scrunching at the smell wafting through the room.

"Not for us." Her voice was calm even as tension settled in the space between her shoulders. She'd lost her most important mark in this godsdamn bar last night.

The man turned, the color draining from his face as he registered his company. Tavern owners made it a point to know Gianna's Tría. It didn't bode well to be caught unaware.

"Apologies. How can I be of assistance?" There was a slight tremor in his voice. Perhaps Aya wouldn't need to persuade him after all.

"Two tradesmen were caught fleeing your bar last night after making illegal trades outside of the Council." Aya leaned a hip against the bar, her hands sliding into her coat pockets. "The supplier is missing. And given you so generously hosted these meetings, we thought you might be willing to give us the information we need."

The man's hands trembled as he reached for the rag he'd slung over his shoulder. He twisted the cloth nervously. "I didn't know they were doing anything illegal."

Tova's laugh tinkled through the space. She flipped her hair over her shoulder and gave the man a friendly wink. "Shall we take a look at your books, then? See how ethical this business really is?"

"Are you checking other establishments?"

"Other establishments aren't playing host to a weapons supplier willing to sell to Kakos," Aya answered. The man blanched further. No one wanted to be caught with any sort of tie to the ostracized kingdom. Not if they wanted to live to see another day.

His eyes were pleading as he looked to Tova, as if she were the one he could reason with.

"I never saw them," he stammered. "Only the tradesmen and their guards. Whoever they were meeting used the side entrance. I didn't know they had anything to do with Kakos."

Tova leaned forward, bracing her arms on the bar, her brows rising. "You never thought to investigate?"

The owner had the nerve to look sheepish. "It's usually best we don't."

Tova snorted, muttering something about honor as Aya considered the man. She hadn't touched her affinity. She didn't need to. Her training taught her how to read people, and the man wasn't lying.

Which means we've gotten nowhere.

She could bring him in for further questioning, she supposed. Tova could take it from here. At the very least, she'd see if there was anything Aya had missed in her time staking out the bar.

She doubted it.

"She has some questions for you," Aya said, her chin jerking toward her friend. "Should you decide not to cooperate, Her Majesty's Enforcer will handle the rest of the discussion."

The man's throat bobbed.

"When you're done here, send for a few Incends," Aya continued to Tova. "We'll want someone here round the clock." She cut her gaze to the owner. "If we sense one ounce of your allegiance has swayed, they'll burn this hovel to the ground. If you refuse to answer her questions, she'll do the honors now."

Tova smirked at the man as fire sparked at her fingertips. Aya resisted the urge to roll her shoulders, to shake off the tension that had her muscles pulled taut as she walked toward the door. She was halfway there when the man found his voice. "You'll scare away the customers! No one will come if they know the Dyminara is here."

As if they didn't know how to remain unseen.

Aya glanced over her shoulder, her gaze sweeping across the debris littering the room. Tova watched, mischief dancing in her hazel eyes. Aya's lips pulled into a small smirk as she met the man's gaze again. "Pity about the mess."

She waited until realization dawned on his wrinkled face, indignation setting his cheeks a scathing red, before she turned on her heel and left.

6

TOO FULL. HER MIND WAS TOO FULL.

Which is how Aya found herself racing through the towering redwoods and evergreens of the Malas, the soft silence of winter muffling the sound of leaves crunching beneath her boots. Snow flurries whirled in the air, her breath searing in her lungs as she kept a grueling pace.

A twig snapped, pulling her attention to her left. She caught a flash of gray through the trees and put on a burst of speed, her thighs screaming as she ran further up the trail.

She threw herself around a moss-covered boulder, her feet sliding on the rocks at its base as she scrambled to avoid the predator.

Aya hit the ground hard, her arm searing in pain as it took the brunt of her fall.

The wolf was on her in an instant. His powerful paws framed her face as he bore down on her, his breath hot on her cheek.

He'd herded her like a sheep straight toward unstable ground.

"Cheater," Aya panted through jagged breath.

Tyr's brown eyes narrowed, and he knocked her jaw with

his snout for good measure before letting her up. She let out a hiss as pain lanced through her shoulder, her arm hanging awkwardly at her side.

Dislocated.

Aya gritted her teeth as she stared up at the patches of pale-gray sky peeking through the thick of the tree branches. She'd intended to train longer. Her body still hummed with anxious energy, her mind still reeling.

She'd tapped her sources down at the docks. Her best spies would convene with Tova once she was done at the Squal. If the supplier was someone from Tala, she'd need to tread carefully—which meant sending others into town, in case the supplier knew to be on the lookout for Aya.

But she couldn't shake the fury that had etched itself into her very bones.

Her queen had counted on her to finish the mission last night, and Aya had failed.

There'd been only one other assignment in which Aya had made such a misstep. It was early in her role, when she'd been discovered by a source and nearly killed.

Her knife had found his skull first, before she could get the information she needed.

She remembered standing in the queen's sitting room afterward, her hands drenched in blood, her eyes unable to meet Gianna's. She had expected anger. Disappointment. Something other than the gentle understanding she received when Gianna tipped up her chin, forcing her to meet her gaze, and smiled sadly.

"You remind me of her, you know," her queen had remarked. "Your mother. You look just like her, of course. But you have her spirit as well. Warm. Kind. Proud. I often felt Eliza should have been born an Incend."

Aya had stood there speechless for a long moment. Her mother had indeed been warm. And kind.

She hadn't had the strength to correct Gianna on their likeness.

"You knew her?" she finally breathed instead.

Gianna had nodded. "I met her on a visit with my father to the farmlands. And again in a few of the local trade gatherings I was allowed to attend at that age. She was exceptional. And always spoke so highly of her young daughter. Of your wit, your intelligence, your pride. I was thrilled to see you not just rise in the Dyminara training but thrive. She would be proud, Aya. As am I, to have you defend my kingdom."

It was forgiveness, Aya supposed, for the botched assignment. And a confirmation of sorts, too. That Aya had chosen her path correctly; that this was what she was made to be.

It made failure taste all the more bitter.

Tyr nudged Aya's hip with his head, drawing her attention back to him.

"You just want to go lounge with Akeeta," she grumbled.

He'd taken an immediate liking to Will's bonded, and despite her many efforts, Tyr would not be dissuaded. Legend said that the gods created the sacred wolves to protect Tala, the Original Kingdom, alongside the Visya. They were to be their equals, their sacred kin. And to build that kinship, the gods made the Athatis immune to Visya affinity, for only through true vulnerability could this bond be made.

Whether it was truly the gods' will for the wolves to be immune, or they simply had magic of their own to protect them, Aya didn't know. What she *did* know was it made dealing with a stubborn wolf like Tyr damn near impossible at times.

Every member of the Dyminara took a bonded. No one had wanted the gray runt of the litter when it came time for Aya's class to choose. But she'd seen what the others hadn't: what Tyr lacked in size, he made up for in spirit.

Her bonded shot her a knowing look as Aya gave her arm a swing and nearly doubled over from the pain. She certainly wasn't training any longer.

She'd seen far worse injuries. In fact, she probably could set her shoulder herself; she'd done it before. But with her muscles still aching from her last assignment, her body wasn't going to tolerate a botched healing. Better to let one of the Anima take care of it.

Tyr kept a slow pace as he led her down the mountain, and Aya's legs were trembling by the time the Athatis compound finally came into view. The wolves had over half the mountain to themselves, as well as the sprawling lands that led to the Pelion Gap. Their haven sat far from the Quarter, and further still from the city itself. A wall forged by the Zeluus separated this part of the mountain from the lower region. The sacred wolves were dangerous to those untrained to handle them. One wrong interaction could turn deadly, especially if an Athatis was in a hunt.

It helped that the wolves despised the cobblestone streets, the brine of the river, and the chaos of the docks. Tyr especially. But Aya's bonded hated most things besides fresh air, raw meat, and her.

She preferred his company to most people, too.

Her skin prickled as she approached the large wooden barn. The power of the gods was strongest here.

While the gods created the veil that separated the mortal realm and the Beyond from their own power—a measure that kept them from interfering in mortal affairs and the mortals from chasing heavenly life too early—Aya swore she could still feel their presence at times.

Like in the old dockside temple when the light reflecting off the river made the stained-glass windows sparkle. Or in the subtle nudges she sometimes felt from Saudra whenever Aya used her affinity. Or when she walked through the Athatis compound or looked into Tyr's deep brown eyes.

The gods might have left the mortal realm after the War, but Aya liked to believe they weren't gone—not truly.

7

WILL HAD LOST TRACK OF HOW LONG HE'D BEEN SITTING in the barn, his fingers dragging rhythmically through Akeeta's white fur.

Gianna had cornered him after the meeting. She always preferred a private, detailed report of his questionings.

"You look tired," she'd observed when he'd finished, laying a hand on his arm. "Is there something else on your mind?"

He'd stared at that hand, let it rest there for a breath before he gently pulled away from her. "It was a long night."

He had hoped it would serve as an explanation and an excuse. He was too exhausted to walk that precious line today, to hold her interest without crossing too far into territory that would surely risk his place as her Second should he misstep. He couldn't afford such errors.

Such a careful game he had to play. Pushing just enough, but not too much. Always cautious, always watching, always *waiting*.

Will leaned his head back against the stable wall. The echoes of pain lasted longer this time; perhaps because the tradesmen kept their truth buried so deep. Or perhaps he simply had to face a bitter truth: the issue with his shield was getting worse.

He let his eyes fall shut as he exhaled a steady breath to calm the tremors, but his aching body tensed as he sensed someone step into the barn.

Their near silent footsteps stopped abruptly.

Godsdammit. Only one person could move like that.

"You could at least say hello," Will drawled. He fixed his gaze on the mountains. "Have some manners."

"And distract from all that energy it requires you to think?" Aya asked lightly. "That'd be cruel."

He couldn't help the laugh that huffed out of him. He heard Tyr leave her, the small wolf coming to nudge Akeeta with his snout before walking into a stall.

"What are you doing here?" Aya asked.

"Seeking peace and quiet." His eyes flicked to her. She'd changed into her fighting leathers, the black fabric hugging every inch of her as she stood there, her proud face stern.

She sketched a mocking bow. "By all means."

She was almost to the door before he spoke again. "I want an update on the supplier by this evening."

She pivoted back to him, her lips pressed into a thin line. "Give me another order," she dared in that lethal, quiet tone.

Apparently, she was itching for a fight.

Will let his eyes flutter shut again, another long breath escaping through his nose. He was too raw, too overstimulated, to deal with this.

"It's not an order, Aya, merely a request. But by all means, take it however you please. Gods know you will regardless."

He heard her take a step toward him, and he opened his mouth to bite out something that would make her leave, but pain pierced his shoulder, the sting as sharp as a knife. Will jerked as he whipped his gaze to her.

"What?" Aya demanded.

He scanned her from head to toe. Her arm hung

awkwardly at her side. He hadn't seen the injury; hadn't been able to brace himself. "What happened to your shoulder?"

Aya opened her mouth, the words dying before they ever left her lips as her frown deepened. Her jaw locked, as if she were steeling herself, and then she moved faster than he could object. He hissed at the pain that stabbed him as she swung her dislocated arm.

"Stop," he said through gritted teeth.

"But I don't feel your affinity. You're not trying to sense me."

"I can still feel it," he snapped. Will's eyes found the rafters, his teeth grinding as he leashed his temper. He'd always taken care to avoid anything that could give this weakness away, especially as it worsened. Normally he could keep it contained, but lately, after long interrogations…

Worse. It was so much worse.

And now Aya had more ammunition to use against him.

She took a step toward him. "What do you mean you can feel it?"

The barn blurred as his affinity thrashed inside of him, as if under assault. Too much. He'd felt too much during the interrogation last night.

Screams and pain and half-truths and lies and—

Was he still in the barn?

"Will." Aya's voice cut through his daze like a blade, brutal and precise. He blinked once, taking in her leather-clad body, her sweat-stained face, her eyes, which were staring at him with a healthy amount of skepticism.

"I can feel it," he said coolly. "Every ounce of fear, every stab of pain. When the sensation is acute enough, my shield can't stop it. And lately, the echoes of the sensation last. It makes my affinity more sensitive. Hence this," he explained with a wave of his hand toward her.

Her blue eyes flared as she connected the pieces; as she realized it wasn't just *her* pain he was feeling now, but the sensations he inflicted in every interrogation he led. "But… surely there's something you could do with your shield."

"You think I haven't tried?" Will forced his voice to remain calm—bored, even. Because yes, every Visya learned how to shield. It was one of the first things they were taught when their affinities presented themselves in childhood, and it was crucial for those with sensation affinity. Because Sensainos could feel sensation just as easily as they could manipulate it, and could become overwhelmed by it before they learned how to shield.

Before they learned that they could *control* when they felt someone else's state.

Will was one of the most powerful Visya in the history of the Dyminara. Shielding was second nature to him. And yet the more he used his affinity, the weaker his shield had become over the years.

When a sensation became too intense, too *strong*…he might as well not have a shield at all.

This was a weakness. One no healer had ever been able to explain. One he'd already had to reveal to Gianna when she'd made him her Enforcer.

He couldn't stand the thought of another person who could exploit it. Better to make Aya think it didn't matter.

Will gave a blithe shrug as he stood. "The gods demand balance. Apparently, this is how Pathos gives me mine." A fitting punishment from the god of sensation. Will patted Akeeta before striding to Aya, stopping just inches away. "I guess he decided it wasn't fair for me to be perfect," he mused, his fringe brushing his brow as he looked down at her. "Don't worry. All other parts of me function *exceptionally* well."

"Doesn't this bother you?"

"No."

It wasn't entirely a lie.

Aya blinked at him, a scoff bursting from her lips. "Of course not," she breathed. "Why would I expect anything else from Dunmeaden's Dark Prince? You bask in using your affinity to inspire fear."

She stepped closer, her chin lifting as she met his gaze. "You like it, don't you? The self-importance of it all. The fact that people tremble in your presence. The fact that you can *feel* the fear you cause."

He could feel the heat radiating from her body, could feel her chest brush his as she sucked in a breath.

"You're sick," Aya hissed.

She made to step away, but he grabbed her arm, tugging her back to him. Aya yelped at the sharp heat that radiated down her arm—the same one that echoed in his own as she pressed up against him.

"I don't need an affinity to inspire fear, Aya love," he hissed before shoving her away. Cold air rushed between them as he stalked to the barn door. "You'd do well to remember that."

8

"YOU'RE GOING TO SPOIL YOUR APPETITE, *MI COUERA*." AYA'S father wiped his brow as he shut another pie in the oven. Apple and cinnamon wafted through the small kitchen, the heat adding to the warmth that burned from the stone hearth in the living room. Her childhood home was small and unassuming. It looked nearly identical to the other farmhouses that dotted the valleys. But her parents had always made it a grand home.

Not in the ways of the merchants in town, with their stately town houses and perfectly kept flower boxes. But through yellow paint that made the walls feel as though they held the sun. Through the scent of a home-cooked meal always flowing from the tiny kitchen. Through laughter and singing and a love stronger than she'd ever known was possible between two people.

The magic of her mother still flowed here. It was often what kept Aya away.

Sure, she blamed her training and her duties. But even before she moved to the Quarter, Aya made herself scarce around the house.

Her father, ever the soft and generous soul, understood—or

at least thought he did. He knew that the hole her mother had left bit at Aya, even to this day. That the lasting, joyous memories that filled this house were too much for his stoic daughter.

Aya never bothered to correct his assumptions. Never bothered to tell him that she could still hear the words she'd screamed at her mother—the last words she'd ever said to her—before she'd boarded that godsforsaken ship.

"Don't they feed you in that palace of yours?" Pa pulled out a worn wooden chair across from Aya, sinking into it with a light sigh.

"Your cooking is better," she said through a mouthful of meat pie.

It was a high compliment. Elara was no novice chef.

Pa's laugh rumbled in his chest, his eyes crinkling as he smiled at his daughter. He, like most people who knew Eliza, always told Aya she was the spitting image of her mother. Where his skin was olive, theirs was pale. Where his eyes were a warm brown, theirs were a cool blue. Where he was tall and broad, they were short with subtle curves. Where his hair was black, theirs was a deep dark brown.

But Aya could easily see the features Pa had given her.

His long dark lashes. His full mouth. His straight nose. His downturned eyes. The way they crinkled when he smiled.

"She speaks the truth," Tova's voice chirped from the small sitting room. Her friend had long since abandoned baking to curl up with a book instead, and her long legs draped over the arm of the leather chair she'd sunken into. "She also never stops eating."

As if there had been time to eat anything between training with Tyr and getting her shoulder fixed.

Aya threw a biscuit at Tova, grinning as her friend shrieked.

"She trains hard. You both do." Pa's voice was filled with pride as he looked between the two friends. "The break for the festival will be nice."

The Dawning marked a night of worship and celebration for everyone—farmers, weapon-makers, tradesmen, merchants, the nobility. The Royal Guard and the Dyminara. Some even traveled throughout Tala to reach the capital for the ceremonies that lasted until dawn.

Aya had been raised on stories of Evie's sacrifice. Of how her parents, some of the worst of the Decachiré practitioners, had chased immortality: the truest sign of a god. They attempted to achieve it through a horrific ritual that sacrificed their mortal lives. Evie tried to put a stop to the ritual, but her parents died, and their power passed to their young daughter, making her the most powerful Visya to ever exist—the likes of which this realm had never seen before.

Years later, when the War reached its pinnacle and all seemed lost to the Decachiré, Evie, rumored to have power to rival the gods', climbed to the tallest peak of the Mala range and managed to summon the veil.

She tore it open, calling in the gods to erase the Decachiré from the realm.

The effort killed her.

But the gods banished the Decachiré practitioners to the seven hells and bound each Visya to a single affinity, so that none could use raw power to push the limitations of their wells again.

Before they retired to the Beyond, before they sealed the veil once more and vowed that the next time they were called to interfere, there would be no sparing the realm… they scattered the Visya across the lands and decreed none would rule again, only a human.

The Visya's purpose would be to use their affinities in service of the gods and protection of the humans of the realm—the innocents who had suffered in a conflict that was not their own.

Of course, the interpretations of such roles had evolved over the centuries and across the kingdoms. Many had long since abandoned the Old Customs of worshipping the gods, expanding the use of Visya affinity, especially in Trahir, where most Visya used their affinities not to protect and serve, but to enhance and prosper.

But Tala had held true to the gods' intentions since the War. The Visya of her kingdom understood their power was a blessing from the gods. It was an honor to protect humans and serve their realm. And while not all Visya served in such a way—some were merchants, and Gale had even risen to a position of power in Tala Council—they were still the Original Kingdom. The birthplace of the Visya. They cherished the gods more than most.

Aya let out a long breath as she sat back in her chair. Festival aside, she wasn't sure there'd be much of a break, especially if Will had his way.

Tova sighed dramatically, as if following her train of thought. "If we make it. With three more days of training, the issues with Trahir, and the demonstration at the school, I may die of exhaustion before then."

The Dyminara were expected to visit the Visya school the next day to lead training exercises. As the strongest of the Visya, it was mostly so they could impart wisdom. But they'd also look for any standouts who might make a good addition to the elite force in the years to come.

"Trouble with Trahir?" Pa frowned.

"It's nothing, Pa," Aya said lightly, shooting Tova a look.

Her friend knew better than to run her mouth.

Tova gave a slight shrug. Pa made it too easy to be comfortable.

"Well, either way, a night of feasting and dancing will do you some good," Pa said, changing the subject. "It is deserved."

Aya snorted. "Don't encourage her to dance. You know what happened last time."

Tova flipped her silvery hair over her shoulder and

settled back behind her book. "I don't know what you're talking about."

"You nearly broke poor Nel's foot." A flush crept up Tova's cheeks. She raised the book even higher, hiding her face completely.

"She had no rhythm. And that table was far too close to the square. Who puts wine near the activities, anyway? It's hazardous."

"Hazardous to anyone who dances like you. That merchant's wife screamed so loudly, I thought someone had died." The woman's white dress had been doused in wine when Tova twirled Nel right into the refreshments. Needless to say, the dress was ruined.

Nel and Tova called things off shortly after—from Tova's pride or Nel's desire for a...*calmer* life, Aya wasn't entirely sure.

"Should I warn poor Danté about what he's in for?"

Tova had been flirting with the handsome young merchant for weeks. Aya knew she was coveting a dance or two with him this evening.

Or a victory romp of her own.

The book snapped shut. "I will burn you alive," Tova growled.

"If you'd be so kind, Tova dear, please do it outside the house and away from my garden this time. The winter roses are partial to water, not fire." Pa's eyes sparkled with amusement. Like Tova's sister Caleigh, Pa was a Terra. Even when winter was at its harshest, he made sure his garden didn't falter.

Tova groaned, closing her book as she sank further into the oversized chair. "Is it really *that* bad?" she muttered from beneath the arm she'd tossed over her head.

Aya glanced at her father before they turned to Tova in unison.

"Yes!"

9

DO YOU THINK HE KNOWS THEY'RE IMAGINING WHAT HE looks like shirtless?"

Aya could hear the amusement dancing in her friend's whisper as she followed Tova's gaze across the large open training room where the Visya students were gathered.

The students that had returned to the Quarter after they'd finished with basic affinity demonstrations at the school were interested in combat. They included three teenage girls who were sitting in front of the raised training ring and staring at Will.

"They look like they want to eat him."

"It would save us the trouble of having to kill him one day," Tova quipped.

Aya coughed, trying to hide her grin behind her raised fist. Galda shot her a scathing look from her place in the center of the training ring, and Aya's cheeks burned. The trainer was small, her black skin weathered, her curly hair shocking white. And yet her round dark brown eyes still held the fiercest stare Aya had ever seen.

She may have aged, but Galda still managed to put the fear of the gods in her.

Will lounged against the far ropes, looking gloriously bored as he toyed with a loose thread on his worn black fighting leathers. Their suits were flexible in all the right places and reinforced in their weakest—the perfect armor for the weapons that they were.

"You're just as bad as they are," Tova breathed, following Aya's gaze. Aya's jaw clenched, and Tova winced as her elbow met her gut.

"You're disgusting."

Tova rolled her eyes and bid Aya goodbye as the students were dismissed. Aya watched her friend go, Tova's long hair swishing in its ponytail as she followed the other Elemental Wielders to the outdoor ring.

The Corpsoma followed shortly behind the Dultra, as they also needed plenty of space to practice with their physical affinities.

Which left the Espri, the Manipulators of Mind and Sensation, inside. Aya sent up a silent prayer of thanks that they got to stay indoors. The Ventaleh had yet to release its icy hold on the city.

Will had asked Liam and his twin, Lena, to join the demonstrations. Cleo, another Sensainos, had been eager to assist as well. She stood toward the back of the ring, her sleeveless fighting leathers hugging her supple curves like a second skin. Her brow was pinched in concentration as she surveyed the remaining students.

The three girls remained, their smiles widening as Will shoved himself off the ropes and strolled toward the center of the ring to explain the drills.

"We'll start with a few defense demonstrations and exercises. Then we'll see what you can do with your affinities." He nodded to Liam and Cleo, and they stepped into the center of the ring, each unsheathing a long blade.

Cleo tucked a piece of her short hair behind her ear, giving Liam a tentative smile.

A trick—to look soft and unprepared. Aya had it in her arsenal as well. And it was why she wasn't surprised when Cleo suddenly lunged, her body uncoiling like a snake primed to strike.

Liam raised his blade in time to block her, and soon the only sound in the room was the clang of metal on metal as they sparred. Liam was handy with a sword, but Cleo… Her footwork was far superior. She had him on the ground in the span of a few minutes, her blade pointed at his throat.

"And that's why I told you to work on your footwork," Galda growled from the corner of the ring.

Aya bit back a smile. She remembered being a student in this very room, watching the older Dyminara go through drills and get scolded by Galda even though they were supposed to be the teachers for the day.

Of course, Aya had already been training with Galda by then—had been for years. But it didn't stop the awe that overtook her when she watched the trainer instruct the Dyminara as she did now.

Cleo and Liam started again, going slowly as Will marked each move for the students, before he broke the group into pairs, Galda passing out wooden swords so they could practice.

Aya wove between the students, correcting quietly as she went. She stopped only when one of the girls from the trio disarmed her partner spectacularly.

"Well done."

The girl whirled to face Aya, sweat shining on her brown skin, her hazel eyes wide.

"What's your name?" Aya asked.

"Yara," the girl breathed, tucking one of her ebony braids behind her ear.

"You've been practicing, Yara." Aya could see it in the way Yara's movements were smooth where most others' were stilted.

Yara nodded, and Aya's affinity lashed out. "Drop your

sword." Yara's hand spasmed, her sword nearly falling out of her grasp before she caught it. Her shield could use some work, but…not bad.

"I thought we weren't using our affinities yet," Yara said darkly, shooting Aya a glare.

"A Dyminara is always expecting the unexpected. And they *always* shield."

Yara's eyes grew wide, a look of awe settling over her features.

"That is what you've been practicing for, isn't it?"

"I'm going to take the oath one day." Pride coated her tone as she lifted her chin, as if daring Aya to deny it. She wouldn't. She'd had that same determination, that same drive. There was no other place for Aya; no other home that made sense.

"Work on that shield some more. Ask Galda to help you. She doesn't bite. Often."

Yara nodded vigorously, clenching her sword tighter as she turned back to her partner.

After a few more rounds, they moved on to affinity work. Lena and Will led the demonstration, walking the students through the complexities of the shield and different offensive and defensive maneuvers. The group broke into pairs again, and this time Aya watched from afar, marking each time Yara managed to slice through her partner's shield and douse them in sensation.

"She's talented." Will took up a spot next to her on the wall, folding his arms across his chest as he followed her gaze. "Shield could use some work, though. I got through too easily."

"With some more practice she'll be fine. I want Galda to work with her," Aya muttered, tearing her eyes away from the young Visya. "You better have been mindful of the pain level. She's just a kid."

"She's fifteen. A year from now, she'll be training in

the qualifications and will face far more than a moment of discomfort, as you and I both know." He frowned as he met Aya's gaze. "Besides, I know *you* may be unfamiliar with positive sensations, but my affinity does include them."

Aya raised a brow. "Is that the only time people feel joy in your presence?" she asked coolly.

Will leaned in, a response primed on his lips, but Galda interrupted from across the room.

"The final demonstration, you two," she barked.

His mouth twisted into a slow, vicious grin. "Let's see if you can back up all that venom you spit, Aya love."

Aya pushed herself off the wall, her gaze pinned on the space between his shoulder blades as he sauntered to the center of the ring. A single flick of her wrist, and her knife would be embedded there before he even blinked.

"Control," Galda growled from the corner of the room. She'd read the tension in Aya's steps, the violence in her gaze.

Aya nearly rolled her eyes. She wouldn't *actually* kill him.

At least not today.

But Galda's face was set, so Aya dipped her head in assent and unsheathed her sword. Will gave her a lazy smirk as he drew his.

And then he was in front of her, unleashing a vicious offense. Their swords clashed with a deafening clang as she blocked his assault. She used his momentum against him, turning so she could force him off her.

She heard his deep chuckle as he turned back to face her, his eyes bright with the thrill of a fight. They circled each other like cats, marking each and every movement. Will lunged again. Again. Again.

They matched each other stroke for stroke. She knew his fighting style like the back of her hand—had spent months studying it all those years ago when they'd become locked in competition for the Tría.

Will's smile was gone, his jaw clenched in concentration

as they parried. The calm, calculating cold of a fight crept through Aya's veins, filling her head with such a blissful peace. She gave herself over to it completely, letting her instincts drive her as they fought. Aya managed to push him back, to put him on the defensive, her arms trembling at the force of his blocks. Her affinity lashed out, looking for weakness in his shield, looking for some maneuver she could persuade him into that would work to her advantage. She hissed in frustration as she found none.

Will's blade came for her side, and Aya ducked under his arm, getting close enough to bring the butt of her sword into his wrist. Will was stronger—but she was faster. His sword flew from his hand. Her arm rose as she prepared to bare her blade at his throat, but he tackled her. They hit the ground with a thud, his hand pinning her sword arm.

She writhed underneath him, her left fist swinging up in a vicious hook, but he blocked it, pinning that arm down, too. His weight was solid against her, his body nothing but taut muscle and battle warmth as he pressed into her. "Nice try," he whispered, his face close enough that she could count each individual lash that rimmed his eyes. His chest heaved against hers, and her heart hammered hard enough that she knew he could feel it.

Something in his eyes shifted as he looked down at her, and Aya froze, the moment suspended between one breath and another as she scanned his face.

And then she felt it: a blanket of soft silence, like the peace that flooded her during battle without the hard edges that came with violence. It settled into her bones, relaxing each muscle as her breath came in a long relaxed exhale. It felt like holding a steaming mug of chaucholda. Like sitting next to the fire on a cold night. Like coming home.

Will smiled faintly. "Told you," he murmured.

And just like that, the sensation vanished as Aya snapped her shield into place with a vicious snarl. She cursed him colorfully, taking advantage of his gloating to hook her leg around his and flip him on his back.

I think there's something else there, isn't there, Aya love? Something you'd rather not explore.

Her fingers dug into the fabric of his leather suit as she tugged his upper half toward her waiting fist.

This…this *weakness* had nearly cost her her very place in this room to begin with.

"Enough!" Galda's voice cut through the raging in her head. Aya immediately released the vice grip she had on Will's chest, letting him drop to the ground. Her breath was ragged as she stared down at him. Gone was that smoldering stare. In its place was a smirk that had her seeing red. Galda moved to the front of the ring, explaining the dynamics of fighting both with body and affinity, and Aya shoved herself from the ground, her hands tingling as she stepped away from Will. He stayed where he was, tucking a hand behind his head.

"Always a pleasure, love."

"Get your lazy rump up before I mop this floor with you," Galda growled, stepping past him as the class broke into pairs one final time. He rolled his eyes but did what she said nonetheless. Even Dunmeaden's Dark Prince didn't argue with Galda.

Galda waited until he strode off before turning her piercing gaze to Aya. "Your shield is usually impenetrable. You got sloppy." The words sent a burning through her veins. It was true—shielding was second nature. It would take most people, even Galda, a great deal of effort to weaken her defenses.

But Will…

You could persuade me to fess up, I suppose. That is…if you could get through my shield as easily as I get through yours.

Aya's hands curled into fists.

"A tangled mind is a defenseless mind," Galda reminded her before walking off. Aya stared after the trainer, turning the lesson over in her head.

"You can always join my shielding lessons," Yara chirped from where she'd appeared at Aya's shoulder. Aya glanced at the girl, noting the teasing smile she fought to keep off her face. Bold, this young Visya. She didn't flinch under Aya's gaze, her mouth only pressing tighter into a thin line as a long moment passed.

Finally, Aya's lips tipped into a smirk. "Our general is going to love you."

10

Aya watched as the fiddlers in Main Square began their upbeat number, partners rushing to the center of the cobblestones to begin the first dance. Large torches lined the square, the fire from the Incends providing a warm blanket over the celebration that stretched into the smaller markets. The Caeli had also lent their powers, constructing a shield of warm air over each square to keep the bitter winds at bay.

The High Priestess, Hyacinth, a woman of Gianna's age, had just finished the Dawning Ceremony, calling forward those who wished to start anew to lay their burdens before the altar of Evie. She reminded them that darkness had no reign in their realm. That the gods had been gracious in sparing them, and that it was up to each and every generation to continue to keep the darkness from consuming the world once more.

Because mortal greed…it could never truly be eliminated.

Yet the Conoscenza also spoke of the gods' mercy. Of how they hadn't truly underestimated mortal lust for power, and had ensured there would be one last failsafe, one final stand, should evil rise again.

Should darkness return, the gods hath not forsaken us. For a second of her kind will rise, born anew to right the greatest wrong.

Of course, there were laws to help guarantee the Decachiré stayed away, especially in the Original Kingdom. Anyone in Tala found with even a simple relic of the Decachiré was killed immediately. No trial, no second chance. It was an archaic law, one that hadn't been applied in over a century. Whether that was due to a fear of death or a reverence for the gods, Aya wasn't sure.

Aya had knelt before the wreath of evergreen just as she did every year: head bowed, stomach heavy, mind blank.

She'd long since learned the Dawning Ceremony was far too short to relieve her of what haunted her.

Tova pressed a glass of wine into her hands, pulling Aya from her thoughts. "And who will have the pleasure of whisking you around the square? Elias, perhaps?"

Aya's eyes tracked to where he stood slightly apart from the older nobles. His rich blue coat paired marvelously with his peachy complexion. He tugged a hand through his dirty blond hair, eyeing the nobles warily. Having only recently inherited his title, the older generation clearly had yet to warm to him.

"Cranky old bastards," Pa used to call them, before reminding Aya to keep such language out of her mouth. She had her mother's proclivity for swearing.

Elias was a bit soft for Aya's typical tastes. And while she'd found herself exhausted next to his sweaty body twice in the last week alone, their time was coming to an end. Elias would make a decent match for someone who truly wanted one.

Besides, she could only imagine his shock at the number of blades she had strapped beneath her leather pants and tight cream sweater tonight.

Stifling a laugh, she turned to tell Tova she'd rather spend the night watching her wreak havoc with her dancing when a gravelly voice cut in.

"Aya. A moment?"

Mathias Denier stood at her elbow, dressed as finely as any merchant or nobleman. His black jacket hugged his tall lean form, the silver threads matching his cropped hair. The crime lord was strikingly handsome, and he wore it as a mask the same way Aya had learned to wield clothes as weapons—all to hide the monster that lurked beneath.

His pale, angular face was clean-shaven and stoic as he bowed once. "I hate to interrupt, but it's urgent."

Aya glanced around the square. It wasn't the first time she'd been approached by the king of Dunmeaden's underbelly. She knew better than to have this conversation here. "Of course. Somewhere more private?"

He nodded, turning on his heel to lead the way.

"What happened to a night of *not* working?" Tova grumbled. Aya just shook her head.

"I'll be back in five minutes. Besides, what are you still doing here? Danté's been eyeing you since we arrived. Spare him his yearning and go dance with him."

It was true. His eyes had found Tova immediately, and it was no wonder why. Tova looked resplendent in a red dress that hugged her lean, muscled figure. Her hair was pinned to one side, showing off the long column of her neck. And Danté, in a tailored red jacket embroidered with his merchant house's sigil and a crisp white shirt that was unbuttoned just enough to show the dark skin of his chest, looked every bit the perfect gentleman to court her. He ran a nervous hand through the thick waves of his black hair as he eyed her again before pretending to seek interest in the conversation.

"Who can blame him? I look fantastic."

"You do. Now go. I'll be back soon. And after this, I promise I'll enjoy an evening of debauchery." It was an empty promise—they both knew it. Aya had never been the vibrant one. But Tova nodded anyway, giving her a small wave as she made her way across the square.

Aya followed Mathias down the alley she'd seen him disappear into. She felt eyes on her, but when she looked over her shoulder, Tova's gaze was planted solely on Danté, who was leading her into the center of the square for the next dance. Aya scanned the area again, her attention snagging on Will.

With his raven-colored hair, his fitted black jacket, and his black pants, he looked sculpted from night itself. He leaned against the stone face of a shop, shifting forward to hear a pretty redhead as she spoke over the music. He must have just arrived. She'd noticed he hadn't deigned to attend the priestess's ceremony. Typical of him to only care about the frivolity afterward.

His head tilted back as he laughed at something the woman said. Aya wondered if, like those intense spikes of pain he couldn't shield against, he could feel the woman's desire.

Aya could see it from here.

She shook off the thought and ducked into the alley.

Mathias waited in a small alcove, his tall frame partly hidden in shadows. "Make it fast, Mathias," Aya sighed. He bristled at the command, his jaw tightening as he stared down at her. At forty, Mathias was nineteen years older than her, and he wielded that age difference like a knife.

"Ronan is dead."

Her blade was in her hand before she could think, her body slamming his into the brick wall as she set the knife against his throat.

"What did you do?"

Mathias held up his hands, his palms facing her in a gesture of innocence.

"Nothing, my dear. I merely meant to inform you so there isn't any, ah, confusion about who is responsible. I can assure you my men had no hand in it."

"Bullshit."

Blood beaded on the knife.

"I swear it before the gods. Narina found him in his hotel room this afternoon. She had a standing appointment with him. It appears he was stabbed and died days ago. He checked in over a week back under a false name. She left him for your inspection."

It explained why Ronan hadn't been at his post at the Squal.

Mathias gripped her knife arm lightly, and she allowed him to pull it away from his neck.

"As you know, we don't leave such traces."

It was true—Mathias's assassins didn't make obvious kills. If a body *was* found, it was likely poisoned. Otherwise, there was only blood. It was his own sick calling card of sorts.

"Narina says he spoke often of playing cards near the docks. Do you suspect he owed money?"

It was likely. Ronan's thirst for booze, sex, and money wasn't exactly a secret. She certainly wasn't surprised to hear he had a standing appointment with a courtesan.

Mathias took her silence as confirmation. "Well then, I suggest you look to the gamblers. It wouldn't be the first time those lowlifes caused trouble."

"That's rich coming from you," she retorted.

He pushed himself off the wall, taking her chin in his hand. Aya's skin crawled as he tilted it up toward his. "I, my dear, am a gentleman. I don't cheat my way into money," he said with lethal softness.

"No. You just kill for it." She ripped her face from his grasp and backed away. "I appreciate the tip, Mathias. We'll be investigating the matter ourselves. You can expect to hear from us should we find your proof to be insufficient."

"I expect nothing less from those trusted with our protection. Especially when a Royal Guard member was harmed. What *does* that mean for the safety of us average citizens?" He gave a mocking bow. "Happy Dawning, my dear. Gods be with you." And then he was gone, whistling as he strolled back through the winding alley that would lead to the celebration.

11

There wasn't enough liquor in the world to make Will want to stay at this festival a moment longer. The redhead he'd been talking to—Sara, if he remembered correctly—had been pawing at him for over an hour, begging him for a dance. Now that he'd finally pulled her into the square, he couldn't figure out how to leave without causing a scene.

She whispered something in his ear, her breath hot and sticky, but his focus was on the alleyway that Aya was storming out of. She stalked to the drinks table, grabbed a glass of amber liquor, and downed it in one.

Clearly Mathias had pissed her off.

Will turned his attention back to the woman in his arms. *Zena, not Sara.*

Honestly, he couldn't remember. He'd been distracted when she'd whispered her name in what he was sure she thought was a sultry tone.

"Are you even listening to me?"

"Of course," he said smoothly, plastering a smile on his face. He let his arms band tighter around her and she grinned, quickly contented.

If only everybody could be soothed that easily.

"I need a word."

Will tensed as Aya appeared at his shoulder, looking like she wanted to murder someone. Zena—Sara—glared at her, her grip on Will tightening possessively. "As you can see, Aya love, I'm a little busy."

A high-pitched giggle bubbled from the woman's lips as he pulled her closer.

The disgust that flickered across Aya's face mirrored his own at the sound, but even this was better than facing down whatever fury Mathias had stoked in the spy.

Aya grabbed his arm and yanked him away from the woman. "And as you can see, I'm not asking. A word. Now."

The girl grabbed for Aya, her hand skimming her cream sweater. Faster than an asp, Will stepped between them and hauled the girl back, his arms wrapped firmly around her waist as a startled yelp burst from her lips.

"I wouldn't do that if I were you," he warned, marking the way Aya's eyes narrowed. "She may look harmless, but don't let her small stature fool you. I'd hate for you to lose that hand of yours. I know I personally would be disappointed should that happen."

The woman huffed as she marched off, her hips swinging with each brisk step.

"She seems lovely."

"You wouldn't know what lovely was if it held a knife to your throat," he grumbled as he stalked toward Aya, his jaw clenched.

One night of damn peace. He couldn't remember the last time he'd had it.

The music dropped into a slow, honeyed rhythm, the dancers around them folding into their partners. The flames from the torches and candles in the windows cast the square in a warm, sleepy glow, serving as the main source of light on the moonless night.

Will's hand curled around Aya's hip as he tugged her roughly into him, the sliver of skin between her leggings and sweater warm as his fingers settled there.

"What are you doing?" she demanded.

"You've snuck down an alley once tonight already. Twice would be a bit conspicuous, don't you think? We'll have this conversation here."

His other hand found hers, her skin so at odds with her; soft and warm and buzzing with something he couldn't make out with his affinity.

Aya blinked up at him as he started to move them to the beat of the music.

"And they call you a spy," he chided.

She stumbled, her body stiff in his arms. Will merely pulled her closer, his fingers weaving through hers.

"It might actually kill you to let me lead," he smirked as he spun her once before pulling her back into his chest.

"I'd resist only to deny you the pleasure of my death."

"Lovely," he muttered. "You're going to draw even more attention than you did by strutting off with Mathias if you don't at least pretend you can stand being near me."

Aya gazed down at their bodies. He could feel every warm line of her.

"This is far more than *near*," she said flatly.

"Humor me." He bent his head, his chin pressing against her temple as they swayed. She took a deep breath, and he felt her muscles relax slightly; then more as the song continued, her body eventually molding to his as the music crested and fell and crested again.

To anyone else, they were just another pair swept up in the slow, dripping melody that wove through the winter air. They'd have no idea they were discussing something—or that Aya was likely debating shoving the blade strapped to her back into his chest.

Will's fingers slipped to the base of her spine, her skin

pebbling beneath them as he brushed against the hilt of the knife there. His chuckle rumbled against them both. "I should've known." His lips brushed the shell of her ear as he whispered, "So what's so urgent, Aya love?"

He didn't want to think about why her body shivered.

"Ronan is dead."

Will knew she could feel the way his muscles tensed, but she didn't bother to look at him as she continued. "Mathias vows they had no involvement in it, and that Narina found him this afternoon with a stab wound. They suspect he's been dead for days."

"Prior to the Squal?"

She nodded.

"Doesn't mean the bastard isn't lying," Will muttered.

"I'll get Lena on it." The Persi could persuade her way through the city without blinking an eye.

"No." The word was out of his mouth before he could stop it. "Let me talk to her," he continued, forcing his tone to smooth. Lena owed him a favor—one he'd have to redeem for this mess. He didn't need Aya meddling in this any further.

Surprisingly, Aya didn't press him on it. She merely tilted her head back, her blue eyes searching his. "If Mathias is somehow involved in whatever is unfolding with Kakos..."

"I know what's at stake." He didn't need her reminding him of what had to be done—of what *he'd* have to do, should the worst come.

They paused as the music came to a close, a smattering of applause breaking out across the square while the band readied for another song.

"See," he said, his arms still wrapped around her waist, his fingers marking steady circles on her skin before he could convince himself to stop. "You didn't die. In fact, I'd say you enjoyed it."

His eyes dragged down her body, taking in every place she'd sunken into him.

Color stole across Aya's cheeks as she opened her mouth, likely to curse him, but the words died on her lips as a piercing howl ripped through the air.

It was followed by screams.

They whirled toward the smaller square a few blocks away, Will frowning as he scanned the streets.

"Is that…?"

"The Athatis," Aya breathed. "The Athatis have breached the town."

12

Tova was at Aya's side in an instant, flames weaving through her fingers. Her voice was steady as she said, "We have to evacuate."

People were already stumbling over each other as they pushed for the main road, the screams growing louder in the distance.

The Athatis were dangerous on an ordinary day. But when hunting, they were lethal. It was nearly impossible to pull them out of their frenzy unless you were interacting with your bonded. And with a Dawning hunt…

"Get these people out of here. I'll go—"

Another howl cut off Will's orders, and Aya stiffened. She knew that call as well as she knew her own pulse.

"Tyr."

She didn't wait for them to respond before she shot through the crowd, the chaos drowning out Will's shouts for her to return.

She wove through the panicked townspeople who were fighting one another to get as far from the wolves as possible. Their cries echoed between the brick and stone buildings as Aya dashed around the corner and into the next square.

She skidded to a halt, her eyes taking in the carnage that lay before her.

Debris was everywhere. Shards of crystal littered the ground, as if someone had thrown glass after glass to keep the Athatis at bay. A small group of villagers formed a line, broken legs of chairs and tables in their hands as they faced the oncoming wolves. Behind them, three bodies lay still on the ground.

Aya darted to them first, her feet splashing in their blood. Their flesh was torn in chunks, but…they were breathing. She stood, pushing in front of the villagers and unsheathing the knife at her back.

"Get them to a healer," she ordered. The villagers didn't need telling twice.

Four wolves prowled forward, their teeth bared and hackles raised. Brien, a shaggy brown wolf renowned for his vicious hunting prowess, led. Two wolves flanked his shoulders. And behind them was Tyr.

She couldn't kill them. The Athatis were sacred, and Tyr—

She cut off the thought before it could even take hold.

Her voice was pure command as she called his name.

Tyr ignored her, his eyes gleaming in the Incend light. Dark—they were so, so dark. Hardly a hint of the warm brown she usually saw there.

Brien took another step forward, loosening a growl that raised the hair on the back of her neck. Blood dripped from his maw, his teeth gleaming as he bared them.

Help me, Saudra. On my oath, help me.

Slowly, Aya sheathed her blade. She raised her hands before the wolves.

"Tyr, stand down."

It was no use.

Brien lunged.

Aya hit the ground hard as she rolled away from him, scrambling back on her feet to keep the wolves in front of her. Her skin burned where the shattered glass had cut into her back, her arms, her face, but she pushed the pain away, her eyes tracking the wolves as they split into two groups to herd her toward the wall.

If she could draw them into the mountains, perhaps they'd pick up an animal's scent to hunt. She'd just have to outrun them. And with all her training with Tyr, perhaps she could—if she had a head start.

She couldn't match their speed. But she could beat their endurance, and maybe, gods willing, she could keep them in the chase long enough to get them out.

Guide me, blessed Saudra.

Aya sidestepped slowly, inching her way toward the nearest alley. A crash echoed through the street she'd come from—a villager knocking into a cart as they tried to escape.

It was all she needed.

Aya ran.

The wolves gave chase, their growls reverberating off the shops that lined the cobblestone street as she tore through the alley, throwing her body around a corner and into the next street that led to the outskirts of town. She had to keep moving. Had to keep away from the crowded residential areas where citizens were still fleeing to their homes.

She dashed around another turn and into a larger road with restaurants on either side. The scrape of tables and chairs echoed as the wolves closed in, scattering destruction in their wake. Away from the celebration, the cobblestones were slick with ice. She slid on the next turn, cursing the soft suede shoes she wore.

Brien was closing in behind her. She could feel it.

She heard him stretch into a lunge, felt his hot breath on her neck—

Something hard slammed into Aya from the side, sending her hurtling toward the ground. Arms wrapped around her waist, twisting so she avoided the brunt of the impact as they rolled, coming to a stop a few feet from where Brien had almost ripped out her throat.

"Are you out of your fucking mind?" Will snarled as he stared down at her, his eyes ablaze with fury. His gaze raked over the blood on her face, as if he were counting each and every slice from the glass.

A warrior assessing his soldier.

He pushed himself up, tugging Aya with him. The wolves turned, their pace slow as they prowled toward them.

"We have to get them to the mountains," she wheezed. The fall had knocked the air from her chest, and she struggled to get it back in the harsh cold.

Will ignored her, drawing a blade from the sheath at his thigh. The hard set of his jaw told Aya enough.

"Get out of here," he muttered, his eyes glued to Brien.

Aya stepped toward the wolves. "Tyr!" she tried again, hating the way her voice cracked. But she would beg him if she had to. She would fight for him, would do whatever she could to keep him from the blade Will now held out in front of him.

But Tyr just bared his razor-sharp teeth.

"Godsdamn you, Aya. Leave." Will didn't take his eyes off Brien, who took another step. Then another. And then, just as Will opened his mouth to command her to go, Brien struck.

Will shoved her, hard, out of Brien's path. Aya stumbled, slamming into a restaurant table. She caught herself before she hit the ground, swinging around to see Will a few yards away, crouched with the knife out. Brien circled behind him and Tyr...Tyr crept closer. The other wolves held their distance, waiting for the hunt to come to a close.

Aya ran, sliding between them before Tyr could lunge, before Will could plunge that knife into the heart of her wolf.

Will swore, his arm like a band of steel as he ripped her behind him.

Tyr snapped his jaws.

Will angled his knife.

"Don't hurt him," she snarled, tugging his knife arm down. Will threw her a murderous look, and it cost him. Brien lunged again, Tyr on his heels.

Will and Aya scattered, Aya skidding across the cobblestones, her feet sliding on the ice.

She heard Will's shout of pain before she hit the ground.

Brien had him pinned down, his teeth inches from Will's neck as blood seeped around him. Tyr's eyes gleamed as he closed in behind his hunter.

Aya didn't think as she threw her power out, desperately calling to the wolves.

To me, to me, to me.

She knew her affinity was useless against them. It didn't stop her from casting everything she had into the flow of persuasion that rippled across the stones.

Brien paused his assault, his head whipping in Aya's direction.

It was…impossible. But the wolf held her stare, as if waiting for something.

Aya seized the moment, scrambling backwards to put more distance between them as she threw every ounce of herself into that persuasion.

To me, to me, to me!

Brien took a step away from Will. Then another. And then he bounded forward, Tyr and the others close behind him. Aya stumbled to her feet as she broke into a run, her body screaming as she tried to draw them further away from Will.

She wasn't fast enough.

Brien's powerful paws pounded the road as he darted forward, and then he was on her, his body slamming hers to the ground. A sickening crack reverberated across the alley as Aya's head smacked into the slick cobblestones, sending stars bursting across her eyes. Brien's breath was hot on her cheek as he snarled, Tyr growling behind him.

Through her wavering vision, Aya's gaze found Will's. He had gotten to his feet, and he staggered toward her, his shirt soaked with blood, his eyes bright with pain.

His…and *hers*.

He'd be able to feel it. Every moment.

Because with that issue with his shield…her death would rush toward him, and he wouldn't be able to escape it.

He wouldn't be able to escape *here*. Pain like that…it would be debilitating. The Athatis would finish her and then him.

Aya cast an arm out, searching for something, anything to use against the wolf pinning her to the ground. Her fingers grasped a loose piece of cobblestone and she wrenched it from the ground, swinging it with all her might at Brien's head.

The wolf snarled as he reared back, and Aya hoisted herself onto her elbows to scramble free. But again, the wolf was faster. He slammed her back to the ground, her head exploding in pain as it snapped against the cobbles.

The last thing she saw was Will drop to his knees, his hand clutching his chest as he bellowed her name.

13

Someone was roaring. Over and over, their voice a mixture of terror and pain. It floated through the muffled silence that filled Aya's head—no, filled her very body, the weight of it crushing. She struggled to break through the murkiness, to calm that desperate plea.

I'm here, she wanted to say. *I'm here.*

But the silence sucked her under, drowning out everything until there was only darkness.

14

WILL GAVE HIMSELF AN HOUR.

An hour to wash the blood and grime from his skin, an hour to rewrap the bite on his bicep that Suja, the healer for the Dyminara, commanded he keep covered, an hour to slowly reel back into himself and try to shake away the biting emptiness he could still feel echoing in his chest.

An hour was all he could afford before he had to face his queen.

Gianna rushed to him as soon as the door to her chambers closed, her white silk robe billowing enough that he knew she wore nothing beneath.

"Are you alright? What the hells happened?"

Will lowered himself to a knee, keeping his eyes resolutely on the ground.

"I'm fine." His voice was hoarse, his throat raw from the cold. His entire body ached.

"And Aya?" She tugged him up and dragged him to the love seat, where she settled beside him in Aya's usual spot. Her hands yanked up the sleeve of his black shirt, revealing the bandage around his bicep more fully.

"With Suja. She'll be fine." The words felt heavy on his

tongue. Suja had forced him from Aya's room with orders to rest, claiming the spy would likely be unconscious for hours as she healed, and was in good hands with her and Tova.

"Praise be to Mora," Gianna breathed.

Yes. For once, the goddess of fate seemed to be on his side.

"What happened?" Gianna repeated sharply, the flames from the sconces on the wall casting her face in flickering shadows.

It wasn't a question. It was a command.

So he recounted the story, answering each and every push for detail with the type of precision for which she'd come to depend on him.

What was the path of wolves? Straight through the heart of town.

Why didn't you let Aya proceed alone? Because he didn't think she could outrun them. Because he took an oath to defend those who fought beside him.

Why did the Athatis stop their pursuit? He didn't know.

How did you both survive? He didn't know.

Her brow furrowed, concern lining the delicate planes of her face as she rested a hand on his thigh. "Lena found significant damage to the Athatis wall," she said. "It's likely that's how those four wolves escaped. I've sent her to search for the perpetrator with her bonded."

Will tried not to bristle, tried to keep his muscles from locking under her touch. But Gianna's brows rose as she added, "Is there a problem?"

"I'm more than capable of leading the hunt."

"And if I ask Suja for her opinion on the matter?" Will gave her a blank stare, and Gianna's face softened in an understanding smile. "Rest for today. Your assistance will be required soon enough."

Of that he had no doubt.

Her smile faltered as she marked his locked jaw, and Will forced himself to relax back against the love seat, his arm draping across the green velvet back, his fingers brushing Gianna's shoulder. A knock at the door had her hand falling into her lap, and the attendant stepped in a moment later, his head bowed.

"The High Priestess will be here in thirty minutes, Majesty."

"Excellent," she said as she rose. "I'll meet her in the formal chamber." Her brown eyes flicked to Will, and he barely had time to erase his frown.

Gianna often sought counsel from her spiritual advisor, but to meet with her at this hour…

He didn't press her on it, though. Not when she eyed his still-lounging form as the attendant left. "You could stay," she offered.

He wasn't entirely sure of the intent of the invitation. Her eyes were wide. Innocent. But her fingers toyed almost mindlessly with the sash of her robe, as if…

Will pushed himself up, his body aching in protest.

"If only there were enough time for what that could entail."

It was more brazen than he'd ever allowed himself to be. One of her golden brows rose, a small smirk tugging at the edge of her pink lips.

"If you need more than thirty minutes, William, then you have no idea how to pleasure a woman."

Will grinned. "If you haven't lasted thirty minutes, Majesty, then you have no idea how to experience true pleasure."

He marked her small shudder as he backed toward the door, but he knew better than to give in.

Gianna loved a chase.

And he was intent on giving her one.

15

GODS, IT WAS BRIGHT.

Aya's eyes burned as they opened slowly.

Everything hurt.

Her head pounded, her breath pierced her side, even her skin felt like it was on fire. And beneath it all was a bone-deep ache that made her long for the gentleness she had just left.

If this was death, the gods had lied—it was not peaceful.

Are you surprised that hells claimed you?

Her mother's tearstained face rose before her, and Aya blinked, the image dissolving into a pale-gray ceiling.

She took in the white comforter. The window, which the sun streamed through, casting everything in a bright glow.

Not the seven hells.

Her room. She was in her room.

Aya sat up, her head swimming with the small movement.

"Easy. Your brain's been rattled." Tova leaned forward in the rough wooden chair she'd dragged to the bedside. Her hair was limp, dirt and blood clotted in the white strands, her Dawning dress torn from her calves to mid-thigh.

Tova let out a long breath as their eyes met. "Praise Mora."

Her chair scraped against the floor as she dropped back against it. "I really didn't want to have to find a new best friend."

Despite herself, Aya croaked a laugh, wincing as pain shot through her side.

"Broken ribs. And let's see, a handful of glass Suja had to pick out of your body, a nasty cut she wove back together on your scalp, and, oh yeah, a concussion." Tova ticked each injury off on her fingers.

Aya touched her side lightly, wincing at the tenderness. Suja was one of the best healers in Dunmeaden. But even she couldn't erase the aching from mending bones. It would be sore for a while. As for the concussion…healers weren't gods.

"How long have I been out?"

"Eight hours."

Aya swore softly as she took in Tova's dress and dirt-streaked face again. "Have you been here the whole time?"

Her friend's nostrils flared as she gripped the arms of the chair. "You look like shit too, you know. Suja thought you were dead when Will carried you in here."

So he'd made it out alive. But did that mean…

"Tyr is fine," Tova said, her voice softening. "They're all fine. They made it back to the barn."

Aya let out a breath she didn't realize she was holding. She'd never live down Will having to carry her back to the Quarter, but it didn't matter. Tyr was safe.

"Liam came by a couple of hours ago," Tova continued. "The wall was wrecked. Gianna had Lena searching the Athatis territory for whoever did the damage. Her bonded caught a scent. They found the man trying to escape through the Pelion Gap."

Aya started. No one traveled the Pelion Gap unless they were desperate. Not with the Athatis, and not in winter. Surviving the vicious cliffs and freezing winds was nearly impossible, to say nothing of the wolves. It was no wonder Lena and her bonded had caught him within hours.

"Who was it?" Aya's question was quiet and cold.

Tova sighed as she sat back in her chair. "That's what Cleo is trying to figure out now."

Aya frowned. Cleo was one of the best Sensainos in the Dyminara, but she wasn't Will. If ever there were a time for the Enforcer's talents…

"Why isn't Will leading the questioning?"

It was as close as she'd get to asking after his well-being.

Tova shrugged. "Suja says he needs rest. I thought she was going to murder him. He wouldn't stop flitting around here. It was like he didn't believe her when she said you were okay."

Aya felt her shoulders tense. She didn't think she'd imagined the flicker of shock on his face when the wolves left him. Something oily curled in her stomach. The Athatis were supposed to be immune to their affinities. To influence one would be an unnatural, vile act. To even *try* was an abuse of the partnership between them—an abuse of the power the gods had given.

Yet Aya hadn't thought twice. And Brien and Tyr had inexplicably, *impossibly* followed her command.

I was doing my duty. I was defending those I serve beside.

Did Will know what she'd done? Did he want Suja to uncover some unnaturalness lurking inside of her?

Aya's mind snagged on the memory of her bonded. It was well known the Athatis could be lethal to those untrained to handle them. It was why they set so many precautions to keep them away from the townspeople. Whoever had released them must have had intimate knowledge of the wolves. They must've known where the barrier was, how to remove it, and, for the most carnage, to do it during a hunt.

But none of that explained Tyr's behavior. She'd seen him in a hunting frenzy before; had been able to pull him out with a simple command. But last night his expression had been vacant.

She met Tova's gaze, and it was fear on her friend's face as she whispered, "You could have been killed."

The truth sat heavily between them. Death wasn't a stranger, but that didn't make it a friend.

Aya grimaced and waved her off as she swung her feet out of bed, the motion sending another spike of pain down her side. She eyed the maroon rug, wondering if her legs were strong enough to hold her.

"I'm fine. But you...Another Dawning, another dress ruined."

"This isn't a joke. On my oath, Aya...what the hells were you thinking?"

"He would've killed Tyr." The words felt like ash on her tongue.

She forced the other images away—those of Will's blood seeping into the cobblestones and the way he staggered toward her, dropping to his knees through her pain. How she'd felt that spike of panic when she remembered he'd feel every moment of her death. How she'd desperately thrown out her power to save him, not even thinking of the impossibility of it or why she cared to in the first place.

I was doing my duty. I was defending those I serve beside.

Aya took a steadying breath as she gripped the mattress.

"What do you think you're doing?" Tova watched her skeptically from her chair, her arms folded across her chest.

Aya shoved herself off the bed, gritting her teeth as the room swirled.

Slowly. She'd just have to go slowly.

She took a shaky step forward, using the iron nightstand to guide her. "I'm going to see my bonded." She grimaced as pain lanced her ribs, but she took another step. "Did Liam have any news on Ronan?"

"Yes. Apparently Will sent someone else to speak with the gamblers since Lena was searching the territory. They said Ronan paid his debts a week prior and was bringing new business consistently to the docks. They had no reason to kill him. Liam did see the body earlier this morning though—he said the wounds were made with a peculiar blade. Will wants him to check with the bladesmith today and see if she can tell us who purchased it."

Aya grunted as she took another step toward her birchwood dresser. She shucked off her dirt-and-blood-splattered clothes, trading them for a pair of dark pants and a long-sleeved black shirt. She limped slowly into her small bathing chamber, the marble floor freezing against her bare feet. She turned the sink until the water ran just as cold and splashed her face. A bath would have to wait.

"Has the queen sent for me?" she asked Tova as she eased back onto the bed, her hands trembling at the effort of tugging on her boots.

"No. She met with Will just after the attack. She wants you both to *recover*." Aya ignored her as she scanned the room for her coat and gloves, frowning as she found them tossed on the floor. "I needed somewhere to sit," Tova added defensively.

Aya huffed a laugh as she eased into both with infuriating slowness. But Tova's face was troubled. She bit her lip as if considering what she wanted to say.

"How did you get away?"

Aya froze, her fingers stilling on the edge of the glove she'd just finished tugging on. "Will didn't regale you with the thrilling tale?" she asked lightly.

"He said he didn't know. That one moment they were on him and the next they went for you, and that when you passed out, they snapped out of whatever daze they were in."

Aya's hands moved to the pockets of her coat as she gazed at her friend. She could lie. Gods knew she was an expert at it. But this was Tova—her best friend. Her only friend. One she already held too many truths from.

"I think I persuaded them."

The light in Tova's eyes flared slightly as she grappled for words. "You... That's not... *How* ?"

Aya pressed her lips together as she turned over the

theory that had been building in her mind. "My guess is that someone didn't just let them out…they poisoned them. Tyr hardly recognized me—his mind, it wasn't right."

Tova didn't look convinced.

"What?" Aya hated the edge in her voice.

But Tova merely pushed herself from the chair and took Aya's hands. "With Kakos ordering weapons and their history of experimenting with affinities, you know people are going to be looking for *any* sign of darkness."

Aya recoiled, her hands jerking in Tova's grip. "You think I'm dabbling in dark-affinity work?"

"No!" Tova's eyes were wide as she held tight. "Gods, no. I'm just worried for you. I don't want you getting caught up in something that has nothing to do with you."

Because with those archaic laws that would allow for immediate execution…

Aya repressed a shudder.

"Just…keep this to yourself," Tova ordered softly.

"You're asking me to lie to our queen?"

"I am asking you to not say anything that you don't know with absolute certainty. Let Will's explanation suffice."

His explanation being that he didn't know what had happened.

Did *she*? Was she sure they'd been affected by someone else, and *that* was why she'd been able to use her affinity in such a forbidden way? Was it possible that it wasn't her persuasion at all, but the noise she'd made that had caused them to get distracted? Perhaps Saudra had answered her call for help; perhaps her patron goddess had granted her this mercy.

I was doing my duty. I was defending those I serve beside.

Tova squeezed her hands again, drawing Aya from her thoughts. "Promise me you'll lay off the recklessness, okay?"

Aya fought against the uneasiness growing in her as she forced a teasing smirk to her lips. "When do I *ever* do anything reckless? Besides, you should speak for yourself. You really do look like shit."

"I still look better than you," Tova grumbled, clearly satisfied. She released Aya's hands as she headed toward the doorway. But she paused, her eyes finding Aya's again. "I'm glad you're okay."

Aya smiled at her, a real one this time. "Me too."

Each step up the steep mountain path felt like a dagger in Aya's side. Suja would kill her when she found out Aya was out of bed. But there was too much at stake to simply rest.

Aya froze as she finally crested the hill to the compound, her breath coming in heavy pants.

The hole ripped through the wall was massive. And while it explained how the Athatis had left their haven, it still didn't explain why. Aya knew her bonded—nothing would have inspired him to leave the mountains to wander the streets. Nothing except for the frenzy of a hunt. They had been lured into the city.

On her oath, she would kill the man responsible for it and anyone else involved.

Aya's thumb skimmed the thin scar on her palm, the raised skin there looking paler in the gray midmorning light. She found the permanence of the mark grounding. Nothing could remove a blood oath. Well, nothing except the punishment for forsaking it, which involved carving out the scar with a knife.

By my blood and before the gods, I pledge my life to protect the Original Kingdom, its citizens, and those who serve beside me.

She knew it was their oath that had sent Will to her defense—and that their oath wasn't enough to quell his fury that she'd ignored his orders to leave.

Which was fine. She was furious, too.

At his willingness to kill her bonded.

At his demand that she leave so he could wield that knife in a way she'd never be able to.

And perhaps at her own weakness, too.

Aya stepped through the hole in the wall, her body slick with sweat from the climb. Tyr wasn't in the barn—but Akeeta was. And her blue eyes were piercing as she stood and stretched. She looked over her shoulder once, her message clear.

Aya followed her as she wound through the forest. The wolf led her to a small meadow, where a stream with patches of ice floating between its gentle rapids spilt through the rocks and grass. Next to it, his head resting on his paws, lay Tyr. He stared at the water, not bothering to move as Aya approached him slowly. But he knew she was there—Aya could feel his awareness shift to her as soon as she stepped into the clearing. And when she lowered herself onto the ground next to him, kneeling by his side, he finally turned his gaze to meet hers.

Her heart ached at the devastation there, at how lost and desolate he looked as he took her in. He let out a low breath and lowered his head once more.

"It's not your fault." She curled her fingers into the thick fur behind his head, leaning over to peer at his face. "I'll find out what happened to you," she swore. "On my oath, I'll make them pay."

Slowly, Tyr pushed himself into a sitting position. He pressed his forehead against hers, a guttural growl rumbling from his chest.

His own promise that he'd make them pay, too.

16

Will stationed himself to the right of Gianna's empty seat at the head of the long mahogany table in the formal meeting chamber, the High Priestess having taken the left. He drummed his fingers on the polished surface, Hyacinth remaining silent as they waited for the rest of their party. Every so often, her maroon robes, just a shade darker than her red hair, rustled, marking her fidgeting.

And though her face was covered by a sheer veil of off-white, it wasn't enough to hide the tension there.

Whatever Cleo had uncovered, it was bad.

It should have been me in that interrogation.

The thought was bitter, and furious, and tinged with a sort of tension that kept his muscles tight. Because now…

Five damn years of waiting; five damn years of biding his time, only to be pushed out the very moment he needed to be in the most. The careful control he'd crafted was slipping through his fingers.

His gaze cut to the door as Aya and Tova arrived, and he scanned the spymaster once, fighting against the way his jaw locked.

There was still fucking blood clotted in her hair.

Aya slid into the chair next to him, staring resolutely ahead, while Tova dropped into the seat next to the priestess.

Gianna followed shortly behind them. Her white dress swished against the cobblestone floor, her fingers tugging at the delicate gold necklace that sat at her throat. Her lips were pressed into a thin line as she settled into the high-backed chair at the head of the table.

"The man is a Diaforaté from Kakos. He used strength and persuasion affinities," she finally said. "Kakos has found a way to replicate raw power."

Will stiffened in his seat.

Too fast. Things were unraveling too fast.

He forced his face into cold contemplation as he focused on his queen. Gianna's voice was heavy as she continued.

"I fear this is the beginning of the second rise of the Decachiré."

A tense silence followed her words, and Will looked to the priestess. Her hands were clenched in front of her, her knuckles white. He could just make out the tightness around her eyes through the veil and the bright red spots that marred the usual soft golden glow of her cheeks..

Hyacinth was angry.

"You think they're readying for war," Aya finally breathed. "You think they're going to challenge the gods again. A return of the Decachiré."

Hyacinth dipped her chin. "The Conoscenza does warn of a return of darkness. When the gods bound magic to a single affinity, it was done so that Visya would only have access to a single power and therefore would not have enough to destroy their wells. We think the Athatis were a test for the Diaforaté to see if their dark power is truly effective in breaking the bounds of the Order, so that they might begin to erode their wells and achieve limitless power."

Her lilting voice was colder than Will had ever heard it.

"And is it?" Tova asked.

The priestess pursed her lips in contemplation. "Yes. And no. He did present both strength and persuasion affinities… that indicates raw power. And his persuasion went far beyond what any ordinary Persi could accomplish. Persuading the Athatis should be impossible, which would lead one to expect his well is far deeper than we've seen before. But dark-affinity work has always had consequences. The man was weakened by the use of his power. And the persuasion wore off the wolves, as is evident by your survival," she explained, nodding to Aya and Will.

Will saw Aya's jaw shift from the corner of his eye, but he kept his stare firmly on Hyacinth.

"Had the raw power truly worked, the persuasion would never have been broken. I suspect it means Kakos hasn't found a way to stabilize raw power enough to be a significant threat *yet*," the priestess continued. "But it's only a matter of time. And when they're successful…" Hyacinth trailed off, her lips pressing in a tight line.

"How are they replicating raw power?" Aya demanded.

Hyacinth shook her head. "He has not confessed to their methods."

"Cleo will question him further," Gianna cut in. "Perhaps he'll be forthcoming on how far their experiments have gotten with the right…motivation."

Will braced his elbows on the table as he looked to the queen. "I'm more than capable of handling the questioning," he said. Gianna's brows rose. "Majesty," he added.

"I need you three searching for the supplier," she replied tersely. "I want to ensure that shipment does not fall into their hands, and that anyone who is willing to work with Kakos is imprisoned immediately. We cannot allow the Southern Kingdom to build their weapons supply."

Will didn't fail to notice that she was cutting him out at every turn.

Careful. He'd have to be careful. Gianna wasn't a fool—if

anything, she was far more cunning than most gave her credit for. And his goals hadn't changed; not truly.

Find the supplier. Find the supplier, and make your next move.

"They're not one and the same?" Aya asked, her eyes darting between Gianna and the priestess. The queen shook her head.

Cleo must have garnered that during her questioning.

Gianna's attention shifted back to Will. "I'm moving up your trip to Rinnia to meet with King Dominic. You'll leave at the end of the week at the latest. While you're there, I want absolute assurance that they had nothing to do with the two tradesmen, and I want their commitment to aid. War is coming, and we will not survive without them."

Will shifted in his seat. Dominic would not take kindly to Gianna's further interference. The king was partial to neutrality. Will doubted he would risk Trahir's wealth to aid in a struggle so far from his isolated lands, allies or not.

Gianna continued, as if reading his thoughts. "Tread carefully. I know Dominic; one Diaforaté with unstable power will likely not be enough to convince him of a significant threat. Our partnership is delicate. Bide your time. Use your status on our Council to appeal to him, and use the trade negotiations as a starting point. Be mindful: we cannot afford to lose them."

Tova opened her mouth, likely to argue against the slow approach, but Gianna held up a hand, her eyes still fixed on Will. "I've sent word that you will be arriving earlier than anticipated. They're prepared to welcome you for a prolonged stay. Make it count."

"Tova," she continued, facing her general, "I want you to begin recruiting subtly for our forces. We'll need numbers, especially if Trahir does not lend their support. Look for the fighters—those who can be trained. In the meantime, I want all three of you searching the docks before Will leaves." Gianna's eyes scanned Aya. Perhaps she noted the blood too, because her voice softened as she said, "I'm sorry we cannot afford more time to rest."

She looked ready to say more, but Will tugged a hand through his hair, his voice a mere rasp as he interjected. "We should get started now. If the supplier is still in the city, the news of this man's capture will likely cause them to flee."

He couldn't very well afford that.

Gianna nodded, her exhale steady as she looked at each of them in turn. "I know you will not fail me." As one, they raised their left fists to their chests.

Will could feel his fingers brush the thin ridge of the scar on his palm. A reminder of all he had done to get here. Of all he would lose should he fail.

"By my blood," they murmured in unison.

17

THE DOCKS WERE BUSTLING WHEN AYA, WILL, AND TOVA arrived. The late afternoon sun flashed off the water as dockworkers unloaded goods from the foreign kingdoms. Those seeking early pleasure wove through the workers, shouting to one another about where they could score the latest deal and which tables were hot as they made their way toward the gambling halls of the Rouline.

This part of the town never slept. And it continued to flood with people as the three of them made their way through each establishment, searching for more information on the supplier.

"I hate the Rouline," Tova grumbled, eyeing a boisterous group of travelers with disgust. She'd nearly torn the head off a man who'd bumped into her a few blocks back, and she became more irritable the further they wandered, stopping every so often at bars and brothels to see if anyone had a story to tell. Aya couldn't blame her. They'd been at it for hours, it was cold, and they'd learned nothing. Aya could feel a headache coming on.

She looped an arm through her friend's, gently tugging her away from the group she was still glaring at. The last thing they needed was Tova drawing a sword on a bunch of tourists.

Will stalked on ahead of the two women, leading the way through the groups of travelers clustered along the main road lining the docks. Besides snapping at her to wash the blood from her hair before they'd left the palace, and murmuring a few questions to club owners, restaurateurs, and madams, he hadn't said a word. But his body was as taut as a bowstring, his lips pressed in a thin line as they moved from place to place.

"He's a real charmer today, isn't he?" Tova muttered, watching as he ducked into another bar without a backward glance. "Make this one fast. I'm tired of standing here and waiting for nothing. It's cold and I'm hungry."

"And cranky," Aya said, nudging her side. "You could come in, you know."

"And leave your backs unguarded? Where is your battle sense, Aya?"

Aya rolled her eyes. "You just hate dives."

Tova shrugged as she leaned against the brick wall. "I'm partial to the finer establishments."

"Snob."

Aya pushed through the door. The room was dark and damp, and her nose scrunched at the brine of the river mixing with the sour smell of ale.

Will was sitting at the bar. Aya swallowed a noise of frustration as she stepped around him and slid onto an empty stool as the keep reached for a bottle of liquor on the higher shelf.

"You think we have time for a drink?"

Will kept his gaze forward, his eyes tracing the bottles behind the bar. "I think *I* have time for a drink." The keep placed a glass of amber liquor in front of Will and raised a questioning brow at Aya. She shook her head.

"We have work to do," she reminded him under her breath. Will took a sip from his glass, letting out a hiss as the liquor burned his throat.

"What do you think I'm doing?"

"Wasting time. We have at least three more stops to make, and Tova's patience is wearing thin. As is mine."

"Tell her to go ahead to the next place. Between the two of us, we have this covered."

"Like hells I'm staying here with you," Aya muttered as she slid off the stool. Will stood, blocking her path toward the door. "What is it?" she spat, her patience wearing thin. "You're pissed because Cleo is leading the questioning? You miss out on one person to torture, and it's the end for you, is that it?"

He set his glass down with a thunk, the green flecks in his eyes flaring in the dim light of the bar as he glared down at her.

"Stop talking and sit down," he growled. "Before I make you." He turned and walked away from her, ducking out of the bar, no doubt to send Tova off. Aya bit down on her simmering anger, falling back onto the stool and swiping his drink.

She was itching for a fight; for some sort of release from the tension inside of her that had been steadily building since she'd awoken after the wolves.

She downed his drink instead, signaling the keep for another.

When Will returned a few moments later, his face was lined with frustration.

"I take it that went well," she said sweetly, sipping from his glass.

He lifted a shoulder as he slid onto the stool.

"She left, at least. About time she does something useful."

"She's been guarding our backs all day."

"I don't need help with that."

Aya rolled her eyes, forcing the uneasiness in her to settle. Tova was more than capable of looking after herself as well, but…

"You think it's wise to send her out alone?"

"I think it would be less wise to let *you* out of my sight," Will muttered as he tracked the barkeep to a table in the back corner of the dive. "And I think that the quicker we can get this over with, the better."

Aya gave a pointed look to the drink in her hand, a retort bubbling to her lips. But he spoke again before she could.

"You should've killed them." The words were soft, but they cleaved through the air like a blade. He still wouldn't look at her.

"The Athatis are sacred," she replied lowly. "Tyr is my bonded."

"I don't give two shits about your bonded," Will snapped, his eyes flashing to hers. He was in some sort of mood to let his temper show like this.

"If it were Akeeta—"

"I would've done my duty." Indeed, that was fury in his voice, which dropped another octave as he said, "I ordered you to clear the square. I ordered you to leave, and yet you put yourself in danger on sentiment."

"Is that what this is about? You're angry because I *disobeyed* you?"

"You took an oath to Tala and the gods. An oath to protect this kingdom and its citizens—"

"And *you*," Aya growled as she set her drink down. "I am honor bound to protect *you*, and I would've been able to fulfill my oath if you hadn't involved yourself."

Will's chest rose and fell rapidly, as if he couldn't quite catch his breath. "Tell me," he seethed quietly, "how *did* the Athatis back away from me? Did I imagine the rush of power I felt against my shield just before your runt of a wolf tried to rip out my throat?" His voice was a lethal caress, a promise of violence masked beneath the soft tone.

And the way he was looking at her…

He knew.

Dread curled in the pit of Aya's stomach, writhing like a snake.

She's too dangerous.

"The priestess was right. It *does* seem as though darkness is returning," Will breathed. "And I imagine it looks a lot like persuading a sacred animal the gods have deemed impossible to affect. And you know what happens to those that display even the slightest hints of darkness, Aya."

She lifted her chin, her hands tingling as she wrapped them around her glass. She wouldn't let Will intimidate her with baseless threats.

Even if…even if Tova had said nearly the same thing hours ago.

Even if she'd been reminding herself with each and every breath that her actions were born out of duty: duty to her realm, duty to her gods.

She forced a sneer, her voice dropping low as she said, "The Dark Prince of Dunmeaden wants to accuse me of heresy?"

Their faces were inches apart, glares equally marked with hatred.

"Perhaps you're the savior then? The one marked by divinity?" His lips twisted into a sarcastic smirk as he looked her over. "No," Will breathed. "You and I both know it's not light that drives you. I've had the broken bones to prove it."

The words landed like a blow.

Aya jerked back, her heart pounding in her chest.

But it wasn't the vision of his broken arm that haunted her in that moment. It was the way he'd watched her all those years ago as the messenger delivered the news of her mother's death. The way he'd cocked his head, the way his brow had furrowed, like he—

Will nodded to a table behind her. "There's the owner. Let's go." He stood without another word.

Aya gave herself a moment to force down the anger that was still simmering inside of her. She was halfway off the barstool when she heard the shouts.

She glanced toward the door, frowning at the sound of

boots pounding on the cobblestone street. Will caught her elbow, a look of irritation etched on his face. "Leave it; we have work to do."

"This is our work," she shot back as she ripped her arm from his hold. "Besides—"

A hoarse yell cut her off.

Aya froze, her blood chilling as she registered her friend's voice. She was out the door in an instant, her body smarting in pain as she launched herself toward the Artist Market, following the sound of shouts.

The market was usually filled with artists and vendors and visitors, especially on a clear day like this. But it was empty now save for seven members of the Royal Guard. Two of them held a struggling Tova between them. They dragged her toward the tall guard in the center, a look of grim satisfaction on his face as he watched.

"What is this?" Aya demanded, her breath coming in uneven pants. Her side seared with pain, but she swallowed it as she marked how every door was closed, every blind drawn.

"The Queen's General is under arrest for treason," the man said, not taking his eyes off her friend.

"Like hells," Aya growled.

Will strolled up next to her, his hands in his pockets. His voice was cool and calm as he said, "This seems to be a matter that's beyond you and the Royal Guard, is it not, Finnias?"

The guard bristled with the insult. "We were sent by Her Majesty with orders to retrieve the general. We have proof that she's conspiring against the kingdom."

"Show it then, you rat," Tova hissed, spitting at his feet.

Finnias just grinned. "We found the blade matching Ronan's injuries in your room, General."

Aya blinked. Will had sent Liam to track down the owner

of that blade just this morning. She glanced at him, but his face gave away nothing.

Fire sparked in Tova's palms as another guard stepped toward her.

"Stand down, Tova," Will ordered, his voice firm. Tova glared at him, and the guard took the opportunity to dart forward, her hand reaching into Tova's satchel. Her expression was as hard as granite as she pulled out a roll of parchment.

It almost looked like…

"Orders. For weapons perhaps?"

Aya's muscles locked as she stared at her friend.

"That…that isn't mine." Tova caught Aya's gaze. "That isn't mine."

"Search her," Finnias murmured to the guard. Tova struggled against the two men holding her, her eyes growing panicked.

"That isn't mine!" she yelled.

Aya felt Will's hand press into the small of her back, his eyes fixed across the market.

More Royal Guards filed in. At least fifteen filled the square now.

"Found something!" The guard searching Tova tugged a small leather-bound book from the bag. The book was worn, its binding cracked. The leather was a deep navy, so dark it was almost black. And on the front cover, in thin silver stitching, was a crescent moon, tilted so it rested on its two points.

The mark of the Decachiré.

The silence lasted a heartbeat, if that, before chaos exploded throughout the square. Shouts echoed between the buildings as more guards advanced on Tova, her flames flaring as they surrounded her.

Aya made it all of one step toward her friend before Will hooked an arm around her waist and dragged her back. She struggled against his hold as the guards' shouting rose. Tova thrashed, her hair whipping out behind her as she tried to break free. One of the guards screamed as her fire burned him.

"Aya—"

"I'm not leaving her!"

"For once in your godsdamn life, listen to me!" Will whirled her to him, his face inches from hers.

There was a thud, followed by the scrape of metal as a sword left its sheath, and they both turned toward the sound. Will swore at the sight of Tova forced to her knees, one guard holding her in place, another with his sword in hand.

They were going to enact that archaic rule.

They were going to kill her.

Right here. Without a trial.

They were going to kill her.

The world slowed, each moment stretching into an eternity. The guard raised his sword and Tova's eyes met Aya's. The hopelessness in them had a scream ripping from Aya's chest. She fought against Will's grip, her feet leaving the ground as he tugged her backward, refusing to give in.

Will shouted something at the guard, something Aya couldn't hear above the rushing in her ears. And then that rush became a roar so loud that she could *feel* it in her veins, could feel it coursing through her as the guard's sword reached its peak, glinting in the sunlight before arcing down toward her friend.

Aya exploded.

18

A DEAFENING CRACK RICOCHETED THROUGH THE SQUARE, followed by a flash of light so bright it erased Aya's vision completely. Will shoved her to the ground, his body covering hers while shouts echoed with clashing of armor. The guards scattered, their screams reverberating against her skull until…

Silence.

Aya blinked her eyes open. Fire and smoke filled the square, a putrid burning smell searing her nose and making tears blur her vision. The ground was littered with injured guards, their moans starting to break through the muffled silence in her head.

In the middle of the square was Tova, a shield of fire around her.

Four guards lay dead at her feet.

Their flesh was raw, sections of it charred completely, their faces contorted into screams of terror. Or pain. Or both.

Her friend scrambled back from their smoking bodies, her eyes wide with fear. Fear that did not leave her face as she gazed across the gore-splattered cobblestones at Aya. Tova's shield was burning on and on, just like the flames that devoured the easels and carts and injured bodies throughout the market.

She was looking at Aya as if *Aya* had…

No.

Aya didn't have flame, and Tova had been fighting, and…

Flame wasn't blinding like that.

Tova continued to stare at her, horror etched on her face as her shield of fire dropped.

Aya tore her gaze away from her friend and took in the moaning figures on the ground; the dead guards beyond them, no more than lumps of red and black. Cracks had formed in the cobblestones, spreading directly from where Aya lay on the ground, like roots growing from a tree.

You and I both know it's not light that drives you.

A high-pitched ringing replaced the roaring in her ears. She recognized a hard clicking noise beneath it. She searched for it, eyes scanning the damaged market, before realizing it was coming from herself, from the way her trembling body made her teeth chatter.

She clenched her jaw, and it was silent again.

Will slowly pushed himself off her, his eyes fixed on the curling smoke as he stood. He was still for a heartbeat. But as the guards who had made it to the alleyways flooded back into the market, faces full of vengeance, he grabbed Aya, hauling her off the ground, his grip tight enough to hurt.

She didn't care. A numbness settled in her, as if whatever had filled her moments ago had ripped all sense of feeling from her.

"We had the wrong heretic," one of the guards sneered as she pulled Tova off the ground and her comrades rushed to help the injured members. Her gaze traced those cracks in the cobblestones that led straight to Aya. "I've never seen a Persi wield light."

"I say we slit both their throats for good measure," another hissed as he grabbed Aya from behind, yanking her away from

Will, the edge of his sword kissing her neck. Before she could even flinch, Will's knife was on the guard's sword hand, his vice grip still on her arm.

"You move this hand, and so help me gods I will saw it from your arm slow enough that you feel every single sunder." His voice was low, and the guard loosened his grip slightly. But not enough. "She's mine," Will snarled softly, violence flashing in his gray eyes.

The guard released her, backing away with his palms raised.

For a brief moment, hope flared in Aya's chest.

Our oaths bind us. He'll get us out. He won't—

"Fools," he called to the guards. "You kill them, and whatever information they have dies with them. They're of better use to Her Majesty alive than dead." He watched them, as if waiting for someone to defy him.

No one did.

Finnias glared from where he'd emerged from the alleyway, but even he remained silent under the Enforcer's stare. That flicker of hope vanished as Will turned his gaze to hers, coldness written in his face.

This. This was Dunmeaden's Dark Prince. The Queen's Enforcer. There would be no escaping this—no escaping *him*. Aya's heart raced, something like panic threatening to obliterate her senses even though she couldn't detect a whisper of his power.

I don't need an affinity to inspire fear, Aya love.

Something flared in Will's eyes then, as if he too was remembering the words he'd said to her mere days ago. His grip tightened on her arm. "We take them to the palace. Their fate rests with our queen."

19

THE SCREAMS WERE DEAFENING.

They reverberated throughout the dark corridors of the prison, piercing the cold, dank air like a sharp blade.

Aya slammed herself against the rough wooden door hard enough to make it rattle, her shoulder aching as she hit it again.

Again.

Again.

She knew these cells were impenetrable. The door was reinforced with iron forged by the Zeluus. There were no windows, the only source of light coming from Incend flames that sat in oval basins too high up the walls to reach, eliminating any chance of a prisoner using them for leverage.

There was nothing. Nothing but stone walls, that wooden door that would not break, and those screams. The pain in them. The pleading. It was enough to cleave through to her very core, to have her throw herself against that immovable door until her body ached, until her throat was raw from her own shouting.

The screaming didn't cease.

Aya backed away until she hit the rough stone behind her.

She covered her ears and slid to the ground, her teeth digging into her lip until she tasted blood.

Tova's screams were deafening.

And Aya was breaking.

It could've been minutes later. Or hours. It felt like an eternity either way by the time it finally stopped. For a moment, the only noise was a violent retching, followed by fading footsteps. Then the dungeon fell silent. Aya's eyes were glassy as she stared at the door.

She felt nothing. None of the aches from the Athatis. None of the pain from Will throwing her to the ground. She felt nothing but the numbness that radiated throughout her body, which trembled no matter how tightly she hugged her knees to her chest.

There were no cries from Tova's cell. There was no noise at all save for the steady drip of water somewhere in the hallway.

She had to be alive. Aya had to believe that she would've felt some shift in the world if Tova had died, some crack in the realm if he had truly taken her life.

She had to be alive. The alternative was too unforgivable.

But the blade. The papers. The book.

She refused to believe it. Refused to believe her friend was conspiring to destroy their home. Someone was framing her—someone *had* to be framing her. The fact that it was even in question, that Gianna would order *this* done to her general…

Aya closed her eyes as she rested her head against the wall behind her.

She should stand. Should prepare to face whatever was coming her way. Because he was coming for her next, of that she was sure. And it would be worse. It would be so much worse after what had happened in the market.

She'd be surprised if she lived to see another day.

Aya forced a breath, unable to bring herself to spend more than a few moments contemplating what she'd done. Every time she tried, her shaking grew worse. Perhaps she was still in some sort of shock. Or perhaps it was because with Tova's screams still ringing in her ears, she couldn't quite hold on to a thought anyway. Except for this:

That once again, she'd brought pain and suffering to someone she loved.

That if today was any indication, the question she'd been asking herself for thirteen years was true.

She was, indeed, a monster.

Forgive me, Divine ones. Forgive me.

Aya forced herself to her feet, her legs trembling beneath her. She steeled herself as she stared at that door. Slowly, she let her sleeves unravel from where she'd twisted them around her hands, her thumb brushing her left palm, seeking the soothing comfort of the raised skin there.

There was nothing.

Aya froze, the world slowing as she glanced down.

Her scar, the blood oath she'd taken to the Dyminara, was gone. Her thumb ran over the skin again, her nails digging into her wrist as she held her palm closer to her face, looking for some sign of the white ridge.

Her palm was bare, as if she'd never pledged those words. As if the gods knew she'd forsaken her oath.

As if they knew her very existence was an affront to the order and peace they had created.

Her chest began to heave, and before she could think of the pain in her ribs, she wrapped her arms around her middle as if she could contain her panic.

She didn't even flinch at her own vice grip.

It's the adrenaline, she tried to reason. But her fingers trembled as she lifted her sweater to inspect her side.

No trace of the bruises from the Athatis.

It was as if she'd never been injured at all.

"What's happening to me?"

The question was choked, her voice thick as her hysteria rose just as quickly as that burning in her veins in the market.

What's happening to me what's happening to me what's happening to me?

Cold sweat coated her body, her stomach twisting tightly as her vision blurred. A frantic prayer raced through her mind as she tried to steady herself—tried to reach for those calming techniques she'd learned—but Aya only retched as she emptied the contents of her stomach onto the floor. Panic raced through her, building like a wall of terror that threatened to consume her as she heaved again.

Distantly, footsteps approached.

Fear masks all senses—it renders one dead before a blow is even struck. It was what Galda used to say whenever the Sensainos unleashed their greatest fears on them during training. Aya forced a breath into her lungs.

You're better than this.

She twisted her sleeves around her palms again, fighting the heaving in her stomach at the thought of the smooth skin there.

You have been trained better than this.

Aya forced herself upright, her eyes fixed on the door as she pushed that panic down—further, further—until all that was left was an empty buzzing in her head, a cold sort of focus that she settled into as she waited for her due.

Will looked like hells. His black shirt was wrinkled, his skin wan in the flickering dungeon light. The door clicked shut behind him, and for a moment, there was nothing but silence as he watched Aya warily, his jaw tight.

Her body trembled under his gaze. Not with fear, she realized.

But rage.

Pure, undiluted rage.

Will stepped away from the door, keeping a wide berth as he moved into the cell. "You're going to want to take a deep breath." He ran a hand through his already-mussed hair with a sigh. "As angry as you are right now, I think you'd regret adding another death to your tally today."

Aya was across the cell in the span of a breath, her hand reaching for his throat. Will grunted as she slammed him into the stone wall.

"I won't regret a single moment spent ending your miserable life," she snarled, her nails forming white crescent moons as she dug into the soft skin of his neck. "And I'll take my sweet time doing it."

She'd kill him—but her rage consumed her, making it easy for Will to break her hold. He spun, slamming Aya face-first into the stone, her arm trapped between her back and his chest. Her cheek stung as it scraped against the rough wall.

"It's been a long day, and I'm not in the mood," he growled as he leaned into her. "So I'll say this only one more time. Take. A fucking. Breath."

She struggled against him, bucking and thrashing and writhing like a feral animal. "She's innocent!" The scream ripped from somewhere deep inside of her—the same place she'd locked that fear away.

"I know," he seethed, his breath hot on her ear. "She's alive because of it. If Kakos truly wanted to deal us a blow, what better way than killing our general without getting their own hands dirty."

So he agreed. Someone was framing Tova. Yet he'd tortured her anyway.

"You're a piece of shit," she snarled, wrestling to break free. All she managed to do was rip her skin further on the stone. But her anger was far easier to face than the layers of fear that threatened to overwhelm her entirely. "You're a sadistic piece of shit."

"Go ahead," Will breathed, his grip tightening on her arm. "Tell me what a monster I am so you don't have to face the fact that you're one, too."

He shoved her away from him and walked to the other side of the cell.

Aya's chest heaved as she forced air into her lungs, her fists clenching and unclenching at her sides. She reached blindly for whatever force had ravaged through her in the square, but all that was there was a hollowness that echoed into every part of her body. Will watched, his dark chuckle filling the space between them. "Having affinity issues, are we?"

"I'll use my bare hands if I have to."

He let out a long breath as he leaned against the wall across from her, his arms folding across his chest. "You're not going to kill me. The guards you injured are fine, by the way," he added lightly.

Fine, except for the four she'd killed. Aya repressed a shudder.

"A healer tended to them," Will said and let his arms drop to his side. "I know you didn't mean to hurt them."

"That's the difference between you and me," she hissed.

A simmering rage flashed in his eyes, barely held at bay as he pushed himself off the wall. "I was under orders—"

"I don't give a damn about your orders."

"You should," he snapped. "Or perhaps the guards in the market were right. Perhaps you *have* forsaken your oath. Tell me, Aya, how did you get entangled with Kakos?"

You and I both know it's not light that drives you.

"You lecture me on my oath, and yet you tortured someone you've sworn to protect." Bile rose in the back of her throat again, and Aya's jaw ached as she gritted her teeth. She'd kill him for what he'd done to Tova.

"I questioned her on Gianna's orders," he shot back. Wrath coated his tone, his temper finally slipping its leash. "Kakos has infiltrated this kingdom—there is no room for doubt."

"You disgust me," Aya seethed.

"I'm well aware. It's been a *joy* not to have to sense it for an entire godsdamn day!"

She stilled, and Will watched her intently, as if her face held the answer to some riddle. She knew that look—it was the same one she used when pressing a source for information.

"What do you mean, you don't sense it?" she said finally, the words practically a growl.

Will angled his head, his black hair brushing his brow. "I can't read you."

The air in the room seemed to tighten. Even with the cold of the cell, she could feel beads of sweat forming beneath her sweater.

"Like right now," he continued softly as he took a single step forward, a predator fixed on his prey. "I can see the panic on your face. But I feel nothing. I haven't been able to feel you since the Athatis attack. One minute I could feel your pain as if it was my own. The next..."

Her thumb brushed that healed skin, her heart beating furiously in her chest as she retreated, her back hitting the wall.

He agreed someone was framing Tova.

Perhaps he thought it was her.

She knew exactly how he'd try to confirm his suspicions, and now that he couldn't sense her...the issue with his shield wouldn't matter.

The pain wouldn't even reach him.

"Well I guess that makes your job here easier," Aya breathed.

Will went deathly still—as still as she'd ever seen him, the light in his eyes winking out. But a knock on the door sounded before his power could touch her.

He glanced toward it, his jaw working in frustration. And then he was in front of her, his fingers curling around her upper arm as he swung her around to face whatever lay on the other side.

20

Aya's stomach clenched as the door opened and Gianna stepped into the dungeon, her brown eyes alert as they swept the space. The High Priestess followed, her steps swift, likely here to read Aya her final passage of the Conoscenza before her soul departed this realm.

Aya would not be greeted by Saudra in the Beyond. She knew that now.

"Release her," Gianna commanded, her voice firm.

It seemed the queen wouldn't even bother to use her Enforcer, Aya thought. Not after what happened in the market. Perhaps she'd be sentenced to death immediately.

Will's fingers slowly uncurled from Aya's arm as Gianna stopped before them. "The ship is waiting at the docks."

Ship?

Was she to be exiled rather than killed? Could the gods truly be so merciful?

Gianna grabbed Aya's left hand, her soft skin cold in the dank air of the dungeon.

Aya braced herself for the sting of the knife, for that scar to be dug out of her palm as a marker of her treason. But then—

"My gods."

Gianna's voice was soft; almost reverent. Her eyes were wet as she dragged her gaze from Aya's palm to the priestess. "It's true. The Divine have not forsaken us."

Hyacinth stepped forward at the words, and Aya repressed a shiver as she ran a finger over where the scar of oath had been, her face contemplative beneath her veil.

"Born anew," the priestess breathed. "It's begun."

Aya blinked, the words taking a moment to register. She felt Will stiffen beside her, his arm shifting where it pressed against hers.

"What...what are you saying?" Aya finally managed.

"Aya," Gianna said, squeezing her hand, eyes shining as she stared at her, "darkness has begun to rise. And the Conoscenza states that when it does..."

A second of her kind will rise, born anew.

Aya swallowed, her heart racing so quickly her chest ached.

Surely Gianna couldn't possibly believe...

The prophecy called for a saint. And Aya...

She glanced to Will, who remained at her shoulder. His feet were braced, his shoulders square, and gaze unfeeling as he stared at Gianna. But she could feel the way the muscles in his arm were coiled, as if he were waiting to strike.

"We have been waiting for such a sign," Gianna was saying, her voice sounding muffled against the roaring in Aya's head. "And when William described your power..."

"The Conoscenza," Aya breathed, hardly listening. "The Conoscenza says..."

"That 'when darkness arises, the one the gods have chosen will be born anew, with the power to right the greatest wrong,'" Hyacinth finished for her. "Not even a healer can remove the scar from a blood oath. You are unmarked, child."

Aya could feel her pulse beating in her throat.

A mistake. A horrible, horrible mistake.

Tell them.

Gianna squeezed Aya's hand again, as if sensing her doubt. "Your pain from the Athatis, your bruises…gone too, yes?"

Tell them why it can't be you.

It wasn't possible. It couldn't be.

"Majesty," Aya whispered. "I can't be—"

"You question your gods?" the priestess interrupted. Aya could just make out the downturn of the priestess' lips as she stared at Aya from beneath her veil. "They say the Second Saint will lead the righteous should war unfold. They say the Second Saint will right the greatest wrong should the Decachiré arise once more. You would deny the realm a chance at survival?"

Aya couldn't breathe. Her lungs ached as she tried to force air in, as she tried to steady her pounding heart.

"What other explanation could there be for the power you displayed, Aya?" Gianna asked, a gentle smile lining her lips as she dropped her hand. "We've just seen the toll dark-affinity work takes on someone. The Diaforaté was weak and showed visible signs of his power's corruption. We know you have done no such thing. You…you are a blessing."

A lie.

This was not the confirmation they thought it was. She did not deserve such words of praise. If anything, she deserved their scorn. She should be on her knees, begging her gods for forgiveness.

Begging Mora for a different fate.

Tell them.

"But it is true that further confirmation is needed. We *must* be certain that we are correct in our assumptions that you are who the prophecy speaks of."

Gianna turned to Will. "She leaves for Trahir with you. Tonight. The Saj of the Maraciana will be able to sense her power, and their studies could aid in developing her affinity. Perhaps they'll have specific instructions on how it is to be used in the coming war."

The Saj were the keepers of knowledge, blessed by Sage, the goddess of wisdom. Some used their affinity to study the religious law; some even became priests and priestesses themselves. But those who studied *power*...they lived in Rinnia, where the grandest libraries, the Maraciana, had been established after the War. They dedicated their lives to maintaining and increasing knowledge around affinities.

And while they didn't concern themselves with the Old Customs of the gods, there was said to be no one who understood Visya power better. The Saj of the Maraciana developed their power so that they could identify an affinity in a Visya instantaneously.

Trahir suited them well.

"Do not speak a word of her power. Dominic is expecting you to discuss the trade terms, but I'll send word ahead that Aya is joining you to meet with the Saj to help us understand what's unfolding in Kakos. Perhaps our signs of preparation will encourage him to take the threat seriously, and will help *you* gain the commitment of their forces should Kakos attack."

Too fast.

Things were moving too fast.

"I can't leave," Aya uttered, her voice hoarse. "Tova. Majesty, she's innocent. You cannot—"

"Yes," Gianna cut her off, her gaze turning steely as she looked back to Will. "I told you to *question* her. Surely you must have known how easily that information could have been planted on her. Your severity was unwarranted."

Will's jaw shifted, his gray eyes stony as he focused on the queen. "My apologies for misunderstanding your orders, Majesty," he finally said slowly.

"Nevertheless," Gianna continued as she met Aya's gaze, "I cannot take any chances. Darkness *is* rising. And if you are indeed the one the prophecy speaks of, we must know how your power is to be used. I tried to warn my father when the rumors first arose of Kakos experimenting with affinities, that they would not be content to keep their heresy confined forever."

"And Tova?"

Gianna's face was grave. "Lena will lead the search for the supplier here. Until we find who is responsible…we must let whoever framed her think they were successful. It's far safer for her in here. We'll ensure her comfort."

Wrong. This was all wrong. Her friend would be disgraced.

"Yet you know she's not behind any of this," Aya started, her brow furrowing as she stared at her queen. Will shifted slightly, his arm pressing into hers further. A subtle warning.

"I will not be seen as weak," Gianna replied evenly. "And allowing my general to walk free after being caught with such a relic would do just that. Not to mention the perpetrator might make another attempt on her life." Gianna smoothed the folds of her white gown. "Tova will take responsibility for the fire to keep you protected. The guards will be persuaded to the same story. Those who are not amenable will be dealt with."

Tova would be dishonored in the eyes of their kingdom. There would be rumors of treason. She would be forced to stay here until the true threat was found. How long would that be?

Aya should be leading this search. She could be clearing her friend's name.

Because this…this would cost Tova her reputation. It would cost guards their lives if they couldn't be persuaded.

Her tally of suffering and dead kept growing.

"She will be well cared for, Aya," her queen promised. "I will see to it myself."

Aya's hands curled into fists, if only to contain the tremors that had started racking through her.

"Kakos could be searching for Aya, Majesty," Will

interrupted, stepping between them. "We should leave. I doubt they had eyes in the market, but if word somehow spreads…"

Tell them, dammit.

But Aya couldn't get her throat to work, couldn't fight past the panic rising in her chest.

"Go straight to the docks," Gianna replied.

The queen turned, and Will gripped Aya's arm, pulling her alongside him as they followed her out of the cell. Aya stumbled at the clipped pace, her legs having trouble keeping steady beneath her.

"Do not delay," the queen continued. "Stop for nothing. And do not let her out of your sight." Gianna turned to face Aya, her brown eyes softening slightly as she tipped her chin up. "We have waited a long, long time for you, Aya."

Aya couldn't fight through the emptiness in her head, couldn't overcome the way her mouth refused to voice her resistance.

Will came to a stop before the door. "By my blood, I will keep her safe."

And then he pulled her into the night, to the ship that waited beyond.

The roaring was back.

It rushed through Aya's mind like a river, muffling the sounds of the crew readying the ship as Will dragged her onto the main deck.

Even his vice grip, which had felt as tight as an iron shackle as they raced through town, had faded to nothing but a mere whisper against the burning inside of her.

She hadn't been able to form the words—hadn't been able to get her mouth to *move*, to tell her queen the truth, that there was no possibility that she could be the one the prophecy spoke of.

Not after all she'd done.

She'd failed not just Gianna, but her gods, and the devastation of that truth had kept her silent and numb.

She glanced up at Will, marking the tension lining his face.

He of all people would know she couldn't be the Second Saint. He'd practically spat it at her in the tavern mere hours ago.

It's not light that drives you. I've had the broken bones to prove it.

He'd had the words to damn her to the seven hells. But he hadn't said a thing in the dungeon.

Why? Why was he going along with this when he knew—

Aya's blood went cold as a thought took hold.

He knew.

Will was saying something. Something about the minutes they had left before they set sail. But she couldn't hear him over the raging in her head.

He knew.

He knew she persuaded those wolves. Had deemed it a sign of darkness itself. But he hadn't said a word about the incident to Tova. Or Gianna.

Just like all those years ago, when she'd sent him hurtling from that wall.

Will knew from the moment he fell that she was different. That there was something in her that wasn't right. He *must* have suspected it then. And he'd wanted her removed from the Dyminara. The easiest way to do it would've been to tell someone that her power had gone beyond her affinity. Beyond anyone's affinity.

He'd called her dangerous.

Told Galda she was unpredictable.

Said she lacked control.

But he'd never mentioned the one thing that would have guaranteed her removal.

It was as if…he'd never *wanted* them to know.

As Will led her from the main deck down a long dark hallway, Aya felt herself settle into that cool, dark place that often brought her vicious clarity. He was still speaking—his words a low buzzing in her ears as they walked past a row of small staterooms.

He knew.

He knew Ronan was on duty at the Squal the night she caught the tradesmen; and the guard had wound up dead.

Will had been missing from the beginning of the Dawning ceremonies; and the wolves had escaped.

He had tasked Liam to find that dagger, had insisted she stay behind while Tova went off on her own; and her friend had nearly been killed.

He had been there at each and every turn.

Perhaps they wouldn't need Lena's investigation into who was colluding with the Kakos.

Not if he was on board this ship with her now.

How?

How had she not known?

He steered her into a small stateroom lit by a solitary lantern. It was a cramped space, with a wooden desk bolted to the floor and a small bed anchored to the wall on the left. It was there that Will led her, his touch surprisingly gentle as he forced her to sit at the foot of the bed.

He crouched down before her, his gray eyes scanning her face. There wasn't a speck of green to be found in them.

"Aya."

Her name was a match to the fury burning inside of her.

She snatched the knife from his belt, her shoulder knocking him backward as she stood. He tried to keep his feet beneath him, and Aya used it to her advantage as she raised the knife and made to slash it viciously across his face.

Will raised his arm just in time.

Blood splattered from his forearm as the blade sliced through his skin.

His shout of pain only fueled her anger more.

Distantly, she heard Tova's screams in the back of her mind.

The floor jerked, and Aya stumbled.

The ship…it was moving. And it was just the distraction Will needed.

He grabbed her wrist as his foot hooked behind her ankle, and Aya crashed onto the bed behind her. Will managed to wrestle the knife from her hand as he pinned her, and she felt the cool kiss of the steel edge as it settled against her throat.

Aya lifted her chin, feeling the edge of the blade pierce her skin. "Do it," she challenged softly.

He wouldn't. Because Will needed her. Perhaps he thought she'd help his cause.

She'd rather die.

His grip tightened on the wrist he kept pinned to the mattress, her other arm held in place by his elbow. His bared teeth were a flash of white in the low light of the lantern. "Have you lost your mind?"

"How long?" she spat, her chest heaving. "How long have you been aiding Kakos? Have you ever been loyal to Tala? To the gods?"

She felt Will's muscles go taut, each line of him coiling tight as he continued to press that blade to her throat. Silence stretched between them, growing tenser with every moment he stared at her. An emotion flashed across his face, there and gone before she could place it. His breath brushed her lips as he tightened his grip on the blade.

"It's not like you to be so off base, Aya. Are you losing your touch?"

Aya bucked her hips, but Will didn't give an inch. His body was a warm, immovable force. "You insisted I stay behind with you," she said. "You knew they were coming for her."

"Liam discovered that dagger while we were at the docks," Will snarled. "He went straight to Gianna. That's why she sent in the Royal Guard."

"On your orders."

"You think I planted those papers on her? If I had, I wouldn't *have wasted so much time*."

Aya laughed, the sound cold and wrong. "And yet you've suspected my affinity was different for years, and you've never said a damn thing."

Silence fell between them, so tense that the air seemed to visibly tighten. Will's eyes darted between her face and the blade at her neck.

"Once again, you've jumped to the wrong conclusion," he ground out.

The sharp sting of the knife disappeared as Will rolled off her and stalked to the far wall. He hissed as he took in the gash on his arm, the blood running down his skin in red rivulets. "What was your plan—to get my confession of treason as I bled out?"

Yes.

She couldn't break through her anger enough to care that she had been about to go against years of training. She knew better than to eliminate a source of information. Yet her rage had overtaken her entirely.

"I know it's you," Aya growled. "I just don't know why I didn't put the pieces together sooner. Or why you've waited this long to act."

Will's eyes flashed with anger. "Exactly. If I were working with Kakos, I would have taken you away from Tala the minute you shoved me off the godsdamn Wall."

"You wanted me out of the Dyminara, and yet you didn't use the one thing that could have guaranteed it."

"I wasn't about to risk *my* place to do it. We were weeks away from taking our oaths and competing for a place by Gianna's side. I didn't know for sure why you'd been able to make me jump. If it had been an issue with my shield, I wasn't about to reveal a weakness like that."

His words washed over her, her mind fighting against the logic in them. Her marks lied all the time. "And what of the wolves? Why didn't you raise the alarm when you met with Gianna?"

He stiffened, but his tone was dangerously composed as he chided her. "So many questions, Aya love."

"Answer me."

Will prowled back to the bed, his jaw tight as he braced an arm on either side of her. "Because as I already told you in the bar, if anyone should have been suspected of dark-affinity work, it was *you*," he seethed. "And what better way for me to confirm my suspicions than to not let you out of my sight. Obviously I was wrong," he said with a hint of disgust as he waved a hand toward her, his eyes scanning her once, as if he could see every place a scar from the last three years had disappeared.

Aya blinked up at him, her body going utterly still as her mind raced to find some gap in his reasoning.

Had he been silent not because he wanted to wield her like some dark weapon...but because he thought she might be a threat?

Because he'd never thought, even for a moment, that the prophecy could have spoken of someone like her?

"Then why try to get me out of the market today?"

He scanned her face, and she felt his hands flex where they gripped the mattress. "Because once I saw that damn book and the horror on your face, I knew it wasn't you. I wasn't going to let you die."

"But you can't say the same for Tova, can you?"

Will straightened, his face tight as he took a step back. "No. I can't." The words were cold. Detached. Heartless. "I had an oath to abide by, and for all I knew in that market, Tova was a threat to our kingdom."

Aya's hands curled at her sides, her knuckles pressing into the mattress, as if she could keep herself anchored as her rage built.

I can make him hurt. Release me, it begged.

Will barked a frustrated laugh, his fingers snagging on his onyx strands as he dragged a hand through his hair. "Think about it, Aya. I have direct access to the queen. If I were working on behalf of Kakos, I would have killed her *and* you. It would be far easier for them to win the war with you dead, and it would've saved me years of the godsdamn agony of dealing with you."

Release me.

Aya's arms trembled as she gripped the mattress. Rash. She had been rash in attacking him—rash in trying to end him when there were still so many unanswered questions.

"You think I'm going to just trust your word?"

"You don't really have a choice, do you?" he snapped. "You don't get to the Saj without me."

Aya had no desire to see the Saj of the Maraciana. She knew exactly what they would tell her. And when they revealed that truth…when they sensed that there was something dark inside of her—something no saint could possibly have—what would she do then?

She'd never be able to return home again.

Will frowned, as if he could read the thoughts flitting through her mind. "Should I send word back to Gianna that you need extra motivation to complete your assignment? Perhaps she'll rethink Tova's comfort," he growled.

Aya bared her teeth as she stood. "You wouldn't dare."

Will bared his right back. "You've seen exactly what I'll dare to do. Try this shit again, and I'll send a godsdamn letter faster than you can bury your knife in my chest."

Aya's chest heaved as they stared each other down. He had her and he knew it. She'd never risk Tova. Which meant it didn't matter what Aya believed—saint or not, she would go to the Saj. What other choice did she have?

Triumph gleamed in his eyes as he smirked. "Now that we understand each other, here's how this is going to go: you're going to stop trying to kill me, and you're going to stay in this stateroom until I can stand the godsdamn sight of you, and when that happens, you're going to work on a plan with me, or on my oath, I will make Tova pay."

He tossed the blade onto the floor between them. Aya glanced between him and the knife, her gaze wary.

"Take it," he urged. "Consider it a peace offering. Like I said, if I had wanted you dead, I would've used it a long time ago."

Aya snatched the blade off the ground. "I hope you rot in the seven hells," she hissed as he headed to the door.

Will let out a low, bitter chuckle, the sound skittering across her bones.

"Trust me, love, I'm already there."

PART TWO

Enemies and Allies

21

AIDON COULDN'T STOP THINKING OF BLOOD.

It was almost as if he could hear the steady drip of it as he blocked his sister's blow, the metal of her sword flashing in the bright sunlight that beat down on them.

It had been Josie's idea to train on the small half-moon beach that sat on the far side of the cliffs. With the bluffs behind them and the ocean stretching for miles toward the horizon, there was little chance of anyone stumbling upon their session.

Aidon hadn't bothered to object. Dominic hated to find Josie training, and given how furious their uncle was at the moment, Aidon wasn't keen to do anything to worsen the king's mood—even if the rivulets of sweat now pouring down his body had him regretting his decision even more.

Aidon hadn't been in the throne room when Peter, the King's Second, read Queen Gianna's letter. He and Peter had been friends since they were boys. Aidon knew him well enough to know he did not exaggerate when he said the queen had been thorough, both in the execution and her recounting of it.

A traitor's death, she'd said, fit for those who conspired

with the heretics. Aidon wasn't sure if his uncle's fury was because the queen had handled their tradesmen's execution, or because, despite Tala's Enforcer receiving confirmation that the two men acted alone, he was on his way to Trahir with the queen's spymaster in tow.

The Queen's Eyes.

At least now Aidon would finally be able to put a face to the name.

"So they still think we're involved," Josie said flatly as she parried. She barely showed a hint of sweat on her umber-brown skin, despite the heat and her light brown fighting leathers.

Ridiculous. She could out-train most of his troops.

"Will was due here anyway to discuss trade terms, and they claim Gianna's Third has business with the Saj of the Maraciana."

Josie snorted before she whirled, bringing her sword down hard. Aidon blocked the blow, but she moved again, her foot hooking behind his and sending him stumbling through the sand. She had him disarmed a moment later, her blade directed at his heart.

"Distracted, brother?" She tilted her head to the side, the sunlight casting hues of red into the dark brown of her mid-length curly hair. Aidon rolled his eyes as he held up his hands in surrender.

"Uncle wants me to mark her," he said by way of explanation as he walked to the large rock where he'd discarded his shirt. He used the tan linen fabric to dust sand from his brown skin, a shade lighter than his sister's. He took a swig from the waterskin he'd tossed there before handing it to Josie. "You know how much I loathe politics."

Crown Prince he may be, but Aidon was better suited to the barracks and battlefields. He wanted to be training with his forces, or checking the city patrol, or doing anything, gods, *anything* other than listening to merchants squabble, or nobles preen, or whatever political posturing spying on Gianna's Third would entail.

"I don't trust them," Dominic had murmured as he paced his office, Aidon sitting straight-backed in the chair across the desk. "Who is to say they haven't framed our men for their own benefit? To use as an advantage in the Enforcer's negotiations? Do not think for one moment, nephew, that they're not here to further their own interests."

"Do you think our men were trading with Kakos?" Josie asked, drawing his attention back to the present as she took a seat on the rock, her gaze fixed on the choppy blue water. Aidon followed her stare, studying the small sailboats that dotted the horizon.

"Father seems to think not," he mused. "Though he's been reluctant to share much on the matter." As the head of the Trahir Merchant Council, Enzo would be the one to know. And, according to Dominic, *should* have known that they had two traitors in their midst. The argument between the two brothers regarding the rogue tradesmen had lasted for what seemed like hours. There were accusations of irresponsibility, and callousness, and a whole host of other heated words that Aidon could hear echoing out of Dominic's chamber.

It came to a head when Enzo seemed reluctant to alter the upcoming trade terms in retribution.

"You refuse your king, brother?"

That had been the end of the discussion.

Aidon's mother always said that something had shifted drastically in Dominic when he lost his wife, Madelyn, ten years ago. That when Madelyn died of her illness, Dominic's dreams died with her—dreams of a family. An heir of his own.

But Aidon hardly remembered a time when his uncle *wasn't* this way.

Stubborn. Arrogant. Cold. The antithesis to everything Madelyn had been.

Yet the tension between the brothers did seem to be getting worse of late.

"I asked what *you* think," Josie pushed.

"I don't think Will is one to make mistakes when it comes to securing the truth," he confessed quietly.

"*Don't* start. You two could stand to be civil. Especially if he's going to be here for a prolonged stay."

Aidon's mouth dropped in mock outrage. "*I* am *always* civil. Besides, it was a compliment."

It wasn't, and Josie knew it. She, for whatever reason, could stand the Enforcer. Aidon didn't necessarily dislike him. He just found Will to be…grating.

"Civil," his sister scoffed. "You're a rogue disguised as a charmer."

Aidon dropped onto the rock next to her with a sigh. "Is that what they say about me in town?"

"I try not to listen." She grinned at Aidon's frown and dusted sand from her leathers. "It must be *so hard* to be the trusted and favored one," she teased as she nudged him with her shoulder, her golden-brown eyes twinkling with amusement.

Aidon forced a laugh.

He'd petitioned his uncle on more than one occasion to allow Josie to fight, but the king refused, keeping her cloistered away in state affairs. They were but chess pieces, moving across the board under their uncle's calculated hand in the name of duty and responsibility to their Crown.

Aidon knew what it was to be duty bound. The rules of the realm were clear: only the eldest sibling could rule before the crown passed on to the next generation. It was how it moved through generations rather than staying stagnant—how it passed to *him* rather than his father.

Josie, who was two years younger, would never inherit the crown and never wanted to, but still suffered in her own way, with her own stifling responsibilities that she was forced to adhere to, wants be damned. He wondered if his father felt the same—if there was something more he'd rather do than lead Council meetings. Or what his mother would be doing if she weren't the King's Advisor.

A peacemaker between two quarreling brothers, more like it.

But that was beside the point.

Aidon, trusted and favored? He wasn't so sure his uncle would agree. For all of his arrogance and stubbornness, Dominic was the paragon of a king: cold and proper. Aidon was warm and bucked tradition. He loathed any marker of royalty, including the golden crown he used as a paperweight on the desk in his room. Needless to say, it infuriated his uncle, and made the lectures from his father ever present.

Duty.

Responsibility.

Loyalty.

They were the values that had been iterated in every lesson and lecture for as long as he could remember.

One day, Aidon, you will rule…

Aidon tugged his linen shirt over his head. "I'm due to meet with the City Guard," he said as he stood. Josie's brows shot up.

"The Bellare again?"

"They vandalized a restaurant in the Old Town owned by a young Visya couple."

Her face scrunched in disgust. "Why the sudden increase in activity?"

Aidon shrugged as he tugged on his shirt. The rebel group had been around for years. They were made mostly of humans—and a few devout Visya—who rejected the modern ways of Trahir, most notably Visya using their affinity outside of what the Conoscenza specifically decreed.

Religious zealots, his uncle often called them. Aidon was inclined to agree. The Bellare took their beliefs far further than even those who worshipped with the Old Customs.

And while the Bellare had mostly been harmless, recently

there'd been a surge in activity from the group in Rinnia. A vandalism here. A fight breaking out in a tavern there. Nothing incredibly dangerous, but enough of a change that Aidon wanted to ensure the Guard kept an eye out.

Perhaps the Bellare had caught wind of what was unfolding in Tala. Even Aidon had heard whispers of it in the bar he frequented with Peter, and that was before Gianna's letter arrived. Gossip always traveled faster than royal missives.

Their own general behind bars, rumors of dark-affinity work stirring, the brutal attack by their sacred wolves…

It was just the sort of thing the rebels would cling to as an indication the gods were angry, and they should repent or else.

Well, at least things are about to get interesting.

"Aidon," Josie called after him as he headed toward the steep rocky path that would take him up the cliffside. He shielded his hand against the sun as he glanced back at his sister. She looked every bit a warrior sitting there with her sword braced against the rock, her back ramrod straight, her fighting leathers cut precisely to her curvy build. She took him in for a second, a frown creasing her brow.

"Be careful," she said.

So she'd felt it too, then. The subtle sense of foreboding that had begun to settle over Rinnia.

The tradesmen. The Bellare. Tala.

Something was indeed unfolding.

Aidon gave his sister a reassuring grin. "I will be."

22

"I hear all this talk of your persuasiveness, Aya, but you know what I think?" Will shot her a lazy grin as he hopped up on the worn stones of the Wall, the strands of his black hair damp with sweat from their training for the Dyminara qualifications.

Visible from the port, the Wall was a beacon of might and power, even in its dilapidated state. Entire sections had been destroyed during the War, but there were still blocks that rimmed the palace grounds, some wrapping into the mountain face itself, as if the structure had been born of the granite of the Malas.

It was common for children to climb the ancient ruins, daring each other to get higher and higher. Those dares became outright challenges on the more treacherous points when they grew older—that is, when they weren't using its nooks and craters to get into other sorts of trouble that drew in teenagers with developing powers and bodies.

It was one of those high points on which Will balanced, his arms outstretched as he danced back and forth, mischief glittering in his eyes.

She hated the way he was looking at her—the way her stomach tightened beneath his gaze.

There was something unsettling about Will, some secret he kept hidden behind the seductive smiles and flirtations. She caught glimpses of it in the way he fought, in the way he made even senior members of the Dyminara tremble with a mere whisper of his affinity. There was something untamed in him—a beast he kept carefully locked away. It scared her that she recognized it so easily; that maybe, all those years ago, as he stood on her doorstep and watched her receive the news of her mother's death…he recognized something similar in her, too.

"Go on, tell me. Gods know you will anyway," Aya finally sighed. The training session with Galda had wiped her out entirely. The rest of the trainees were further down the mountain, a steady stream heading into the city. She'd been content to walk alone, but Will had been dogging her steps since they left the training compound.

"I think you couldn't persuade a bird to fly." Will spun once, his footsteps light on the crumbling rock. He shot her another taunting grin. "I think this gossip about your talent is all talk."

Aya rolled her eyes, turning her back on the Wall. He could talk himself off the ledge, for all she cared. His taunts had become endless the closer they got to qualifying—especially when it became known they were both being considered for Gianna's Tría.

"There it is, that wave of disgust I've grown to love," he called after her. Aya spun back to him.

"Get out of my head."

Another wicked grin. "But it's so fun to feel you war with yourself. You hate me, that much is obvious. But I think there's something else there, isn't there, Aya love? Something you'd rather not explore."

Aya tensed, fists curling at her sides. Her shield was up—her shield was always up, except for the few incidents when she felt any emotion too strongly. And if anyone could get a strong reaction out of her, it was the arrogant prick in front of her.

A weakness. One she hated.

"You're too in love with yourself to recognize when what you're feeling is your own self-obsession." Her voice was dangerously low as she took a step toward him.

Will just shrugged. "Maybe. Or maybe I'm right, and you're just ignoring it because that would mean you'd have to look at me like an actual person instead of the monster you've made me out to be." He shoved his hands in his pockets. Even standing on a ledge, he looked at ease. "You could persuade me to fess up, I suppose. That is…if you could get through my shield as easily as I get through yours."

"Fuck you."

"You'd love to, wouldn't you?"

Her pulse quickened. "You know what I'd love?" Aya snapped, taking another step toward him. Her lips curled. "For you to jump off this cliff."

Will's smile vanished as her persuasion hit him, her affinity having rallied without her even feeling it. And then he was falling, and she was screaming, and inside, a voice was whispering that she was right, that the reason she recognized darkness so easily was because she had it, too.

Aya was outside of her body, watching as she dashed to the edge, her shouts echoing through the still mountain air.

She knew what came next—had replayed this nightmare enough times to remember exactly how it would unfold.

The trainees would hear and come running. She would race down the hill, willing her legs to move faster as she stumbled on the rocky path. She would find him clutching his arm, his face as white as the bone that protruded from his skin, his teeth gritted against the pain. She would drop to her knees before him, hands outstretched desperately to stop the bleeding, to do *something* that could take back what she had done.

"Stay away from me," he'd growl, just as the rest of their companions reached them. They'd ask what happened, demand answers, and he would watch her for a moment before turning to the group and saying, "I slipped. Stop gawking and someone get a godsdamn healer, now."

And later, when the rest of the group was gone and Aya dragged herself to his father's town house to check on him, she'd wait in the hallway, listening to Will argue with Galda inside his room, urging her to remove Aya from the qualifications before she could hurt anyone else.

"She could've killed me," he'd snap. "She's too dangerous."

A long silence would follow before Galda's raspy growl would reply, "You should've kept up your shield."

Will wouldn't disagree.

"Interesting, isn't it," a voice remarked from her shoulder, drawing Aya back from her thoughts. Aya turned away from watching herself sprint down that hill, her eyes landing on the raven-haired healer.

She knew immediately which version of the nightmare she was in.

Not this one. Please, gods, not this one.

But the woman had never spoken before. She had a soft and steady voice and a kind face.

"What's interesting?" Aya asked cautiously. The healer fixed her blue eyes on her, her lips pursed as she considered Aya.

She was younger than Aya had thought—late twenties, at most.

"It's interesting you never realized it then," the woman answered. "He did." A nod to the Wall. "Or were you just too afraid to accept your fate?"

A chill stole over Aya, and she rubbed her hands across her arms.

"What fate?"

But before the woman could answer, Aya's own anguished cry pierced the air.

She knew that sound. Knew exactly what her screams meant.

Will was dead.

23

Aya lurched forward, her breath coming in a sharp gasp. The small stateroom was dark save for the moonlight that streamed through the porthole she kept locked tight, but she didn't need it to find the bucket next to her bed.

Aya lunged across the mattress, her stomach writhing as she vomited nothing but clear liquid.

The wind howled through the small cracks around the porthole, and she ground her teeth at the sound.

Whenever Aya's mother returned from her voyages, she would put Aya to bed with whispered tales of mermaids and sea wisps that danced around her ship, ensuring safe passage across the sea. "Velos's wind sings on the ocean, *mi couera*," she'd say, a wistful look in her eyes that told Aya that, while she was happy to be home, she could hear the wind of her patron god calling her back to sea again—back to some new adventure that filled her soul.

Aya would listen to her soothing voice and cling to her warmth, memorizing her caramel scent, hoping that if she held her tightly enough, her mother wouldn't disappear again. But the wind's song always won.

Aya found the wind didn't sing here. It shrieked.

Her breath came in short unsteady rasps as she settled back against her pillows and tried to remember which particular terror had drawn her from sleep.

Two weeks they'd been at sea, and each night her dreams were haunted by screams. Mostly Tova's or those guards in the square, but sometimes her mother's, too—as if Aya had been with her when her ship sank to the bottom of the Anath Sea.

It was agony, reliving these memories each night. And yet perhaps it was warranted; a payment for the sins she had committed.

She glanced at the small wooden desk bolted to the floor, another untouched dinner sitting atop the worn surface. Someone always came at mealtimes, but the various faces of the crew were indistinguishable in her mind. She didn't bother to speak to them, nor they her—except for the man this evening, who told her that she was expected in the second stateroom at dawn.

It seemed Will had decided he could finally stand the sight of her. He hadn't deigned to visit since she'd taken that knife to his forearm. With no healer on board, she'd half wished he'd do her a favor and bleed out and die.

She'd played along with his game. Had taken his order to stay in her room and would obey his summons. She'd do whatever she needed to keep Tova safe.

Besides...Aya was a master at lying in wait.

And Will...Will was hiding something. His rationale had been strong, strong enough that Aya's certainty of his guilt had begun to waver. But not enough for her to trust him.

Because there was some piece missing.

His explanations were thorough, but they didn't quite add up. All of that secrecy, and for what? To protect his reputation? To ensure that *he* would be the one to eliminate the threat when he suspected her darkness?

She knew Will to be arrogant, but these felt like half-truths, told to hide full lies.

Just like my own.

Aya straightened, pushing the thought aside.

That's what she'd dreamt of: the Wall. But something was different this time…the healer had spoken to her.

Aya's fingers curled into the rough fabric of her thin sheets as she remembered the healer's mention of fate.

She'd had two weeks to wrestle with Gianna's words. Two weeks to play her past on repeat as night bled into the early hours of morning and wonder if perhaps the gods had a different destiny for her. Two weeks to try to suffocate the tiny seed of hope that had taken root inside of her, the one that said perhaps Gianna was right about her power.

Because if her queen *was* right, if the prophecy did indeed speak of her, then that meant—

Aya cut off the thought immediately. It did her no good to cling to foolish hopes. Gianna could claim what she wanted. Aya knew the truth.

She was no saint. She was not the light her mother used to whisper about in those tales she told late at night about Evie and her equal.

Would her mother have ever imagined that one day someone would think her prideful, stubborn daughter was the one the Conoscenza spoke of; the one the gods would choose?

No.

Even then, Aya had been a serious, reserved child. The winter wind to her mother's warm and comforting spring breeze. *A cautious soul*, her mother had once whispered as she tucked her into her side. *But with a burning flame of love saved for those who warrant it.*

But whatever flame she had sensed in Aya had been doused as soon as her own had been extinguished on the waves of the Anath Sea. And Aya had buried her fear, her pain, her guilt, and leaned instead into the only things that made sense.

Control. Discipline. Distance.

She had found her place in shadows and darkness, in cold alleyways and dilapidated bars, in the smooth handle of a dagger and sharp steel of a blade.

She was not a beacon of light.

She was not a savior of nations or realms.

If the gods had chosen her, they had chosen wrong.

But Will had been right. She *was* dangerous.

So Aya would do what she did best. She would bury her fear and hone her anger into something cold, and quiet, and lethal.

Something that slipped through the night without detection.

Something that people never saw coming.

Something that could loosen secrets, and win allies, and maybe, just maybe, channel what was inside of her to aid in the coming war.

For Tova.

For her queen.

For the oath she had taken to protect her kingdom and serve her gods.

And perhaps for herself, too.

24

SHE'D TRIED TO KILL HIM.

Two weeks had passed, and Will was still bitter about it.

He sighed as he sat in one of the large staterooms, his fingers drumming on the battered mahogany table. He'd just barely caught it—that flash of something *else* in her eyes when she'd attacked him.

Aya had always been cold. But this…this was a fury so frigid it burned.

He leaned his head on his fist and glanced toward the portholes lining the wall. Nearly dawn. He wondered if she'd even bother to show up. She'd taken him seriously, it seemed, and stayed away. He hadn't seen her since he'd slammed her stateroom door so she could curse him without him having to hear it.

It was an impossible task, this journey of his. To get close to Dominic, to push through the trade terms, to get Aya to cooperate, to find a way to mask each and every betrayal he'd commit.

It was a fucking impossible task.

The door to his right clicked open.

Right on schedule.

Aya's footsteps were near silent, her face tight as she settled into the chair opposite him. She was in her leather pants, but she'd donned a white shirt—*his* white shirt that he'd had an attendant give her because her clothes had been covered in smoke and ash—and it slid off her shoulder as she leaned her elbows on the table, her hands clasped in front of her.

Her face was drawn and gaunt. He knew she hadn't been eating. He had seen those untouched plates being carried out of her room and heard her hurling her guts up each night, and he wasn't naive enough to think it seasickness. Not with the haunted look that had turned her icy eyes a dull shade of blue.

His affinity reached out instinctively, and he suppressed a shudder as it met nothing. Will couldn't feel a whisper of her, not even the cool essence of her shield. It felt like missing a step while walking down a long staircase. But he didn't need his abilities to read the anger simmering in her steely gaze.

She still didn't trust him. He couldn't blame her.

"No knife this morning?" Will asked lightly.

"It's strapped beneath the shirt. Will a strip search be part of your requirements too?"

Will's laugh was low, his brows rising as he lounged back in his chair. "Don't be a sore loser, Aya. It's not my fault you behaved rashly."

Aya leaned forward, her jaw flexing. "Don't speak to me like a child."

"Then stop acting like one," he snapped, his frustration unusually close to the surface. "You let your hatred cloud your judgment. We can't afford that in Rinnia."

Will reached for the scrolls on the table. "The trade agreements," he explained, unfurling the first one. "And everything I know about the Trahir Court," he said as he handed her the next. "Burn that after you read it."

Aya's brows rose as she peeked at the paper. "This is… thorough."

"It should be, I've been working on it for the better part of a fortnight."

That and avoiding that glorious look of hatred on your face.

Will folded his arms as he leaned back in his chair, the wood creaking beneath him. "We can't bully Dominic into lending us support in the coming war, especially with the trade agreements on the line. But his nephew, Aidon, may be amenable."

Aidon was the King's General of Trahir's armies. The perfect way in.

Aya scanned the papers again, her brow creasing as she studied the ink. "You want me to mark him."

It wasn't a question, but Will dipped his chin in confirmation anyway.

"Why?"

"Because his relationship with his uncle is fraught with tension, and I have a feeling we can use that to our advantage. Aidon lacks his uncle's callousness. Perhaps we can play on his tender sympathies."

"I thought you said bullying wouldn't be effective."

"And I thought you were a spy. Don't tell me you suddenly have a moral compass."

She leveled him a look as she rolled up the scroll, the meaning behind it evident—he wasn't one to be questioning morals.

"What of the Saj?"

He cocked a brow. "Come around, have you?"

Aya didn't bother to respond. He rubbed his jaw as he dragged his gaze back to the porthole. The Saj of the Maraciana knew far more of the affinities than anyone did—but there was one that rose above the others.

Natali was the brightest of them all and the most discreet. He had known them for years; which meant he *also* knew that they could be difficult to work with, especially if they felt one was unworthy of their knowledge.

"I have a contact there. I'll send word once we dock that

we'd like to meet with them. It may take some time. We'll review the Maraciana customs tomorrow."

Will was certain that once they sensed Aya's power, Natali would be more than accommodating, regardless of Aya's reluctance. Not from any deep devotion to the gods—no, the Saj of the Maraciana were far more interested in the laws of power than those of religion. But to study an affinity like Aya's?

Any Saj of the Maraciana would be delighted.

At least, that's what he was counting on. If not...he wasn't sure what he'd do.

"You don't honestly believe I'm a saint." It wasn't a question, but Aya's voice had that probing note that made him raise a brow.

"Since when do you care what I believe?" His evasion did nothing to soften her piercing gaze. "Clearly *you* don't want to be a saint, so what does it even matter?"

A probing of his own, he supposed. Because he had no idea what thoughts were circling in that head of hers.

"Do you even believe in the gods?" she asked.

"You can't be serious. First you accuse me of treason, now heresy?" Aya was unmoved by his frustration, which only grew as he glared at her. "Of course I fucking believe in the gods. Think what you want about me, but I'm no heretic."

Her voice was soft and vicious as she said, "Is that what you cling to in order to live with yourself?"

Sometimes, he thought he might actually hate her.

"Funny," he seethed, "I was going to ask if your utter devotion was your way of avoiding taking any responsibility in your life."

His heart hammered as anger, hot and heavy, pooled in his gut.

It was as if she knew...as if she could hear the arguments that raged in his head late at night.

Lately, Will didn't thank Pathos, his patron god, for his power.

He cursed him.

Aya's eyes flashed with anger. But he continued on before she could land another verbal blow, his chin jerking toward the parchment in her hands as he stood. "Either way, I suggest you start reading. You have a lot to get through."

"Enforcer?"

Will glanced up from the book in his hands, another historical fiction the captain had loaned him. He'd read four during their time at sea. It wasn't as if Aya was willing to socialize with him outside of the times he'd demanded they review their plans over the last week.

"We've just anchored," the first mate said from where he stood in the doorway of his room. "A skiff will be here within the half hour to take you to shore."

With the imposing cliffs that surrounded Rinnia, docking a ship of their size would be impossible. So smaller skiffs traversed the choppy waters, ferrying merchants and visitors from larger vessels to the small harbor on the far side of the shoreline.

Will nodded, closing the book with a snap before heading to the main deck. Aya stood at the railing, her dark brown hair whipping in the warm breeze. She was back in the black ensemble she'd left in, looking like a speck of night against the backdrop of the city, which sprawled up from the crescent moon beach, its buildings an explosion of color. Coral pinks and bright yellows and blinding whites and rich blues covered the landscape, lining the twisting paths that wound up the towering cliffs and stretching far into the city.

"Impressive, isn't it?" he said by way of greeting, following her gaze to where a shimmering sandstone palace, all arches and open windows, sat on top of one of the cliffs. She nodded, her hands tugging at her shirt. "The heat takes some getting used to. A lighter wardrobe will help. There are some shops we'll head to after we get settled in."

His brow furrowed as he watched a small skiff approach a neighboring boat. He'd had weeks to prepare for this. It wasn't enough. It never was.

He hated this city.

"We'll head to the castle first. We'll be expected to greet the royal family before settling into our rooms."

"I know," Aya muttered, her gaze fixed on the town.

"They'll likely ask us to join them for dinner—"

"I know," she cut him off again, moving to stalk past him. Will caught her arm, hauling her back.

"Then you *also* know that I'm about to remind you what's at stake. I need Dominic's favor, and you need access to the Maraciana. Don't screw this up."

She shoved past him, her shoulder all angles and bone as it rammed into his.

He'd have to work on that. The not eating. The nausea.

It was an impossible task, this journey of his. A fucking impossible task.

25

AYA STOOD WITH WILL IN THE MAIN HALL OF THE CLIFF-top palace, the pale marble floor glistening like sand and seeming to shift beneath her feet after so long at sea.

Open archways were rimmed by gossamer curtains that blew in the ever-present breeze, which carried the cries of the gulls and crash of the waves through the airy space. It was blinding, the brightness that flooded this place.

Aya marked the sentinels in the king's emerald-green livery, their backs ramrod straight as they guarded the entrances to the four halls that split from the atrium.

A new addition, if Will's notes were to be believed.

So much for trust between allies.

Aya couldn't really blame the king.

"It's an honor to have you with us, Prince." The attendant, a man with creamy skin and wiry chestnut hair who introduced himself as Ezekiel, gave a polite bow. Aya raised a brow at the title. "And you, madam. His Majesty is thrilled about your stay with us. He sends his apologies, but his greeting will have to wait. He's been pulled away to address a matter in the countryside but looks forward to seeing you at dinner this evening."

"Let's not lie to our guests, Ezekiel," a smooth voice drawled. "The old man is likely hunting."

A tall, lean man strolled toward them, his wide brown eyes sparkling with amusement. He was dressed casually in tan britches and a loose white shirt that showed off the brown skin of his toned chest. His dark brown curly hair was cropped close to his head, his cheekbones high, nose broad, his jaw square.

And the way he held himself, tall and proud…

Aidon. The Crown Prince of Trahir.

"That, or he's nursing his pride over this mess we've found ourselves in with our rogue tradesmen," the prince added lightly. "You know how wounded he gets." He stopped next to Ezekiel, the attendant bristling at his flippancy. Aidon's eyes were bright with mischief as he gave a slight nod of his head to Aya and Will. "No offense meant, of course."

"Your Highness," Will responded, bowing. "It's our hope to keep the mess to a minimum."

Aidon grinned, stepping forward to clap him on the shoulder. "Don't bother posturing, my friend. It's good to see you. You look well." He turned to Aya, a brow raised as he looked her over. "I heard you were bringing a friend." He let out a low whistle. "So *this* is the Queen's Eyes. You can understand why some might be…*alarmed* at your presence."

He winked.

Ah. So the guards *were* for her.

"You should be more alarmed if my presence is undetected, Your Highness," she replied as she bowed.

"Touché." Aidon grinned, his hands finding his pockets. "Please, call me Aidon. I hear it's your first time in Rinnia?" Aya nodded, and his smile grew as he snapped his fingers. "Then we must take a tour. Arrange us a carriage, Ezekiel?"

"Perhaps our guests would like to get settled first, Your Highness. I have yet to show them to their rooms."

Aidon's expression was hopeful. "Afterward?"

Will shrugged, the gesture easy and loose. "Unfortunately Aya's luggage didn't make it onto our ship. We planned to head into town to get her some clothes. We'd love for you to accompany us."

It was strange to see Will like this—somewhat amiable—especially having watched him tense at every mention of Aidon on their journey here. But Aya could still see the signs of tension. The tightness of his jaw, the way his smile didn't quite meet his eyes… The closer they'd gotten to Rinnia, the worse it had become.

But Aidon didn't seem to notice or care. He merely rubbed his hands together as he said, "Excellent. I'll meet you back here in an hour." And then he was off, a light whistle on his lips as he strolled from the main hall.

Ezekiel suppressed a sigh as he watched his prince go, before leading them to their rooms on the upper floors.

Aya's was first. Ezekiel pushed open the white double doors to reveal a spacious, circular sitting room. A velvet magenta couch and two pale blue oversized armchairs sat on either side of a jagged glass table, its base sparkling with what looked like seashells. Large colorful cushions and rugs were tastefully scattered throughout the space, and on the far side of the room, sheer white curtains marked two open doors, which led onto a large terrace that looked as if it hung over the sea.

"The bedroom is through there." Ezekiel nodded to the doors on the left side of the room. "And the bathing room as well." He turned his attention to Will. "We have you situated a few doors down, Prince. If you care to follow me…"

Despite Aidon's casual demeanor, they'd made sure to keep their rooms separated. Aya tucked that insight away as she stepped onto the faded terra-cotta tile of the terrace. The sandstone marble balustrade stretched the length of the suite, another set of doors leading into the bedroom. She had a completely unobstructed view of the sea.

Aya watched the waves crash into the cliffs below. The

horizon stretched on endlessly, and as she scanned it, she'd never felt so small. She hadn't truly thought of how little of the world she'd seen; of how comfortable she'd become in the sharp peaks and valleys of the Malas.

Aya turned away from the sea, making her way into the bedroom. A large four-poster bed with a plush white comforter and navy pillows took up most of the room, a mirrored dresser nestled against the wall opposite. A tall marble-lined mirror stood in the corner nearest the balcony. To the left of the room was a door that led to the bathroom—a bright white chamber with an enormous tub, double vanity, and separate toilet chamber.

The queen's palace always seemed grand, with its dark stone passages and cavernous halls, its fireplaces and stained-glass windows. But this…this made the palace feel quaint. Aya went to one of the sinks, letting the cold water she splashed on her face calm her spinning head. She heard the click of her bedroom door, followed by footsteps padding toward her. Will appeared, leaning against the doorframe as he watched her in the mirror.

"It's a lot to take in," he murmured as she splashed her face again. Aya reached for a fluffy white towel, patting her face dry before meeting his gaze through the mirror. The easy smile was gone, as if he had taken off his courtier mask and slipped back into his usual calculating self. "The color and the noise. It can be overwhelming."

She leaned a hip against the counter as she faced him, ignoring his attempt to settle her. "Aidon seems charming," she said lightly, folding her arms across her chest.

"That's the general consensus."

They stared at each other for a moment, the subtle crashing of the waves filling the silence between them.

"But you don't agree."

He shrugged. "I have my own opinions on the prince. And I know you well enough to know you don't actually care what they are."

Fair enough.

She pushed herself off the counter, angling her body to squeeze past him. But she paused as she dragged her eyes up to his. "You're right, *Prince*," she breathed, their bodies close enough that her chest brushed his. "I don't."

Will grabbed the doorframe, blocking her path forward. "Do not," he growled, leaning into her, "call me that."

Aya raised her chin, refusing to shrink away from him, even with the doorframe digging into her back, the firm lines of his body pressing into her front.

"But it's an honor, isn't it?" she asked, his warmth seeping into her. "Your reputation precedes you."

The doorframe groaned slightly under his grip.

"I don't think you want to start talking about reputations, Aya love." His eyes flared as he stared down at her, his breath caressing her mouth as he whispered, "Do you?"

Aya raised a hand to shove him off her, but his gaze darted to her wrist, his gray eyes sparking as he took in the flames wreathing her fingers—flames she hadn't even sensed. Some part of her recoiled from the sight, and it was like dousing her hand in a bucket of water. The flames vanished.

"Interesting," he murmured, taking a step back. He tilted his head, his hair sliding across his forehead as he considered her. "Do you need to stay hidden until Natali teaches you some control?"

Aya bristled at the taunt. "You can't hide me away without the king suspecting we're up to something." Will's eyes narrowed, and Aya smirked. "What a warm reception he gave you."

"Us," Will corrected as he strolled toward the door, his hands sliding into his pockets. "I'll meet you in the front hall in a half hour. Don't be late."

26

THE STREETS OF RINNIA WERE AS CHEERFUL AS THEY WERE colorful. A fine layer of sand covered the cobblestones, as if the beach couldn't help but want to be near the citizens who strolled along the main thoroughfare, many with their faces upturned to the sun.

"It's been an unseasonably cold winter," Aidon explained, following Aya's gaze to one such couple. "We're grateful for the return of our usual mild temperatures. Though I suppose to you the past month would have felt pleasantly warm."

Aya wasn't sure she'd have called it pleasant. Beads of sweat gathered at the nape of her neck despite having braided her long hair back. But she forced a smile regardless, the muscles around her mouth twinging at an expression that felt foreign after the last few weeks.

They continued further into the heart of the city—the Old Town, Aidon explained—stopping at various clothing shops filled with light and revealing fabrics that marked the typical Trahir fashion. Aya knew she should pay more attention to what she selected. Her wardrobe would be another weapon in her arsenal. But with the heat bearing down and her body exhausted from the journey, she had little energy left to care. She flipped through the clothes quickly, her head swimming with the brightness that assaulted her senses.

If the shop owners were surprised to see their prince among them, they didn't show it. In fact, they greeted him with a warm familiarity he returned, remembering each by name and asking after their various affairs.

Aya, Aidon, and Will made their way into another plaza, this one marked by a small fountain in the center and rimmed by quaint cafés, each with a different-color awning to keep its patrons shaded from the harsh sun. It struck Aya that her mother must have loved this city. She'd never thought to ask, to learn if she found the heat of Rinnia preferable to the cold of Dunmeaden, to hear what foods she had tried and what they drank in lieu of chaucholda. Perhaps Aya had been worried the question would make her mother leave all that sooner.

"What happened here?" Will's voice tugged her from her thoughts, and she followed his gaze to a small cerulean-blue restaurant that sat vacant. Its large window had been shattered, shards of glass still littering the stone floor inside.

"The Bellare," Aidon said darkly, his brow furrowed as he took in the beechwood door hanging haphazardly on its hinges as if someone had tried to pry it off entirely.

"The what?" Aya asked.

The prince heaved a sigh. "They're a group of rebels. They claim to be devout worshippers of the gods and reject any modernization. They believe that by allowing Visya in the Trahir Council and other positions of power, or any not *expressly* outlined in the Conoscenza, we're going against what the gods intended. They claim to have humans' best interests at heart; that by ensuring Visya are kept in their place, they're protecting the vulnerable."

"Aren't they harmless?" Will frowned, his gray eyes sweeping over the damage.

"They were. But we've seen a recent surge in activity." Aidon nodded at the restaurant. "The couple who owns this place are Visya. They've been too frightened to return, even with the City Guard watching the plaza."

Aya's stomach roiled. Tala may be more traditional in their adherence to the gods' desires, but this…this was a perversion of the Conoscenza.

"They attacked them because they own the restaurant?" Aya pressed.

"They're zealots," Aidon muttered. "My uncle…and his father before him…and his mother before *him*…they held a different vision for our kingdom. We have long since learned that if we are to prosper, if *all* of our people are to prosper, then we cannot treat the Visya as our servants. We must be equals. The Bellare hate it."

"Servants," she said flatly. "The Visya were never meant to be such. We serve the gods."

The Visya in Tala sought to uphold their sacred duty. It was an honor.

Aidon frowned, his head tilting as he regarded her. "I only meant we don't believe the Visya's purpose is so… prescribed."

"Sorry to interrupt, Your Highness." A woman appeared at Aidon's shoulder, her green livery marking her as an attendant of his court. But it was Will she looked at as he continued to survey the wreckage with a frown.

"Councillor Lavigne wishes to see you, Prince. He was informed of your arrival and wishes to discuss the recent tariffs prior to tomorrow's meeting."

Will swore under his breath. "Can it wait?"

"I'm afraid not. Avis was quite insistent."

"I'll be there in a moment," Will replied tersely. The woman bowed and took her leave.

Aya frowned as she surveyed Will. "Council business already?"

A muscle in his jaw flickered. "Unfortunately."

"I'd be happy to continue the tour," Aidon interjected.

"Now that we're done shopping, there's another spot I'd love to show you."

She should go with him; it would be rude to decline. Yet she was more than curious about Will slithering off just as they'd arrived.

One of Aidon's guards cleared his throat and stepped forward, his face nervous as he glanced between Aya and Aidon. "We'll accompany you, Your Highness."

Aya bit back a grin, but Will didn't bother to hide his laugh. "Do they always follow you around like dogs, Aidon?"

Aidon's answering smile was tight. "Only doing their job, Prince. But I'm perfectly capable of defending myself. If memory serves me, you've had the black eye to prove it."

Will merely shrugged. "Whenever you'd like a rematch, Your Highness, you know where to find me."

Aya stepped to Aidon's side and took his outstretched arm. "I'll see you later," she said pointedly to Will. She didn't bother to wait for his response as she let Aidon pull her away from the wreckage.

"Forgive me if I misspoke back there," Aidon said as he led them out of the plaza. "I meant no offense."

Aya's shoulders lifted. She knew how other kingdoms mocked Tala's ways. She'd heard enough tradespeople remark on how outdated their beliefs were. "Don't think twice about it," she assured him. "But tell me...was it your plan all along to get me out on my own?"

Aidon chuckled, the sound reverberating through her as he steered them down a narrow side street. "As much as I'd love to take credit for the interruption, I can't. Though I won't deny being glad for it. I find you *far* less pretentious than William."

"How long have you known each other?"

"Seven years." A couple squeezed past them, and Aidon

nodded his hello. They were the only other people on the street, which began to steepen as they made their way further into the cliffs on the outskirts of the city. "We met when we were sixteen. His father brought him along on a Council visit. Will thought me the spoiled son of the head of the Council; I thought him the cocky son of a man whose only motivation in trade is one born of greed."

It spoke volumes, she supposed, that in a kingdom of such wealth and prosperity, Gale's greed was discernible.

"We both skipped the Council dinner that night and got rip-roaring drunk at one of the taverns in town. Our fathers were furious. It was the first time I realized that perhaps we had more in common than I thought."

"A tendency to make poor decisions?"

"That, and very complicated relationships with our fathers." Will had mentioned Aidon's tension with Dominic, but had said nothing of the strain with Enzo. She tucked the information away, unwilling to press too hard too soon. As for Will…she'd never considered his relationship with Gale. They always seemed to get along fine, but then again, she never saw them together outside of Council affairs.

"So where does the black eye fit in?"

"Ah. *That.* That was two years later. I invited him to train with me and my forces. We got it into our heads that we should spar, and well, let's just say we were both young and hotheaded and gloriously foolish."

"And now?"

He paused, and his dark brown eyes, rich and warm, sparkled as he looked down at her. "Older, more mature, and yet…still gloriously foolish, I would imagine." The corners of her mouth twitched, and Aidon cleared his throat, turning back to the building they'd stopped in front of. "We're here."

"Here" was a small white temple that faced out to sea on the edge of the cliffs, its stained-glass windows winking in the late afternoon sun. Aidon led her inside to where an unassuming pulpit stood against a wall of windows, giving an extraordinary view of the ocean. On either side of the old wooden pews were stained-glass windows, each depicting one of the Nine Divine.

There was Nikatos, god of war, wielding his legendary sword. Next to him was Mora, goddess of fate, her healing glow surrounding her like a veil of light. Then Hepha, goddess of flame, wreathed in fire. Next to her, Velos, god of wind, with his arms out, a fierce gust swirling around him. Then Cero, god of earth, a flower stemming from their palm.

And on the other side of the temple stood Aquine, god of water, a single tear of rain on his face. He was followed by Pathos, god of sensation, his heart visible through his skin. Then Saudra, goddess of persuasion, a coy smile on her lips. And closest to the pulpit was Sage, goddess of wisdom, a crown of scrolls sitting on her head.

The rest of the windows were clear, all except for a small stained-glass square that sat at the top, directly above the altar. It was a deep navy-blue save for a burst of bright light that radiated from its center, as if the sun had exploded when it touched the pane.

A homage to Evie.

Aya shivered as she gazed upon the symbol of the saint.

"This is my favorite place in all of Rinnia," Aidon murmured as he wandered toward the front of the temple, his eyes fixed on the sea. "It's quiet. And quaint. Somewhere I can just be. Plus, the view is spectacular."

"It's beautiful," she agreed.

Aidon shot her a grin. "I know our kingdoms have our differences. But we're not heathens, you know. We hold the gods in high regard."

He pursed his lips as he surveyed the interior, his brow furrowing slightly, as if he was considering his next words. "Though I will admit," he said slowly, "I don't know of any kingdom that rivals the devotion of yours."

She hadn't dared touch her power since the market. But reaching for her persuasion now was second nature. Aya's skin prickled, a wave of cold coming over her as she pushed her power toward Aidon in the hopes of loosening his tongue further.

"I do fear our commitment to the gods will be called into question soon enough," he added.

Aya's fingers gripped the back of the pew until her knuckles turned white as she tried to steady herself. Her affinity buckled as it reached the prince, and she let out a shaky breath.

Aya let her power drop, fighting against the cold curling in her gut.

"How do you mean?" she managed to say.

Aidon let out a long breath, his hand rubbing the back of his neck. "I've heard the rumors of what's unfolding in Kakos. I suspect they're why the Bellare is starting to cause problems. And though my uncle enjoys our isolation, I think the world will insist on our involvement in these affairs, or else *some* might think us sympathetic to a darker cause." He gave her a pointed look, but his features softened as he scanned her. "Are you feeling all right?"

Aya let her eyes close as the room tilted.

"I think the heat is taking its toll. Do you mind if we return to the palace?"

Aidon was at her side in an instant, his hand warm as it pressed against the small of her back. "Of course not. I'll send for a carriage. Let's get you some water in the meantime."

She let herself lean in toward him as he led her from the temple, a wave of relief swooping through her as she left the gazes of the Divine. She glanced up at him, taking in the lines of his handsome face, his scent—like embers in the sea breeze—settling over her. And as his hand slid from her back to her waist, his arm wrapping around her more fully to steady her, she could easily see why so many flocked to him. Aidon was warm and sturdy and kind.

And while she would do what she needed to gain his trust, there was something about Aidon that was soothing and solid. If the way the townspeople had reacted to the prince was any indication, they felt it, too.

It was as if he were the sun, and those around him were simply stretching to be near his light.

27

Will lounged on the magenta couch in Aya's sitting room, one arm tucked behind his head, his legs draped over the rounded arm. Bags and boxes from various shops littered the floor around him, and he couldn't help but raise a brow as he surveyed the damage Aya had done.

Clothes *were* weapons, he supposed.

His gaze roved to the white ceiling, his mind churning as he stared at nothing.

Less than five hours in this city, and he already wanted to hit something. The meeting with Avis hadn't helped. He'd tried to hold his tongue, especially given Avis's daughter, Helene, was in the other room. But Will had more important things to be doing than stroking the egos of fragile councillors.

The Bellare was on the move. That was an interesting development. One he could use to his advantage. If they were already irritating Dominic, he could—

The brisk snap of the door jarred him from his thoughts. Will was on his feet in an instant. Aya paused in the doorway, her face flushed as she took him in, whips of hair stuck to her damp cheeks.

"What is it?" Will asked. She darted past him as she headed toward the bedroom. "Aya."

He heard the bathroom door click shut, her retching echoing off the marble.

He found her slumped over the toilet, her head braced on her arm. She looked so small curled up like that, her body trembling. Will kneeled behind her and placed a tentative hand on her back. She didn't flinch. Slowly, he began to rub soothing circles there. The heat of her skin radiated through her shirt.

"You're overheated. You need food and water. And a change of clothes."

Aya tensed as she emptied the contents of her stomach again. "Can't eat," she rasped. He moved his hand to her neck, his fingers massaging the tense muscles there. It was a testament to how poorly she felt that she let him.

"You didn't vomit in front of the prince, did you?" he teased, sitting back on his heels as she sat up a moment later.

"Save it," she said wearily, dragging the sleeve of her shirt across her damp forehead. She looked like hells.

Will frowned, his eyes searching her face. "Did you eat or drink anything while you were out?"

"I wasn't poisoned."

"Can't be too careful. Especially given the less-than-warm reception we received from Dominic. And if there are rumors that the Second Saint has been found and Kakos has heard, who knows what they might do..."

"Don't call me that," Aya muttered, her jaw set as she stared past him. "And Trahir is our ally."

Will's brows flicked up. "Is that what Aidon was whispering in your ear on your little stroll?"

Her eyes were cold as they met his. "I know he's marking me. I'm trained to recognize such things. I'm not a fool."

"No, you're not," Will agreed as he pushed himself off the floor. He reached a hand down to help her, but Aya brushed him off, her face tight as she hauled herself up. He stayed near her as she moved to the sink. She looked a breath away from going unconscious.

"I'll send for a tonic to help with the nausea."

Aya merely turned the faucet on, her gaze dull as it met his through the mirror. "Don't you have Council business to attend to?"

"That's an odd way to say thank you," Will mused.

Aya closed her eyes. "Please just go away." The words were soft, and the exhaustion in them had his lips pressing together as he scanned her again. He stepped toward the sink, his arm reaching across her to grab one of the washcloths and run it under the cold water. A slight tremor worked through her as he placed it at the base of her neck.

"I'll see you at dinner," he said softly.

28

"Are we drinking yet?" Aidon asked as he strolled through the formal dining chamber, the marble floors so polished he could nearly see his own reflection. A breeze blew in from the five open arches that made up the back wall, the terrace beyond them basked in the dusk glow.

Josie turned in her seat and threw him a grin as she raised her wineglass. "Will and I were just getting started."

Aidon nodded to the Enforcer as he approached his seat at the head of the golden table, his fingers making quick work of the buttons on his emerald jacket.

"Why even bother with it then, Aidon?" Josie asked as he flung it over the back of his oak chair and sat down with a sigh.

"I couldn't let you two look better than me, could I?"

His sister was indeed dressed for their guests in a resplendent suit of wine red, the jacket buttoning at her sternum and showing off her bare skin beneath. Will had donned his usual fitted black jacket and pants, his fingers tugging at the collar of his white shirt. Josie smirked. "Is our Prince of the North having trouble acclimating to the weather?"

"If only I had your fashion sense, Josie."

Her brown eyes twinkled with amusement, but the sound

of the door opening had her whipping her head around as Aya entered the room.

She wore a dress with short sleeves and a loose bodice that cinched at her waist before dropping into a flowing, floor-length skirt that pooled on the floor. Aidon scanned the emerald-green fabric. The attendant had chosen nicely. They might as well have been a matching set.

"Green suits her, don't you think?" Aidon muttered to Will as she approached.

He hadn't missed the way the Enforcer had frowned when she entered, his finger circling the rim of his wineglass as he took in her dress. Will shifted his attention to Aidon, his face neutral as he took a sip of wine. "I prefer Aya in black."

"Aya!" Josie pushed her chair back and pulled the woman into a hug.

Aidon watched as Aya tensed, her arms stiff as they circled Josie.

"I'm so glad you joined Will on this trip." His sister pulled back with a conspirator's grin. "These two are a pain in the ass to deal with alone."

Aidon couldn't help the chuckle that rumbled through him as he lounged further back in his chair. "I'm wounded, Josie. We've always made such lively company for you."

His sister rolled her eyes as she tugged Aya to the seat next to her.

"What he's really trying to say is they're always getting into trouble, and I'm always having to pull them out."

"And here I thought you mentioned being older and more mature," Aya teased, a small smirk on her lips as she peered at Aidon. Light-gray shadow covered the lids of her kohl-lined eyes, the soft pink of her lips pairing nicely with a touch of rosiness that had been added to her cheeks. Her hair was in loose curls that hung down her back, one side pinned behind her ear with a silver comb.

Josie snorted into her wine. "Did you really, Brother?"

"I might have said something along those lines," he said lightly. He felt his own lips tip up as he regarded Aya again, marking the way she leaned one arm on the table, her body angled toward his.

This was a game he could play—and one he could play well.

"You look like you're feeling better," he remarked. He let his eyes scan her dress again. But before he could continue, a small oak door on the far side of the room swung open, revealing his parents and the king.

His uncle led their small procession, and even though Enzo and he were twins, born merely two minutes apart, it was never difficult for Aidon to point out the stark differences between Dominic and his father.

Dominic was broad, with pale skin, a square jaw, and beady green eyes that held a look of constant calculation, which seemed to intensify as he looked at Aidon and Aya, as if measuring the distance between them. His black hair was short, wavy, and speckled with gray, and topped with the bone-white crown he was rarely without. Tonight, he wore a gray linen suit and white shirt.

Enzo stood a few inches taller than his older brother, his build lankier, his green eyes a hint warmer than the king's. His hair had long turned gray, and he only donned the silver crown that currently topped his head during state occasions. Apparently tonight qualified. He sported tan linen pants and a matching jacket, his white shirt beneath it unbuttoned at the collar.

Aidon and Josie's mother, Zuri, walked arm in arm with their father, Enzo. Her gown was of pure white, tied around her neck, its fabric open and flowing, showing off her curves and black skin. Even in her silver heels, she was several inches shorter than Enzo, the point of the green emerald at the apex of her silver crown level with his nose. Her long hair was braided and fashioned into a bun at the back of her head.

The four already seated stood, greeting them with a bow

as Enzo led Zuri to the chair at Dominic's right before settling to his left. Lead Councillor. King. Advisor. "Welcome," Dominic said to Will and Aya, his voice smooth and deep from his place at the head of the table. "Please be seated."

The attendants, who had been waiting in the wings, snapped into action, hurrying to the kitchens to grab platters of food. Dominic held up his glass and smiled. "To enduring friendships," he toasted. An edged greeting, if Aidon had ever heard one. But Will merely raised his own glass and answered smoothly, "To your generous hospitality, Majesty."

The wine they sipped was sweet and bubbly, the perfect pairing for the warm breeze that blew in through the open archways.

"It's a pleasure to welcome you both to our kingdom," Zuri said, her eyes landing on Aya. "Aidon tells us this is your first visit to Rinnia, Aya. How do you find our city?"

"It's beautiful." She turned to Dominic. "Thank you, Majesty, for agreeing to my stay."

"I must say," Dominic drawled as an attendant lifted the lid on his plate, "I'm surprised Gianna sent *two* of her most trusted Dyminara to our shores. Especially after I assured her the two tradesmen were operating independently of our kingdom."

Will cleared his throat. "Aya is in need of knowledge from the Saj of the Maraciana, Majesty. We felt it would be better not to inconvenience you with two separate visits, given I'd already be here to discuss our ever-flourishing partnership."

Aidon bit back a grin at Will's silver tongue, but Dominic wasn't impressed. He hardly repressed his scoff. "Gianna says Kakos has progressed in their attempt to create raw power."

Aya dipped her chin. "I'm sure you've heard of the Diaforaté attack on the Athatis, Majesty."

The king's eyes sparked as he took a sip of his wine. "Aided by your general, if the rumors are true. We hear she was found with a relic of the practitioners."

Silence rippled across the table, tense and tight. Such an act was the worst type of dishonor. Aidon watched Aya's face carefully, but the spy didn't so much as blink. She was as steady as she'd been in the temple when he'd alluded to the trouble in the Southern Kingdom.

"And what will happen to your general for such a crime?" Dominic continued.

Will's grip tightened on his glass for the briefest of moments, but his voice was as smooth as silk as he said, "I can assure you our queen has her own plans on how to handle the infiltration. In the meantime, Aya's research will be crucial to helping our army prepare. We'd be happy to share any findings with your forces."

The king waved a hand at the offer. "We have no need to take such drastic actions."

Aidon stiffened in his seat. "I wouldn't call preparing my soldiers drastic, Uncle," he interjected.

"Here we go," Josie muttered, stabbing a piece of asparagus onto her fork. Their mother shot her a look, but she looked equally wary as Dominic and Enzo stared Aidon down.

The disapproval in their gazes was identical.

Aidon knew they were his uncle's troops. His uncle's people. But Aidon would be damned if he'd let Dominic speak for him in front of their allies this way.

"With all due respect to our esteemed visitors, it sounds as though this conflict is for Queen Gianna's forces to sort out," the king remarked, dismissing Aidon as he turned to face Will.

Aidon's hands curled into fists beneath the table.

Will sat back in his chair, an easy smile on his face. "We understand your hesitation, Majesty. Perhaps over the coming weeks we can discuss the matter more." He flicked his gaze to Enzo, who merely stared impassively back. "For now, we are simply grateful to have access to your kingdom and continue to strengthen our partnership."

Calm. Will was utterly calm, and Aidon thought he might hate him for it. Already his uncle was grinning, his shoulders loosening as they moved away from talks of conflict. Aidon didn't know how to stay so unaffected, so visibly unruffled, when his uncle cut him off at the knees. But Will…he didn't seem to give a damn.

"I look forward to Enzo's updates on your conversations with the Council, William," Dominic purred. "It's always such a pleasure to meet with Tala's most trusted advisor and the queen's…*closest* confidant."

The words were light and friendly, but it didn't stop them from settling in the space like a stone. Aidon had heard those rumors, too. He watched Aya glance at Will, the first crack in her carefully curated mask.

But Will just grinned, his voice slipping into an easy drawl as he said, "Thank you, Majesty."

29

"Not a complete disaster" was all Will muttered about dinner before stalking to his room and closing the door with a sharp snap, leaving Aya alone to ruminate on all that had occurred.

She peeled off the emerald dress and slid into the short gray nightgown the attendant had left. She'd heard Aidon's comment about the color choice and hadn't missed the way his eyes roved over her when she leaned toward him at the table.

A flirt, she reminded herself. He was a flirt, and a very good one at that.

As was she. It did surprise her, though, how little she had to try with Aidon. As if her flirting weren't forced at all.

Don't act like you'd kick him out of your bed.

Aya pushed the thought away, rolling her neck once. She didn't have time for such distractions. Especially now they knew how slow a process it would be to get Trahir to commit their forces should Kakos attack.

There hadn't been any more talk of Kakos. Will had warned that Dominic wouldn't warm easily, and that per Gianna's instructions, they should take it slow. But Aya was still surprised at how dismissive Dominic seemed.

She knew Trahir to be more focused on riches and modernizing their empire than serving the gods, but even Aidon had remarked on Trahir's maintained reverence for the Divine.

It seemed Will was right: the prince would be a helpful ally indeed.

Aya glanced in the mirror as she made her way to the bed, her steps slowing as she marked the sharp angles in her face.

She hadn't been lying when she told Will she couldn't eat. It was as if the power that exploded out of her in the market hadn't just burned through the square... It had burned through her, too. She wasn't quite sure what had been left in its wake.

She could almost hear Tova's exasperated tone. "*Always so dramatic.*"

The thought of her friend turned the dull ache in her chest into a piercing pain. Word of Tova's alleged treason had reached even here. Which meant in Tala the soldiers she led would be trading whispers about their beloved general, wondering how they could have missed the signs. Her family would be the object of scorn.

And Aya and Will would be the heroes who apprehended her. Who saved their kingdom from the evil of Kakos, saved Tala's armies from falling before war had even begun.

A lie.

It was disgusting.

It was despicable.

It's your fault.

Aya's body felt heavy as she settled under the sheets of her bed.

At least she could find some small comfort in Gianna's promise that Tova would be cared for. She could only hope that when they met with the Council, they'd learn something to help in Lena's search for the supplier.

It wasn't enough to stop her from wondering...when this was all over—when Aya found a way to use whatever was inside of her and return home—would Tova forgive her for leaving?

Aya kicked off the covers as she shifted in the bed. Even with every window and door open, the heat felt oppressive. Her head throbbed. The sparkling wine had left her mind feeling full and empty all at once, the small morsels of food she'd managed settling uneasily in her stomach after her vomiting this afternoon.

She shuddered as she thought of what happened in the temple. Her affinity had never felt like that. And when she'd tried to persuade Aidon…

Broken.

Her affinity felt broken.

Something had changed after the market. It was as if her well of power was a festering wound that prodded her frustration and anger until they were always right there beneath the surface, close enough to cloud her clarity and rationale.

That anger that she'd felt when she'd attacked Will… She was no stranger to rage. But this time, it latched on to her, its vise grip nearly more than she could control.

And Aya knew that nothing was more important than her keeping control.

She rolled in the bed again, her pulse pounding a steady beat in her throat. Will had written to Natali when they arrived. What awaited her when they responded to the request to visit the libraries?

She told herself the faster she learned how to wield her power, the sooner she could return home…

And yet part of her hoped they'd take their time.

You're just avoiding the truth they'll bring you.

Aya frowned at the bitter thought.

No. She *needed* time with the Council. She still wasn't sure what to make of Will, or the tension that had descended on him when they'd arrived in the city. She wasn't about to let him investigate the Council without her. And she'd be able to get to know Aidon, too. To learn what made the prince tick, and how he could assist in gaining the alliance.

This was what she was meant to do. Gather information. Track sources. Pick marks and slip through their defenses.

This was what the gods had blessed her with.

Anything else felt more like a curse.

30

"You *had* been complaining about things getting boring around here," Peter whispered to Aidon as the prince pinched the bridge of his nose.

They sat at the long rectangular table in the circular meeting room of the Council building, the oak-paneled walls bathed in the afternoon sunlight that streamed in from the second-story windows. They had been in session for hours despite it being their second gathering since Aya and Will arrived two weeks prior.

Trahir's Merchant Council smelled blood.

They were relentless in trying to renegotiate Tala's trade terms given the upheaval in the kingdom. Aidon wasn't sure he agreed with their tactics. If war was truly coming, surely they had more important things to argue about. But his father, though he disagreed with Dominic's directive, wouldn't take kindly to Aidon's interruption. Aidon was here for one reason only—and it was the woman who sat across from him, her expression bored as she traced a line in the table.

"You must understand, *Prince*, that given the situation in Tala, we have our…*reservations* about the current trade agreements," Avis said to Will, his deep voice rumbling across the space, disdain dripping from every syllable. A flush crawled up his peachy cheeks as the arguments wore on.

Will leaned back in his seat, the wood creaking as he tilted the chair onto two legs. "If anything, Avis, I'd expect you'd want to increase your orders. Or are Trahir's armies well and truly stocked?"

The councillor's face went red, his blond hair glinting in the sunlight as he glared at the Enforcer. Aidon's jaw clenched at the murmurs that ran down the table. He didn't need Tala spreading fear among his people—or questioning his armies' abilities.

Next to him Peter sighed, his skin looking wan in the fading lamplight. Even his wavy hair, normally perfectly combed to the side, looked awry. Peter ran a hand along his broad jaw as his eyes narrowed at Will. "I thought your intentions were to maintain the agreements we've been preparing."

Will grinned. "They are. But you and yours seem keen on renegotiating, so perhaps we should do the same."

Aidon cut a glance at Aya. She was slouched in her chair, her fingers toying with a thread on her white sleeveless top. One look down the table told him no one else paid her any mind. Aidon suspected it was exactly what she wanted; for the Council to think her no more than disinterested and unqualified while she soaked in each and every detail.

"You're staring," Peter said under his breath. Aidon gaped at his friend, who merely continued to track the argument between Avis and Will.

"Am not," he muttered.

Peter sighed as he ran a hand through his thick hair. "If I reminded you that playing with fire is *dangerous*, Aidon, would you refrain from doing so?"

Aidon at least gave his friend the courtesy of pretending to think it over. "Probably not."

"I figured."

But Aidon wasn't a fool. He knew better than to chase after a woman who likely had more steel strapped to her than he did. Although *where* she would be hiding it beneath that thin shirt and matching white pants that hugged her curves, he had no idea.

He merely found Aya a challenge. This was the woman who served as third in command to the Queen of the Original Kingdom. They said she could move like liquid night, could infiltrate any court, could silence any source who became a detriment to their cause.

Gods, she likely had eyes in his own city. Maybe even in this damn room.

It would be foolish to look at the woman sitting across from him and see anything but a potential threat to his kingdom.

But Aidon had to admit…he loved a challenge.

Aya let out a long breath as the Council finally broke for the day, her fingers massaging her temples while the councillors filed out of the room.

They were getting nowhere.

While the Council had been genuine in their regret over the two tradesmen, they were all too happy to use the situation to their advantage to argue the pending deals. It was telling, Aya realized, that while Dominic was reluctant to see Kakos as a true threat, the Merchant Council was all too willing to capitalize on the potential instability of war to negotiate better terms.

When Aya and Will weren't in Council meetings, they had been in town, meeting with merchants in bars and markets and wherever else their conversations wouldn't seem conspicuous or under the ever-present gaze of Enzo. Still, she didn't dare touch her persuasion—not after the temple. Not with the dreams that hauled her from sleep.

The healer had visited her again, this time in the temple.

These are the gods you worship? she'd asked. *Why don't they help you?*

Aya hadn't had an answer.

Will claimed he felt no trace of deceit from those they questioned. And while Aya had been reluctant to believe a word that came out of his mouth, she hadn't been able to disagree. She saw the merchants for herself, identified their tells quickly over their conversations through planted questions and known lies.

Those they'd questioned had been truthful. They knew nothing of the deal the rogue tradesmen had enacted, or the supplier.

Aya had been so desperate for a different answer that she'd hardly felt relief.

It wasn't as if she *wanted* Trahir to be involved. She'd much rather have them as an ally. But their innocence meant another dead end, another day Tova spent locked away in prison and dishonored in the eyes of their kingdom.

It meant more waiting. For news from Lena, whose scouts were searching the Midlands and attempting to reach the southern border in search of the supplier. For Natali, who had yet to respond.

It meant more unanswered questions about Will. If he *was* involved with Kakos, would it not make more sense to cover his tracks? To make Aya think Trahir *did* have information on the supplier so she'd be caught up in a fruitless chase that kept her occupied and her focus away from him?

This helpless feeling felt like drowning.

"That was excruciating." Will sighed. He leaned against the doorframe of the empty room, his fingers tugging on the collar of his white shirt as he unbuttoned it. "Avis Lavigne is a particular form of torture, isn't he? He could do with some reminding of his place." He jerked his head toward the busy street. "I need a drink. Care to join?"

Aya lifted her head from her hands, her voice weary as she said, "Is there someone else we're questioning?"

He frowned. “No.”

“Then no.” Her limbs ached as she pushed herself out of the chair, her body sore from so many hours of sitting on the rough wood.

Will’s frown deepened as he took a step back into the room. “It’s a fucking drink, Aya.”

Her anger simmered. It wasn’t just a *fucking* drink, and he knew it. She would tolerate his presence when it was warranted. She’d do what she needed to for her kingdom. But anything beyond it…

It wasn’t just the healer who haunted her dreams. She still heard Tova’s screams.

Will scanned her face, his gray eyes cloudy with some emotion she couldn’t place. “I am not your enemy,” he said softly.

“You have done *nothing* but try to take away everything I have ever loved,” she snapped, her hands gripping the edge of the table.

Her position in the Dyminara. Her bonded. Her best friend.

“Tell me,” she bit out through gritted teeth, “that doesn’t make you my enemy.”

A muscle in his jaw worked as he bit back a retort before shaking his head and ducking out the door, leaving her to trek back to the palace alone.

31

Aya didn't bother going back. Instead, she found herself wandering through the Old Town, which was crowded with people on their way to an early dinner.

She kept her pace slow, her hands shoved into the pockets of her white linen pants as she took in the various restaurants and shops around her. Cerulean paint across the square caught her eye. She was back in the plaza Aidon had shown them on their tour.

Aya glanced at the townspeople milling around. They gave the restaurant a wide berth, as though it was dangerous to even be near it. She picked her way across the plaza and slipped down the narrow street that ran alongside the building. A battered side door hung open, as if no one could be bothered with security after the vandalism.

Aya peered over her shoulder before ducking inside.

She found herself in a small kitchen, its counters utterly pristine except for a fine layer of dust that had settled over them, which she swiped a finger through as she wandered further into the building. The attack must have come after hours then, when everyone had gone home. A small mercy.

She stepped into the main dining area, careful to stay in

the shadows as her gaze swept the room. The space was small, and had it not been for the upturned tables and chairs, it would have been inviting. Aya frowned at the splintered wood on the ground. Some of the furniture had been destroyed completely. She crouched down, her fingers trailing the chips of wood.

"Horrible, isn't it?"

Aya whipped her head around, her gaze landing on the tall figure standing in the short hallway to the kitchen.

"Aidon," she breathed, her hand coming to her chest. "Gods. You scared me."

"Imagine that… *You* don't like people sneaking around." The prince's teasing grin didn't quite meet his eyes.

Aya stood and dusted off her palms. "I didn't mean to overstep," she winced. "Force of habit."

"By all means." Aidon gestured to the room. "Maybe you'll find something I didn't."

She spun in a small circle, her arms crossed as her eyes scanned the space. "The City Guard didn't hear any of this?"

He shook his head. "The guards patrol a wide circuit. By the time one crossed the plaza, the Bellare were gone." His brow furrowed as he watched her. "Why?"

"Between the damage to the furniture and the lack of sound, a Zeluus and a Caeli had to be involved at least. Unless…" Her teeth dug into her lower lip as she hesitated.

"Unless?"

"Unless the Diaforaté have made it to Trahir." She watched as Aidon stiffened, the warmth that usually filled his gaze absent as he considered her. "It's just a theory," she said placatingly. "But either way, I have a hard time believing that a guard wouldn't hear or see such destruction until after it happened."

The prince's sigh was heavy as he rubbed a hand over his jaw. "It's something we should consider. I'll bring it to the Guard."

Aya nodded once, stepping over a pile of debris as she made her way to his side.

"I suspect your uncle won't enjoy the theory."

Aidon grinned, his hand finding the small of her back as he guided her toward the side door. "I can handle him."

She was nearly asleep by the time she heard Will's footsteps in the hall. Aya rolled over, her eyes squinting to see the clock on her wall in the dying Incend light. Two hours after midnight.

His quiet knock on her door had her gritting her teeth, but she knew better than to ignore him. He'd do something foolish, like break in. Aya shucked the covers off and grabbed the emerald silk robe that hung by her bedside, throwing it over her white slip as she stalked to the door.

"What?"

Will's eyes were glassy and his hair ruffled, as if he, or someone else, had been running their fingers through it. He made to step into the room, but Aya raised her arm, blocking the doorway.

"What," she snapped.

Will groaned, his head leaning against the doorframe. "Has anyone told you how *lovely* you are?" he drawled.

"You're drunk. Go to bed."

Will lifted his head, his eyes squinting as if he could hold her in place with his stare. "You know Aidon was tracking you, right?"

Gods above.

Aya grabbed Will's arm and tugged him into the room. He stumbled as she shoved him onto the couch, a muffled *oof* escaping from him as he bounced on the cushions. His hand was around her hip, tugging her so she fell with him, her legs on either side of his lap.

"You're being reckless," she hissed as she went to shove off him.

Will's hands held her in place, his eyes bright as he grinned up at her. "You knew, didn't you?"

Of course she knew. She knew the prince had marked her just as she had marked him. She also knew that, like her own initial attraction to him, that spark in his eye when he looked at her wasn't forced. So tonight, when she'd walked past where Aidon and Peter had just settled for a drink, she kept walking toward that plaza, knowing full well he'd follow.

"I needed to bring him back to the wrecked restaurant. I wanted to search the space. And I suggested a Diaforaté was behind the attack."

Will squinted at her, his thumb arcing almost mindlessly against the space right above her hip bone. "Do you actually think that?"

Aya planted a hand on his chest, shoving him back as she stood. "No." It was more likely that the City Guard had gone lax on their patrol. But a gentle prod toward the possibility might get Trahir thinking seriously about Kakos. Or, at the very least, nudge Aidon in the right direction. "This could've waited until the morning."

"Ah," Will said as he reached into his pocket. "But this couldn't." He handed her a small piece of parchment. "Natali has accepted our request."

Aya's jaw locked as she read the messy scrawl. They were due to meet them tomorrow.

Will sighed, his hand dragging through his tousled hair as he slumped back against the cushions. He glanced up at her, his fingers stilling in the strands. "You could have told me *why* you dismissed me so thoroughly."

"What are you talking about?"

"This afternoon after the Council meeting. I get not wanting anyone to overhear what you were planning, but..." Will's voice trailed off, his lips parted as he registered her confusion. A laugh, short and bitter, escaped him. "Of course." He pushed himself to his feet, his body swaying slightly with the sudden movement. He fell into her, and her arms slipped under his as she held him steady.

"What's gotten into you?" She frowned up at him. His shirt was untucked, the collar wrinkled, as if he hadn't been able to stop tugging on it. It wasn't like Will to be so unkempt. So frazzled.

His face was a mere breath away from hers, his gray eyes darkening as he took her in. She could feel his heart pounding against his chest—against *hers* as he leaned into her. "You truly hate me, don't you."

It wasn't a question, but Aya opened her mouth, the *yes* primed on her lips. "Does it matter?" she asked instead.

Will's weight disappeared as he righted himself, his hand tugging again through his mussed hair. "No."

His voice was cold—empty.

"Good night, Aya," he muttered as he ducked out her door.

32

The Maraciana, the main libraries of the Saj who studied in Trahir, sat nestled on the western cliffs of Rinnia, partially built into the cliff face, far past the small temple Aidon had shown Aya. It looked more like a small palace than a place to study. Two tall rectangular buildings alongside the main complex stood before her, their facades connected by an open bridge many stories above the ground.

"The dormitories," Ezekiel explained.

The attendant had offered to escort them here, given a carriage was needed. He'd chattered happily throughout the ride, pointing out various parts of the city. Will had remained quiet, his face contemplative as he stared out the window.

Perhaps his hangover lingered.

Aya had also remained silent, letting Ezekiel's facts about Rinnia wash over her as she focused on steadying her breath.

To meet with the Saj of the Maraciana was an honor, he'd said.

She couldn't help but feel it was more like a sentencing.

"And that's the main library, there," Ezekiel said as he nodded to a third building, shorter than the other two but by far the largest. Its white facade stretched around the cliffs, further than Aya could see. "The rest are on the other side. You won't be able to see them from here."

The main library looked to be about three stories, the front of each made up entirely of arches that stretched the length of the building. The top was lined with spires above each arch, subtly masking the domed gray roof that glinted in the sunlight.

Ezekiel left them as they began to pick their way up the small pathway that wound through the structures. Aya glanced ahead, noting someone standing in the doorway of the main library.

"You must be Aya. I'm Natali," they said as she approached, giving her and Will a small bow that they returned. "I'll be your guide throughout your time with us." Strands of their chin-length gray hair whipped around their lined face in the breeze. Their complexion matched that of the sand that dusted the courtyard path, even this high in the cliffs. And while their voice was warm enough, their eyes—large and round and a rich amber—were wary as they scanned them both.

"Enforcer." Natali nodded in acknowledgment to Will.

"Always a pleasure, Natali," Will answered smoothly.

"Don't lie, Enforcer. It's unbecoming, even for you." Natali beckoned toward the library. "Let us not waste our words where the wind whispers."

Aya followed them as they stepped into the large atrium. They were led into a massive library, the dark-green-and-white-checkered marble floor stretching as far back as Aya could see. Lines of towering mahogany bookshelves bordered the atrium, reaching all the way up toward the domed ceiling. Every so often, the rows were broken up with small study nooks, some of which looked out over the sea. Aya followed Natali as they passed through the atrium and took a left. They led the way up a ramp to the second floor, through some of those towering bookshelves, and back to a quieter wing of the library where a cluster of offices sat.

"Please, have a seat," Natali said, holding the door open for them. Aya and Will sank into the two small wooden chairs, watching as Natali adjusted the books on the shelf before settling behind their desk. They pressed their palms together, surveying them above their fingertips, and waited.

Aya cleared her throat, her fingers toying with the gauzy material of her loose gray pants. But the words wouldn't come.

Will leaned back in his chair, his ankle propped over his knee as he said, "As I mentioned in our letter, we're interested in learning more about the prophecy of the Second Saint."

"You've come a long way for something you could read in a book. Surely Tala, in its devotion to the gods, has such texts. And Saj who can help you in your religious endeavors."

"True. But our queen feels it is essential for us to gain greater knowledge of it with the threat arising in Kakos," he answered smoothly. "Hence our request to see you."

Natali tilted their head, their amber eyes pensive. "We've heard whispers of what's unfolding. It's familiar." Aya tried not to flinch under the steady gaze that seemed to strip her bare. "And what connection to all of it do *you* have?"

"You tell us," Will drawled, his relaxed posture not enough to hide the tension in his jaw. "Your affinity identifies others' powers. Don't act like you didn't read us both as soon as we stepped into this room, Natali."

Natali merely laughed.

"So eager for answers, but unsure of the right questions," they chided. Aya tried to keep her breathing steady as Natali's eyes roved over her again. "I sense much anger in you, Daughter of Secrets. Those who study the religious law say the Second Saint is one of light. But you…"

Aya felt a chill race up her spine.

"Don't bait her, Natali," Will interrupted. "It's… *unbecoming*."

Natali's brows rose. "Let us both be straightforward, then.

Are you not here to learn what I sense in her, Enforcer? To discover if she is indeed the one the prophecy speaks of?"

Will grimaced, but he raised his hands in a gesture of compliance. Aya swallowed her surprise. She'd never seen someone leash Will so quickly.

"We are," Will said evenly. "And you can understand the...*sensitivity* of the matter, yes? We wouldn't want word getting out, given there are those who might cause her harm."

Natali's lips twitched. "Trust me, Enforcer. I have no desire to bring Kakos to our door. Your secret is safe with me." They leaned back in their chair, their hands steepled once more in contemplation as they regarded Aya. "The prophecy does speak of one like you, with raw power in their veins. Here to right the greatest wrong."

Aya's chest tightened. "So...it's true then? I'm a..."

She couldn't bring herself to utter the word. She hadn't let herself consider the possibility for more than a few spare moments, hadn't let herself think too long on what that could mean, what that could *change*.

Natali merely stared at her, the silence settling heavily between them. "They say *this* one will accomplish what the other could not," they finally said slowly.

Aya frowned. "Evie banished the Decachiré."

"The gods banished the Decachiré. And the prophecy speaks nothing of it. It speaks of another who can master raw power so that the greatest wrong might be righted."

More riddles. More semantics. More frustrations Aya did not have time for.

"Is it true?" she bit out, her fingers curling over the arms of her chair.

Natali gave a long sigh. "Perhaps." A raised brow at Aya. "Let's see what you can do."

33

NATALI LED THEM THROUGH THE LIBRARY AND INTO another building of the Maraciana. "The Affinities Complex," was all they said. From what Aya could see, it looked like a school. There were various classrooms and training areas, with Visya involved in affinity exercises.

"Some send their children here to study," Will murmured as they walked along the main hallway. "Others come here later in life to further their craft."

"You know a lot about the Saj of the Maraciana."

Will just shrugged. "I've paid attention on my visits."

Natali led them to a winding staircase, which they followed down so far that Aya's head was spinning by the time they reached their destination. It looked like a dungeon—the cold, dark space long and uninviting. Aya suppressed a shudder as a chill crept over her. The hall was similar to the dungeons in the queen's palace, the air damp. But there were no cells lining the stone walls, just rooms, and it was into one of these that Natali led them.

Aya's eyes adjusted to the dim light of the lanterns that were already lit while Will huffed a laugh, glancing around the bare space. "You certainly have a flair for the dramatics, don't you, Natali?"

"We're less likely to be interrupted here," they said as they shut the door. Their long pants swished against the stone floor as they moved to the center of the room. "It was my understanding you didn't want news of your suspicions to get back to your hosts."

Will muttered some response, but Aya could hardly hear him. Her gaze was fixed on the stone floor, the pattern an exact replica of the floors in Gianna's prison. She curled her hands into fists, her nails digging into her palms.

Peace from the Divine, steady me.

"Like all affinities, raw power was contained in a Visya's well," Natali was saying. "But the prophecy says the Second shall mirror the First. *Your* power should match Evie's. Practically limitless."

Distantly, Aya could hear Tova's screams. They rang in the back of her mind, a steady chorus to Natali's continued instruction and the prayer she silently repeated. "We'll know more once we *see* it. In theory, pulling any affinity works the same. You'll draw inward, from your well. Except your well is depthless."

"Aya," Will muttered. She shifted her gaze from the tiles to find him watching her. His brow furrowed at whatever he found on her face. "What is it?"

"Nothing," she lied. She rolled her shoulders back as she turned her attention to Natali.

"Sense it," was all they said, motioning for her to begin.

Aya closed her eyes as she drew in a long breath. She had done these exercises as a child—looking inward, getting to know her well of power so intimately that reaching for it, pulling from it, was second nature.

It felt almost foolish now.

There was the surface of her well, smooth as glass and cold as ice.

"Deeper," Natali commanded.

The screams were growing louder, their ringing like alarm bells in the back of her mind.

Aya broke the surface. Went even deeper.

Paused.

Because beneath that cold place she often settled into—beneath the lid she kept locked on herself so tightly…

It was a raging inferno.

Aya's eyes flickered open. Will was still frowning, his face intent as he monitored her. She'd seen that look. It was the same look he'd worn on her doorstep thirteen years ago.

Fury built with the heat inside of her, the emotion so quick, so severe, it would have taken her by surprise if she'd been able to pull herself from its thrall.

The screaming was clearer now, as if Tova were merely doors away from her.

"Aya…" Will started, his voice deep and low. A warning.

"What do you feel?" Natali asked, their voice drifting to her from somewhere far away. Their eyes darted between Aya and Will, noting the way her gaze refused to move.

Aya felt too much. The pain, the rage, the guilt…it would burn her from the inside out.

And then it would burn the world.

Flame rippled across her skin, sending a flare of light through the dim space. She was a living torch, burning with every fear and despair inside of her.

And the screaming… It wasn't just inside of her. It *was* her, the hair-raising sound leaving her as pain ripped through her. Will moved, hissing as he cupped her face, but his hands remained, his gray eyes flickering in the flames that danced along her skin.

"Breathe," he commanded. She forced in a breath that burned her lungs, and the flames were banked. Pain. There was so much pain. It ached in every corner of her.

"Again."

Aya sucked in air, trying to match Will's steady rhythm. She continued until she could vaguely make out the feeling of his calluses against her skin.

The flames vanished, leaving her cold and nauseous, her legs shaky beneath her. She stumbled back into the wall, and Will released his hold on her as he whirled to face the Saj. "What's happening to her?"

Natali merely stared at Aya, their head cocked to the side. "Is this how your power has been reacting as of late?"

Aya forced the trembling in her limbs to still with another aching breath. "It hasn't been predictable." A skilled evasion. Because it was more than that. This power was draining her—stealing away bits that she wondered if she'd ever get back. Forcing her further into that cold, dark place inside of her. "Why is this happening?"

Natali merely blinked at her. "I'll need to visit the library," was all they said.

"I thought you knew about this power," Will growled.

The Saj raised their brows. "You forget, Enforcer, that *knowledge* is the truest form of power. What runs in her veins has not been seen in centuries." Natali flicked their eyes to his hands, the skin red and blistered. "Unless you'd like *that* to happen again, I suggest you let me get on with my research." Their eyes cut to Aya. "Come back in two days' time. Alone."

Will let out a string of curses as they left. "Pretentious know-it-all," he muttered. He turned and caught Aya staring at his palms. "It looks worse than it feels."

"Why didn't you shield?" Her fire was affinity-born. With a proper shield, he shouldn't have been harmed.

"I did." He rolled his neck. "Not fast enough, apparently."

Gods. In mere seconds, she'd nearly ruined his flesh. And she…she had been on fire, the pain of it enough to draw a shrill scream from her chest. But her skin remained whole. Unburned.

Will frowned as he considered her, silence stretching between them before he finally said, "Your nausea had nothing to do with the heat that day, did it?"

He'd already seen her weakness. She supposed there was no harm in telling him. "I tried to persuade Aidon."

Will's jaw shifted, his gray eyes narrowing further. "You should have told me."

She aimed for the door. "I guess we both have our secrets, then."

"How were your studies?" Josie's voice rang out from across the palace courtyard, jarring Aya from her trance. She hadn't even noticed the princess sitting at a small iron table, a canvas in front of her. She'd been too focused on getting back to her room, having left Will as soon as they reached the palace gates.

Josie's smile faded as she took in Aya's disheveled appearance. Several strands had come free from her braid, likely from the number of times she'd run shaking hands through her hair on the ride back. She was sure her eyes held the glazed look of someone who wasn't fully there. Aya had been afraid of the truth she'd get today. What she hadn't expected was to feel more confused than ever.

Is this what Evie had gone through when trying to use her immense power?

Because you're a saint now, is that it? Aya almost snorted at the thought.

The princess laid down her brush slowly, a grimace on her face. "That bad?"

Aya smiled faintly. "I'm not sure Natali likes me very much."

Josie waved a hand. "They don't like anyone," she said easily. "Except Aidon, but everyone likes Aidon."

Aya was certainly starting to see why.

"Sit," Josie urged, nodding to the chair across from her. Aya hesitated, the heaviness from the day pressing down on her. But Josie smiled at her so earnestly that Aya couldn't help but sink into the chair, letting out a long breath through her nose. The table was covered with tan paper, each inch of it splattered with paint. In some areas, there were large swaths of color where she had clearly used it as a palette.

Josie followed her gaze. "They *hate* me in the studio because I always make such a mess. But I like to take up space."

"What are you working on?"

Josie carefully lifted the canvas, turning it so Aya could see. It was a face, all sharp angles and defined features. And yet the wide blue eyes were soft and inviting, if not a bit mischievous. The figure had close-cropped black hair, their skin a pinky hue that popped on the gray canvas.

"Her name is Viviane," Josie explained. She frowned as she stared at the painting, her teeth sinking into her lower lip. "I never can get her eyes right."

"Who is she?"

"My partner. It's her birthday next week, and she's always asking me to paint something for her. Vi loves art. She owns a gallery in town." Josie let out a sigh and shrugged as she put the canvas back on the small tabletop easel. Aya remembered staring at a piece of art like that. She used to finesse a single carving, going over and over the tiny lines with her knife until her fingers cramped, until her back ached from being hunched over for so long.

She swallowed the lump in her throat, her voice a bit hoarse as she said, "I think it's beautiful."

Josie waved her off, but Aya didn't miss the flush in her cheeks, or the small smile as she started packing up her supplies.

"I'm going to the gallery tomorrow. You should come. I know Vi would love to meet you. She's obsessed with the Mala range. She has at least five different paintings of the mountains in the studio, and honestly, I think she secretly keeps increasing the price so no one will buy them."

Aya didn't bother to tell her it was more likely that no one else in Rinnia appreciated the rugged beauty of the north.

"I can meet you at the Maraciana, and we can go together."

Aya's fingers twisted in her lap. "I won't be going to the Maraciana tomorrow."

She couldn't decide if it was a relief or not.

Josie grinned. "Then it's settled. We'll go together from here in the afternoon." She reached across the table and took Aya's hand, giving it a tight squeeze. "Tomorrow will be better," she assured her.

It was strange how comforting it was to feel the pressure of that hand against her own. To have someone look at her and see not a prophecy, but a person.

Aya merely nodded.

Tomorrow will be better.

She wasn't sure she believed her.

34

THE SPARRING POST RATTLED AS AIDON THREW ANOTHER combination at it, the sting on his knuckles the sweetest sort of pain. *One two. One two. One two.*

A miscommunication. That's what the City Guard had told him when he presented the possibility of a Diaforaté in their midst. Apparently, the patrol that night had been in disarray. The attack hadn't just happened in between rotations. A guard had missed his post entirely and hadn't come forward until now.

He'd fired the guard. And they were back to square one.

One two. One two. One two.

He'd have to report it to his king—and his father would surely have a lecture waiting as well.

Aidon had long grown used to butting heads with his uncle. Dominic could be pompous, and stubborn, and aloof, and so damn aggravating that Aidon wondered how anyone managed to get through a conversation with him without an unending litany of swear words playing in their mind.

But his father…

A lecture from his father was different. Those conversations were deeper, and riddled with high standards, and tinged with a weight Dominic couldn't muster, because this wasn't his king lecturing him, but his father, and it meant something more.

Aidon wasn't just his son, but the successor to the throne, and with that came the responsibility of sharpening him like a knife as he prepared Aidon for all that lay ahead of him.

One two. One two. One two.

These early hours in the farthest wood-paneled training room of the barracks were a special type of bliss, when the hiss of his breath and the rhythmic thud of his fists hitting the wood were the only sounds in the entire complex. Aidon loved a good time as much as the next person. He found joy in the nights in town with his friends, when Clyde and his husband, Lucas, often took him for all he was worth in cards. He loved sailing around the coves with Peter, or chartering the barge for those particularly raucous afternoons on the water, or even attempting to paint with Josie as she and Viviane laughed at his technique.

Yet true peace was found for Aidon not in total stillness, but in stolen quiet moments. Like the archery sessions in the woods, where the creak of his bow interrupted the murmured conversations with his father as they aimed at their targets.

It hadn't always been this way between them. Of course, there'd always been *some* tension—the kind that typically followed fathers and their sons. There was a reason Aidon and Will had understood each other so thoroughly all those years ago, a reason Aidon had watched him with Gale and recognized the frustration that came with having a father that not only wanted the best for you but demanded it.

And Gale was worse, far worse than Enzo would ever amount to.

But as the time of Aidon taking the throne loomed closer, his father grew more persistent.

One day, Aidon, you will rule…

As if he didn't know. As if he hadn't been reminded every

day of his godsdamn life. As if he couldn't tell that their hopes of a better ruler landed squarely on his shoulders.

A low cough interrupted his combination. Aya hovered in the doorway, dressed in a set of sleeveless brown fighting leathers he was willing to bet Josie had borrowed for her.

"Someone's up early," he said, his bare chest heaving as he tried to catch his breath. He didn't miss the way Aya's face flushed slightly as he stepped around the beam, or how she tried to keep her eyes fixed firmly on his face.

"I hope I'm not intruding."

"Of course not. I'm merely trying to keep up with the rest of my troops. I'm afraid they train harder than I do these days." She looked tired. As if she hadn't slept at all. "Rough night?"

Aya glanced down at her leathers, her brows raised slightly in surprise. "Are you suggesting I look poorly, Your Highness?"

"I wouldn't dream of it, my lady."

Aya snorted at the title, her arms folding across her chest as she strolled around the room. She stopped at a wooden panel with tiny scratches marking its surface.

"It's our tally," Aidon explained from where he stood in the middle of the ring. "A tradition Josie and I have kept over the years. We keep score of who wins our duels."

A faint A and J were carved above lines of markings that were nearly evenly matched.

He loosed a breath. "Josie would much rather join my forces than spend another moment shaking hands on behalf of the Crown. But my uncle..."

Aya glanced over her shoulder. "He won't allow it."

"She thinks he finds her weak."

"Does he?"

Aidon frowned. "Sometimes, I wonder if he finds weakness in everyone but himself." It was a bold confession to make, but harmless. Anyone who met Dominic could grasp the basics of his character. "But," Aidon sighed, giving his head a slight shake, "it's about duty, not ability. He's nothing if not committed to our roles in the kingdom."

Duty.

Responsibility.

Loyalty.

We all make our sacrifices, his mother had once told him. He wondered if he imagined the longing on her face. If, like her daughter and son, she secretly despised the boxes that *duty* seemed keen to force them all into.

Aya tilted her head as she watched him. "Will you value the same? Duty above all? Will you keep people confined to their traditional roles?"

He jutted his chin toward the tally. "After *that*? I'd be a fool. Though I expect it's yet another reason my uncle fears me taking the throne."

Aya's brows raised. "Another? How many are there?"

He waved her off. "Too many for one conversation, that's for sure. I'll bore you with the details later." He scanned her leathers again, sensing the perfect opening.

"You know...if you're looking for a training partner, you're more than welcome to join me in the mornings. I may not be a member of Dyminara, but as history has shown, I am quite capable of holding my own against one."

The corners of her mouth twitched. "Will might see that as a challenge."

"And you?"

"I definitely do." Her finger traced the grooves on the wall again, as if she could feel the pride carved there. "You have Visya in your forces," she remarked suddenly.

"Our kingdoms may hold different ideas around how Visya should use their gods-given power, but again, I wouldn't deny a warrior their chance to wield a sword."

"And how do you train them?"

"Ah," he said, finally catching her meaning. How could

he, if he didn't have powers? He settled onto the bench against the far wall, his legs stretching out before him.

"I'm well versed in the affinities. If I'm to lead, I must be familiar with the weapons in our arsenal. I suppose it's no different than your general learning the strengths and weaknesses of the humans she trains."

She stiffened at the mention of the Queen's General, and Aidon winced. He had forgotten the woman was dishonored. "Besides," he continued quickly, "if we need to train with affinities, there's a tonic the Visya can take to help them control their powers until we find our rhythm as a unit."

Her gaze cut to him, her mouth pressing into a thin line. "A tonic?"

Aidon's eyes went wide. "I suppose saying it aloud makes it sound inhumane, but no one is forced—"

"No," Aya interjected, shaking her head, "I just haven't heard of such a thing."

Aidon rubbed the back of his neck. "That's because it only exists here. Our healers hold the formula. My uncle hopes to leverage it in trade one day."

He didn't miss the grimace that crossed her face.

"All of that aside," he plowed on, "I have enough confidence in my own abilities to stand my ground against you. So are you going to let me see what all the talk is about?" He stood and stretched, biting back a grin as Aya's eyes flickered across him once more. Her cheeks were flushed as she faced the rack of swords.

"If you insist."

He hadn't been joking, Aya realized. Aidon didn't need Visya affinity to be a deadly contender. It was clear he was the general of his uncle's forces for a reason. Not only did he know his way around the battlefield, but he fought with a technique to rival some of the best Dyminara.

Aidon grinned as they parried, the clanging of their swords the only sound aside from their uneven breathing. He was smooth and graceful and quick and vicious, and it was all she could do to keep blocking, to keep moving, to keep dodging his lightning-quick strikes.

Too long. It had been too long since she'd trained. And Aidon was going easy on her. She knew he could see the moments she winced at the stitch in her side, could sense how the blade, which often felt like an extension of her arm, sat heavy in her hand.

"Don't coddle me," she ordered through pants as they came together again, swords clanging. The last three weeks were starting to show. Her footwork was slower, each step feeling like trudging through mud.

"Let's break," he said as he dodged a low swipe to his side. "I'm exhausted."

A lie, but…weak. She had let herself become weak. She backed off, her chest heaving, and nodded. Her body was coated in sweat, her hair sticking to her neck as Aidon racked their swords, the muscles of his back rippling. She rolled her wrist, wincing slightly at the soreness there.

Aidon frowned as he caught the movement, his long stride gobbling up the space between them as he took her arm lightly, pulling her toward him to examine her wrist. "Are you injured?"

"It was a long time ago. I broke it, and by the time I got to the healer, it hadn't set correctly. She had to break it again. It still aches sometimes."

Aidon dragged his thumb along the inside of her wrist, his eyes warm as they met hers. His ember and sea breeze scent settled over her, heat radiating off him as he stroked her skin again. Something tightened in her stomach at the touch.

"Sounds like quite the wound."

Aya swallowed. "It's the inside ones I struggle with more," she confessed, the words falling from her lips before she could stop them. She wasn't sure why she'd said it. Perhaps because of what he'd confessed of Dominic earlier. Perhaps because she needed him to trust her. Perhaps because she needed someone to hear it.

He took a slight step toward her, his chest brushing against hers. "And what helps with those?"

Again, she was struck by that *something* about him. He was handsome, anyone could see that. And an obvious flirt, though he could say the same of her, she supposed. But there was something there that drew her in—that had her pulse fluttering slightly as he continued to meet her gaze.

"This," she breathed, her eyes scanning the planes of his face.

Aidon grinned, and Aya cleared her throat. "Training," she clarified as she gently pulled her hand out of his grasp. She tucked a piece of hair behind her ear as she took a step back.

Too close. They'd gotten too close. And yet she found herself sharing another piece of herself. "I can't always settle. It's like there's this constant energy and it's trying to claw its way out. It's not just my power. It's my mind. My thoughts race and I just..." Her voice trailed off as she picked at a piece of dirt on her leathers. "The training settles me. It helps me feel in control."

The prince held her gaze, his face open and earnest. "You always seem so steady."

Aya pressed her lips together in grim agreement. "I have to."

And the way he was looking at her...it was as if he understood.

35

WILL SAT ON ONE OF THE IRON CHAIRS ON HIS BALCONY, a glass of water in his hand as he watched the sun rise. He'd found a healer outside of the palace yesterday; one who didn't care who he was or why his skin was blistered and burned.

The burns were gone, but his palms still itched terribly.

He hadn't expected Aya's training to be easy. But he certainly hadn't expected her to become a godsdamned living torch.

I guess we both have our secrets.

So much for progress, then.

A knock at the door had him suppressing a groan. *Please, gods, just leave me alone.*

The attendant Sion entered, his blond hair slicked back into a ponytail, his tanned skin weathered from the sun. He was always assigned to Will whenever he traveled to Rinnia. Will couldn't tell who hated the arrangement more—him or the attendant.

"Prince," Sion greeted him, giving Will a shallow bow before heading to the armoire against the far wall.

"Would it do me any good to remind you that I'm capable

of dressing myself?" Will called to the attendant, sulking further into his chair.

"I'm afraid not, Prince."

Will didn't bother to correct him on the title either. The Trahir Court always claimed it was a sign of respect—something Gianna had started years ago. Thanks to her, the moniker followed him not just through Tala, but across continents. Thanks to her, people quaked in his presence. He supposed it was thanks to her that people treated him with a morsel of respect. Most didn't take kindly to Gale's son holding such esteem on the Council.

"They won't dare mock you when I'm done with you," Gianna had promised. And oh, had she delivered.

Will traced the steady rise and fall of the sea, a thought crossing his mind, unbidden and filled with such intense desire that he tried to rid himself of it immediately:

He hoped that one day the title would fade entirely, that respect would be earned not from fear, but from truth.

He hoped one day simply his name would be enough.

That *he* would be enough.

His grip tightened on his glass. He didn't have the luxury of such hopes. Nor did he have the time.

"Shall I draw a bath?" Sion called from the sitting room.

"No. I have somewhere I need to be."

Will was surprised to find that Dominic didn't insist on having this meeting in the throne room. Given his usual pomp and circumstance, it seemed a rather obvious choice. But instead an attendant led him and Aya into the king's private study; a circular room lined with bookcases that ended at two tall windows lined with crimson curtains. In front of the window sat an ornate wooden desk, and behind it sat Dominic. Zuri stood at his shoulder, her hands clasped behind her back.

Aya still looked shaken and pale, as if the effects of

yesterday's training with Natali hadn't quite worn off. Although he supposed that's how she typically looked these days. She hardly ate, and with the dark circles that lined her eyes, he knew she wasn't sleeping. She hadn't said much to him when he had met her in the main hall. But he hadn't missed the way her gaze darted to his hands, taking in the newly healed skin.

"I suppose you're here to encourage me to go to war," Dominic began as they settled into the two seats across from him and Zuri.

Will draped an arm across the back of his chair. "With all due respect, Your Majesty, war is coming to *you* whether you want to be involved or not."

Dominic chuckled darkly. "I've always admired your brazenness but let me be clear: I will not tolerate threats to my kingdom."

"It's not a threat, Majesty," Aya cut in, her voice soft yet firm. "If Kakos is able to fully revive the Decachiré again, war will reach every part of this realm. Do you think they'll spare you in their vengeance? Trahir was equally involved in the embargo that destroyed their kingdom."

"An act that seems to have not been effective," Dominic muttered, "if this threat is to be believed. And yet you still offer no proof."

"The illegal trades by *your* tradesmen and the Diaforaté in our kingdom is all the proof you should need," Will retorted. "And the Bellare certainly seem riled about something."

Dominic didn't rise to his bait. "Ah, yet the Diaforaté didn't perfect their raw power, did they? You both survived that attack." From the corner of his eye, Will saw Aya's hand stiffen on the arm of her chair. Dominic grinned. "Come now, surely you know how rumors spread. You two are becoming quite notorious. First you survive the wolves, then capture your general." The king leaned back in his chair. "And yet there's still much we don't know about

Kakos's experiments. It's a shame that the Diaforaté died in his questioning."

Will blinked—the only sign of his surprise.

Dominic pounced. "You were unaware? Gianna mentioned it in her letter regarding your arrival," he said with a nod to Aya. The king pulled a piece of parchment marked with the Tala royal seal from his desk drawer and cleared his throat. "'We learned that the Diaforaté are attempting to achieve raw power by siphoning power from other Visya.'"

From the corner of his eye, Will saw Aya stiffen. "How?" she demanded.

Dominic held up a finger before continuing. "'It was his final confession before he succumbed to his sensations during his questioning,'" he read. "'I implore you, Dominic, to consider what is at stake should he not be the only one. Your forces will be crucial in aiding our cause…'"

Will fought the urge to grind his teeth as his irritation rose.

Zuri was watching him carefully, her brow furrowed. "You seem surprised, Enforcer, about this letter," she remarked. "Did you not know of his death?"

Will held her stare as he sank further back in his chair, forcing his muscles to ease. "It is not my Queen's duty to play messenger to me, Lady Zuri."

He was, of course, furious.

The Priestess had said the man was weak due to his dark-affinity work. And sources had succumbed to their sensations during questioning before. But to have such a massive misstep…

And Gianna had told him to take his time, to introduce their concerns slowly, yet she had already pushed for Dominic's support. She was undermining his ability to build trust with this court; was creating more obstacles he'd have to overcome. And by the smug smile on the king's face, Dominic knew it. He was relishing sharing this news and, in doing so, reminding Will that, though the title of Prince followed him from kingdom to kingdom, he was no more than a servant bending to the will of his queen.

"I find it strange, Majesty, that you so frequently question the word of your ally," Aya observed, her head tilted as she considered Dominic. "We've brought you assurance that Kakos is building their forces. We have seen proof of dark-affinity work in our kingdom. Their heresy is growing, and yet you ask if a threat is legitimate."

"I ask," the king growled, "because you ask *my armies* to get involved. Allies we may be, but that does not entitle you to call on our aid for every issue that impacts your kingdom. Was it not *your* general working with the heretics to begin with? Who's to say *you* didn't frame our tradesmen to push us into supporting your war?"

Will's jaw twitched as he fought to keep his frustration in check. "Given the problems it's created for us with your Council, Majesty, that would be a foolish plan indeed."

Dominic didn't waver. "Even still, this sounds as though this is no more than a continental skirmish, with Tala at the center and insubordination in your ranks. It's not as though we ask *you* to intervene with the Bellare."

"Let's not speak in hypotheticals, then," Will urged as he leaned forward, bracing his arms on his knees. "What does the situation need to look like for your armies to be involved?"

"Until I know for sure that this is a true threat to my people, and not a one-off incident, I will not guarantee you anything, Prince," Dominic replied.

Well. Will supposed it was only a matter of time until Dominic got exactly what he asked for.

36

AYA NEARLY HAD TO JOG TO KEEP UP WITH WILL'S BRISK stride as they left the king's study. Will was pissed—that much was clear. He hadn't done a good job of hiding his surprise at hearing Gianna's missive, just as he wasn't doing a good job of hiding how furious it made him now.

He hit the courtyard with impressive pace, his eyes fixed on the palace gates.

"Where are you going?" she inquired.

"Out." He didn't bother to spare her a glance. Perhaps he hoped his taciturn mood would scare her off. Aya wasn't moved. She simply followed him, nodding to the guards as they started down the path that would lead them into town.

"You anticipated this," Aya reminded him. "You knew Dominic wouldn't jump to a formal agreement."

Will cut her a look, a muscle in his jaw working. "It doesn't make it any less frustrating." He tugged a hand through his hair, letting out a long breath through his nose. "Contrary to what you accused me of, I don't relish the idea of thousands dying for this war."

She opened her mouth to correct him but found herself coming up short. What excuses could she give? It was exactly what she had suggested when she accused him of partnering with Kakos.

"Why press Dominic in her letter?" she asked instead. "Aren't you supposed to be leading the effort for allyship? She told you to bide your time."

Will laughed, the sound low and hollow as he swung around to face her, his lips twisting into a sneer. "That surprises you, does it? Our queen knows Kakos's activity is a threat not just to our realm, but to the gods themselves. She'll leave nothing to chance."

It was telling, though, that Gianna didn't trust Will to secure the alliance without her involvement, especially given how close she had always kept him to her affairs. Her Second had seemed to be her closest confidant, and Aya always assumed that was because the queen trusted him implicitly.

Will turned, gripping the rusted iron railing that ran along the cliff edge, his brow furrowed as he considered the sea. "Gianna is ambitious and severely untrusting," he finally murmured, as if lost in thought.

"But you're her Second," Aya pressed. "And..."

And her rumored lover.

His eyes were dark as they cut to her. "You and I both know nothing stands in the way of Gianna taking what she decides is hers."

The words settled heavily between them. Unease flooded Aya's stomach as Will turned his gaze back to the ocean, his hands tightening once on the rail. But before she could push him further, he was turning again, aiming for the path. "I think I've had enough inquisitions for one day," he muttered. "I'm going to the tavern. I'd ask you to join me, but I know how much you adore my company."

Aya rolled her eyes. It was hardly noon. "You deal with your disappointment in such productive ways."

Will glanced at her, his jaw tight with anger. "Kakos is *siphoning* Visya power. They'll be experimenting on humans next. An attack is surely imminent. We are on the brink of war, negotiating an alliance with a king who can't get his head out of his ass, all while Gianna undermines our efforts in the name of the very gods we seek to protect by stopping this threat," he ground out. "Our most important source is now *dead*. I'll deal with my disappointment however I like." He started down the path, hands shoved into his pockets, shoulders bunched.

"You should be careful," Aya called after him. "The woman you mock is our queen."

He didn't bother to turn around. "Even I, Aya, would not be foolish enough to openly mock our queen."

A liar, Aya tried to remind herself as she watched him disappear around the bend. Will was a masterful liar; almost as masterful as she was.

But the thought was hollow.

Aya was trained to trust her intuition. To question the logical and expected. To truly *see*. And what was she seeing of him?

His frustration wasn't forced. With the Council, with Dominic, with Gianna.

Nor was his restlessness. Will wanted answers as badly as she did.

And Aya wasn't sure where that left her.

37

WILL CLOSED HIS EYES AS HE LEANED HIS HEAD AGAINST the cool stones of the sea wall. He took a second to thank whatever gods still bothered to care that he'd found a spot of shade. It was sweltering, making his skin feel as though he was about to burst and turning the dull thud that ached behind his eyes into a persistent, piercing pain.

He should've gone to the bar like he told Aya he was going to. It was foolish to be here—to seek this help. But he was desperate.

Perhaps he'd simply take Aya and leave this godsforsaken place without a word. He'd help her wrangle her power some other way, and Gianna… Well, he'd have to find a way to deal with his queen regardless.

He had no plans to return to Tala.

"You look like shit," a voice drawled from the shadows. Will let out a heavy sigh, enjoying a moment more of blissful darkness before turning to face the tall figure with tawny skin and silken charcoal hair. Despite the smirk twisting his lips, his hooded eyes were wary as they scanned Will.

"Ryker," Will greeted the boy tersely.

But he wasn't a boy anymore, as the several feet he'd

grown over the last five years clearly showed. No…Ryker was a man now. And it was a man's voice that said, "Heard you were in town. I figured it was only a matter of time before you'd come sniffing her out. Why she agreed to see your sorry ass is beyond me."

Will pushed himself off the wall. Gods, Ryker was taller than he was now, despite being three years Will's junior. And though he was lanky, Will could see the cut of his muscles as he folded his arms across his broad chest. He'd always thought Ryker would've made a good fighter. Perhaps would've even made the Dyminara, if they took humans and the boy had grown up in Tala. But Ryker had other allegiances.

Will's eyes flicked to the rose tattoo on Ryker's bicep, the bottom petal peeking out from his shirt. So it was official, then. Last he'd seen Ryker, he was merely following the Bellare around like a lost pup.

"I see she's still having you play errand boy," Will mused, matching Ryker's smirk with one of his own. The younger boy's vanished as his features twisted into a glare.

"She relies on me for protection. Given no one else has bothered to—"

His words were cut off with a mere brush of Will's affinity, a strangled yell escaping as he clutched his chest. Will might not truly be able to manipulate the body like the Anima, but he could mimic the sensation of a heart attack well enough. He didn't particularly care that Ryker was human. Not when he couldn't very well run off to the Royal Guard. Not with that tattoo on his arm—not these days.

Ryker's eyes flared, not with panic, but with fury. Definitely no longer a boy, then. Will hated to admit he was impressed. It didn't stop the horrible calm that entered his voice as he said, "I'd advise you not to finish that sentence, Ryker." He waited until Ryker forced a single tense nod before releasing him from his power.

"You're a piece of shit," he hissed. He tugged on the collar of his linen shirt, straightening it into place. Will merely gestured down the street.

"Let's get this over with, shall we?"

Lorna's house was a tiny stone cottage rammed between two ramshackle beach bungalows. The first and only time Will had been here five years ago, he'd thought it looked like a gray stain in the midst of so much bright color. It was far better suited for the Mala range. It was surprising that Lorna had found a house that paid homage to her home kingdom. She detested Tala and its queen.

The house sat on a street that was blocks away from the hustle and bustle of the main thoroughfare of Rinnia, and even though he couldn't hear the ocean from this far back, sand still littered the cobblestones.

Will stared at the light wooden door, weathered from the salt in the air. Ryker didn't bother to say goodbye as he stalked off down the street, likely to wait at some bar until this meeting was over.

Brave of her to assume she won't need her guard dog.

Will had barely finished knocking when the door swung open, a small woman blinking up at him. Her pale face looked exactly as it had the last time he'd seen her—the last time she'd refused to give him what he needed. Except now he could see the signs of age starting to settle in; the wrinkles in the corners of her blue eyes, the wisps of gray in her long, wavy black hair.

"Lorna," he greeted her gruffly. She merely stepped aside, inclining her head to invite him in. He followed her into the cramped circular room, noting the kettle of tea on the worn wooden table before a hearth that had likely never once seen a fire.

She padded into the small kitchen, calling over her shoulder, "I made sandwiches if you're hungry."

"I'm not." Will lowered himself onto the leather couch, clasping his hands in front of him as he waited. Lorna brought the sandwiches anyway, serving him tea before she finally settled into the scratched leather armchair to his right.

"It's good to see you, William. Although I must say I'm surprised."

He returned his teacup to the tray. "I assume you know why I'm here."

"I have my guesses." Lorna sighed. "Rumors reach even these parts of the city." She took a long sip of her tea, her eyes searching his face. Will resisted the urge to look away from that piercing stare. "If you're here to ask us to pressure the king for an alliance, then you must have forgotten that I have no involvement with the Bellare."

Will scoffed. Perhaps she didn't—but Ryker did. And they'd both made it known Lorna was a second mother to the boy after his own parents had been killed by pirates at sea years ago.

"I'm not interested in the Bellare and their agenda." If he were, he would've questioned Ryker days ago about the vandalism. But like Dominic had said, it wasn't their problem, and Will had more pressing matters. "You have knowledge of the prophecy of the Second Saint. I need it."

How Kakos hadn't hunted her down by now was beyond him. She could vow she wasn't tied to the Bellare all she wanted, but he had no doubt they were responsible for her protection. That, or perhaps she truly had kept it to herself all these years.

"Well, then you already know my answer, I'm afraid."

He raked his fingers through his hair. Pointless. It was fucking *pointless* to have come, to have even wasted his breath. And yet he forced his voice to remain steady. "You have studied that prophecy for years. You knew that your research would be crucial—"

"My research is none of your business. I should never have spoken of it to you."

"Then why bother to see me now?" he asked tightly.

She shrugged. "It's been too long. I thought we could catch up. I was hoping you'd left such ambitions behind."

Will didn't bother to hide his bitter laugh. "Charmed as I am, if you're unwilling to help, I'd rather spend my time in the Maraciana than waste it here." At the mere mention of those libraries…

Yes. There it was. Annoyance flashed in those blue eyes.

Lorna had the making of a Saj of the Maraciana. And yet she had refused to join them when she arrived in Trahir. She used their libraries. She honed her affinity. But something kept her from giving herself entirely to the study of power.

Perhaps there was more Tala in her than she cared to admit.

Her voice was level as she said, "Even the Saj of the Maraciana have limits."

"What is it that you want, Lorna? What will it take for you to give me what I need?"

Her face was grave as she regarded him for a long moment, her lips pressed into a firm line. Finally, she set her teacup down. "Nothing. There is nothing that you could give me that would change my mind."

"You seem to forget that I have other methods of doing so." He was not the boy he had been five years ago. She'd seen to that.

"I *had* heard you've built quite the reputation for yourself since I last saw you. The Dark Prince of Dunmeaden." She observed him with a critical eye. "They say you're not just second in command, but a close personal friend to Gianna as well."

Will's voice was hardly more than a snarl as he stood. "*You don't speak to me about Gianna.*"

Lorna didn't so much as flinch. "My mistake, Prince," she breathed.

The door opened with a bang, and Ryker glanced

between the two of them. "I told you I should have stayed," he growled.

Lorna just smiled at the boy. "The prince was merely expressing his displeasure with my loyalties, Son."

Will could feel his jaw aching, his teeth grinding together so hard he thought they might break. Enough—he'd had enough.

"One day, Lorna, you'll have to find a way to live with yourself. Gods know you'll have plenty of time to figure it out in the seven hells."

Will had almost made it to his room when Aya intercepted him in the hall, Aidon following her out of her suite, a deck of cards in his hand. The prince bid her a good night, a jaunty grin on his lips as he nodded to Will before leaving them.

"Your absence was noted at dinner," Aya said.

He didn't care. This entire court—no, this entire city—could burn in hells. He didn't bother to respond, yet his silence did nothing to keep her from following him to his door. Will silently counted back from ten.

One night's peace. That's all he was asking for.

He tugged on the brass handle of his suite door, but Aya's hand met the polished surface, snapping it closed.

"Where have you been? And don't bother saying the tavern, because I don't smell a whiff of alcohol on you."

"I didn't realize I had to run my agenda by you."

"You do when I'm forced to answer questions about your whereabouts. Aidon—"

"*Aidon* can mind his own damn business," Will interjected, whirling to face her. The prince's name was kindling to his temper. "You two seem to be getting awfully comfortable together," he spat out as he jerked his chin toward her room.

Aya's face flushed at the implication, her brow furrowing as she glared at him. "You were the one who wanted information on the court. You were the one who encouraged me to get close to him for this alliance. It's not like you were able to sway Dominic this morning."

His anger rose sharply, like a cresting wave. "Well I don't recall asking you to fuck him—"

Wind, hard as a wall, slammed him backward against the door, making it rattle against its hinges. Aya's eyes were bright with cold anger as she took a single step toward him, her voice a mere hiss as she said, "You disgust me."

Will winced, his body aching as he peeled himself off the wood. "Did you mean to do that?"

She was already stalking away.

"Aya!"

She ducked into her room, the door closing hard enough that a sharp crack echoed through the hall.

38

NATALI DIDN'T BOTHER WITH NICETIES WHEN AYA ARRIVED in the small training room the next morning. They merely crossed their arms, their brow furrowed as they observed her. "Angry already?"

Aya rolled her shoulders. "I'm fine. Did the library share wisdom on how to not become a living torch?"

"It gave me theories. Let's begin."

Aya bit back her annoyance as she shut her eyes and tried to settle herself.

For years, her control was the only thing that had kept Aya from splintering. But bit by bit, that control was slipping. She could feel it in the way that power thrashed inside of her.

Perhaps she'd never truly had it. If she had, she wouldn't have sent Will falling to his near death. Her best friend wouldn't have looked at her like she was a monster. And her mother...

You know that I never want *to leave you.*

Aya drew into her power, calling that raging well forward.

She'd thrown that gust of wind last night without a second thought.

It terrified her.

Natali was saying something. But Aya couldn't hear them with the ringing in her ears, couldn't see with the darkness that crept into her vision. Cold surged through her, as if her very blood had turned to ice. There was nothing in her mind but her own vicious tone.

That's what you always say. But you always leave. You're a liar.

Hands were on her shoulders, shaking her hard enough that her teeth clattered.

Aya.

Aya.

"Aya!" Natali's voice pulled her to the surface. Aya was on the floor, her lungs searing as her vision focused. Natali knelt over her, their amber eyes wide. Aya's head swam as she sat up. "I was afraid of this," the Saj murmured.

"What happened?" Her lungs were burning, but her voice was steady and cold.

"You stole the air. I shielded but…you could suffocate an entire room should you wish to."

Aya gritted her teeth as her stomach turned. She was a warrior. A weapon, when needed. She was willing to do what it took to adhere to the oath she'd taken to her kingdom and the Divine. But this…

Could she bear this level of destruction?

How could *this* be a gift from the gods?

Aya's vision swam as she pushed to her feet. "Why do I feel like this?" she rasped, the stone wall she leaned against the only thing keeping her from sinking to the floor again.

"Raw power can take *more* from you."

Visya affinity wasn't limitless, and it wasn't equal. Some were born with deeper wells than others, and every young Visya had to learn how to manage their affinity, how to find their limits, build their reservoirs, and feed their power with their energy. Like all things in nature, there was a balance.

A Visya who refused to touch their affinity would become ill. Without an outlet, the power could consume its host. But for a Visya who didn't master their affinity correctly—who didn't know how to use their power steadily, who emptied their well too fast, or became too entranced by their power, or didn't take time to recover—the effects could kill them.

"So I'm, what, burning out faster? I thought this power was supposed to be nearly limitless?"

Natali shook their head. They pulled a small book from their pocket, opening to a page they'd bookmarked. Aya gagged at the grotesque drawing of a man whose eyes had sunken into his head, his skin in patches of decay. He seemed to be screaming in agony.

"When the Decachiré practitioners pushed against the bounds of their wells, their raw power began to devour. It fed on their wells, deepening their power beyond what the gods allowed."

But if these pictures were true, then the power didn't just feed on their wells...

"It fed on *them*," Aya breathed, her eyes scanning the images on the page.

Natali made a contemplative sound. "Some say it ate away at their very *essence*, that they were inherently dark, and the practice pushed them further into that darkness, which further fueled their corruption. It's the inverse of Visya who use their well correctly. Inner and outer. It's all a science. A balance."

Aya's stomach clenched, her fingers digging into her palms as the Saj met her gaze.

"Is that what you sensed in me? Darkness?"

Natali cocked their head, their amber eyes pensive as they considered her. "The Saj of the Maraciana can identify affinities. We can sense the depth of a well. Of course, we've never sensed raw power before. You're the first to show such power in centuries."

They sighed, their brow furrowing as they continued. "When you use your affinity, there is a...darkness...that fuels it. An energy I haven't sensed before. I'd hoped perhaps it was the Enforcer affecting you," they murmured. "That his darkness was calling to yours and affecting your power in some way. You have a likeness in you. It's why I suggested you train alone."

Go ahead, he'd once told her. *Tell me what a monster I am so you don't have to face the fact that you're one, too.*

"But Evie..."

"Evie's power was nearly boundless. It also wasn't fueled by the dark acts of the practitioners. Her *essence*, if it did indeed help further her power, was light. Perhaps it's *why* she was able to wield such great affinity." Natali didn't have to continue for Aya to know what they were implying.

Whatever was in Evie, it was not found in her.

You didn't think you could be a saint, did you?

"But the prophecy says a second of her kind," Aya pressed, fighting to keep the tremor out of her voice. "So if I'm not like Evie—"

"The prophecy is layered. Complex. Misunderstood by the devout and by the Saj, regardless of what we study. Your power is raw, like Evie's, and it is far deeper than any well I've sensed before. All would indicate you are the one the prophecy speaks of. But the prophecy says nothing about one's essence and how such power is fueled. And this power...it is also killing you."

Aya stilled as Natali's words washed over her, her pulse pounding in her throat.

Had the gods truly chosen wrong?

"What does that make me? Some sort of dark saint?"

Natali shook their head. "I do not know."

Her throat constricted, her next plea burning beneath her panic. "So...so help me fix this. Surely the practitioners found some way to offset these effects. Their forces were rumored to be over a thousand strong."

The Saj snapped the book closed. "While the Saj of the

Maraciana may not adhere to the Old Customs, there are sins even we don't dare speak of," they said sharply. "We don't concern ourselves with the inner workings of dark-affinity work."

Aya's eyes narrowed. "You're the Knowledge Keepers. You have studied the affinities for centuries."

"I cannot train you."

Aya's breath punched out of her lungs. "You can't be serious," she breathed as dread, heavy and unrelenting, pooled in her stomach.

"Using small amounts won't hurt you. And physical exertion can help offset the pressure of your unused power. But the power you would need to make a difference in the coming war could devour you entirely."

"And yet you don't even truly know how the saint's power is to be used at the helm of an army to right the greatest wrong, do you?" Aya snarled. Natali didn't bother to answer. Aya swore as she stepped away from the Saj, her anger rising rapidly. She whirled back to Natali, her fingers digging into her palms, as if she could contain her rage. "I cannot aid in the war if I do not understand my power!"

"And you cannot understand what you refuse to acknowledge," they snapped.

That death has always followed in my wake. That I've never been one filled with light.

"I will not help you feed yourself to an insatiable host, nor will I unleash another wave of darkness on this realm."

"*I am not practicing the Decachiré!*"

Her fury seemed to linger, ringing in the silence that followed her outburst.

Natali raised a brow. "Yet your power reacts just the same. And the Saj of the Maraciana have limits. We do not study darkness."

Aya's hands shook as she unclenched her fists. Her power did react the same. Because it wasn't just feeding on her energy. It was taking parts of her, pulling her deeper into a darkness she had tried desperately to keep locked away.

"It would be far safer for you, and the realm, for you to stay far away from this war," Natali murmured.

"So, what?" Aya seethed. "The entire prophecy gets ignored because the gods chose wrong? Darkness wins regardless, is that it? I cannot simply stand by."

"Your power alone does not fulfill the prophecy. You forget the Second Saint must *rise*."

Another nonanswer. Another riddle she couldn't parse.

Her fingers tangled in her hair as she raked them through her strands. "What does that *mean*?"

No different. She was no different from the Diaforaté the realm condemned today; from the practitioners who had caused the destruction of peace centuries ago.

Perhaps this power hadn't come from the gods at all. Perhaps she had done this to herself, had somehow corrupted her affinity and created…this.

Because her gods…her gods would not condemn her in this way.

Gianna would not accept this.

She would not accept this.

Not when she had been so close.

So close to what? that voice inside of her whispered. *You've known this truth all along. You will never be their saint.*

Natali tilted their head, a mournful look passing across their face as they watched her. "Whatever you're holding on to…it will destroy you." A heavy sigh left their lips. "You may use the library for research. Perhaps there is still information there that can aid your armies."

And then they departed.

Aya swallowed, the silence in the training room more like a defining roar.

I thought it was the Enforcer affecting you.

Not his darkness.

Hers.

It's not light that drives you.

Was she really surprised? Natali said that the Decachiré practitioners were rumored to have an inherent darkness. Perhaps Aya had begun the descent into hers thirteen years ago.

For centuries, people had expected a second of Evie's kind. A Saint of Light. But now, what were they left with?

Whatever you're holding on to…it will destroy you.

It had been hope.

Hope that had wedged its way into her.

Hope that people had clung to for centuries.

And Natali was right. That foolish hope would destroy them all.

39

Thirteen years before

SHE WAS GOING TO ERUPT. THE HOT, RAGING FEELING WITHIN her was growing, boiling her very blood until she swore she could smell fire as she fell to her knees in the clearing.

Dead. Her mother was dead, and Aya…

Aya wrapped her arms tighter around herself, the rage building and building and building until she couldn't take it anymore, until she bowed over her knees and screamed, her throat searing with the intensity of her cries.

Her head swam, her vision blurring with tears and a heady haze that had her slumping to the ground, consciousness sliding from her in one fell swoop.

When she awoke, she was on a hard cot in a small sparse room she had never seen before. A woman towered over her, her face stoic as she stared down at Aya.

Galda. Trainer to the Dyminara.

Aya peeled her tongue off the roof of her mouth and swallowed, the taste of ash coating her throat as she croaked, "Where am I?"

"The Quarter," Galda answered. She tilted her head as she observed Aya's tearstained face. "I found you facedown in the woods. You're lucky you're alive, girl."

Alive.

Aya winced at the word, and Galda's frown deepened.

"What happened?" Aya asked. The last thing Aya remembered was screaming her rage, and then…nothing.

Galda crouched down by the cot, bringing her face level with Aya's. "You were overcome." Aya went to question her further, but Galda held up her hand. "You're quite a powerful Persi. Did you know that?"

Aya shuddered, tears building behind her eyes once more.

Yes, she knew it. It was a blessing from Saudra. And yet what would her patron goddess think of what she had done?

Galda ducked her head to meet Aya's gaze. "But do you know what makes a Visya truly powerful?"

Aya frowned. "The depth of their well."

Galda's laugh was like gravel, her eyes bright as she shook her head. "No." She braced her arms on the bed, her lips lifting slightly as she considered Aya. "Control. The most powerful Visya learn to control their affinity and all that affects it. They channel their emotions and hone their power into something as sharp as any blade. They are rulers of their body, mind, and spirit."

Aya's breath caught in her chest as the trainer stared down at her, as if she could read every thought circling inside her head.

"You, girl…you could learn control. And you could be sure that the only thing that has power over you is yourself."

Aya sat up, her voice a mere rasp as she said, "Teach me."

Galda leaned back on her heels, her brows high. "I am not a gentle trainer. My methods are hardly fit for a child."

Aya stood, her fists clenched in determination. "Teach me."

The trainer stared up at her from her crouched position, considering every inch of her as if to see all there was to work with. Hardly anything, at merely eight years old.

But finally she stood, her gaze raking over Aya one final time. "We'll start tomorrow."

40

AYA STUMBLED THROUGH TOWN, THE NOISES AROUND HER a murmur against the roaring in her head. She'd barely made it through dinner at the palace, and afterward…

A night in her room left with nothing but her thoughts felt suffocating. So she found herself in the entertainment district, the streets lined with bars and upscale brothels. The citizens of Rinnia were preparing for a raucous night, and she hoped the steady hum of music and drunken revelry would be enough to drown out that voice inside her head—the one that hadn't quieted since Natali confirmed everything Aya had ever feared.

She was dark. She was bitter. She was cold. And she would bring nothing but pain to those she loved, just as she always had.

The healer in her dream had asked why her gods weren't helping her. Perhaps Aya finally had her answer.

Perhaps she always had.

I never want to leave you.

Aya buried the memory of her mother as her gaze landed on a white building, its windows dark. She could hear the sensual music from the street, the steady rhythm of the drums almost hypnotic.

She wanted an escape. Wanted to be someone else—*anyone* else who hadn't committed her sins.

Aya ducked into the bar.

The space was dark and seductive, the various sitting areas decorated with dark leather chairs and deep-maroon accents. The music from the band in the corner pulsed through the space, loud and slow enough that she could feel it in her bones. There was a carnal energy here.

Aya signaled the barkeep at the dark wooden bar. The whiskey burned her throat, but she downed the drink as she scanned the space, her eyes landing on a dark-haired man with tawny skin standing away from where couples were writhing against each other on the dance floor. He dragged his eyes across her tan top, the neckline plunging between her breasts as the fabric twisted and tied around her back. Her midriff was bare, and white linen pants hugged her hips. His lips twisted in an appreciative grin as he prowled toward her.

"Another?" he offered as he nodded at her empty glass. Aya tilted her head back, taking in the sharp angles of his face.

"Please."

Aya lost track of how many she'd had by the time the man coaxed her onto the dance floor. All she knew was that her head was blissfully empty as she moved against him, her hips grinding in time to the music. She was lost in the feeling of his hands on her, content to distract herself in any way she could.

"Let's get out of here," he murmured against her ear, his breath hot on her neck.

That would certainly be a welcome distraction. She went to nod, but a voice cut in, deep and firm. "She'll be leaving with me."

Aya drew back to see Will standing behind the stranger, his hands in the pockets of his black pants. The sleeves of his white dress shirt were rolled to his elbows, the buttons carelessly undone to below his collarbone.

The man turned, his brows rising as he took him in. His gaze darted between him and Aya. "She's with you?"

"Leave, Ryker." There was enough menace in his voice that the man backed away.

Irritation surged in Aya, her hair sweeping over her shoulder, as she watched the stranger go. "Thanks for that," she muttered darkly as she turned to Will. "You just ruined a perfectly good evening. How do you know him anyway?"

He sighed as he approached her. "An old acquaintance." He peered down at her, his gray eyes wary. "I went to the Maraciana today to meet you after your training. Natali refused to see me. What happened?"

The music throbbed in time to her unsteady heartbeat. "Nothing."

"Nothing," Will repeated as he stepped closer. "So you're just here. At a bar. Alone. For nothing."

"I'm here to dance."

A muscle worked in his jaw, and Aya could swear his eyes darkened as they skimmed over her. "Let's go, Aya."

She couldn't. She couldn't face this truth.

She swallowed, the heat of the room pressing in on her as she fixed Will with a glare.

"I told you, I'm here to dance." He read the stubborn tilt of her chin, his lips tightening as he realized she wasn't moving. A server passed them, and Will grabbed a drink off the tray he held aloft, downing it in a single gulp.

"Fine," he growled as he plopped the glass back on the tray. He closed the distance between them, his hand settling on her hip. "So dance."

Aya didn't move. Will laughed, his breath brushing across her lips like a caress, his eyes glinting with a challenge, as if daring her to step away. "Unless you've changed your mind."

Like hells she'd let him drive her out of here.

Aya slid a hand behind his head, her fingers curling around the base of his neck, fingers grazing the ends of his hair that curled in the Rinnia heat.

You have a likeness in you.

She shut out the thought as she moved her hips in a slow, sensual circle to the beat of the music. Will's eyes flared, his body going tense as she moved against him. "Aya…"

"Changing *your* mind, William?" she taunted as her hand dragged up his chest, her hips swiveling against his again. His hand slid up her arm, his grip tight, as if he were going to tug her hand from behind his neck. But he paused, his jaw shifting as she rolled her hips again, her breasts pressing against his chest as she breathed, "Did you take on more than you can handle?"

She expected him to step away. To back down and leave.

But he bent his head toward hers, his voice low. "I can handle every bit of you."

And perhaps it was the liquor, but her skin burned as he slid that hand from her hip to her waist, his fingers trailing across her bare skin as he turned her roughly and tugged her against him. Will started to move, his body rocking against hers as the music continued its seductive rhythm.

Aya's hold on the back of his neck tightened as he slid his hands to the front of her hips, his grip warm as he pressed her against him.

She was used to fighting him, but this…this was an entirely new type of battle. Will ducked his head, his nose grazing her neck as his hand splayed across the bare skin of her abs. She shuddered under his touch, her body burning like the flame that had devoured her in the training room.

She was losing herself entirely, her body melding into his as he ground into her, her fingers sliding through the soft strands of his hair.

"Gods," Will murmured as she moved against him. She could feel every inch of his arousal. And though she told herself she hated him, her body went loose with desire, her core throbbing as he shifted his hips against hers.

His lips skimmed her neck, and *godsdamn her*…she tilted her head without a second thought, urging him to take more. Will's low laugh rumbled against her throat. "What do you need, Aya love?" His breath against her ear made her shudder. Her very blood was on fire, her mind swirling with lust and desire and alcohol. She needed release; she needed to forget.

She turned in his hold, her hips molding into his as she writhed against him, his hardness pressing into her core and sending a spike of pleasure through her. Will groaned, his hand tangling in her hair as he cupped the back of her head. "This is going to escalate very quickly if you don't stop that," he said tightly.

"I don't care." The words were breathless, her movements quickening with the beat of the music. But something in them had Will tensing, his fingers curling on her hip as he gently pushed her back.

"Wait." His breath was uneven, his eyes wide and bright, as if he couldn't quite figure out how they'd gotten here. His fingers stayed woven in her hair, his thumb pressing against the base of her head. His brow furrowed as he searched her face. "What happened today?"

It was ridiculous how easily he could read her, and how furious it made her. Her vision swam as she stared at him, her chest rising and falling with jagged breaths.

Aya jerked out of his hold.

"You want to know what Natali told me?" she panted, that old instinct to cut him rearing its head. "Apparently, I'm just as dark as you are." She barked a laugh, the sound brittle and harsh. "Worse, if you can believe it."

Her eyes dragged over him, taking in the flush of his skin, the evidence that her fingers had been in his hair. "Perhaps that's what explains this," she said more to herself.

Because the draw between them…she had never been

able to truly ignore it. Even when it sent him falling from the Wall. Even when she'd wanted to kill him for what he did to Tova.

"Well? Go on," Aya urged, swaying as her arms flung wide. "Aren't I the perfect weapon for Kakos? Shouldn't you whisk me away to the Southern Kingdom now?"

She didn't believe the accusations even as she spit them out.

Because for weeks now, she'd been forced to slowly reckon with a truth that had been steadily growing since she'd attacked him on that ship:

If Will were sympathetic to Kakos, he wouldn't care. He wouldn't be vigorously questioning the Council; he wouldn't be furious about Dominic's refusal to consider this threat seriously.

He had been right that day in the ship's stateroom; she had let her hatred cloud her judgment. She had been driven by her desperation to avoid her own demons, her own fate.

It had been so much easier to think Will guilty, to focus on his faults rather than face her own.

It's what she'd been doing for years.

Will's frown deepened as he took a step back from her, something shifting in his eyes. There was anger there. But beneath that…

Hurt.

Will looked hurt.

He slid his hands into his pockets, his shoulders tense and his voice low as he said, "You can be a real bitch, you know that?"

She did.

He disappeared into the crowd, and Aya couldn't place the emotion that writhed in her gut as she watched him go. It didn't come to her until she was lying awake in her bed hours later, her mind refusing to rest.

Shame. That's what she'd felt at his words.

It was shame.

41

AIDON COULD TELL AYA WAS DISTRACTED. SHE STOOD before him in the training room, her sword locked against his own. It was another early morning for them both.

She looked like hells. There were bags under her eyes, which were a pale, dull blue in the dawn light. He'd tried to get her to talk to him about whatever was weighing on her so heavily, but Aya had merely picked up a sword and motioned for him to begin.

An inside wound, then.

Aidon grunted as her blade came against his, the impact reverberating up his arm. She fought with a vehemence he hadn't yet seen in her. He parried, his blade knocking hers aside and whipping back toward her weak spot.

But Aya twisted. "Fuck!" she yelled, her hand moving to her cheek.

"Shit," Aidon hissed, dropping his blade at once. Blood coated her fingers, a long cut angling up her cheek where his blade had sliced her. "I am so sorry." He grabbed a spare rag from the wooden bench and pressed it to her face. "I didn't expect you to turn like that." It was an amateur mistake, really. One a Dyminara had far too much experience to make.

Whatever was occupying her mind, it had her fully in its thrall. "I am so sorry," he repeated.

Aya took over applying pressure as she sucked in a steadying breath. "It's not your fault. It was an easy block. I've gotten slow."

Aidon dipped his head, his fingers settling on her wrist as his gaze caught hers. "Are you truly alright?" He wasn't just talking about the wound.

"If you think this is the worst injury I've sustained while training, then you insult me." She glanced at the rag, marking the blood.

"I'll take you to the healers."

She waved him off, but Aidon insisted until she relented. She pressed the rag to her cheek again, wincing slightly. "I'm afraid all this royal treatment has made me lazy." Aya sighed.

Aidon's answering laugh filled the training room. "I'll get you back into tip-top shape," he said as he stepped away from her to hang up their swords. She smiled, the expression not quite meeting her eyes.

"I'm counting on it."

Aidon paused by the weapons rack, his eyes sweeping over her. She still had that weary look to her, that hollowness that clouded her eyes.

"Let me make this up to you."

She raised a brow.

"Dinner. Tonight. As an apology."

Her eyes flicked across his face, the corner of her lips lifting slightly as she considered him. "As an apology," she repeated, some question hidden beneath the words. Aidon allowed himself to return to her. Allowed himself to trail his thumb beneath that cut on her face, her skin soft and warm and smooth.

"Perhaps the apology is merely an excuse," he admitted, his voice low. He waited, watching her blue eyes search his.

She inhaled, her breath steady as she released it. "I'd love to."

The sparring with Aidon had helped in a way, but Aya's mind still refused to settle. So after her trip to the healer, she took to the winding cliffside paths, her muscles aching with the sudden effort of her run, her head still pounding from the liquor she'd drunk the night before.

She'd seen no sign of Will yet today. She was relieved, and she was fairly certain that made her a coward.

Aya's body screamed in protest with every step, but she didn't dare let up. Not when the exertion was settling her, clearing her mind and taming that well inside of her. She ran until she couldn't demand another step from her trembling legs. Only then did she return to the palace. She managed to find a quiet spot on one of the lower terraces before sinking to her knees, her head pressing against the cool stone of the railing as she gasped for air.

"Should I send for someone, or are you just taking a moment?"

Aya raised her head to see Josie in a long yellow dress, the fabric loose and flowing in the sea breeze, smirking down at her.

Aya offered up a weak grin. "I'm taking in the scenery."

The princess scoffed. "Be honest. You're three seconds away from hurling your guts up on my mother's favorite terrace." A laugh huffed out of Aya as she grasped the hand Josie extended and stood on wobbling legs. Josie frowned as she dragged her eyes across her. "You look as bad as Will did this morning," she said dryly.

Aya's mouth tightened. "You've seen him?"

"He went stomping out of here earlier."

Aya swallowed as a wave of uneasiness passed over her.

"I'm sure he'll recover, whatever it is," Josie mused, as if reading her thoughts. She scrunched her nose. "Besides, if you're planning on seeking him out, you might want to bathe first." Josie let out a noise of protest as Aya shoved her lightly, her grin only growing as Aya started toward the door.

"I'm going to track down some lunch. Care to join me?" Josie called after her.

Aya paused in the threshold. It would keep her out of the palace—and away from Will.

"Why not."

It was late afternoon by the time Josie and Aya returned so that Aya could prepare for dinner with Aidon. Josie had persuaded her to try the fried fish down at the docks, and though she'd been skeptical, Aya found it delicious. They'd also stopped by Vi's gallery and browsed the artist's plaza, pausing at a few stalls for Josie to restock her painting supplies. Tova would have loved it. The fish, Viviane, the frenzy of the artist's plaza. Her friend would have loved every bit of it.

Aya sank deeper into the bath she'd drawn when she returned, her fingers curling around the lip of the tub. There was still no news from Lena on the search for the supplier. Every day wasted here felt like just another moment that kept Tova in that godsforsaken prison.

But at least...a plan. Aya had the workings of a plan.

It certainly wasn't her strongest, but she'd take whatever she could get. Because she needed to get home to her friend. And she couldn't do that until she found a way to wrangle what was inside of her.

This power...it was pushing Aya further into that cold and dark place she couldn't seem to pull herself out of. It had been easier to do so before the market. Before the prophecy. Then, that icy anger had felt like a mask—something she could tap into when she needed it.

Now it felt like a second skin.

Her attendant arrived shortly after Aya roused herself from the tub, Josie following with a sly smile. She strolled to

Aya's armoire and flung it open. "I'm choosing your outfit," Josie announced.

Aya glanced at the attendant, who fought to keep the annoyance from her voice as she said, "I reminded Her Highness that as a royal attendant, it is my duty to—"

"And I reminded *you* that my friend is going on a date with my brother, so *I* must be the one to dress her. I feel horribly left out already," Josie added with a wink to Aya.

"It's not a date," Aya said flatly. Josie snorted. "It's not. He's being hospitable."

Something clenched in her stomach as she said it. Aya knew they were mere marks to each other, and that Aidon would likely be pressing for information on her activities at dinner. It's what she would do. But…

Perhaps the apology is merely an excuse.

Something was shifting between them, blurring the lines between sources and friends and perhaps even something more.

Josie cocked a brow. "Was William invited to this hospitable dinner?" Aya pressed her lips together and Josie grinned. "See? A date."

"Are you going to show me what devilish plans you have for my outfit, or do I have to dress myself?"

42

AIDON CHOSE THE QUAINT RESTAURANT IN THE BACK OF the Old Town because it was small enough that they were likely to be undisturbed.

He loved how comfortable his people were in approaching him. But sometimes he wanted to enjoy a meal without dropping his fork every few moments to greet another couple, or hug another child, or inquire about another mother who had fallen ill.

Besides, he had a feeling that Aya wouldn't take well to strangers popping up at their table unannounced, and the last thing he needed after a long week was her pulling a knife on someone.

He also simply loved the food here. He'd known the chef for years, having first met him when he and Josie had been sent to bed without dinner for misbehaving at a particularly stuffy court affair. He'd dragged his sister into town to stop her whining, and they'd found the lovely hidden eatery while wandering near the residential streets. He'd made a point of coming back at least once a month since.

Aya sat across from him in a short-sleeved pale blue dress. The sheer sleeves were cuffed with a white band at her elbows, the light chiffon skirt cut in layers and brushing just above her knees. The bodice swept in a deep V and was held together with a white sash that tied at the back of the dress. It made her look softer. He wondered if she'd done that on purpose.

She glanced around at the space, her eyes scanning the small wooden tables and rough stone walls. He expected to have to draw her opinion from her, but she slid her gaze toward him, a small grin on her lips.

"I love it."

"I thought you might."

"What's good here?" She scanned the menu, tucking a strand of long brown hair behind her ear. He was relieved to see her cheek was smooth once more.

"Everything."

Another rare smile from her as she pushed the menu away. "Then I trust you to guide us in the right direction."

Aidon shot her a teasing smirk. "Something tells me it's unusual for you to relinquish control. Should I be worried?"

A quiet laugh rasped from her. "Perhaps I'm changing my ways."

Something in the way she said it was tinged with heaviness, but he knew better than to pry. Too soon. Perhaps later she would share more of herself with him. So instead he passed the time by asking her about her home, about the legendary Athatis wolves who protected the Dyminara, about their traditions.

In Trahir, families no longer cremated their dead, but erected tombs gilded in gold to honor their memory as they went to rest with the gods—at least the most prosperous merchants did. Other families buried their dead in wooden boxes. Aya had nearly spat her drink out at that. In Tala, it seemed, burning was a way to release a soul back to the earth; back to the gods. Those that didn't were rumored to become trapped in the veil itself.

Aidon knew Tala's devotion to the gods was unparalleled, especially among the Visya. But to *see* it, to truly witness it in the way Aya spoke of their sacred duty to serve the gods and protect the humans of their realm…

He knew enough Visya in Trahir to know they would balk at it. That they would see it as subservience. But it didn't sound that way when Aya spoke of her devotion to her gods and people. In fact, it reminded him of himself, in a way. She was a committed warrior whose loyalty was something he would admire in his own soldiers. Did it matter that she felt that loyalty was decreed by the gods? Was his own not decreed by his family? By his birthright and position?

At the end of the day, did they not honor the same Divine…just differently?

"Your commitment to your duty is admirable," he said carefully, letting the earnestness he felt show in his face. They'd worked their way slowly through their meal, and he laid down his fork as he focused on her fully. "But do you ever want something just for yourself?"

Perhaps the question was far too personal for whatever this was growing between them. He wasn't even sure who he was asking it for. Maybe them both.

Aya's face was pensive, her finger trailing the rim of her wineglass as she studied him. "It chafes, doesn't it?" she remarked, her voice far gentler than he'd ever heard it.

"What does?"

"The responsibility." She leaned back in her seat, her eyes fixed steadily on him as she continued to toy with the glass.

He lifted a shoulder. "It's all I've ever known."

She nodded. "Then you know perhaps better than I do that it does no good to wish for something that can't be." There was a heaviness in her voice that had him leaning toward her, a frown on his face, but Aya's lips tightened before she plastered on a tight smile, as if she'd just caught herself. "Sorry. That's more than enough heaviness for one evening."

"So I shouldn't ask how your research with the Saj is going?"

She blew out a breath, something like a laugh lost in the sound. "It's slow," she confessed. "Natali speaks in endless riddles, and they certainly take their time with things."

"Will they be able to help?" He kept his tone light—intrigued. Again, that contemplative look settled on her face, her full lips pursing as she considered him. Considered how much to tell him, Aidon realized.

Because their flirtations aside, they both had roles to play. Duties to abide by.

But whatever reassurance she was seeking, she must have found it in his face, because Aya sat back in her chair and said, "I don't know. How much does anyone truly know about the Decachiré?"

Aidon chuckled. "Your best bet would be tracking down the Vaguer, but we all know how that would end." Aya's blank look was enough to send him sputtering, "You can't be serious. You've never heard of the Vaguer?"

His parents had told him and Josie enough horrific bedtime tales to dissuade even Aidon from tracking down the small group of devout worshippers not of the gods, but of Evie, the First Saint. There were myriad rumors surrounding them. They were said to be nearly impossible to find—that one had to travel through the Agaré rain forest, the Blood-Red Mountains, and the Preuve desert. And even if the voyage didn't kill the seeker…the Vaguer would. They were rumored to be keepers of a relic of Evie's. He told Aya as much, watching her frown become more critical with every word.

"What's the relic?"

Aidon lifted a shoulder. "Some say it's her sword—the same one her parents used in the horrific ritual. Others a shard of her bone. No one's ever found out."

"No one," Aya deadpanned. "Sounds like a scary bedtime story."

"Speak for yourself. I grew up on stories about the Vaguer, and just talking about them makes me uneasy." Indeed, a shiver raced down his spine. "They're said to have no bounds in their thirst for knowledge. They were excommunicated from the Maraciana over a century ago for their willingness to study dark-affinity work. They claimed it was essential to understanding Evie better, to worshipping her more fully. Obviously it was...*controversial*, and not just to the Saj of the Maraciana, but to the kingdom. We may not worship the Divine in the same way, but we still adhere to their decrees. Dark-affinity work has no place in this realm, and while they honor the First Saint, their practices border on heresy. And yet, even still, over the years, the most desperate have attempted to seek the Vaguer out."

"For what?" Aya asked, an amused smile tugging at her mouth.

"Knowledge. Power. Miracles. Who knows? It's a fool's errand."

She took a slow sip of her wine, her eyes sparking with something that looked like mischief. "Well, thank the gods I'm not a fool, then."

His eyes flicked over her, watching the way her tongue ran across the bottom of her lip. "You certainly are not," he murmured. He watched with no small amount of satisfaction as a flush crept over her cheeks, those blue eyes brightening in the lantern light. It was senseless, really, how she sent his pulse racing. How that look in her eyes heated his blood so quickly, as if he were no better than a young whelp who had just discovered the charms of a woman.

Still, he knew Aya's purpose here and suspected he was no more than a source of information. He'd told himself the same thing about her when he'd invited her out this morning. She was a mark—an assignment from his king.

But he couldn't deny that flirting with her was like stepping onto the battlefield. Strategy could only get him so far. The rest was giving himself over to the dance of the fight and hoping he could keep up.

Always chasing, never disciplined, his uncle loved to growl. Aidon supposed he was right in a way. He was a general, after all. And while that came with obeying orders and giving commands, it didn't change the fact that there was something in his blood that craved adrenaline.

There was a particular thrill that came with battle. And Aya…

She felt a lot like the excitement of violence.

But before he could act on the tingling beneath his skin, there was someone at their table, clearing their throat. A City Guard. Aidon's eyes narrowed as he straightened.

"What is it?"

"It's Helene Lavigne, Your Highness. She's been taken."

43

THE COBBLESTONES WERE CAKED WITH BLOOD.

Aya pulled up short outside the white town house, home to Councillor Avis Lavigne and his family. The door hung off its hinges, giving an unobstructed view to the entryway, where upended chairs and shattered crystal littered the space.

It was as if Avis's daughter had tried to fight her way out.

"Gods," Aidon breathed as he took in the mess. His grave face said enough: they'd be lucky if Helene was alive. Members of the City Guard had cordoned off the area, but that didn't stop anxious townspeople from craning their necks to catch a glimpse of what was going on. "This is a nightmare," he muttered, his frown deepening as his sister pushed through the guards.

"Vi and I heard Claire Lavigne's screams from the art studio," Josie said when she reached them. "I've just got her settled in one of the healing shops down the street. She's in shock."

"But you didn't hear Helene?" Aya asked. Josie shook her head, and Aya turned back to the front stoop, her eyes scanning the entryway again. Whoever broke in was strong.

Not necessarily Zeluus strong but…strong enough to leave a path of destruction in their wake. And they obviously didn't care about covering their tracks. As if they were leaving a message.

"Where's Avis?" Aidon asked, his voice low. Josie nodded her chin to where the councillor stood, his face purple as he berated one of the City Guards.

"What can I do?" Josie asked, but Aidon was already in motion.

"Go home." He turned to Aya, his expression hard. "Make sure she gets there safely." Josie went to argue, but Aidon wouldn't hear it. "I don't know who they're targeting. This was a bloodbath, Josie. Go home. Now."

That voice… It wasn't the warm baritone Aya had grown used to. It was the voice of the general.

"Come on," Aya said, tugging lightly on Josie's arm. "This is about to become a scene." There were more townspeople gathering behind the Guard, and their eyes had found the prince and princess easily.

Josie silently fumed as they walked back, her lips pressed into a tight line. She remained silent until they arrived in her suite, where Josie immediately took up a steady pacing as Aya settled on the turquoise quilt of her four-poster bed.

"You're angry," Aya observed.

"He says he doesn't agree with our uncle. He believes me perfectly capable to serve in the forces. And yet at the slightest hint of danger, he sends me home. And he asked *you* to escort me, so clearly he must think me incapable of handling myself."

Aya didn't want to think too much about the fact that Aidon had trusted her with his sister's safety. She couldn't take a moment to consider what that might mean; not now, not with Josie's building fury.

"Have you shared this with him?"

Josie waved a hand, the gold rings on her fingers catching

the bright light of the candles flickering in the chandelier. "In passing."

"Perhaps it warrants a more serious conversation."

The princess hummed noncommittally, her gaze troubled as she finally sank into a vibrant blue armchair across from Aya. "Things like this don't happen here."

The words settled heavily between them.

Aya's fingers twitched, seeking the comfort of her blades. It had taken everything in her to leave the Lavigne house and accompany Josie back up to the palace. But she willed that buzzing in her veins to settle, willed her face to stay calm as she turned over the facts again.

This wasn't just a kidnapping. This was a statement.

A knock sounded on the door and Will's head popped in, his gray eyes alert as they found Aya immediately.

The brief pause as their gazes met seemed to stretch for an eternity, the memory of the night before like a physical barrier between them.

"Can I steal her, Josie?" Will finally rasped.

Aya paused from where she'd already stood, her eyes darting to the princess. She would stay if Josie asked her to. It's what Josie would do if their roles were reversed. What a *friend* would do.

"It's fine," Josie said, as if sensing her hesitation. "I'm fine. There's no point in both of us twiddling our thumbs."

Aya nodded. "I'll be back if I hear anything about Helene."

Will's pace was quick as he led the way to his room. He didn't speak, not even as the door snapped shut behind him. He just let out a long breath and nodded to the terrace. Aya followed him, her arms crossed firmly around her middle as she wrestled with the shame that began to gnaw at her insides.

It was far easier to stifle it when he wasn't standing before her.

But that burning feeling faded as Will dragged a hand through his hair. A hand that was covered in blood.

"What the hells happened?" she breathed, snatching his hand and turning it over to inspect his palm. No cut, no bruises. Just blood.

Will's brow furrowed, his fingers curling around hers gently, as if on impulse, as confusion settled on his face. It lingered a moment before his eyes narrowed.

"Say it," he rasped. Her hand fell to her side as he released it. "If you're going to accuse me of it, then have the nerve to fucking *say it*."

Aya blinked at him. "I'm not accusing you of kidnapping Helene."

"Bullshit—"

"But coming back here like this is foolish when you've made your disdain for Lavigne clear," she pressed, her voice soft and measured.

He stalked away from her, taking up a space on the far side of the terrace. The muscles in his back rippled as he grasped the smooth stone balustrade, his hair brushing his brow as he bowed his head. His laugh was cold and harsh. "You honestly think I'm a monster, don't you?"

The words tugged on another memory. *You truly hate me, don't you.*

Aya swallowed. "Why is there blood on your hands?"

"Because I was helping your precious prince investigate," Will hissed. "Ask him yourself. I got there shortly after you left."

He pushed himself off the balustrade, anger glinting in his eyes as he stared at her. "And you want to trade secrets, Aya love? Let's talk about this darkness you supposedly have."

Aya's jaw clenched, her hands curling into fists at her side.

"I went back to the Maraciana," he continued. "You failed to mention Natali refuses to train you."

Her heart pounded in her chest, her fingers tingling as he stepped closer.

"I can't help you if you won't *trust* me."

"Trust you?" Aya asked, her voice rising with his frustration. "A few weeks ago, I was certain you were working for Kakos. You expected me to *tell* you that the raw power is feeding on me? That it'll destroy me just like it destroyed the Decachiré practitioners?"

He shook his head. "You are nothing like those people, Aya. Perhaps if you practice, if we do some research..."

"I am not some *thing* for you to test your theories on," she spat out as she faced him fully. "This is my life."

He was before her now, his hands finding her shoulders as he peered down at her. "Exactly! It is your *life*, and I'm watching you waste away. You think I don't notice what's happened to you since the market? How you're slipping deeper and deeper into some place I can't haul you out of?"

"I thought you couldn't sense me," she seethed.

"I don't need to sense you," he said roughly. "I can see it."

"You only care because you can't fail Gianna."

And though it made her a hypocrite, the words hit exactly where she wanted. The air between them tightened as he stepped back, his arms falling to his sides. He was silent for a moment, the waves crashing into the cliffs the only sound.

"This has nothing to do with her," he finally bit out. "But perhaps you *should* share your anger with our queen."

Aya's laugh was cold. "That's your excuse? You're going to use the woman you love—"

"I *do not* love her!" He flung the words with enough venom that Aya paused, so caught off guard by his vehemence that the retort on her tongue disappeared entirely. All she could focus on was the brightness in his eyes and the way his chest rose and fell rapidly, as if he couldn't catch his breath. A vicious twisting started in her gut and spread to her lungs, her throat constricting as she gazed at Will.

Pain.

She was feeling his pain.

"I feel you," she rasped.

He was everywhere. From the bitterness that clenched her heart, to the sorrow that pooled in her stomach, to the anger that stole her breath, to the *burning* that coursed through her blood as she stared and stared at him.

Will's eyes went wide, and in the span it took him to blink, the feeling of him vanished, leaving Aya empty and cold as she doubled over, gasping for air.

Pain. So much pain.

And beneath it…him. His essence had been everywhere, perhaps even inside her very soul. Will was panting, his breath as unsteady as her own as he said, "You tapped into your Sensainos affinity."

He had done it again. He had provoked her enough that she had lost control and acted without thought. But she was still reeling herself back in, still collecting her pieces and sorting through what was his and what was hers, so much so that she couldn't find words as she panted.

This wasn't the pain of her power. This was the pain of *him*. His agony. His frustration. And beneath it all, something deep and burning and so completely full that its absence made her heart cleave.

Will took a deep breath, his face slipping into a cold mask of indifference as he met her gaze. "Not fun, is it?"

No, it wasn't. She felt raw, and shaken, and so unmoored that the ground seemed to tilt beneath her. She pieced herself back together as much as she could, forced herself upright, and took another shaky breath.

"I'm sorry."

His brows shot up, disappearing beneath his hair.

"I didn't mean to… I shouldn't have…" She could still feel the bitter ache of sadness that had settled in her like a weight. It had been the worst sort of intrusion. What she had felt… She hadn't known what was raging beneath his skin.

It was agony.

That cold mask gave way to wariness as he watched her for a few moments.

"I understand that I have given you little reason to trust me, Aya," he finally said. "But believe me on this: That perfect ideal of Gianna you cling to? It's a lie."

She blinked at him, her eyes stinging in the sea breeze.

"It's late. You should go."

She hesitated.

"Please." And the word was so soft, so broken, that she left without another word.

44

WILL'S HANDS SHOOK AS HE PEELED OFF HIS SHIRT AND grabbed a washcloth, the faucet set to the coldest setting. They didn't stop trembling, not as he washed his face and neck, the icy water that dripped down his chest and back not enough to calm him. He chucked the cloth into the sink and gripped the edges of the porcelain basin, his knuckles white, as he tried to steady his breathing.

I feel you.

If the thought of it didn't make him sick, he would've been impressed. Emotions were complex things: layered, intricate. Newer Sensainos often had trouble accessing just one. But he knew by the way she'd been left gasping for air that Aya hadn't just sensed his anger. She'd gone deeper.

How deep, he wasn't sure. And that terrified him.

He'd have to work with her on managing her state. It was easy to become overwhelmed by someone else's emotions. The sensations could be debilitating if she didn't learn how to sense them without embodying them as her own, as she'd already experienced tonight.

As *he'd* experienced that night of the Athatis attack, when he had thought her dead.

He inhaled deeply, blowing out the breath through his nose. He did it again and again until the tremors stopped, until he peeled his aching fingers off the rim of the sink. He lifted his head, meeting his reflection in the large oval mirror. His hair was mussed from where he'd tugged his hands through it in frustration, his eyes dark, jaw tense.

The way she'd stared at him tonight…the pain he'd seen on her face…

He didn't think her reaction was just because of the sensations. She was reacting to *him*. She had seen him, truly seen him, and what she beheld shocked her.

It should've given him some relief, he supposed. But instead all he could feel was dread. It sat heavily in him as he stared at his haunted reflection in the mirror.

He had spent years building his walls against Aya. He had come to terms with it all: That he would have to do things he never imagined doing. That she would hate him, and he would continue to stoke that flame of hatred until it burned too brightly for her to look at him and be able to see anything else. That he would never be able to explain it all to her—why he begged for her removal from the Dyminara, why he taunted and pushed her, why he let the world and Gianna think he was interested in being the queen's plaything, why he'd followed those orders to question Tova, and why he'd been sick enough to vomit after the ordeal.

Even if he could explain, he'd always doubted she'd care enough to listen. Not that it would matter anyway. It wouldn't take away the things he'd done. It wouldn't eliminate the pain he'd caused or the sins he'd committed.

Will wasn't afraid of meeting the gods in the end. He knew what awaited him, despite the sacrifices he'd made, despite the fact he'd fight with his dying breath to protect the innocents of this realm.

It wasn't the gods he feared.

It was her. Her knowing the truth and hating him still.

He could bear the layers of the seven hells. Would welcome them gladly if it meant that he could avoid the moment when she saw him fully and looked at him with disgust anyway.

45

AYA SLID A HAND INTO HER POCKET, HER FINGERS WRAPPING around the small vial of tonic as she stood in the middle of the abandoned paddock and surveyed the space.

It had been all too easy to step in front of Aidon's blade, ensuring he cut her enough to warrant a trip to the healing rooms. Easier still to prod the eager young healer who tended to her cheek to share enough about the work space for Aya to deduce where the tonic was kept; to allow her to slip back late last night and steal a small amount, just enough to remain inconspicuous.

She hadn't even needed to touch her affinity.

Aya paced a small circle, her hand grazing the rotted wooden fence that surrounded the paddock. Josie had mentioned a spot where her mother used to sneak off with her to train. From the looks of it, the paddock hadn't seen much use in years. Perhaps Zuri and Josie had found another location.

There was little breeze this far from the cliff face, and while the thick forest shielded the paddock from view, it created a dense bubble of heat that had Aya sweating in her fighting leathers, despite the early hour.

She took a steadying breath as she uncorked the vial.

She didn't know what to believe—whether the gods had chosen wrong, or if she had somehow corrupted her affinity with all she had done.

She supposed it didn't really matter. Darkness was darkness in the end.

But there was still no word from Lena on the supplier. The longer Aya waited, the longer she was kept from helping Tova. The longer the realm waited for a saint that would never come.

And the closer war crept.

Aya had taken an oath—to her kingdom, to her realm, to her gods.

Perhaps this tonic would allow her to keep it; to use her power safely.

You are nothing like those people.

Years. Years she'd spent hating him. Years convincing herself Will was no more than the arrogant, cruel monster people said he was, and that he had no regard for anyone but himself. Years hating how hard she had to fight the allure of him, how something in him called out to her. She clung to those notions of him and never allowed herself to challenge them. But now…

She couldn't escape him by running off on a mission, or put Tova between them, or use the queen's attention as an excuse to stay the hells away from him. And the pain she'd felt from him at her assumption of his love for Gianna…

It was fury. And rage. And hurt. And some deep ache that felt so familiar, she hated that she couldn't name it.

She had misjudged him, and he had never bothered to correct her.

Aya ignored her flicker of unease as she raised the tonic to her lips and took a small sip. It tasted like water.

She paced the paddock again, kicking at the rocks strewn across the dirt as she waited for some sort of sensation. Two minutes passed. Then five. She frowned up at the sky, her arms folded across her chest. She didn't feel any different.

Finally, she rolled her neck and shook her arms loose as she closed her eyes and reached inward.

There.

That raging sea that made up her well of power had calmed, its essence now smooth like glass. Aya's heart stuttered as she looked at her hand, pulling a single drop of the power forward while she held the image of her friend in her mind.

Suddenly, a flame appeared in her palm, flickering gently like the lit wick of a candle. Her own shocked laugh startled her, and the flame vanished. She willed it to return, her jaw clenching as she pushed her power to the surface and urged the flame to grow.

Calling this raw power was simple, but keeping it—maintaining it, controlling it—that was far more difficult than using her persuasion. It felt slippery. Sweat dripped down Aya's neck as she forced the flame to wreath her wrist. It stuttered and fought with a stubbornness to rival Hepha's own, but eventually it succumbed, forming a perfect, flickering circle. She pushed harder, forcing the flame to encompass her arm, her teeth gritting with the effort.

Difficult, but…

No darkness clouded her vision. No screams rang in her ears. No tremors or nausea racked her body.

It was working. The tonic was working.

Aya stayed in the paddock for hours, steadily working her way through the Order of the Dultra. She tested each elemental affinity and found she was partial to ice.

Unsurprising.

Fire was a close second.

She worked on earth now, attempting to coax the moss on the paddock rail to expand. Her hair was plastered to her sweat-stained cheeks as she panted, her affinity shifting through her like mud.

She'd hit a wall, unable to push her power further. Aidon's tonic certainly did its job well. If she took a larger dose, she had no doubt it would nullify her affinity completely.

But now, just beneath that heaviness...her well began to churn once more. She could feel it in the way her muscles cramped, in the way the affinity seemed to be scraping along her insides.

Aya stormed away from the moss and let out a noise of frustration, her arm arcing downward in a vicious slash. The ground beneath her split, a shallow cut appearing in the earth.

"Impressive."

She whirled.

Will leaned against a tree just beyond the paddock. He wore his own fighting leathers, brown and light and sleeveless like hers. His hair, curled slightly from the humidity, clung to his forehead; his body was covered in a light sheen of sweat, as if he'd just finished his own training. She tracked the rippling of his biceps as he pushed off from the tree and hopped the paddock fence. "I see you took my advice on practicing."

He kept his face neutral—amused, even. But Aya could see the tension in him even with the space he kept between them.

"How did you find me?"

"I was running through the forest. Did you not want me to?"

"I didn't want to get your hopes up," Aya admitted. "I can hardly dive deep enough for it to matter."

"I just watched you move through the elemental affinities as easily as breathing."

He'd been there for a while, then. Aya swallowed as a welcome breeze blew through the paddock.

"So the negative effects are gone?"

And perhaps it was the hopeful note in his voice—the possibility that all of this could be solved so easily—that had her pushing the vial of tonic deeper into her back pocket, unable to admit the truth. She toed the line she'd cut in the ground, a frown on her face.

"Natali says light affinity use shouldn't be too harmful. It's the deeper work that's the problem."

His voice was solemn as he said, "You should have told me."

But he didn't press her about why she hadn't. Perhaps there was an answer he didn't want to hear. He considered her for a long moment, hesitation written in his gaze. "I meant what I said last night. You're not alone in this. I'll help you. The answers are somewhere."

There were bags under his eyes, the dark purple worse than when they'd first arrived. He usually hid it easily enough behind his swaggering confidence and arrogance, but today, in the stillness and quiet of the paddock, Will looked haunted.

"I shouldn't have read you."

He gave an easy shrug, the lightness of the gesture not quite reflected on his face. "It wouldn't have happened if I hadn't pushed you. Consider us even." His throat bobbed, those gray eyes still locked on her. "I'm sorry. That I made you doubt where my loyalties lie. For—"

He cut himself off, giving his head a small shake. "I'm just sorry."

Aya stilled. She had never heard those words from him. Not once.

Will watched her warily, gauging her response.

"Tell me about Gianna," was all she said.

He let out a long breath and leaned against the paddock fence, his foot resting on the rail behind him. A muscle in his jaw worked, as if he were considering his words before he spoke them. "You know as well as I do that Gianna wields manipulation like a knife. That *we* often do it for her."

The truth of his words settled heavily in Aya. Of course she knew; it had been her job for the last three years.

Will's gaze was steady on her as he continued: "She's far

too cunning not to know what keeping Tova would do to you. And even if Lena found the supplier, I have no doubt she would keep Tova for as long as it suited her."

"Until I master my power." It wasn't a question, but Will nodded his confirmation anyway. "You made the same threat," she pointed out.

"I know." The words were heavy, a look of disgust twisting his features. "And it was despicable. I needed you to stay on that boat, and I knew that if I threatened Tova, you'd comply."

"Would you have acted on it?"

Will shook his head once as he stared hard at the ground, as if he couldn't bring himself to meet her gaze. "But it doesn't mean I haven't done horrible things to get what I want."

Aya remembered the sadness that had flooded her the night before. Perhaps there was guilt in it, too. She knew it intimately.

Silence stretched between them, too full for her to know where to break it. "I tried to stop it, you know," he finally confessed. "I argued with Gianna. And when she sent me down there anyway, I told Tova to scream—to act like I was questioning her. Because I knew…" His voice trailed off, his gray eyes dark as he looked at her. "But Gianna came down to see the questioning for herself. And she brought Cleo."

And Cleo, with her Sensainos ability, would have been able to feel Tova's lack of pain.

Aya closed her eyes.

Gianna had scolded him in front of her for his treatment of Tova. She had made it sound as if he had overstepped and used too much force. Had lied, and for what?

Because she knew I would obey her as long as I trusted her.

"You should have told me."

"Should I have done that before or after you kept trying to stab me?" She opened her mouth to say something, but the corner of Will's mouth lifted slightly. "I'm joking," he reassured her.

But Aya cocked her head, her brow furrowed as she took him in. "You let people think you're involved with her. Why?"

Will's face was carefully composed as he pushed off the fence. "That's a tale for another day. Shall we train?"

It was a skilled evasion, but…time. It would take time, she supposed, for them to adjust to this fragile peace. To learn how to navigate its spaces and its strength.

"Perhaps we start with the library at Maraciana," she answered smoothly. Because that tonic had worn off entirely, and she wasn't about to test her limits on him.

Will let out a dramatic sigh. "I find I'm jealous of Aidon's monopoly on your physical activities."

"Why do you hate him?" The words were out of her mouth before she could take them back.

Will stilled, his feet braced apart as studied her. "I don't hate him."

"You certainly don't like him."

The silence stretched long enough that she wondered if she'd overstepped, if she'd broken that fragile peace before it had even truly begun. But his voice was low as he finally said, "Because he is unburdened by powers."

Will leaned a hip against the paddock rail, his arms folding across his chest. "Because despite their bickering, his father cares about him. Because his people adore him. Because he is *good*. Because he is everything a man—a true prince—should be."

Do not call me that.

It was a mockery, compared to someone like Aidon. At least, she supposed that's how Will saw it, what he felt every time someone addressed him with those words.

How many times had she heard it since they'd arrived here? And she had spat that title at him herself and mocked him in her anger.

"Don't look at me like that," Will breathed. Pain lingered in his voice, on his face. "I don't need your pity."

She swallowed the lump in her throat. "I don't pity you."

It was true. It wasn't pity that was coloring her thoughts. It was something far worse.

She'd always assumed Will took pride in his reputation, thought he basked in the glory of the title that followed him. But he was made by Gianna. Just as she was.

Weapons, the both of them.

She had been fine with it. Had been proud to serve her queen and her gods.

But now, she wasn't so sure.

He scanned her face, as if reading the thoughts there. "I have always known, Aya, that there would be consequences for my choices."

She wished she could turn away from the intensity of his stare, but she was locked there, trapped in whatever spell of his she couldn't seem to escape from. "Then why make them?"

Something softened in his gaze at that—some emotion flickering across his face, there and gone in a simple blink. His voice was hoarse as he said, "Because they allow me to protect what matters." He pushed off the fence, his movements graceful as he hauled himself over the railing. "I'll come with you tomorrow to the Maraciana. We'll figure this out together."

"Where are you off to now?"

"To prepare for a meeting with the king." He threw her a grim smile over his shoulder as he headed toward the palace. "You were right. It was foolish of me to return covered in blood. As you once pointed out, my reputation precedes me. I figure it's best to get ahead of it lest he suspects I was involved with Helene."

Wrong. She had been so, so wrong.

"Do you want me to come with you?" The offer surprised him as much as it did her when it left her mouth of its own accord. Will froze, glancing back at her as if he hadn't quite heard her. Aya felt her lips twitch. "What? We're bound by an oath, remember?"

Will grinned. "Charmed as I am, I'd hate to give Dominic two people to bully."

"You think me incapable of handling him?"

Will shook his head, his expression softening. "I think you incapable of nothing, Aya love."

He started toward the palace again, and Aya peered after him, the vial burning in her back pocket as she watched him go.

46

IT WAS AMAZING, AIDON THOUGHT, THAT EVEN IN THE KING'S throne room, Will still managed to ooze arrogance. The Enforcer stood between two of the marble pillars that lined the walkway to the throne, his hands shoved casually in the pockets of his black jacket. Aidon stood at Dominic's shoulder, the king's bone-white crown glinting in the sunlight that streamed through the high windows behind him.

"I assume you have a reason for calling this meeting," Dominic sighed.

Will gave a low chuckle. "I do love your directness, Majesty. It makes it so much simpler to get to the heart of the matter." Dominic's brows rose, but Will continued. "Let us not pretend you weren't going to call me in for questioning after Helene was taken. So I'm here to assure you I had no involvement in the matter."

Aidon kept his eyes on Will as he said, "It's true. He arrived shortly after Helene was taken and helped us in our search."

The king settled back on his throne, his hand scratching his goatee. "And do you have proof of your whereabouts prior to arriving at the house, Enforcer?"

"Really, Uncle, this isn't nec—"

Will held up a hand, silencing Aidon.

"In that small corner tavern Aidon so kindly introduced me to years ago," Will replied. "I'm sure Amelia would be *more* than happy to account for my whereabouts."

"And what of your companion?"

Aidon stiffened as Will's gaze shifted to him, a smirk tugging on his mouth as he realized what Aidon hadn't confessed to his uncle. "Aya was with your nephew last night."

"We were at dinner," Aidon added quickly. It didn't matter. He could see his uncle's jaw tense as he gave a brisk nod. There would be another discussion about this; he was sure of it. Marking Aya was one thing. Courting her...that was out of the question.

Will began to pace, his hands clasped behind his back as he said, "I must say, Majesty, your suspicions wound me. As I'm sure they would our queen." Dominic opened his mouth, but Will leaned against one of the pillars, his arms folding across his chest. He was the picture of impertinence as he drawled, "Perhaps, like you, *we* need to take a look at *our* trade terms with Trahir."

"Are you threatening me, Enforcer?"

Will raised his brows. "Threatening you? I wouldn't dream of it, Majesty." He pushed off the pillar, his hands sliding into his pockets as he neared the throne. "But you're a businessman. You understand how deals might fall through if certain parties aren't sincere in their agreements. Tala has long provided Trahir with generous terms for the weapons that have given your armies their advantage, because you are our ally. Yet you question us at every turn. Perhaps we are mistaken in our arrangement?"

Dominic's knuckles were white as he grasped the golden arms of his throne. "We could make our own weapons, should it please you more."

Will gave a shrug. "By all means. However, I think you'd

find difficulties in creating them at such a scale. Materials aside, the Visya here have become accustomed to a different sort of life, wouldn't you agree? I haven't heard of many of your Zeluus using their strength affinity to create weapons in defense of the kingdom."

Aidon cleared his throat, his chin raised as he cut a glance to his uncle. "Perhaps Will has a point. Let's not forget our friendship in our time of strife."

The king glowered at Will but dipped his head in acknowledgment. "Of course," he agreed. "We wouldn't want our friends in the north thinking we're taking advantage of their generosity."

Dominic's shrewd green eyes tracked to Aidon. "I want extra guards posted around the city," he ordered. "And extra eyes on the Bellare. Be subtle about it. I don't want them knowing our suspicions of them being involved in this kidnapping. Not until we know more."

"Avis Lavigne and his family are human," Will said. "Surely they wouldn't harm those they consider their own."

"Avis is on the Council, and it's well known the Bellare disagree with our modernization and continued focus on growing trade," Aidon mused. "Perhaps they wanted to send a message."

"A poor choice," Will scoffed. "If anyone is a traditionalist, it's Avis."

"Pardon the interruption," Sion chimed in from the back of the room. "There's a man here to see you, Enforcer."

"We're done," Dominic said with a wave of his hand. Will bowed as he took his leave, following Sion out of the hall. The king sighed, his fingers pinching his brow as he rested his head in his hand.

"It was just dinner," Aidon muttered, his eyes fixed ahead. His uncle gave a low laugh.

"It's never just dinner, Aidon."

47

WILL COULD FEEL HIS SHOULDERS RELAXING AS HE followed Sion out of the throne room.

He'd been bluffing about the trade terms; Gianna would never agree to an action that might cost them the alliance. But he *hadn't* been lying about the bar. Amelia, the barkeep at his favorite tavern, would certainly be the alibi he needed. He had been too embarrassed to admit to Aya last night that he'd posted up at the bar, planning to lose himself in beer and a game of cards, only to distract himself from what *she* was doing at dinner.

But extra eyes on the Bellare…

He hadn't mentioned Ryker. Not yet. He had no problem with Ryker rotting in prison. But if it meant losing Lorna's help—help that was already nearly impossible to get…he was too desperate to risk it. He'd visited the Saj again. She hadn't deigned to open the door.

"Who is it, Sion?" he asked as the throne room doors shut behind them.

"A young man who claims he's a friend of yours."

Will frowned. He didn't have any friends in this godsforsaken city, save perhaps Josie.

"Did he give you a name, or am I to guess?" He knew from the smug grin on Sion's face that he found pleasure in catching Will off guard.

"Ryker." His smirk vanished as he watched the change that came over Will, his voice instantly more accommodating. "Should I ask him to leave, Prince?"

"No," Will growled. "Show me to him."

By the time Will made it to the private gathering room—a small circular library of sorts—his rage had grown into something visceral. The door had barely closed behind him before he had Ryker in his grasp. His fingers closed over the boy's vest as he shoved him into one of the leather chairs before the bookcase.

"Have you lost your fucking mind?" he snarled. "What the hells are you doing here?" Ryker struggled against his hold, but Will kept him pinned, willing himself to breathe so he didn't kill him on the spot.

"I came to tell you to stay away from Lorna," Ryker growled.

Will shoved him once more for good measure before stepping away.

"Feeling territorial, Ryker?"

"It's too dangerous."

Will whirled. "Do not talk to me about danger when you show up here. I should turn you in, you piece of shit." The king would be looking for any opportunity to suspect Will of Helene's abduction. At least Ryker had been wise enough to cover his damn tattoo.

Ryker blinked up at him, letting his surprise show only for a moment. "Being a member of the Bellare isn't against the law."

"But kidnapping the daughter of a councillor is."

Ryker's lips tightened, his fists clenching at his side. "You should check your information, *Prince*. That had nothing to do with us. I'll gladly pass that along to the general if it will aid in his search. We have no need to abduct those we try to protect. The Lavignes are human."

It changed nothing. Because Ryker was here, and if he was lying, and the Bellare *were* involved…

"You could get us killed."

Ryker's brows rose. "Us?" He leaned back in his chair, a contemplative look on his face. "This is about the woman at the club, isn't it? Did you tell her how you know me?"

"Leave it, Ryker," Will warned.

"Who is she to you?"

"None of your concern."

Ryker's sneer clouded Will's vision with red.

"I know that look," Ryker said. "It's the same one my mates get when they grow overly fond of their whores."

Every rational thought eddied from Will's mind as he lunged for the rebel and sent them both crashing to the floor. He didn't bother touching his power. No, he wanted to *feel* Ryker's flesh bruise. He got in one hit, then another, and another, and then someone was shouting, and hands were on him, trying to yank him away from the bleeding boy on the floor.

"What the hells are you doing?"

Josie. It was Josie's hands tugging on his arms, Josie's shouts that had echoed through the room. Will immediately backed off from Ryker, his breath coming in heaving pants. Ryker rolled to his side, spitting a mouthful of blood as he groaned. More blood streamed from his nose, his lip swollen and split in two. But he looked triumphant as he stared at Will, red coating his teeth as he grinned. "Typical of you," he wheezed. He grimaced as he stood, his body stooped. "Always showing exactly where to hit you hardest."

Will made for Ryker again, but Josie flung out her arm, stopping him dead. "Leave before I have you removed," Josie ordered Ryker, her voice a mere growl.

The boy kept his mouth shut as he bowed, giving Will one final smirk before he limped out of the room.

Josie gave Will the courtesy of three seconds to gather himself before she whirled on him, her brown eyes bright with anger. "Don't you think we have enough going on without you getting into a godsdamn brawl?"

Will inhaled shakily. "I'm sorry." He sank into one of the seats, his hands rubbing his face. His cheek ached. Ryker must have landed a punch; one he hadn't even noticed in his rage.

He felt raw—as if his shield had been obliterated, and he could feel everything at its highest frequency. This wasn't like him. The Enforcer was not supposed to get riled, and certainly not by something like a petty squabble. But Aya slipping under his shield had loosened something in him.

"Who is he?" Josie asked, the edge in her voice gone. He heard her settle into the chair next to him.

"His name is Ryker." Will sighed as he met Josie's gaze. "We have a complicated history."

The princess snorted. "I'll say. You're not going to tell me what that was about, are you?"

"I wish I could." He meant it. He and Josie had always had a cordial relationship. She was kind, and funny, and loyal.

She surveyed him closely now, her lips pursed. "I saw the blood last night," she said quietly. Will opened his mouth, but she held up a hand. "I know you weren't involved with Helene's kidnapping. And given you've already been beaten up today—"

"He got *one* good hit in."

Josie rolled her eyes as she continued. "I figured I'd tell you that I know you, and I know you didn't take that girl."

Will's throat bobbed. "Thank you," he said hoarsely. He knew he should say more. Josie deserved to know what her kindness meant to him. But his throat was tight, and his head felt heavy, and Josie was squeezing his arm as if she saw it all anyway and already understood.

48

THE SUN HAD BEGUN ITS DESCENT BY THE TIME AYA AND Will left the Maraciana two weeks later, their backs aching from another day spent hunched over books.

Aya had finally fallen into a steady rhythm—the first since she'd left Tala over seven weeks ago. In the early morning she trained with Aidon before he left to continue the search for Helene, his frustration growing each day the City Guard came back empty-handed. And though her curiosity had her wondering if perhaps she should help, she and Will had equally pressing matters. So after her training, they holed up in the Maraciana to research. He was hells-bent on studying Evie, convinced that the saint would hold answers.

"You're supposed to be the second of your kind," he had mused.

I'm not a saint.

Even if the gods *had* chosen her, a true saint didn't need a tonic to survive her power. A true saint wasn't fueled by darkness. But Aya had swallowed the words, forcing them down in the face of Will's optimism. "I'm nothing like her," she'd argued wearily instead.

Will had just blinked at her. "Humor me."

It was fruitless anyway.

There was plenty of texts on the savior of their realm, but nothing of true use to Aya. Will had been interested to learn Evie claimed Pathos as her patron god before the Visya had ever been restricted to a single affinity, and that it sparked rumors that the saint was a descendent of the god, a theory that had been dismissed by the High Priestesses centuries ago.

An interesting tidbit, but utterly useless when it came to learning what Aya was secretly searching for: a way to survive the Decachiré. And if she could find it, she could use whatever was roiling inside of her without the tonic, which only allowed her to delve so deep into her power.

Her nerves grew more frayed with every page that came up short of answers, but Will's optimism was relentless.

Aya usually worked out her frustration at the end of the day during affinity training with Will in the paddock—just enough to keep the edge off her writhing well.

She still hadn't told him about the tonic she sipped before those sessions, just as she hadn't told him what she was desperately looking for within those books. She didn't want to see the look on his face when he realized she was accepting her fate, sinking deeper into the darkness within her.

Today, the early evening was balmy, the breeze from the sea cooling the air enough that they decided to forgo the carriage from the Maraciana and walk back to the palace instead. They sank into an easy silence as they strolled through the heart of the city, keeping off the busy path that followed the crescent moon beach. Will glanced up at the dusk sky, the clouds colored in pinks and oranges and purples.

"Rinnia does have its own beauty, I suppose," he murmured. His hands were in his pockets, his shoulders looser than she'd seen in weeks. He caught her gaze, quirking an eyebrow at her. "What?"

"I've never asked why you hate it here so much."

"I never said I did."

"You think I haven't noticed? You grit your teeth any harder, and you won't have any left."

Will smirked. "I had no idea you paid so much attention to me, Aya love," he drawled. Aya felt her cheeks heat, and she fixed her gaze ahead, refusing to see his smug satisfaction at getting a reaction out of her. Will heaved a sigh before continuing, the teasing gone from his voice entirely. "I don't have fond memories of this place."

"With your father, you mean?" They stepped into a small plaza, and she glanced at him, marking the contemplation on his face.

"I don't remember him always being such a monster," Will finally said. "Greedy, yes. And selfish. But I think something hardened in him after my mother..." His voice trailed off, his mouth tightening. "Or perhaps I was just unable to see it. Which I suppose makes me just as much of a monster as he is."

Aya let his confession sink in, the heaviness in his voice settling over her like the humidity that cloaked the air. All those times he'd carelessly thrown that word around, had accused her of thinking he was such, had it been his own fears taking hold?

Aya knew what it was like to be haunted by the past.

"I'm sorry," she murmured. Will stiffened. "About your mother. The pain of it never leaves you."

"No," he agreed quietly. "It doesn't." He kept his gaze locked ahead as he said, "I'm sorry, too. I'm not ignorant to the role my father played in your mother's death."

Aya drew in a shaky breath. "It's not your fault." She didn't say it to assuage his guilt, but simply because it was true. There was only one person to blame for that, and it wasn't Will.

He stopped, the abruptness of it catching Aya off guard. She was a few paces ahead of him before she glanced back.

"Even still. I am sorry."

Three times now she'd heard those words from him. She

still wasn't sure what to make of it all. But she nodded, which must have been enough, because he strolled back to her side, falling in step with her as they ducked into the narrow street that connected one plaza to the next.

"Would you have taken over his merchant empire had you not joined the Dyminara?" It was what everyone had expected, before Will joined qualifications. She wondered if his father had been surprised, or even angry. Will let out a bitter noise.

"No. I would not have tied myself to him any more than I already am."

She went to press him further, but he changed the subject.

"What do you miss most about home?" he asked, his shoulder bumping hers as a group of children raced around them, towels in hand as they ran toward the beach.

Tova. Pa. Tyr.

But she'd had enough heaviness for one conversation and suspected he had, too. So Aya forced a small smile to her face as she said, "The Ventaleh."

Will laughed, the rich tenor of it seeming to fill the street. "I'm serious."

"As am I," Aya retorted. "I don't mind the cold. And when the wind comes, it means warm fires, and chaucholda, and the Dawning. I used to sit by the fire in the library at the Quarter and carve for hours when the Ventaleh began to howl."

He glanced sidelong at her. "I haven't seen you carve since we've arrived."

She was surprised he'd noticed she carved at all. "It's not like I had time to grab my supplies when we left."

Will's eyes found the street again, his jaw shifting slightly.

"Anyway," she continued, tucking thoughts of that day away, "the Ventaleh has its own peace to it. I find it soothing. Not like..."

She waved a hand in the direction of the beach, where they could hear music and laughter starting. It was nearly sunset, and the townspeople treated the moment like a festival. They gathered to build small fires, where they ate and drank and toasted another day.

"I miss the mountains," Will confessed. "That's where I find my peace."

"And here I thought you were going to say your fancy dinners at Eden."

"Ah yes, those too, of course." He said it with enough sarcasm that Aya couldn't help the grin that tugged at the corners of her mouth. They'd made it to the residential section of the Old Town, the next plaza they walked through more like a small courtyard. It was quiet except for the tinkling of the small fountain in its center, its residents likely by the sea or grabbing an early drink in town.

"So you—"

The words died on her lips as a sharp whizzing sounded near her ear. Aya spun, her hand instinctively reaching for the blade at her hip as she took in the three hooded men, two with swords drawn and one with a bow, its string pulled taut.

Aya's fingers curled around the handle of her blade, but she didn't draw it.

Will stepped forward. "Can we help you, gentlemen?" His voice was calm, but his back was tense, his muscles twitching as he rested a hand on the sword at his side. The men wore the traditional clothes of the Western Kingdom, but so did Aya and Will. If Kakos had found them, if they knew about her...

"You and your father are an insult to the gods," the man in the center snarled, his voice like gravel, his accent marking him from Trahir.

"The Bellare, I take it?" Will asked lightly.

Aya felt a prickling sensation creep up her spine, and she glanced over her shoulder. Three more men prowled down the narrow street behind them, knives and swords drawn.

An ambush. This was an ambush.

"Will," she said under her breath as she turned, her back pressing into his as she watched the men approach.

"I know," he murmured. His hand caught her elbow as she went to draw her knife. "Why don't we have this conversation alone," Will suggested to the attackers. "Aya, I'll meet you back at the palace."

The man with the bow laughed, and Aya heard the string creak as he pulled it tighter. "We'd be happy to let the lady go. Our issue is not with her."

But Aya shifted on her feet, her arm sliding out of Will's grasp as she drew her blade. A silent reminder of the oath that had bound them. And perhaps more—a hand extended, should he want it.

"Rare you're not using that blade against *me*," he muttered. "Truly a first."

Aya moved, throwing her knife with deadly precision. The man across from her didn't even have time to scream as it lodged in his throat, his blood spraying his companions as he fell. She heard the arrow loose, but she and Will were already moving. Will took down the man with the bow, his scream cutting off as quickly as it started as Will's affinity hit him. Aya rushed the two approaching men, sliding under the swipe of one's sword as she snatched her blade from the dead man's neck and slashed it across the gut of the other rebel. His eyes bulged as he clutched his innards, his knees hitting the cobblestones with a sickening crunch as he slumped to the ground.

Two more rebels charged down the street, but Aya whirled, her attention on blocking the blade coming for her neck. She deflected the blow with a grunt, her knife swiping up, the sharp point piercing just under the man's ribs. He staggered, his weight heavy on her as he slumped over. Aya shucked him off, her knife twirling in her hand as she faced the oncoming men.

A shout of pain rang out from near the fountain, and

Aya's gaze cut straight to Will as he clasped his side, his fingers dark with blood. Two men lay dead at his feet, but another three were before him, one with a sword heading straight for his throat. Aya threw her knife without a thought, the blade lodging in the man's eye. He let out a piercing scream, his hands clawing at his face as Will thrust his sword into his chest.

An arm wrapped around Aya's neck, the pressure tight enough to steal the air from her lungs as she was dragged backwards into a firm body. She felt the tip of a blade just below her ribs. Will turned, eyes flaring with rage, but he stumbled as his hand clutched his side.

"Do it, you coward," Aya rasped to her captor.

The man's breath was hot on her neck as he laughed. "I want the little shit to watch," he said. The two rebels near Will grabbed him by the arms and forced him to his knees. He struggled, his teeth bared, but it was no use. One grabbed his hair and yanked, forcing his gaze to Aya. Will's eyes were wide, his breath coming in wet pants.

"Aya," he wheezed. "Use it."

Her power. Because his…his could not get them out of this. Without the tonic, Aya could feel that tempest inside of her, begging to be unleashed. To decimate the rebels, the plaza, perhaps the entire world. It would kill them all.

"Aya!" he rasped again.

"*Duck.*"

It was instinct that had Aya following the cold command that rang out from somewhere behind her. Instinct that had her head jerking to the side as an arrow whizzed through the air and sliced clean through her captor's throat. His body was a crushing weight as they both fell to the ground, the sound of running footsteps filling the plaza.

The City Guard had arrived. And from the hoarse shouts she heard echo across the space, they'd captured the remaining three men.

Aya pressed her palms into the cobblestones, her arms shaking as she tried to lift the man off her. His weight suddenly disappeared, and hands gripped under her arms, hauling her to her knees.

"Are you hurt?" Will's voice was sharp, his hands skimming her face, her arms, her side—each place caked in the rebels' blood. She knocked his hands away and pressed her palm against his wound, the warmth of his blood coating her fingers at an alarming rate.

"Aya."

"I'm fine." She glanced up to see Aidon before them, bow in hand. "Thank you."

The prince nodded, but his brow furrowed as he took in the blood covering her hand.

Aya fought to keep her voice steady as she pressed her hand tighter to the wound. "He needs a healer."

Will covered her hand with his own, his eyes fixed on her face. "I'm fine," he parroted, a weak smirk on his lips. But his weight shifted from where he sat on his heels, his body tilting to the side. Aya wedged her shoulder beneath his, not daring to move that hand against his wound.

"A healer, Aidon. Now."

49

THE LIQUOR BURNED AS AYA SIPPED IT, BUT IT DID LITTLE TO settle her as she stood on Will's balcony, her eyes fixed unseeingly on the sea.

"The pain will linger," the healer had warned. "He's lucky to be alive."

Aya glanced at her left palm, where her oath once was. The skin was raw from scrubbing off the blood.

She downed the rest of her drink.

"You didn't pour me one?" Will's voice was hoarse—a mere rasp over the crashing of the waves against the cliffs. She turned to see him leaning against the doorway, his hair mussed, a pair of fresh black cotton pants sitting low on his hips. An angry red mark marred his side, but his skin was clear of blood. She'd made sure of it.

"I left water by your bed."

Will plucked a glass from the dresser, holding it up so she could see the brown liquor. "I know. So I helped myself instead. Some caregiver you are," he teased as he made his way to her, his steps stiff and tight. His jaw locked as he braced his forearms on the balustrade.

"Are you hungry?" Aya asked. "I can send for some

dinner." She started for the door, but Will caught her wrist, holding her in place. His gray eyes were solemn as they flitted across her face. "What?"

His fingers shifted, his thumb pressing into the center of her palm, in that space where her oath once was. "I know you healed me."

He was lucky to be alive. And *she* was lucky—lucky that no one had seen that flare of light from her palm as she tried to knit his flesh together enough to stave off the bleeding until the healer arrived. Lucky that pulling her healing affinity forward had felt like trying to find light underground instead of the raging well she'd felt just moments before.

"You were bleeding out."

"You risked healing me, and yet you didn't touch your power during that attack. You were willing to die," he muttered. "You could've easily used your power to free yourself from that hold. And don't tell me it was because they were human. We were under attack."

Aya frowned as she tried to read what was on his face. "I told you, I can't use too much—"

"I've watched you decimate an entire square without taking a breath."

Aya tensed as she tugged her hand from his grip. "Is that what you want me to do? Kill everything standing in my path?"

"If it means that you live to see another day, then yes, that's exactly what I want you to do," Will ground out. "He would've killed you had Aidon not arrived—"

"I would have killed *you* had Aidon not arrived!" The words ricocheted between them, the truth leaving her lips before she could stop it. It settled into the growing silence like a stone.

She had no doubt it was the truth; that had she unleashed her power, it would not have cared who lived and who died. She folded her arms across her chest, suddenly cold despite the humid night.

"I don't believe that for a second." His voice was soft as he turned to face her, his hip leaning against the balcony.

"'You and I both know it's not light that drives you.' You said that to me."

Will's face was grave. "I was angry," he confessed. "I didn't actually think—"

"Stop," she demanded. "Stop pretending like I'm not a danger to anyone who gets close to me. To anyone I care about."

Something shifted in his gaze at that, and he took a small step toward her as he set his drink on the balustrade. His hands slid up her arms to grasp her shoulders, his head ducking to meet her gaze.

"I see you," he said roughly, giving her shoulders a light squeeze. "I have *always* seen you. And nothing I see in you is dark, Aya."

But he didn't know that secret she kept buried so deep; the one she hadn't told a soul, not even Tova. Just as he didn't feel the tempest of raw power inside of her—the way it threatened to devour until there was nothing left.

I will destroy everything I've ever loved, just as I always have.

She shook her head, emotion swelling in her chest, but Will pulled her closer. "I'm here. To pull you back from whatever edge you're so afraid of falling over."

"You can't promise me that," Aya breathed. "We don't even know where the edge is."

There was nothing but uncompromising will in his face. "Then I'll go over it with you. To the seven hells themselves, if we must. No matter how far the fall."

Aya blinked up at him. This honesty between them was still so new. But his words felt like a promise. An oath. She brushed her thumb across the bare skin of her left palm, and Will slid his hand down, his thumb pressing against where that mark once was.

"You miss it," he surmised. She still hadn't grown used

to her healed skin—the smoothness that replaced the bumps and ridges from her years in the Dyminara. She'd almost been willing to keep a scar from where Aidon had cut her, if only to feel more like herself.

If only to serve as a reminder that she was not what the world had hoped for.

"I do," she agreed quietly as she brushed a hand over the mark on his side, watching as his muscles jumped at her light touch, his skin prickling as she trailed her fingers across the scar.

"It *is* impressive, isn't it?" he drawled with a wry grin, as if he could sense the levity she so desperately needed.

And despite the tension of the day—the weeks, really—a laugh rasped from her. Will's answering smile was dazzling, the green in his eyes flaring as he stared down at her. "I think we've both been through far worse," Aya remarked.

Will shook his head, that light in his eyes fading as quickly as it had come. "Don't remind me. I thought you were dead that night the Athatis attacked. When I couldn't feel you anymore, I thought they had..."

He shook his head again and cleared his throat, as if the words were stuck there.

A vision of him on his knees rose in her mind, the echoes of him bellowing her name tugging at her memory. Her hand flattened on his side, and Will stilled, his eyes locking on her. She wondered if her own tangled emotions were reflected there: the confusion and the surprise and the hesitation and something else that she was still too wary to explore.

Her throat bobbed as she swallowed. "I never thanked you. For coming after me that night. I would never have made it out if you hadn't found me."

His brows rose. "What happened to, 'I would've been able to fulfill my oath if you hadn't involved yourself'?"

Aya groaned. "Insufferable."

His laugh was a caress against her mouth. "To consistency, Aya love." She could feel the warmth of him, his woodsmoke and spiced-honey scent wrapping around her as a breeze blew in from the ocean. Her heart kicked into an unsteady rhythm as the smile faded from his face, replaced by something else entirely. It tightened the air between them, stretching it so taut that Aya could feel the pull toward him. But Will let out a shaky breath as he shifted away from her, his hand grabbing his abandoned glass. He took one last long sip of his drink. "We should get some sleep."

She blinked, as if coming to. Sleep…of course. Such a thing seemed impossible. But she nodded and bid him good night. She was at the balcony door when he called out to her.

"I got you something. It's in the top drawer of my dresser." She cocked her head, but he merely turned back to the ocean, his figure a dark outline cut against the star-flecked sky.

The parcel was wrapped in simple brown paper held in place with a white ribbon. She tugged gently on it, her breath catching as she took in the small sharp whittling knife and untouched block of wood. A note rested on top, scrawled in handwriting she hadn't realized was familiar:

Just don't stab me with it.

50

AIDON STROLLED ACROSS THE BEACH, WEAVING BETWEEN the unlit bonfires and stopping every so often to greet various townspeople. The night was warm, the dusk sky a deep purple. A quartet had set up near the largest fire, which would serve as the heart of the dancing and celebrating, though the festival stretched all the way down the crescent beach.

He was relieved the Pysar celebration had finally arrived. The city needed something festive. And with two weeks having passed since the last Bellare attack, perhaps the celebratory mood would last.

Even if his was lacking.

Despite his attempted refusals, Aya had taken him to lunch just after the attack—as a thank-you for saving her and Will's lives. He didn't bother telling her he didn't know that he quite deserved it.

The screams from the dungeons had still been ringing in his ears. The Bellare members they'd captured yielded nothing of Helene's whereabouts, even under Sensainos and Persi questioning.

It is not the power behind the blade, but the timing of the strike, his mother loved to say. *Patience, Aidon.*

But he was growing restless.

Aidon sighed and made a silent commitment to put such thoughts to the side, at least for the evening. Because those were flames he saw at the far end of the beach. The Lighting had begun.

He scanned the crowd for Aya. He wanted her to see this, to take in how the flames flickered down the beach, racing toward the central fire, where torchbearers stood ready to ignite the massive structure and officially begin the festivities.

He found her weaving through the crowd in a long, loose white dress that barely dusted the sand. A long slit up the side showed flashes of the golden sandals that laced up her legs. She'd coaxed her hair into loose curls, one side pinned behind her ear and the rest cascading down her back. Josie walked with her in a peach gown of similar light fabric that hugged every curve, the skirt fanning out around her feet.

They each held glasses of sparkling wine, and Josie lifted hers in greeting before wordlessly walking off with a small knowing smile. No sign of Will, though Aidon didn't miss him. He'd invited the Enforcer out of courtesy and perhaps as an apology for the attack. It didn't mean Aidon found his company any more enjoyable.

"So…this is Pysar," Aya said, her eyes scanning the beach.

For a moment, he couldn't find the words to respond. It was as though her mere presence had trapped his voice in his throat, and all he could do was trace the length of the stunning white dress that twisted at her neck, the back entirely open before meeting again just below the small of her back. She cocked her head at him, a quizzical frown on her face. "What?"

"Nothing." Aidon coughed. "Yes, this is Pysar."

She grinned at him. "Are you going to tell me what it's all about?"

Aidon shifted on his feet, his hands sliding into the pockets of his tan linen pants. "We weren't always the leaders in trade that we are today. It wasn't until a group of sailors discovered the spring migration patterns of a fish unique to this region that we started to become known for our delicacies. The festival celebrates that discovery. It's the beginning of the spring season, an awakening."

Cheers began to swell around them, and he placed his hands on her shoulders, her skin warm and soft. "Although *this* is just the beginning," he said as he turned her just as the fires roared faster and faster down the beach, the shouts reaching a joyous level as the main structure went up in flames.

"It's exquisite," she breathed. She scanned the beach once more, a quiet awe on her face. "Now what do we do?"

Aidon smiled as the quartet began to play, his hand finding the small of her back as he guided her forward. "Now, we dance."

51

Aya found Will standing away from the merriment, hiding in the shadows cast from the bonfires.

"Don't you look approachable and fun," she smirked, pressing a glass of sparkling wine into his hand. Truth be told, his white linen dress shirt and tan trousers certainly *did* make him look approachable, despite his lurking in the shadows giving him the distinct air of someone trying to avoid stares—and doing so unsuccessfully. Aya marked the curious glances in his direction, but if Will noticed, he didn't let on. He merely offered her a small grin as he sipped the wine.

"You said we had to come because Aidon invited us, not that we had to enjoy ourselves." His eyes scanned her, taking in her gown before settling on her flushed face. "Though you seem to be having an excellent time."

Aya lifted a shoulder, turning to watch the next dance with him. "Are you pouting because there are no pretty redheads for you to charm?"

Will grinned. "Careful, Aya. I might just think you were jealous."

She turned to face him fully, her lips twisting into a smirk, but any response died on her lips as the smooth sound of the cello cut through the balmy night, its melody slow and deep. The revelers slowed their movements, some shooting confused glances at the musicians as the cellist continued his honeyed rhythm that was clearly not typical of this land. Others merely pulled their partners close to partake in a slow and steady dance with those they loved most, not caring that an unfamiliar tune had begun to swell around them.

Aya stepped toward the fire as though in a daze, her gaze fixed on the quartet. Her breath caught as the violin joined in slowly, driving the melody forward in a heartbreakingly beautiful duet. They continued on before the other violinist wove her sound through them, the viola coming in to add its warmth to the cello beneath it all.

She knew this music, knew this very song. Had danced to it mere months ago on a cold night under a sky full of stars. "This is from home," Aya breathed, her eyes burning as she stared at the quartet. She could feel Will watching her, and she swallowed hard, finally turning to him. "You requested this?"

"I did."

"Why?"

His jaw shifted as he contemplated her question. Finally, he gave a small shrug. "Because I miss it, too." He looked as though he wanted to say more, but there was wariness in his gaze—a wariness she was sure she had put there with all she had done over the years. But whatever he beheld as he searched her face now had him continuing in another breath, the words spilling out on a long exhale, "And because I simply want to dance with you."

The confession settled between them, stretching across the night air like a bridge.

He took her wine, setting it in the sand along with his own. And then he extended his hand and looked at her expectantly, as if he wasn't the least bit afraid of what it might mean, as if he knew, even before she did, that she would accept his offer.

Another step forward, should she want to take it. Another layer of distrust pulled away, should she choose to accept it.

I have always seen you.

His rough palms scraped against her own as she slid her hand into his, their fingers intertwining as he pulled her gently into the midst of those dancing. His arm slid around her waist, pulling her close as they began to move to the music, the deep melody swelling around them. It was as if Aya could feel the strings of the quartet in her very soul, the somber yet sweet composition moving through her blood.

"The last time we did this, I thought you were going to stab me," Will mused.

"Who says I'm not still considering it?" she teased, tilting her head back to catch his gaze. His eyes were bright, the light of the flames making the green in his irises flicker like small sparks of fire. Aya's breath caught as he trailed his fingers down her spine slowly, her skin tingling as he stroked her bare back. He leaned in, his face mere inches from hers.

"That's funny," he drawled, his voice vibrating in every place she was pressed against him. "I don't feel a blade."

"Not where your fingers are now at least," she crooned. Will stiffened as he blinked at her, surprise flaring in his eyes. And then he tipped his head back and laughed, the sound a rich tenor that touched every part of her, sparking something deep in her core—something new, some unfamiliar feeling she hadn't let herself venture into before.

She grinned at him as he spun her once before tugging her back to him, notes of woodsmoke and spiced-honey wrapping around her as fully as his arms, which held her to him.

"Touché, Aya love," he murmured. She let herself relax into him, let the building music sweep through her as Will guided them across the sand, his steps never faltering, his gray eyes never leaving hers. And for a moment, there was simply this: the swelling strings and his soothing scent and a settling deep within her, not unlike the feeling he'd used to disarm her when they were sparring for the young Visya in Dunmeaden what felt like a lifetime ago.

It felt like peace.

52

WILL GAVE AYA A POLITE BOW AND A WINK AS THE SONG ended before strolling off through the revelers. Another song began, this one merry and fast.

"Enjoying the festival?"

Aya turned, the grin on her face fading as she met King Dominic's stare. She remembered herself, bowing low as she said, "Yes, Majesty. I'm grateful to Aidon for extending us an invitation."

Dominic hummed in response, his eyes shifting to the celebration. "It seems Gianna was not mistaken in how similar you two might find each other," he mused.

Aya frowned. "I'm not sure I understand your meaning."

His voice remained carefree as he turned to regard her fully. "Gianna mentioned in her letter that she felt you and my nephew might get along. She was alluding to a match." He chuckled at the blank expression on her face. "Surely you weren't ignorant of your queen's intentions. The amount of time you spend with my nephew has not escaped me."

Aya took a steadying breath. "With all due respect, Majesty, my queen would not see me as a proper match for your nephew. She holds the gods in the highest regard and would never stand for a Visya on the throne."

The king's grin grew wolfish, his eyes glinting in the firelight. "Ah, but, my dear Aya, you are no ordinary Visya, are you?"

Her heart stumbled as he took a step toward her, her hands fisting at her sides.

He knows. How does he know?

"*You* are Gianna's eyes," the king continued. "Your abilities are unmatched."

Vicious relief swept through her, and she forced her face to remain neutral as she said, "You flatter me. But let us not forget Will is Gianna's Second."

"Do not think me naive enough to believe you would claim the Dark Prince more powerful than you. Besides, we all know he holds a *special* place in Gianna's heart. I have no doubt her feelings are reflected in his rank."

Aya could feel her face flush, her lips pressing tight as she imagined all the ways she could silence the king.

Dominic tsked. "I must say, it is *fascinating* to learn how much Gianna keeps from her Tría."

He was goading her. Prodding her for…what? Confirmation of her feelings for Aidon? Gianna's aspirations? Aidon's own intentions?

"I can assure you, whatever she may have alluded to in her letter, Gianna has no intentions with regard to me and Aidon," she said evenly. "She would never stand for Visya rule."

"Ah, but *you* wouldn't be ruling, would you?"

Aya raised a brow. "Did you once share those sentiments with your wife, Majesty?"

It was a cruel jab, and Dominic bristled, but there was a hand on her back, and suddenly Aidon was at her side, a too-easy grin on his face.

"Everything alright?" he asked her lightly. His eyes sharpened as they fell on the king. "Uncle," he said, giving a terse nod. Dominic returned the gesture, his eyes cold as they lingered on Aya before he walked away.

Aidon let out a low whistle as he glanced down at her. "He usually reserves a look of that much fury for me. What on earth did you say to him?"

Aya stepped out of his grasp, her arms wrapping around herself as she walked away from the crowd. She suddenly felt cold. Aidon followed her, a steady presence at her back as she led the way to the outskirts of the festivities.

"Did Gianna say anything about us in her letter?" She fought to keep the accusation from her voice as she turned to face him. She knew Aidon had been marking her… But to keep *this* from her?

The prince's brows rose. "I didn't read her letter. This is the first I'm hearing of it." He tugged at the collar of his shirt, his voice hesitant as he asked, "What do you mean by…us?"

Aya rubbed her face, looking anywhere but Aidon as she gathered herself. "Your uncle seems to think Gianna intended for us to be a match."

Aidon's brow furrowed. "I—" He paused, taking a second to gather himself. "I'm surprised to hear she would support such a thing. That would go in direct violation of what the gods decreed."

"That's what I said to your uncle. She'd never approve of it."

Aidon's frown deepened, his eyes darting across her face as he slid his hands into his pockets. "I suppose if you weren't crowned…"

"Has that ever happened?"

Aidon shook his head, as if drawing himself to the present. "Not that I know of."

Aya turned away from him, letting the breeze settle her. Why would the king even suggest it? Gianna would never stand for it. Unless…

She had already proven she was desperate for an alliance.

If there was a way to ensure Trahir's support without directly defying the gods, perhaps she would.

Aidon's steps were slow as he walked around her, his grasp gentle as he lifted her chin. But his dark brown eyes were probing as he took her in, concern written in his gaze. "What are you thinking?"

"Too much," she admitted quietly. Because to be traded like that…like some object…

The mere thought made her feel hollow.

She truly had become no better than a weapon to be wielded by her queen. And while Aya had always been proud to serve her, to uphold her duty, she was again faced with the gnawing feeling that perhaps her devotion had clouded each aspect of her judgment.

Aidon brushed a loose strand of hair off her cheek, tucking it behind her ear. "I can't believe my uncle wouldn't mention this to me," he muttered, his face still serious. "I thought…I thought in *this*, I'd have a choice." The remark was soft and distant, as if he weren't truly speaking to her at all. She opened her mouth to reassure him, but the words lodged in her throat as her mind raced.

Aidon blinked, his jaw set as he focused on her. "That's not to say that I don't…that I wouldn't…" His hands, warm and calloused, found her cheeks. He was too close—far too close for her to think rationally, to not get caught up in the intensity of his gaze, still slightly frantic with thought, or in his lips that were a mere breath from hers.

"Maybe…we…" His voice trailed off, his eyes darting between her eyes and her lips. There was a question there, a question she didn't have the answer to either.

"Fuck it," he whispered. He closed that distance, his mouth warm as it pressed against her own. Aya's hands slid to the collar of his linen shirt, unsure of whether to pull him closer or push him away. Aidon seemed equally conflicted as his hand slid to the back of her head, his fingers tightening in her hair.

A throat cleared behind them, and Aya stumbled back, putting a healthy distance between her and the prince.

"I hate to ruin the moment," Will drawled. His hands were shoved in his pockets, his face unreadable as he took in the two of them. "But we have a problem."

Aidon glared at Will as if the only problem he saw was standing just before him. But Will was unfazed, his voice grave as he said, "Viviane is missing."

53

WILL COULD FEEL AYA'S EYES ON HIM AS THEY MADE their way through the empty streets of Rinnia, the merry sounds of the festival a distant hum in the otherwise sleepy silence that stretched through the city.

He kept his gaze sweeping the streets, even as the air between them grew taut, their footsteps sharp echoes on the cobblestones as they followed Aidon down a narrow side road.

Josie had found Will on the beach, her dress disheveled, eyes wide in terror as she babbled incoherently. He had picked out the words *Viviane* and *apartment* and *gone*, and had been able to piece the rest together easily enough.

Dominic ordered Josie back to the palace with her guards, and the princess hadn't even seemed to hear him. She just blinked as they led her away, as though the shock had overwhelmed her completely. Will doubted she would dare sit still once it had worn off. The princess was a fighter. She would rather die than sit idly by while someone she loved was in danger.

"Find them," had been Dominic's only order to his nephew.

The City Guard had been dispatched, and Aya, Will, and Aidon had chosen the road near Vi's ransacked apartment to start their search. They scoured the streets until they reached the outskirts of the residential area.

Suddenly Aya flung out a hand, catching Will's chest before he took another step. "Look," she murmured. He followed her gaze to the blood that pooled on the stones of an alleyway.

Will closed his eyes for a heartbeat.

She couldn't be dead. For Josie's sake, she couldn't be dead.

Aidon frowned at the blood, then at the alley stretching into the dark.

Aya stepped around him, her brow furrowed in concentration. She scanned the wall, laying a hand against the rough brick. "It's on the wall."

Will stepped up behind, leaning over her shoulder to follow her gaze. Indeed, those were splashes of blood, nearly invisible against the deep red of the brick.

"Do you think the Bellare are retaliating after the attack the other week?" she asked as she tilted her head to catch his gaze.

"I don't know." He stepped back out of her mint and evergreen scent, steeling himself against the hurt he saw flash across her face.

He wasn't trying to be cruel. He was trying to calm the ringing in his ears whenever he looked at Aidon, and being near her didn't help.

He hadn't been surprised to see their embrace. He'd practically shoved them together, after all. But he *had* been surprised at how it hollowed out something inside of him; the way he felt the ground slipping beneath his feet, as if he had lost some footing he hadn't even known he'd found.

Aidon made his way further into the alley, his sword already drawn. Aya followed, her footsteps nearly silent as she tracked the blood.

"Aya," Will warned. He didn't like this—any of it. But she continued on, her hand tracing the brick wall. Will swore under his breath as he ducked after them. The air was thick and stale here, as if the sea breeze never reached this place.

Will kept to the middle of the wide path, his breath feeling stuck in his lungs. He cast his power out, but it felt like pushing through mud, his affinity sluggish as it pressed against the heavy air.

Aidon drew up short ahead of them, his sword going slack. "It's a dead end," he said.

And then Will felt it.

Pain lanced through his ribs, sharp and deep, and he clenched his teeth against it, a hiss escaping from him. Aya's eyes darted to him, and then she was whirling, a knife appearing in her hand as she faced the direction they'd come from.

Three cloaked figures emerged, two holding the third slumped between them.

Viviane.

The air around them seemed to shimmer and pulse, before the heaviness disappeared and Will could hear the *drip, drip, drip* of blood falling from the knife the man on the left held. They had shielded the air—had blocked their sound completely and herded them to the dead end.

No one would hear them here.

Aya's eyes were fixed on the slumped figure, her voice trembling as she called, "Vi!"

No response. Will tested his affinity again, sensing instead of manipulating. He could feel her pain, her terror.

"She's alive," he murmured to Aya.

"You won't win this fight," the man with the knife said to Aidon, taking another step closer.

"If you believe that, you seriously misjudge who you're facing," Aidon retorted. "We handled the others of your group. We'll handle you, too."

The words twisted something in Will's gut. It made no sense to herd them here together like this. The Bellare who had attacked them in the plaza the other week had them outnumbered. But they had needed to—they had been human…

These men were Visya.

His eyes found Aya's, and he read it there, too. Something wasn't right. She opened her mouth to warn Aidon, but the prince fell to his knees, his sword clattering to the ground as he screamed, the sound reverberating off the shield of air the Caeli had formed. His back arched, the tendons in his neck stretching as he gritted his teeth against whatever hells the other man—the Sensainos—was unleashing on him.

Will ground his teeth as he reinforced his shield to block out the pain. Aya started toward Aidon, but a knife flashed, and Viviane dropped to the ground, her own scream loud enough to shatter windows, to shatter Will's very skull as he dropped with her, her pain his own, her death rushing toward him and obliterating his shield as he doubled over his knees and gasped for air.

Was *this* the trap? To render them both defenseless and finish Aya? Had Kakos found her?

But the Caeli didn't head for her. Not immediately. No, he took that knife he had just plunged into Viviane's heart and raced toward Will.

Will's eyes found Aya's as pain continued to rip through him, as Viviane took her final breaths, the agony peaking until the cold chill of death began to wash over him.

But it wasn't death.

It was a burst of ice that flew from Aya's outstretched hand and cracked the ground beneath her feet, just as fire erupted, lighting the courtyard in a blinding haze. For a moment, all he could make out was fire and ice and pain—so much pain that he thought he surely must be dying. His vision swam, the courtyard blurring beneath the heat and the cold and then… blessed darkness and quiet.

But he fought against its alluring peace, tugging on his consciousness and forcing himself to stay—stay where the pain was still radiating through his body, stay where she was. His breath was sharp through his teeth as he forced his eyes open, gray meeting blue as Aya stood frozen in place, her wide eyes fixed on him, her hand still outstretched toward the Caeli.

A spear of ice was embedded in the Caeli's chest, his body keeled over steps away from Will.

Dead.

Next to her, Aidon was on his knees, his hands hanging limply at his sides as he stared at the charred body before him, not unlike the ones Aya had left in Dunmeaden.

Will pushed himself up, forcing his limbs to steady as he staggered to Aya. He covered her outstretched hand with his own, lowering it to her side as he searched her face. Her skin was as cold as the ice that had cracked across the ground, her hand trembling beneath his.

"Are you alright?"

She gave a small nod. But fear cloaked her blue eyes. Fear, and guilt, and that dull, vacant haze that he recognized as her slipping into herself. So he forced lightness into his breathless voice as he said, "Fire and ice, huh?"

Aya took a shuddering breath as she looked to where Aidon knelt, the prince still staring numbly at the burning flesh. "The fire wasn't me."

Will cut his gaze to the prince. He hadn't seen it before—the scorched stretch of ground that lay in front of the prince, as if the fire had poured directly from where he sat. Aya's hand slipped from Will's grasp as she took a step toward Aidon. "Hepha's flame," she breathed. "You're an Incend." Aidon sat back on his heels, his jaw tight as he turned his gaze to her.

"And you're not just a Persi."

"Later," Will rumbled. It was too dangerous to have this conversation here.

Aidon staggered to his feet, his face still a mask of distrust, and for a moment, Will expected him to argue. But the prince nodded, and Will turned to Vi's crumpled figure, his footsteps growing heavier as he approached the dead woman.

He'd failed Josie miserably.

He crouched before the broken figure and tugged at her hood, his heart stuttering in his chest as he gazed at the face that had frozen in terror in her final moments.

Blue eyes, wide and unseeing. Full lips parted in a gasp of pain. And bright blond hair that he hadn't noticed beneath her hood in the dark.

He swore softly.

This wasn't Viviane.

It was Helene Lavigne.

54

THE WALK TO THE PALACE WAS LONG AND SLOW WITH Helene's lifeless body in Will's arms, the silence so strained Aya could feel it pressing in all around them.

Visya members of the Bellare, Aidon had said as he burned the men's bodies, each marked with a rose tattoo.

Aya hadn't argued. And while Aidon had mentioned that the Bellare *did* include some devout Visya, it still didn't make sense, tattoos or no. This attack had been different than the last.

Aya tucked her suspicions away as they reached the chaos of the palace gates, where guards rushed about. Peter darted through the melee to meet them, his eyes wide as he took in their ghastly appearance. The blood drained from his face as he noticed the bundle in Will's arms.

"Is that—?"

"Helene Lavigne," Aidon cut in. And it was the voice of the general that said, "Get her parents immediately."

Peter swallowed and gave a small shake of his head. "Avis and Claire are already here. In the throne room. Your father sent for them as soon as Viviane was taken."

They followed Peter, their footsteps impossibly loud on the

marble floors. Peter pushed through the heavy driftwood doors to the throne room, where the king, Enzo, Zuri, Josie, and the Lavignes were gathered. Josie whirled to face them, her eyes immediately finding the broken body in Will's arms. Her face crumbled as she lurched forward. "No," she cried. "No no no!"

Aya rushed forward, catching the princess in her arms.

"It's not her," she soothed her friend. "It's not her."

But Claire Lavigne already seemed to know—had caught sight of the whips of blond from under the hood. Her wail of agony tore at Aya as the mother sank to her knees, Zuri moving with her, her arm across the woman's shoulders.

Avis didn't spare his wife a glance. His eyes stayed on Will, his face rapidly changing from white, to red, to a deep purple.

"You," he snarled, his long stride propelling him forward. "You did this, you *murderer*!" His shouts reverberated through the hall, his fury like a cresting wave as he continued toward Will. Aya went to untangle herself from Josie, but Aidon stepped between the men, his brown eyes dark.

"Your daughter was killed by two rebels before we could overcome them."

"Bullshit!" Spit flew from Avis's mouth as his body trembled with rage. "You know who he is. Queen Gianna's Enforcer. You've heard what he's capable of. And yet you allow him to walk among us like he wasn't born straight from the hells."

Will's face betrayed nothing as Avis flung his accusations—just the same grimness that had settled over his features as soon as he'd discovered Helene. But Aidon took a single step forward and pointed to Will.

"This man nearly died trying to save your daughter's life. He saw to it that her body was returned to you."

Avis glared at the prince, but he remained silent as he pushed past him and took his daughter from Will's arms. Aya's heart ached as he stared down at Helene with a brokenness she knew would haunt him.

Aidon looked to his king. "The two rebels have been disposed of, their bodies dumped in the sea. I request your leave, Uncle, to meet with the Guard. We need to check all known rebel outposts. Tonight."

Dominic nodded. "Perhaps our guests would like to rest. They have been more than helpful." And though it sounded like thanks, there was a stoniness glinting in his eyes as he dismissed them.

Aidon bowed before glancing at Aya and Will, his face unreadable as he said, "I'll see you out." He cut a glance at Peter. "Gather the Guard. I want everyone outside the training complex in twenty minutes."

Aidon's pace quickened as they hit the hall, his shoulders bunched as they headed to the guest wing. "I'm coming with you," Josie said as she followed them.

"Like hells you are."

Josie grabbed her brother's arm, a snarl erupting from her. "She is my partner and she is in danger. *I am coming with you.*"

Aidon met his sister's glare, his voice quiet as he said, "They know."

Josie turned, stunned, to Aya and Will. The prince resumed his pace, and soon they were tucked inside Aya's sitting room. The silence was heavy again as Aya and Aidon stared at each other.

"Well?" Aidon finally demanded, his brow furrowed in disdain.

"Careful," Will warned from where he sat in an armchair, his elbows propped on his knees. "Though I'm grateful for your defense to Lavigne's accusation, I won't hesitate to wipe that sneer off your face." Aya shot him a look, and he shrugged. "Unless you'd like to do the honors, Aya love."

Aya let out a long breath through her nose, turning her attention to the siblings across from her. "You know how the Conoscenza speaks of one like Evie rising should darkness return?" They nodded, confusion marking their stares. Aya took another deep breath, her hands weaving into the fabric of her dirty dress.

And then she told them. Everything. The fire in the market. The framing of Tova. The prophecy and the orders to study with the Saj of the Maraciana.

She told it all, except the most important piece—that her power was steadily devouring her. That if Natali was to be believed, then she wasn't the saint they'd all hoped for.

Aya wasn't sure why she'd been able to touch her power tonight without consequence, especially with the tonic out of her system. But regardless, she wasn't about to reveal the truth, especially not when they were so desperate for Trahir to commit their forces.

If the idea of a saint was what encouraged Aidon to press this alliance with Dominic, then to hells with it.

By the time she'd finished, Aidon was slouched against the couch, his fingers massaging his temples. But Josie remained upright, her brows high. Aya didn't miss the note of skepticism in her voice as she said, "I've never been in the presence of a saint before."

"Thrilling, isn't it?" Will mused. But for all of the lightness in his tone, his narrowed gaze was fixed on Aidon, who had yet to say a word.

Aya dipped her head to meet the prince's gaze. "So let me get this straight," he finally murmured. "Your general is innocent. You're the Second Saint. And you're here to study your power secretly with the Saj of the Maraciana. Any more secrets?"

Far too many.

"I meant what I said at dinner," Aya said evenly. "I *have* been trying to study the Decachiré to see how my power might help in the war. Because war *is* coming, Aidon. Kakos is preparing for something. You know it as surely as I do. And if we are not ready for them…I fear what will happen to the realm."

A muscle worked in his jaw as he looked away, his hand massaging the back of his neck.

"I believe you owe us an explanation now, Your Highness," Will drawled.

"You're getting close to the point where I won't intervene if he tries to kill you," Josie warned.

"It's been a while since the prince and I had a go."

"Enough," Aya cut in. Will's baiting wasn't going to get them anywhere. But her order did nothing but stoke whatever anger he'd been leashing beneath his arrogance, and his relaxed posture slid away as he gripped the arms of his chair.

"He wants to talk about secrets? He's been lying to the world for godsdamn years," Will snarled. "Who knows what else they're keeping from us?"

"Rich coming from you," Aidon shot back. "You've been sitting on a weapon that could change the tide of the coming war, and you didn't say a thing. And yet you want me to trust you with my arm—?"

Aidon choked, a vein in his neck bulging. His face grew panicked, his fingers clawing at his throat as he gasped for air.

"What are you doing?" Josie demanded.

Will merely sat back in his chair, his gray eyes cold as he regarded the prince. "Mimicking the sensation of suffocation," he said, his voice dangerously calm.

"Stop it!" Josie's vicious command cut through Aya's shock, but before she could lift a finger, Will dropped whatever hold he had on Aidon. The prince gasped for air.

"Now that I understand you're Visya, Aidon, you'll hear me quite clearly when I say that I have no hesitation in exercising my affinity on you. And that if you refer to her as a weapon again, I won't even bother with it when I cut out your godsdamn tongue. Understood?"

Aidon took another shuddering breath, but it was to Aya he turned, his face drawn as he said, "I'm sorry. I didn't mean that."

He buried his head in his hands, letting out a muffled groan. "This is a fucking mess."

Josie placed a hand on his arm, giving it a gentle squeeze. Something passed wordlessly between them, and Aidon finally cleared his throat and said, "I was sick as a child, and no healer could discover what it was. My uncle sent for one of the Saj of the Maraciana in a last-ditch effort to save my life, and he discovered my power. Keeping it inside had been killing me slowly. Apparently, someone in my family line was Visya."

Aya bit her lip as she surveyed the prince. He met her gaze, a dull smile on his face. "You see, then, why my uncle would want to keep this quiet." He laughed roughly, dragging a hand down his face once more. "A Visya prince. The end of my family's line." Aidon leaned forward, his arms braced on his knees. "I can't take the crown if anyone knows the truth. The gods forbid it."

Will remained silent, his gaze fixed on the prince. She could see the cogs of his mind moving, his fingers steepled together in front of him.

The rules of the realm were set—only the eldest sibling could rule. The crown passing to another family line was something that hadn't happened in over a century.

"Would your uncle side with Kakos?" Will finally asked, that contemplative frown still on his face. Aidon shook his head.

"While we may not be as traditional as the north, we don't condone heresy. If Kakos is trying to revive the Decachiré, then they are a threat not just to humans and Visya, but the gods. He would never support that."

"Even if in their heresy, they support you, a Visya, taking the throne?" Will pressed. "I doubt Kakos gives a damn what the gods have decreed."

"Even then. Kakos's support would not sway centuries of custom and belief in my own kingdom," Aidon retorted.

"My uncle knows that. I think he rather hopes to not get involved—to let your queen fight this religious war on her own, should Kakos truly attack."

It would be the safest option, Aya supposed. Especially if the king's nephew wanted to fight. She knew Aidon would stop at nothing to defend his people, including revealing his power to save them.

"What if you had Gianna's support for you taking the throne?" she asked softly, her eyes fixed on the ground. "Would that get your uncle to agree to the alliance?"

"She would never agree to it," Will retorted.

But Aya kept her focus on a tear in the carpet, her palms gripping the edge of the chair cushion. "If she was willing to offer me in marriage, then I think she might accept anything."

The room grew still, a tense silence descending on them.

"Apparently I've missed something," Josie finally said slowly.

"The king claims Gianna intends for me to match with your brother," Aya explained. "He believes she alluded to it as a potential exchange for an alliance." She refused to look in Will's direction, refused to see whatever was stirring in those gray eyes.

"Gianna would use you in such a way?" Josie asked, the disbelief evident in her voice. "Why?"

Aya shook her head, searching for the words to explain all that she suspected, but it was Will who answered, his voice flat. "Because there would be no greater concession than to give you one of her own."

"But you're Visya," Josie pushed.

"Perhaps she feels differently about a saint on the throne," Will answered for Aya in that same dull tone. "Or perhaps she doesn't believe it to be heresy, because Aya wouldn't be crowned at all."

Aya met his stony gaze. His face was unreadable.

"Reasons aside, if Gianna is desperate enough to offer

me up, perhaps she'd be desperate enough to back a Visya on the throne if it means your uncle lends us his forces," Aya finally said.

"There is another option," Aidon hedged. "One that doesn't involve Gianna at all." His eyes raked over her, as if searching for the power she'd displayed.

"Absolutely not," Will growled.

"If my uncle knows the prophecy is true, he may be more willing to fight," Aidon plowed on. "There would be infallible proof of Kakos rising to power."

"There *is* infallible proof," Will interjected. "We've seen it in our own damn kingdom, and still he refuses to act. The answer is no."

"He's right," Aya pressed. "There are too many unknowns right now. My studies aren't complete. And if word gets back to Kakos, it could accelerate the conflict before we're ready for it."

Too close; they were circling too close to the truth about her power.

No one will follow darkness into battle.

Aya dug her fingers into the arm of her chair as Aidon rubbed a hand across his jaw. "So when will this news be shared?" he asked.

Silence stretched between the four friends, and Aidon let out a hard laugh. "You're joking."

"My power is an advantage," Aya reasoned, desperate to keep Aidon from digging further. "You of all people understand how valuable the element of surprise can be. Gianna will tell the realm when the time is right."

"You'd ask my troops to join this war with no knowledge that a saint exists."

"I'm not—"

"My kingdom needs to know, Aya!"

The proclamation settled heavily in the room, Aidon's voice rumbling with authority. Aya could feel her brows rise.

A king—that's who had been speaking. She hadn't heard that tone from him before. Even Josie looked surprised as she glanced at her brother.

Aidon rubbed at his face, his voice strained. "But fine. For now, I'll talk to my uncle. See what, if anything, would change his willingness to commit our forces."

Aya knew it marked the end of their meeting. Josie was already standing, desperate to find Viviane. Aya walked them to the door, but Aidon lingered, even as Will excused himself to bathe.

"I'm sorry for how I reacted," Aidon finally said after Will left. "I was scared."

Aya raised a brow, a small smirk lifting the corner of her lips. "Finally, you've come to your senses."

Aidon rolled his eyes. "Not of you," he said incredulously. "*For* you. For myself, too. I was scared that you knew my secret. And what yours meant for you." He leaned against the armoire on the far wall, his arms folding across his chest. "You're not all that terrifying, you know."

"Even though I'm a weapon?" She had meant her teasing to sound light, but there was enough heaviness to the words that she knew he sensed how deeply he had cut her.

"I didn't mean that. It's how I've been trained to think of us my entire life. But it's not how I see you."

Us.

Because he was one of them. Visya, just like her.

Aya swallowed, desperately wanting to alleviate the heaviness that had settled between them. But she found herself hesitating, the light verbal sparring that usually came so easily with Aidon suddenly full and thick with implications. He tilted his head as he considered her, a grim smile on his face.

"Gianna's offer is eating at you, isn't it?"

Aya swallowed, her hands twining behind her back. "Do you think it would encourage your uncle to make an alliance?"

"Would that be what sways you to accept the match?"

She knew what the answer was. For Tala—for her people—she would. And yet she found herself unable to make that promise aloud. She told herself it was because it didn't change the danger she'd bring him. But perhaps it was also because of the hesitation she saw in his own gaze as he watched her.

Could he live with that? That their match had been born not out of his duty to the Crown, but of hers to her queen?

Could she?

Aidon pushed himself off the armoire. "Before you answer, remember that this isn't just about alliances, and duties, and *us*. It's about him, too." There was no accusation in his voice, but it didn't stop Aya from instantly rejecting his notion, her mouth opening to argue. Aidon cut her off with a soft chuckle. "You can lie all you want to me, Aya. But at least be honest with yourself. You have feelings for him. For me too," he added with a sly smile. "But ignoring whatever is between you and Will while making this decision would be foolish. And as I recall you saying, you're no fool."

Was it even a decision? If Gianna pushed this, and Dominic accepted, they were merely pawns in a grander game. She knew he felt it too—knew it was what drove the desperation behind his kiss on the beach. They cared for each other, it was true. But…

Haven't you ever wanted something for yourself?

"How are you so calm about this?" Aya asked, her arms folded tightly across her chest.

He shrugged. "I'm no stranger to my uncle flexing his will. And as you once said, Aya, it isn't particularly helpful to wish for things that cannot be."

Like choices they did not have because of their duties.

"Besides," Aidon continued, "there are far worse matches, wouldn't you say?" He grinned at her, but the gesture didn't quite meet his eyes.

"You deserve a choice." She needed him to hear it. She needed them both to hear it.

"As do you. For now, we have more pressing matters. Josie needs me. Let's take it up at Genemai, yeah? Save me a dance?" The Birth of Magic festival was less than a fortnight away.

He rapped the armoire once and was already turning to go when she called him back. "Would the chance of an alliance sway *you*?"

His brown eyes were unreadable as they searched hers.

"I don't know," was all he said before he closed the door behind him.

55

WILL SANK BENEATH THE SURFACE OF THE WATER, LETTING the scalding heat bite his skin. He could wash away the blood that coated his arms and the ash that clung to his skin, but he could not rid himself of the words she had uttered to Josie in that room.

Gianna intends for me to match with your brother.

His rage was a living thing, boiling him from the inside out.

It didn't matter where Aya was, or what she learned to do with her power. She belonged to the queen, and Gianna would never release that which was hers.

Just as Gianna would always own him, too.

Will finished his bath and padded to the bar cart, fully content to forgo a glass and down the whole damn bottle, but he paused, the neck mere inches from his lips as he felt that tug deep within him, the one that told him he wasn't where he was supposed to be.

He lowered the bottle slowly, letting his head fall against the wall. He'd barely kept himself in check an hour ago. He couldn't go to her now—not with his emotions pounding through him so intensely. He was used to feeling, had never been afraid of the sensations, either others' or his own. But *this*... This intensity felt like it might consume him. Like he was out in the waters that roared against the cliffs, and if he didn't master whatever this was, he would surely drown.

Will cursed as he set down the bottle and went back to her room.

He knew exactly where he'd find her: on the balcony, staring at the waves. And by the looks of it, she'd been doing just that since they'd left. She stood with her arms folded tightly around her, her dirt-flecked white dress blowing in the wind. He leaned against the doorframe, letting the sea breeze wash over him as he simply took her in.

"Do you think this is what she wanted?" she called to him, sensing his presence without him saying a word. And despite the hells they were in, his mouth twitched at that. But any hint of a grin faded as he took in the curve of her shoulders and the white marks on her arms as she gripped herself tighter.

"Come inside."

She glanced over her shoulder, and his heart gave a vicious twist at the bleakness in her face. He watched her chest rise and fall in time to the waves, tracing every breath as she tried to steady herself. His affinity reached out instinctively—to calm, to soothe—even though he knew he'd meet nothing. He'd never realized how constant her presence was until it was gone; how much her essence sank into his very being. Even in those times she'd held her shield, he'd still been able to feel *her* beneath it.

"Come inside," he repeated, his voice rough. He wondered if she could sense the plea in his words.

Aya pushed herself off the balustrade and crossed the terrace, pausing for a beat as she passed him in the threshold. Her shoulder brushed against him, her eyes flicking across his face. But she stayed coiled in on herself, so he kept his distance as he led the way into the bathroom. He nodded to the lip of the tub as he turned on the faucet and grabbed a washcloth from the rack of towels beside it. Aya perched on the edge, staring unseeingly in front of her. Will tested the water with his wrist before dunking the washcloth beneath it.

Then he kneeled before her, gently taking one of her arms in his hands and unraveling it from the vise grip she kept on herself. Her eyes moved to him, watching as he ran the washcloth up the length of her arm in long, soothing strokes. He washed the dirt and blood from her, his hands steady despite the pounding in his chest. He moved to her other arm, working in silence as her breath settled into a deeper rhythm, the muscles in her shoulders relaxing.

Her eyes fluttered closed as he cupped her face, gently wiping the streaks of dirt and ash from her cheeks. He ran the washcloth across her forehead, then to the back of her neck, letting the cool water soothe her in a way he couldn't. She let her head drop, her forehead pressing against his, her shaky exhale brushing across his lips.

Will swallowed against the roaring inside of him.

He dropped the cloth into the tub with a wet slap, and she snapped her head up as he backed away and settled against the sink. For a few long moments, they stared at each other, Aya gripping the edge of the tub hard enough that her knuckles went white.

"So?" she finally asked, her voice quivering slightly.

"So what?"

"Do you think this match is what she wants?"

"I don't know." He rubbed his face, a dull pain throbbing behind his eyes.

"Do you think it's even possible?"

"I don't know."

He didn't want to talk about this. Not with her. Truthfully, he didn't want to even consider it—couldn't bear to without wanting to hit something. He was exhausted and angry, and if she didn't stop looking at him like that, he might very well do something he knew he would regret.

But Aya stood, undeterred. "Has it ever happened in the past? A Visya married to the Crown?"

"I don't know."

"Well, do you truly think the idea of a saint changes anything? That people would even accept it?"

Her questions snapped his control, his words rushing from him before he could stop them. "I don't know, Aya! I don't fucking know!"

Aya stared at him, her full lips parted in surprise at his outburst. He swore, pushing himself off the counter and stalking into the sitting room. He should've known better than to come here, especially when he didn't have himself in check.

"And what about you then?" she demanded as she followed him.

"What about me?"

She stepped in front of him, blocking his path to the door. Her eyes glowed like blue embers as she refused to back down. "You told me to get close to him. Did you know all along? Is this what *you* want?"

His hands fisted at his sides as he fought to keep his voice steady, but it trembled anyway as he growled, "What's it going to take, Aya? What more do I have to do to prove to you that I am not your enemy? What's it going to take for you to trust me?" He knew she could see the anger written on his face, could maybe even sense the way it came off him in waves.

He wasn't truly angry at her, but at the mess that was his whole entire fucking life—the mess it seemed the gods would never free him from.

She folded her arms, her voice low as she said, "You didn't answer my question."

"No," he forced through clenched teeth as he stared down at her. "No, I don't want to watch you ensnare him. I don't want to watch him drag his eyes all over you. I don't want to watch him make you laugh and blush. I don't want to watch him touch you like he—"

He bit off his words as if he might choke on them.

She was silent for a heartbeat, her eyes flaring in recognition.

"You're jealous," she breathed.

"He is falling in *love* with you!" he proclaimed, his arms flinging wide. As if the fact could provide any adequate explanation for the agony he was in. As if she understood at all.

"And you're jealous."

He felt a muscle feather in his jaw. She took a step closer to him, her head tilting slightly as she considered him. She was so close—too close. Close enough that her chest brushed against his as she stared up at him, everything he was feeling reflected in her gaze. The trepidation. The nerves. The longing.

It was the longing that had him cupping her face in his hands, his voice low and rough as he said, "And so what if I am?"

A tremor racked her body, her breath coming in shallow pants that matched his own. "I do not belong to you," she whispered, but there was no cockiness to her words. There was nothing but the same burning he felt as her body melted against his.

He smiled grimly, pushing a stray curl out of her face as he considered her; considered how the way she was looking at him was enough to bring him to his fucking knees. Her breath caught as he leaned in and brushed his lips against her cheek.

"You don't belong to *anyone* but yourself," he breathed against her ear, grinning as he felt her fingers dig into his biceps. Her eyes were bright as he pulled back and leaned his forehead against hers, his lips a breath from her own. "Don't you forget it."

It took every bit of his self-control to pull away from her. To let his hands fall from her face and let the cold air rush in as he stepped back, marking the goose bumps that prickled her flesh. She stared at him, her lips parted, her chest heaving as much as his own.

"Good night, Aya."

It had been an impossible feat to pull away from her. To leave her when she had looked at him with that darkened stare that had him wondering if maybe, just maybe the gods hadn't completely forsaken him.

Will sighed, leaning against the rough brick wall. He didn't want to be here, lurking in the shadows outside one of the seedier taverns in town, waiting. But he couldn't shake that insistent feeling that had been pressing in on him since they had been cornered earlier that evening.

And that *look* on Avis's face…

Aidon and his City Guard were checking every hovel and hellhole for some trace of Viviane, but Will was willing to bet his favorite blade they'd come up empty.

And he was going to prove it.

It was only a matter of minutes before Ryker stumbled out of the tavern, his stride brisk as he headed away from the heart of the city. Will followed, waiting until the boy turned down one of the darker alleyways before making his move. But Ryker, it seemed, was expecting him.

No—not him.

Because as the boy whirled, it wasn't to Will, but to a figure that had materialized out of the darkness next to him. Will's blood froze as Ryker yanked Aya against him, his knife bared at her throat.

"Well, isn't *this* interesting?" Ryker purred, glancing over Aya's head at Will. His arm tightened around her waist, as if he sensed how Aya was assessing his hold, looking for a way out. She'd donned her fighting leathers—as if she knew exactly what to be prepared for.

Blood beaded on the knife as Ryker growled, "Don't try me."

There was murder in Aya's eyes as she stilled, and Ryker's nose brushed her ear. "Good to see you again, sweetheart."

Will hadn't gone for Ryker after the Bellare attacked him and Aya. Not because he hadn't wanted to kill him, but because he saw the hopelessness in Aya's face the more they came up empty in their research. He still needed Lorna, but he wasn't ready to play that final card.

But now…

I should have fucking killed him.

"Let her go," was all he said.

Ryker clucked his tongue as he straightened, his dark eyes settling on Will. "I think I'll keep her right here to ensure your good behavior."

Will watched as Aya's fists clenched, but she didn't dare move, not with that knife against her throat.

"What is it you two want?"

"She has no business with you," Will pressed.

Again, Ryker glanced down at Aya, letting out a hum. "So she was following *you* then. Interesting. It's almost as if she doesn't trust you."

The words hit somewhere deep in Will, but he kept his focus on that knife, which Ryker finally loosened ever so slightly. Will slid his hands into his pockets, forcing himself to breathe—to relax into that easy arrogance he knew would draw Ryker away from her.

"I came to save you some time. The two men you're searching for are dead."

Ryker frowned, dropping the knife further in his distraction. "What are you on about?"

"Your friends took it upon themselves to kill a councillor's daughter. So we returned the favor," Will said airily. He didn't have to extend his affinity to know the shock that flickered across Ryker's face was real.

"Helene is dead?"

"By rebel hands," Will drawled, marking the knife as it slid even lower. *Move*, he silently urged her. But Aya's attention wasn't on her captor. It was on him, a small frown creasing her brow as she tried to sort through what was happening. "We caught two of them tonight."

"That can't be possible," Ryker breathed as he lowered the knife completely. Aya stayed exactly where she was.

"Have you already taken a head count then?"

Say it, Ryker. I know you know, so say it.

Ryker bit his lip, true hesitation on his face as he stared at Will. "Avis Lavigne is a member of the Bellare."

Aya broke his hold, and in the span of a breath, she had him on his back, her boot pressing lightly against his throat, his knife pointed at his heart.

"I preferred you from behind," Ryker wheezed.

"And I prefer men on their backs," she snarled, her boot digging into his windpipe.

Will sighed. "I need him alive, love."

Aya shot him a glare over her shoulder. "He might not have killed Helene, but he sure as hells almost killed us."

"I had nothing to do with that," Ryker rasped.

Aya bared her teeth as she leaned over him. "You're lying."

"Let him go, Aya." The look she gave Will was murderous. He supposed he deserved it for keeping her in the dark, but he couldn't find it in himself to be fully bothered. Not when there was still something heated beneath her angry stare.

"For fucks sake," Ryker groaned, drawing her attention back to him.

She loosened her boot from his neck. "Avis Lavigne is a member of the Bellare?"

"Yes." Ryker's gaze shifted to Will. "I told you we had nothing to do with her kidnapping."

"You forgot to mention Avis's affiliation," Will replied as he removed his hands from his pockets, his arms folding as he regarded Ryker. "Do the Bellare have any reason to go after him or his family?"

"Why would I have told you that with the Guard breathing down our necks? And no. He's a highly favored member."

Aya's frown deepened, and Will knew she was arriving at the same conclusion he had suspected.

Someone was framing the Bellare.

He jerked his chin toward Ryker. Aya's jaw clenched, but she stepped back, letting the boy rise. Ryker didn't waste his breath on goodbyes as he disappeared into the night.

Will contemplated going after him, but Aya was staring after the young rebel, her shoulders tense, and he knew the real fight was here. Sure enough, her blue eyes were like ice as she whirled to face him.

"What the hells?" she demanded. Will reached for the wound on her neck, but she smacked his hand away. "How are you involved with the Bellare?"

He snorted. "I'm not. I sensed Avis's shock when Aidon accused them of killing Helene. I was lucky to have Ryker, who could confirm my suspicions."

"You've had an in all along, and you've never said anything?"

Will sighed as he tugged a hand through his hair. "It's complicated. I couldn't very well be seen with ties to the Bellare if we want Dominic's help."

Aya frowned, doubt rising in her eyes with each diversion. Will hated it—hated that he had to put it there.

"He almost killed us, and you let him go."

Will closed his eyes, his breath rushing out of him. "Please, Aya. Trust me. I will tell you everything, I promise. But right now, there are more pressing matters."

It was a fool's hope, he realized, asking her to trust him like this. But she simply frowned, her face taking on that calculated look as she raised a hand to her neck.

She winced as her fingers brushed the cut.

Will ripped a strip of fabric from his shirt, moving her hand away as he gently pressed the cloth to her neck. "Always making a mess," he murmured.

Her fingers brushed his as she took the cloth from his hold. "Someone is framing the Bellare."

Will forced a smile to his face. "I'll give you three guesses who," he quipped. It didn't work to alleviate the heaviness that had befallen her. "Now if only we could prove it."

A grim determination settled over her features as she met his stare, her hand sliding into the pocket of her leathers. She pulled out a key.

"I'm way ahead of you."

56

AYA HAD SUSPECTED IT, TOO. SHE HAD KNOWN SOMETHING wasn't right when those men cornered them in the alley this evening.

She just wasn't sure *what*. So when Will had disappeared from her room earlier, she'd changed. And then she'd followed him.

But not before she'd swiped the key to Dominic's study from an unsuspecting guard for good measure.

The castle was fairly empty, what with the early hour and more guards delegated to the search for Viviane. And yet the silence felt heavy, as if an eerie hush had settled over the halls.

Aya led the way in the dark, her eyes sweeping the empty passageways they crept through as she sent up a silent plea to Saudra to help them in their endeavor. And though their footsteps were mercifully muffled by the thick rugs that stretched the marble hallways to Dominic's study, their movements still sounded far too loud.

She could feel her pulse hammering as they made their way toward the study's door, Will a steady presence at her back.

Nearly there.

Behind her, Will froze.

The muffled sound of boots came from the hall they'd just passed on their left, getting closer and closer by the second. Aya grabbed Will, tugging him forward as they rushed for the study. She had the key out of her pocket and into the lock in one swift movement, the door clicking open as they lunged inside. Aya closed the door silently behind them, their backs resting against the polished surface as they waited for the footsteps to pass.

Aya could feel her pulse in her throat, and her hands tingled as she ran her fingers through her hair once silence returned. Will swore softly, his eyes closed as he caught his breath. "Let's get this over with," he muttered.

A sliver of gray light spilled from between the thick crimson curtains that covered the two grand windows on the far side of the study. Will strode toward the desk, cracking the curtains just enough to let a splash of early dawn light spill onto the ornate wooden surface scattered with papers. Aya locked the door before making her way to him just as Will reached for a set of documents. She lunged, catching his hand.

"Let me," she ordered. "Dominic will be able to sense if something is out of place."

He stepped back carefully as Aya scanned the desk. Trade information, Council correspondence, the usual ledgers... nothing that immediately screamed betrayal.

But Dominic was cunning, perhaps more than they gave him credit for. He wouldn't leave evidence out in the open.

Aya crouched by the desk, running her fingers along the seams of the drawers. She gave each a tug. All locked. Her small knife flashed in the dim light as she swiftly pried each open, her hands carefully flipping through more documents.

"Wait a minute," Will murmured from above her, his eyes fixed on something on the desk. He pushed some papers aside, his brow furrowed. "Never mind. I thought—"

Will stopped, both of their gazes cutting to the door.

Footsteps were coming their way again. "Shit."

They flew into motion, Will setting the papers back on the desk and Aya dropping to the floor to close the drawers. She reached the last one and her eyes snagged on a familiar script. Aya reached for the parchment, even as Will hissed, "Leave it."

But there it was—the queen's letter to the king. The same one Aya had seen Dominic read from when they first pressed him for an alliance. If she could just learn what Gianna had put in that letter, then perhaps...

The door rattled, and Will swore thoroughly as he yanked Aya out of the way, dropping down, closing the drawer and locking it one smooth motion. He grabbed her and pulled her behind the curtains, pressing them as close as possible to the bookcase that lined the wall just as the lock clicked and the door swung open. She could feel his heart hammering against her back, his arms tight around her waist and his breath hot on her neck as he folded them even further into the space between where the bookcase ended and the window started. Aya tried to steady her own breathing as the footsteps approached the desk. Will's grip tightened as the intruder parted the curtains, both of them holding their breath as the curtains drew back further, and further, and further.

They were doomed.

But then...the curtains stopped, their thick crimson fabric still concealing them. Aya's knees wobbled with relief, but she didn't dare breathe—not with whoever it was standing mere feet away. There was the sound of a drawer opening, papers shuffling, and then the snap of the drawer closing once more. Aya continued to hold her breath, waiting until the footsteps made their way back to the door, which was closed and locked with a loud click, before letting out a shaky exhale. She could feel Will's body relax behind her, suddenly hyperaware of how he was pressed against her, his arms still hugging her against his solid build.

His head dropped onto her shoulder, his lips brushing her

neck as he rasped, "I'm going to fucking murder you if you ever do that to us again."

She couldn't help the laugh that bubbled out of her. A real laugh, quiet and perhaps brought on by the immense relief she felt pounding through her, but a laugh all the same. She shook against him, her lips pressing into a thin line as she tried to control the hysterics that were threatening to erupt. She felt Will grin against her neck.

"I'm glad you find this so funny." He gave her a tight squeeze before stepping out from the curtains. "But I'd love to know what was so important that you almost had us found out."

Aya followed him to the desk and knelt before the drawer once more, her body buzzing and hands trembling with the adrenaline that had coursed through her moments ago. She used her knife to flip the lock and gave the drawer a tug.

Will went deathly still beside her as Aya pulled out the letter. "Is that…?"

"Gianna's letter," Aya breathed. It wasn't what they'd come for, but once she'd seen the Tala royal seal, she hadn't been able to wrench herself from the desk.

Her heart stuttered in her chest as she scanned the pages. "He wasn't lying."

Because there, in Gianna's loopy handwriting, was the very implication Dominic had shared on the beach:

> *I imagine she and your nephew will get along nicely. Perhaps there's potential for firmer, more formal friendships between our kingdoms…*

Her eyes flicked to Will, marking the tension that had crept into his stance. He jerked his chin at the drawer, his voice terse as he said, "Lock it and let's go." His steps were clipped as he led the way to the door, as if he couldn't wait to be as far away from the room as possible.

Aya tossed the letter back into the drawer, her hands trembling as she flipped the lock and followed him.

"Will."

She grabbed his arm as he reached for the door. His face was guarded. He shook his head and tugged on the handle, opening the door to the hallway outside.

"Will—?"

"What the hells are you two doing?"

Aya froze.

She had been so caught up in Will that she hadn't even thought to stop him, to make him look, to *listen*, and there stood Josie, eyes wide as she stared at them in the doorway of her uncle's study.

She was still in her Pysar dress, and her eyes were red and exhausted, as if she had just returned from the search for Viviane. She glanced around the hallway, her mouth pressing into a thin line as she stalked toward them. "What the *hells* are you doing?" she hissed again.

Will merely closed the door with a soft snap, his face utterly calm as he drawled, "Wrong room."

"You think me a fool?"

"Josie..." Aya started, watching her friend's fury build. "Josie, please listen."

The princess whirled to her. "My partner is *missing* and you...you raid my uncle's study? What was it you hoped to find?"

Aya opened her mouth, the truth dying in her throat before she could voice it. She couldn't very well share their suspicions until they knew for sure what Dominic's role with the Bellare was. Not with Viviane still missing.

"We were searching for any indication that your uncle may be tied to Kakos," she said instead.

Josie's brown eyes widened, her hands curling into fists as her voice dropped. "Excuse me?"

A numbness settled in Aya's fingertips as she stared at

her friend. "Surely you can understand our suspicions with Aidon's recent revelation."

The words were hollow. Heavy.

Disgust rippled across Josie's face. "We told you—"

"I know," Aya interrupted, the steady calm in her voice so at odds with the whirling in her mind. As if she were outside herself, watching the lies she wielded. "But we needed to be sure before we press Gianna to move forward more formally with suggesting a match in the name of an alliance."

The silence between them was deafening. Josie's gaze darted between Aya and Will, her chest heaving as she wrestled for words. Finally, she let out a bitter laugh. "And to think that I felt *bad* for you earlier. That I thought you were being used. And yet…*you* are the one who would use Aidon in such a way. You're just as bad as the queen you serve."

Aya's stomach gave a vicious twist, but it was Will who snarled, "Careful, Princess."

But Josie didn't seem to hear him, didn't seem to care as she took a step toward Aya, her voice trembling. "You were supposed to be my *friend*."

Aya took a step toward her, and she felt Will's hand graze her arm imperceptibly, as if to hold her back. As if to remind her of her duty.

"I *am* your friend," Aya rasped.

"No." Josie shook her head. "A friend would have been with me tonight, searching for Viviane. A friend would have put her own agenda aside to *be there*. A friend wouldn't *use* someone to push their own wants. A friend wouldn't barter with my brother's future. So make no mistake, Aya. You are no friend of mine."

And then she was gone, her quick stride sending her down the hallway and out of sight as Aya's mind screamed at her to find the words to call Josie back, to make her understand, to make her stay.

Aya turned to find Will watching her warily. She folded

her arms across her chest, swallowing the urge to snap at him. It wasn't his fault. She'd been careless. Distracted. She shifted uneasily as his gaze stripped her bare, as if he could sense the guilt curling in her stomach. He frowned, his hand massaging the back of his neck as he said, "Quick thinking. We should be prepared for questions, though."

Aya nodded once, her arms tightening across her chest.

"Aya..." Will stepped toward her, but she stepped out of his grasp.

"I'm going to bed." He opened his mouth, but she cut him off. "I'll see you later." A flicker of hurt passed over his face, there and gone in an instant. He swallowed and slid his hands into his pockets, rolling his shoulders back as he nodded.

"Later, then."

Aya barely slept.

Not with the anger that continued to work its way through her, gnawing at each part it touched. And when the sun was finally too high in the sky to ignore, she found herself in the training complex, her fists aching as she hit the sparring post again and again, the wood rattling with the fury of her blows.

She'd hoped to find proof of Dominic's framing of the Bellare. Instead, she'd found something far worse.

It had simmered her blood when Dominic suggested her queen would use her in such a way; but to see it, truly see it, in Gianna's letter made her insides burn.

The sparring post shook under Aya's next flurry of punches, her breath coming in uneven pants, emotion rising so quickly in her chest she thought she might choke on it.

Because beneath that anger sat something else, something all too familiar: guilt.

She should be out looking for Vi. Hiding made her a coward. But she couldn't stand to face Aidon or Josie. Not when those fragile friendships had likely shattered. Not when she couldn't scrub the queen's missive from her mind. Not when she couldn't help but see exactly *why* Gianna would suggest such a thing. The logic in it, the reason.

Not when Aya couldn't help but see how it could help *her*, too.

She couldn't use her power without that godsforsaken tonic. But perhaps she wouldn't need to. Perhaps the tonic would provide just enough proof for Gianna to think she'd mastered her abilities, and their union would seal the alliance. And with Aya here in Trahir with Aidon, she'd have an endless supply of it; and perhaps the healers could adjust it to help her go deeper…

You would use him in such a way?

It made Aya sick with herself that she could even consider it.

Aya was no stranger to wielding lies and manipulation in the name of her queen. She'd practically been raised on deceit, having begun training at such a young age. But the lies she told…the people she used…

They were strangers. People she didn't have to face in the morning. People who wanted to destroy what she held dear. What Gianna held dear.

Aidon and Josie were not those people.

They weren't strangers. Or enemies.

They were allies.

Friends.

She had lied to Josie about what they were looking for; about *why*. But there was a reason it had fallen so easily from her lips.

Because Josie was right: Aya *would* consider doing whatever was necessary for an alliance. She would consider it because her queen had commanded it, and that was what Aya did. She obeyed without question. She acted without considering the consequences. She let herself be wielded like a weapon, and she did the same to those she marked.

So yes, Josie was right.

She was no better than Gianna.

And she hated it.

Tears stung her eyes, blurring the sparring post as she threw another combination at the worn wood. Aya gritted her teeth against the onslaught of emotion that continued to rise from her chest to her throat.

Gods. She didn't want to be this way anymore. Cold, and calculating, and nothing more than a chess piece to be moved across the board. And yet she feared she'd have to do so much worse, *be* so much worse, if she were to be of any use in this war.

Aya leaned her head against the post, her hands trembling as they curled into fists.

She would not break. Not now. Not when there was still so much left to do.

She lifted her head, wiping roughly at the stray tears that had escaped down her cheeks.

She would not do this to Aidon. To herself. There was another way to channel what was inside of her.

But there was something she needed to do first. A slate she needed to clear.

She had to tell Will about the tonic.

And she had to do it tonight.

57

WILL'S ROOM WAS EMPTY WHEN AYA ARRIVED THAT night, the door unlocked. She paced the sitting area as she waited, her hands smoothing the fabric of her loose navy pants.

She took a steady breath as she slid a hand into her pocket and pulled out the tonic. He would hate it. He would hate that while he'd been desperately searching for information on Evie, she'd been looking for how to use the darkness inside of her.

He would hate that because she hadn't found her answers in the Maraciana, she was desperate. Desperate enough to consider that last option, that final card she'd been holding on to since that dinner with Aidon.

He would hate that their evening training sessions in the paddock had all been a lie and she wasn't making progress. She was relying on something to control her power.

And once he saw that, he would see that Natali was right.

She truly was fueled by darkness.

But he deserved to know—all of it. He had made her a promise.

No matter how far the fall.

He deserved to know how far that fall could truly be.

Aya sat on the couch, her foot bouncing to a nervous rhythm as she glanced at the clock. Where was he?

He'd probably damned the consequences and joined one of the search parties.

Telling him is the right thing to do.

And yet…

She didn't want to see that warm light fade from his eyes, didn't want that steady faith he had in her to crumble as he finally realized she wasn't what the world hoped for.

Wasn't what he hoped for.

She stood and paced, rolling the vial between her fingers before setting it down on the driftwood desk that sat against the far wall of the sitting room. A flash of crimson beneath a stack of papers caught her eye, and Aya paused, glancing over her shoulder at the closed door before brushing the parchment aside to reveal the royal seal of Tala.

Carefully, Aya unfolded the letter, her eyes darting across the page. It was an update from Lena, dated two weeks ago. It was coded so well she had to read the page twice, her heart sinking with every line.

Lena had found no sign of the supplier. Their contacts had gone dark, and the Midlands were securing their borders—a drastic action for the vast space between Tala and Kakos.

But it was a line at the bottom of the missive that had Aya frowning.

The queen demands an update. Respond.

Her hand trembled as she put the parchment down, her fingers moving the other papers aside.

"Godsdamn it," Aya rasped.

Three letters from Lena. Three updates spanning the last nine weeks. He hadn't told her about a single one.

Aya ground her teeth, her eyes blurring as she took in Lena's messy scrawl. She dropped the letters and tugged on the desk drawer, pulse hammering in her throat as her anger built. She shifted through more parchment, drafts of letters he'd never sent, before finding a thick envelope beneath, its seal broken.

It was addressed to her.

Aya let out a strangled sound, her fury so thick she could choke on it.

Because she knew, she *knew* exactly whose handwriting she'd find as she tugged out the letter.

Tova's.

Aya scanned the page, her eyes devouring each and every damning sentence.

> *Lena says there's been no word. What's happening there? Gianna grows more anxious by the day. Has the Council given anything? What if we've been looking in the wrong place this whole time for the supplier? It was Will's plan to bring you to Trahir. He pushed Gianna for it vehemently... Do what is necessary. Come home!*

Aya staggered back from the desk.

There was such silence in her head. Silence that slowly turned into a dull roar, blocking out every thought, every sense, as her hands curled into fists and she tried to rein in the surging in her veins. It was fueled by enough fury to burn this entire palace to the ground.

"Aya."

She whirled, her knife appearing in her hand in the span of a breath. But Will was ready for her, his hand catching hers and pressing into that spot that had her grip spasming, her knife falling into his outstretched palm. He wedged her against the desk, but he kept the knife lowered, his other hand twisting her arm behind her back.

"What the hells?" he demanded.

She swung at him, but he dodged her easily, pinning her hand to the desk.

"You lying piece of shit." The words were a hiss pulled from somewhere deep within her. Will went deathly still for a heartbeat as his eyes darted to the letters scattered across the polished surface. Guilt darkened his gaze.

"Aya—"

"I knew it," she whispered, her body trembling against his.

"Aya, listen to me."

She threw her weight against him, rocking him off her. She had another knife free in the span of a heartbeat, its blade slicing toward Will's face. But he knew her. Had trained with her for years now. He blocked her blow again, grabbing her arm and twisting her so her back landed against the wall.

"I was going to tell you," he bit out, his body sealing her against the smooth plaster of the wall. She bucked against him, but he was an immovable force against her.

"When it benefited you most, I'm sure."

"When I was sure you weren't going to do anything rash," he snapped, his hips shifting against hers. "Aya, listen to me. Tova's letter, it's not—"

She was too furious to hear him, to take anything that came out of his mouth and dub it as truth. *Gods.* He had kept her distracted, first with Aidon, then with her "training," then with *him*, and she had left Tova to waste away… *It was Will's plan to bring you to Trahir…*

"Were you the one who told Gianna to bring me here?" The question was as sharp as any knife as she thrashed against him. Will swallowed, but he didn't release his hold on her.

"Yes."

He was saying something, something about how it was his only option, but his words were lost again to the roaring in her ears, the *fury* that seemed to cut off her air.

"I trusted you," she choked out, her breath coming in deep heaves. "*I trusted you!*"

Pain flickered in Will's eyes, and he glanced back toward

the desk as if to gather himself. But he froze as he took in the vial, his body going taut against hers.

"What is that?"

A cold, cruel laugh burst from her.

She had honestly thought this *thing* between them was real? That they could *trust* each other?

She was a fool.

She shoved him off her, brandishing her knife. "A tonic to suppress my power." She seethed as Will stumbled back, the blade he'd stolen from her stretched out in front of him. "I took it from Aidon's stores."

Will's jaw tightened, his gray eyes blazing. "You are not some *thing* to be tamed!"

"Not if it ruins your godsdamn agenda," she spat back, chest heaving. "I suppose you would fail Kakos if I couldn't fully wield my power for them, wouldn't you?"

Anger twisted Will's features, a snarl erupting from him. "You can't be serious."

"Why else would you keep these letters from me?" she demanded. "Why else would you keep *everything* from me?"

"Gods, if you'd just *listen*—"

"Why? You've never said one honest thing in your godsdamn life!" Something in her chest was shattering, and she wasn't sure she would survive the pain of it.

"You *are* serious, aren't you?" Will breathed as he straightened. The knife dropped to his side. "You'd look for any reason to condemn me."

The bitterness in his voice twisted her anger into something clear and vicious and so unexpected that she felt her face flush as she took a step toward him. He didn't raise his knife.

"Hate me all you want," Aya said, seething, "but you know as well as I do that you'd make the perfect mole."

His teeth flashed as his arms flung wide. "I have been *nothing* but loyal!"

"Loyal? *Loyal?*" She could feel the heat of his anger radiating off his body as she took another step toward him. "You knew about my power for ages and didn't tell a soul. You tricked me into leaving Tova in that prison to get me out of Tala. You've kept me in the dark for weeks, and for what?"

"They wanted your power," Will thundered. "They have *always* wanted your power! I was trying to keep you safe."

Aya stilled, his words washing over her, heavy and unrelenting. Her knife hand shook as she stared at him. "They didn't know about my power. You're lying," she breathed.

Will shook his head. "I'm not. And you cannot keep punishing me," he rasped. "You cannot keep casting me as the villain in your story. You have no idea what I've done. You have no fucking clue. You're so determined to see me as a monster, as the godsdamn enemy, that you won't open your eyes."

"*You're lying,*" Aya bit out as she grabbed his shirt and tugged him into her, her blade kissing the skin of his throat.

Will didn't move. Didn't raise his blade. He kept his eyes on her, anger and disappointment swirling in his irises. "This is where we always end up, isn't it, Aya love?" he breathed. "You with a knife to my throat."

He kept still, his knife hanging by his side.

"Kill me, or get out." His command was soft and vicious.

Aya stayed rooted to the spot, her chin raised, hand shaking.

She should do it. She should take this blade and drag it across his godsdamn throat.

Her eyes blurred with tears, and she hated them almost as much as she hated that he had been the one to put them there.

Slowly, her grip loosened on his shirt.

"That's what I thought," Will muttered as he took a step back. He stared at her for a moment, his hair disheveled, face pained. "I've spent years trying to protect you. And where has it gotten me, Aya?"

His tossed the knife on the floor between them, the clatter of the blade deafening in the silence.

"It's gotten me nowhere."

Her blood went cold as he turned his back on her and walked toward the bedroom.

"I mean it. Get out."

The bedroom door snapped shut, the lock clicking behind him in a loud and final sound that left Aya utterly alone.

58

AYA DIDN'T BOTHER TO PICK THE LOCK. SHE MERELY kicked the door to Natali's dormitory open. She hadn't felt a lick of guilt when she'd persuaded the young Saj in the library to tell her where they slept. And she didn't feel one now, not even as Natali bolted from where they sat at their desk, clearly startled.

"You could knock," they panted, their hand covering their heart.

"And you could be direct for once in your godsdamned life," Aya growled as she stormed across the room.

Too much time. She'd wasted too much time in this godsdamn kingdom.

And Natali had refused to help. They'd left her to grasp desperately for answers, answers she couldn't find on her own. They'd kept her drowning in this darkness inside of her, and—

Aya grabbed the Saj and thrust them against the wall with one hand, a knife in the other. She pressed it against their ribs, just enough for them to feel its presence.

There was no fear in Natali's face. They just blinked at her expectantly.

"Where do I find the Vaguer?"

This…this had been her last card.

Aya was done with foolish hope. She was no saint. But she didn't have to be—not if she learned to wield the darkness inside of her. And if Aidon was to be believed, there was only one group in this godsforsaken kingdom who studied the Decachiré enough to potentially hold those answers.

Do what is necessary. Come home.

Gianna wanted a weapon. Aya knew exactly how to be one.

Natali barked a laugh, the sound harsh. "So you have a death wish."

Aya pressed the knife tighter to their side. "As do you, it seems. Don't tempt my fury, Natali. I will persuade it out of you if I have to."

"And if I am not inclined to tell you?"

Aya's lips twisted into a vicious grin. "I have ways to make you inclined."

Still, no fear entered Natali's eyes. If anything, there was grim resignation as they nodded to the paper on their desk. "You'll want to write it down. At least then, when they find your body, they'll know exactly what stupidity led to your death."

Aya released the Saj and grabbed the parchment.

"Save your lectures," she growled.

Natali merely cocked their head. "You deserve whatever fate awaits you in the desert."

PART THREE

Sins and Saints

59

THE TAVERN WAS LOUD, THE CROWD OVERLY BOISTEROUS, the music grating on Will's nerves. And yet he'd ordered another drink, and then another, until he'd lost track and the jolliness of the string quartet didn't make him want to stab himself.

He'd left the palace first thing that morning. He couldn't bear to see Aya, not after last night. So instead he'd wandered away most of the day, until he'd found this pigsty of a bar and parked it on a barstool hours ago.

"You look like shit."

Will turned, the room tilting slightly as he watched Josie slide into a seat next to him.

"Thank you." The words fumbled over his tongue, and he squinted at Josie. She wouldn't stop *moving*. He must've noted it aloud, because she let out a dull laugh.

"How much have you had to drink?"

"Dunno. Enough, I suppose." He leaned toward her, his brows furrowing into a deep frown. "Is this when you attack me for snooping? When my guard is down?"

The princess rolled her eyes. "I don't need your guard to be down to best you in a fight."

"Fair enough." Will raised his glass in salute to her as he rocked back in his chair. "That you do not." Josie grabbed the glass from him, swapping it with a glass of water.

"As much as I enjoy seeing you act like a fool, why don't you try some of this for a while?"

Will eyed her warily. "Why are you being so nice to me?"

She had been furious when he last saw her; not that he could blame her. But now, Josie just looked weary.

Weary because she'd likely been searching for Vi all day. "Any update?" he asked gently, silently cursing himself. It should've been the first question out of his mouth.

"No," Josie said heavily. "We have no leads."

She sighed as she crossed her arms on the bar, her gaze serious as she regarded him. "And as for being nice to you… I know that if our roles were reversed, I would've been in that office too, especially given the threats that face us. And I know that regardless of what Aya said, *you* weren't looking for reasons to push this match. You were looking for reasons not to."

He felt his jaw shift under Josie's watchful gaze.

"I've seen the way you look at her, Will. And while I don't condone what you did, I can understand your desperation. Both of yours. My uncle has not made this easy."

Will kept silent as he sipped his water, and Josie took a swig from his beer, shuddering as she swallowed the lukewarm liquid.

"I'm still furious at her," she continued. "And you, for that matter. I just don't see a point in continuing to yell at you. We have bigger issues at hand right now. But I've told Aidon. He deserves to know."

Will picked at a spot on the bar. "I expect no less." He raised his gaze to her, his head tilted as he considered her. "For what it's worth…I would be proud to have you fight at my side."

And he meant it. Josie would make an incredible

warrior—already was one in his book, her uncle be damned. Josie stared at him for a moment, as if testing the statement for its truth. Her shoulders relaxed slightly at whatever she found there.

"You know, it was my mother who taught me how to fight," she admitted. "Aidon was always allowed to train with the forces as a child. I used to throw the biggest tantrums about it. So one night she came to my room and made me swear I wouldn't tell my uncle where we were going. She brought me to an old abandoned paddock past the training complex. That was the first night I ever lifted a sword."

Will knew exactly the paddock she spoke of. He swallowed, his gaze fixed on his water glass. "I'm not surprised," he confessed. Zuri always had that mischievous glint in her eyes. He could just see her leading her daughter into the night to train.

Josie blew out a breath. "Some good it's done me." She sighed. "I can't even protect those that matter to me."

Will nudged her with his elbow. "We'll find her," he promised. He knew she had no reason to trust him—not after what they had done. Knew that was why she didn't respond.

But he said it again anyway. Because despite her anger at him, Josie was his friend. And he wanted to mean it.

"We'll find her."

60

Aya didn't stop until she reached the Agaré rain forest, and even then she felt as if she could've ridden straight through the night. But they'd been riding all day, and the stallion she'd stolen from a stable on the outskirts of town—Fihr was what the nameplate on the stall read—needed rest. His broad chest was heaving after the steady run that'd taken them through the farmland to the rolling hills and curves of the highlands, and finally to the dense trees that marked the border of the rain forest.

The Agaré had a muted sound to it, and while she could make out the hum of the animals that lived here, it was muffled by the damp and heavy air.

She'd managed to find a small cave to curl up in—a collection of large boulders really, just large enough to shield her and Fihr from the beasts that roamed at night. And though she hadn't slept in over a day, though her eyes were heavy and her thoughts muddled, rest evaded her still. Every time her head drooped, the hiss of a snake or the chilled and distant laughter of a forest sprite had it snapping back up, her hand clenching her knife as her eyes scanned the darkness.

Fihr pranced nervously in place, his dark eyes tracing the

black forest. He hated it here. The endless darkness, the wet ground, the constant hum of *something* lurking just beyond; his fear was enough that Aya had to grit her teeth against her fraying nerves.

If Natali was to be believed, they had another day in the forest before they reached the Blood-Red Mountains, and then another half day to cross through the mountain pass and enter the desert. She'd need to be alert; Natali had warned of the Agaré's distractions: the sprites who could lure you in with the comfort of a fire, the berries that looked succulent enough to eat but were poisonous to the touch.

She needed to rest.

But Aya didn't want to know what would visit her tonight in her dreams. If the raven-haired healer would be back with another prodding question as to where her gods were in this mess.

Yet as sleep finally tugged her into its depths, she knew it wasn't the healer she was trying to avoid. It was Will and his look of crushing disappointment she couldn't escape whenever she shut her eyes.

61

I SUPPOSE AYA'S TOO BUSY WITH THE SAJ TO ASSIST IN THE search?"

Aidon's question was light—too light, and it had Will tearing his gaze from the map they were poring over in Dominic's study.

As promised, Will had lent himself to the search for Viviane. He had been surprised when the prince hadn't mentioned their visit to the study. But Will had already vowed not to let such reservations stop him. Helping was the least he could do for Josie. At least, that's what he told himself. It certainly had nothing to do with avoiding Aya.

It wasn't as though she had sought him out anyway. Apparently Aya was avoiding the prince, too.

Aidon sighed as he rolled up the map, the rebel warehouses the City Guard had uncovered marked in red. "If Aya's getting closer to understanding her power, my uncle needs to know."

Will shook his head. There was no way in hells he would give Dominic that information—not when he still suspected the king of framing the Bellare. Will had offered to search the less likely places in the city. The places where the Bellare had no known presence. There was more chance of Vi being there than in any of those circles on the map.

"A sign of the prophecy might sway his hand," Aidon continued as he sat in his uncle's chair. "The rising of the Second Saint shows this conflict is much bigger than he's been playing it off to be. It is proof darkness *has* returned, and that it's a threat to the entire realm."

"And if it doesn't change his mind?"

"Then at the very least, it might tempt him to consider your queen's *other* proposal. I doubt even Dominic could resist the allure of his nephew being wedded to a saint. That union would ensure allyship."

Will went deathly still, his hands gripping the edge of the desk. "And has Aya agreed to said proposal?"

Aidon's mouth formed a tight line, his silence the only answer Will needed.

"Then might I suggest you keep such notions to yourself. She's not an item to be traded."

Aidon blinked at him, his head cocking to the side as he propped his feet up on the desk. "I do care about her, you know. I just wish she'd stop holing herself up in the Maraciana and actually *speak* to me. She's not the only one who wants answers. Who has doubts about all of this. She's not the only one who would be giving something up in the name of her duty."

Will grabbed another map, this one a detailed depiction of the Old Town, and rolled it open. He'd take any distraction over having this conversation with Aidon.

"Besides, I can't imagine that the Saj have been entirely useful," Aidon continued. "It's not like anyone's studied the Decachiré that deeply since the Vaguer."

Will glanced up at the prince, his pulse slowing. "What did you just say?"

Aidon dropped his legs from the desk. "The Vaguer. They're—"

"I know who they are."

Aidon straightened at the edge in his voice.

"Did you tell Aya this?"

"I mentioned them in passing, but I told her not to bother. She was completely disinterested."

Will closed his eyes, his jaw aching as he ground his teeth. Aya *would* appear disinterested, if only to keep Aidon from suspecting he had given her something she wanted. And then she'd tuck the information away until it could be used.

Until she'd be desperate enough to try anything.

"When did you last see her?"

Aidon stood slowly from his chair, confusion written in his face. "Four days ago? The night Helene was killed."

Will swore as he aimed for the door.

He'd been an idiot to think she was wallowing in her own despair. He knew Aya better than that. She didn't hide—not like this.

"I need a horse," Will bit out to Aidon, who had followed him to the empty courtyard. "Now."

"If that's where she's gone, it's a fool's errand, Will. The journey alone—"

Aidon grunted as Will's affinity hit him, and the prince dropped to his knees with a satisfying thud.

Will threw his focus into the pain he wielded, his teeth barred as he snarled, "She wouldn't even *be* there if it weren't for you."

A lie. This was his fault. He had kept those godsdamn letters from her. He had ordered her from his room. He had let her think she was out of options, that she was desperate enough to do something like *this*.

"You forget yourself," Aidon hissed through gritted teeth.

Will let his affinity drop instantly, a hollow feeling ringing in the place where his power had raged. "You're right," he muttered as Aidon stood.

The prince winced, his jaw tight with anger. But he took a steadying breath and said, "I'll show you to the stables."

62

THREE DAYS. THREE DAYS IN THIS GODSFORSAKEN DESERT, and Aya had begun to believe that Natali had doomed her on purpose. She frowned down at the compass Natali had given her, her head aching in the blistering heat. Aya had found the second oasis last night, stopping long enough to let Fihr rest and to refill their canteens. And while, according to the map she'd drawn from Natali's instructions, they should find the Vaguer's oasis today, there was no sign of it. There was no sign of anything except mounds and mounds of sand, interrupted only by the skulls of the animals who'd found themselves lost in the never-ending stretch of beige that seemed to swallow the earth whole.

Her canteens were nearing dangerous levels, and though she'd rationed her food, the saddlebags were getting light. Aya took a deep breath, her lungs aching with the heat and the grit in the air. If she never saw sand again, it would be too soon.

She let Fihr's reins fall from her hands. The horse had taken an easy pace today, and she couldn't blame him. He was exhausted, and if she didn't find a reprieve for them both, she doubted they'd last another day in the desert heat.

The horse's ears twitched, his drooping head rising slightly as he beheld something in the distance. Aya followed his gaze, the brightness of the sun searing her eyes.

There, hazy and flickering, was what looked like trees. She gripped the horn of the saddle and leaned forward, trying to will her mind to stay strong against the tricks of the heat. But Fihr, it seemed, had no such hesitation. The horse picked up his pace, his breath coming in bellowing gusts as he worked himself into a gallop. Aya cursed, her hands fumbling for the reins, the outline of the trees becoming solid as they flew across the sands.

A sprawling, lush landscape took shape as they crested one of the dunes, and Aya let out a long breath of relief.

It was no mirage. They had found the oasis.

63

One day, Aidon, you will rule...

What type of king would he be? Aidon wondered.

He forced himself to remain relaxed as Dominic drummed his fingers on his mahogany desk, his green stare as calculating as ever as Aidon's information settled between them.

Would he play the games of monarchs and know exactly who to use and when?

The silence stretched on, each moment passing with a tap of the king's fingers, but Aidon let it linger. He'd long since learned that he couldn't push his uncle into conversation.

Would he dictate the lives of those closest to him in the name of his kingdom?

Dominic steepled his hands, his face stern as he surveyed his nephew.

Would he want something for himself and be ruthless in taking it?

One day, Aidon, you will rule...

"I've always appreciated your loyalty, Aidon," his uncle finally drawled, the unexpected compliment causing Aidon's brows to flick upward. "There are so few people it seems we can trust these days."

Duty.

Responsibility.

Loyalty.

One day, Aidon, you will rule...

Aidon's jaw flexed as he gripped the arms of his chair and met his uncle's unwavering stare. "What do you need me to do?"

64

AIDON HAD WARNED AYA THAT THE VAGUER WERE NOT TO be trifled with. And as Aya sat with her hands bound in one of the small clay huts that dotted the oasis, she was starting to wonder if she hadn't quite taken his warning to heart.

The Vaguer had converged on her as soon as she slid off Fihr. The exhaustion from the journey had made her too slow for their advance, and they'd taken her easily. They'd blindfolded and bound her before she'd been able to loosen a knife. The blindfold seemed a bit dramatic, though, especially given they'd removed it as soon as they'd bound her to the chair.

The hut was one large simple room, with a bed in the corner, a small stove, and a table. They'd dragged her chair to the middle of the room and left her there.

Aya rested her head back against the chair and let out a steady breath through her nose. She could break these bonds with her power with half a thought. But she sensed the Vaguer enjoyed dramatics. So she waited.

Aya wasn't sure how much time had passed before the older man stepped into the hut. He was pale despite the desert sun, his head bald and his skin weathered. But his eyes were what had some deep warning bell ringing inside her. They were almost completely black: depthless, like the pits of the hells themselves.

He grinned, tugging a chair forward so he could sit opposite her. He wore robes of gray.

"It has been a long time since a visitor braved the desert to find us." His voice was reedy, and a shiver worked up her spine as she held his gaze. "Longer still since one survived. What is your name?"

Aya lifted her chin. "You first."

The man chuckled. "We do not take them here."

She fought the urge to prod further. She had a feeling the Vaguer weren't generous with their information. She wouldn't waste her questions.

"Aya," she finally said, shifting slightly against her bindings.

The man sat back in his chair, testing her name in a breath. "Ay*aaa*," he purred. "And to what do we owe the pleasure, Aya?"

"I wish to learn how the practitioners survived the Decachiré. I hear that in your devotion to Evie, you've studied such things." Her delivery was blunt in a way that would've made Will roll his eyes, and her heart clenched at the thought of him.

The Vaguer laughed again, the sound more like a rasp. "You expect us to assist you in heresy?"

"I'm merely asking you to share your knowledge."

He crossed his thin arms, his brows rising as he settled back in his seat. "And why would you have a need for such information?"

Aya let her flame rise, let it burn away the bonds that held her to the chair. Then she summoned wind, let it scatter the ashes of the rope around them.

"Because like you, I know that knowledge is crucial to defeating the Decachiré."

The Vaguer's eyes gleamed. "What *are* you?"

There was a hunger to the question that Aya wanted to balk from. But she didn't drop the Vaguer's gaze as he continued to stare at her.

"I sense your raw power, but..." Suddenly, he let out a gleeful laugh, the sound cracking through the room like thunder. "A dark saint? Could such a thing exist?"

So he sensed it too—that darkness that fueled her power. Aya swallowed. Aidon had said the Vaguer knew no bounds in their thirst for knowledge. She was counting on it.

"I don't know. But I can't use it," she rasped. "My power. Not fully. It's feeding on me, just like the Decachiré."

The man considered her for a moment, his head tilting as he took her in. "It's not knowledge you seek. It's *confirmation*."

The word rattled between them, settling heavily in the dry heat. Aya frowned, but the Vaguer continued.

"You've heard the tales of Saint Evie. Of the sacrifice her parents were willing to make to become immortal."

"A sacrifice she tried to stop."

"Yes. And the practitioners say that her interference is what caused the ritual to be incomplete."

Aya blinked at the man. "How so?"

The Vaguer leaned forward in his chair, his elbows resting on his knees. Aya fought the urge to lean away from him, to get as far back from those depthless eyes as possible.

"The level of raw power needed to practice the Decachiré leads the affinity to devour its host. Only those that continue to feed it with their darkness can survive."

"I don't understand."

He regarded her for a long moment. "They must yield to the darkness of their soul. They must allow their evil nature to rule them entirely. *That* is how one survives the Decachiré."

It was years of training that had Aya forcing down the fear that made her blood turn cold, years of training that had her focused on the pursuit of facts rather than her feelings.

"Of course," the Vaguer continued, "Evie's parents thought to go even further than stepping into their true essence in order to obliterate the bounds of their wells. They wanted to become immortal and believed shedding their mortal bodies would do it. They used her father's sword, but young Evie interrupted the ritual, and the practitioners believe that it was her parents' concern for leaving their daughter—their love for her—that rendered the ritual ineffective. It was a weakness, they said, for those who are ruled entirely by their dark nature would not be swayed by emotions such as love."

"Their forces were thousands strong. You mean all those people gave themselves over to darkness entirely?"

"A great deal were *followers*, not practitioners. Only those who summoned enough power to bestow powers to humans—or, in Evie's parents' case, seek immortality—were true practitioners. They had obliterated the bounds of their wells. *That* was the Decachiré."

Aya frowned. The history books in the Maraciana had never made such a distinction. "So the followers—what? Dabbled in darkness?"

The Vaguer shrugged. "Those who merely dove deeper into their wells—who pushed the boundaries but did not seek to break them—could live with the negative effects without yielding their souls entirely. Unless, of course, they were digging too deep. It's all relative, you see. All a science. It was a dangerous line to walk—to push power to its brink. To learn how far you could go without it devouring you entirely."

Something curled in Aya's stomach, and the Vaguer's eyes glinted with a hint of annoyance. "History books love to twist the tales, don't they? They'd hate to confess that the Decachiré's forces were so large not because all were true practitioners of pure evil, but because so many people *supported* the practitioners' cause. Many believed the gods should not be the only ones with limitless power, the only ones to twist the threads of fate. But *true* knowledge and power is full understanding. It's why we don't limit our studies here. If something is to be defeated, it should be understood."

And yet it hadn't truly been defeated, had it? Not when a second war was coming.

She turned the information over in her mind, her brow furrowed as she wrestled with what he'd told her. But the Vaguer wasn't done, it seemed. A smirk twisted his chapped lips. "How fascinating you are," he crooned. "You seek to know what you are, and yet still, you don't ask for it. Never has one sought us out and not demanded its power."

Aya's hands fisted on her thighs. "What are you talking about?"

The Vaguer leaned forward, excitement in those depthless eyes. "Evie's sword."

Shock, cold and vicious, thrummed through her.

Impossible.

Aidon had mentioned a relic, but Aya hadn't bothered to believe it. It had seemed too far-fetched, too ridiculous to even consider. Besides, she'd been too focused on finding a source who knew something of the Decachiré, too determined to get just enough out of Aidon about the Vaguer's studies without him suspecting her interest.

The man grinned. "The legends say that when Evie tried to wrestle her father's sword from him, it passed her parents' raw power to her, making her the most powerful Visya in the world. Powerful enough to meet the gods. The essence of that magic still lives in the blade."

"Does the sword…? Will it pass along that power?"

Could it replace what was inside of her? Could it heal the darkness in her enough to let her help in this war?

The Vaguer laughed again. "You ask the wrong questions. The answers you seek are about your *essence*. After all, that's what you're looking to learn, isn't it? What truly feeds your power? What makes up your very *self*? Darkness? Or light?"

Aya swallowed and told herself it was the desert heat that made her throat ache so.

His eyes were as dark as a moonless night as he regarded her. "Tell me, Aya. Would you like to meet your soul?"

65

THE VAGUER WAITED UNTIL THE MOON HAD REACHED ITS peak before they lit the fires. Aya stood before the largest one, a circle of various members surrounding her and the old man.

"A trial of the soul," he had called it. "A touch of the sword, and you will be connected to your true nature…that which fuels your power."

And if yours is indeed dark? What will you do then?

Aya hadn't had an answer for that small voice inside her mind. She had come to learn how to survive the power inside of her. If facing her soul was the way to know if she even could, she would do it, least of all to get the answers to the questions she'd been asking herself for years now.

Aya's heart hammered, her pulse thudding in time to the cracking of firewood as a woman approached them with a long slender object in her arms. It was wrapped in a beige blanket, and as she stopped before the man, she bowed her head, her long dark hair sliding over her shoulders and in front of her face.

She murmured a prayer in the Old Language before handing the sword off and stepping away.

The man held the bundle toward Aya. "You must be the one to touch the blade."

Somewhere deep in the recesses of her mind, she could hear Galda scolding her for agreeing to something so unknown. This sword had been used in the darkest of rituals. And while Evie had wielded it, what did Aya truly know about the magic in the blade?

A tonic made by the healers in Rinnia was one thing. But this…

As if sensing her hesitation, the man put a withered hand on her wrist. "There is nothing to fear. A single touch, and then we begin."

The words did nothing to calm her raging heart, which seemed to beat harder and harder as she unwrapped the blanket. But she'd made her decision. She could not run from it any longer.

The worn silver of the sword glinted in the firelight, its handle worn and plain. There was an inscription she couldn't quite read on the blade, and her fingers paused over it, her pulse fluttering in her throat as she stared down at the relic.

The letter burning a hole in her pocket had her grasping the blade in the next breath.

She felt a stirring inside of her, a great rush of *something* that ran from the tips of her fingers down to the soles of her feet.

The Vaguer grinned.

"The trial begins."

Aside from that initial jolt, the sword had done nothing. At least, that's what it felt like as Aya stood next to the Vaguer before the fire, the roar of the flames droning on and on until it was a dull beat in her mind.

He had her call her affinity forward, first in flame, then in ice, then in wind, and then in the earth itself, creating trenches by the fire until he was satisfied. The elemental affinities, he explained, were the first of the Orders, the closest to nature. They were the easiest way to begin the descent into her well, which was how she would connect to her *true* nature, as her essence was what fueled her power. It made sense, she supposed, that they'd been the ones she felt safest experimenting with, even when she'd been using the tonic.

Aya wiped the moisture from her brow, the sweltering fire sending sweat dripping down her back. Even though the desert night brought a bitter cold, she couldn't escape the heat. It wrapped around her entirely, blanketing the sounds of the Vaguer and their voices until they were a muffled murmur somewhere far, far away.

"What's the point of this?" The impatience was evident in her question, but the old man seemed unaffected. He merely smiled his crooked smile, his eyes like chips of obsidian.

"Still you resist," he mused, more to himself than to her. "What is it about yourself that you are so desperate to escape?"

"I'm not trying to escape anything," Aya growled. But the Vaguer clucked his tongue.

"The lies we tell ourselves to avoid our truth," he said sadly. "You can feel it, can't you? Boiling beneath the surface. You have shoved it so far down you hardly know how to access it."

"My power?"

"Your *essence*." He whispered the words like a lover's caress, his eyes flaring in the light of the flames.

"Who are you, Daughter of Darkness?"

The words weren't his.

They were a hiss somewhere in the recesses of her mind, a soft, probing voice that had the hair on Aya's neck rising. She ground her teeth against the name while the Vaguer stepped closer, those midnight eyes growing wider as he took her in. He was saying something, but his words were smothered by the new voice.

"What is your true nature?"

Aya took a step back, her foot narrowly avoiding one of those trenches. She stumbled, and from the corner of her eye, she saw something that nearly made her lose her footing again.

Darkness crawled across the camp like a haunted mist. It covered the oasis, covered the rest of the Vaguer, covered everything until all she could see was an endless expanse of deep charcoal gray that swirled around her and the man. His skin seemed to glow in it, and he let out a gleeful laugh that had her skin prickling.

"What is this?" Aya demanded.

He grinned. "Let's see what's inside."

She wasn't sure who said it—if it was the Vaguer, whose eyes were gleaming with reverence, or the voice that seemed to be nestled against her ear. Either way, she didn't like the sound of it. But before she could speak, someone was calling her name. She whirled toward that voice—like the sun given sound. And though she knew it was impossible, that it defied every law of nature and the gods, she knew who she'd see standing before her.

Her mother hadn't aged a day. She looked exactly as Aya remembered, down to the brown pants and emerald-green tunic she'd worn when she left. Her long, dark brown hair was tied back with a white ribbon; her pale blue eyes bright as she smiled.

"Ma," Aya breathed. Something was cracking inside of her, some wound reopening in her soul as she stared at her mother.

But her mother wasn't looking at her, Aya realized. She was looking just next to her, where a young girl, eight at most, stood, her blue eyes filled with tears.

"No," Aya rasped.

She couldn't watch this. She tried to move, but her body was rooted in place, as if someone had anchored her there.

"Aya...you know that I never *want* to leave you."

Aya shook her head as her mother's voice filled the air.

This isn't real. This isn't real.

"That's what you always say. And yet you always leave. You're a liar," the girl—*Aya*—spat out, her small hands curling into fists.

Aya reached for the girl in a desperate attempt to stop her, to silence the words she knew would fall from her lips.

"Aya—" her mother started.

"I don't care. Just go!"

"Aya, please."

"Go!"

She saw it then—the wave of persuasion that flew from the girl and enveloped her mother. The look of betrayal and perhaps even fear that flickered across her mother's face as she took a step back. Then another.

Aya's fingers curled so tightly she could feel her nails cut into her palms. Her greatest sin, her biggest regret, was playing out before her, and she could do nothing to stop it.

Aya closed her eyes, but it was no better inside. Because there was that endless well, its power churning violently like the Anath Sea.

"*That's it.*" Somewhere, the voice was speaking to her. "*Feel it.*"

She didn't want to feel this. This was her pain. Her guilt. Her hatred for all that had become of her. This…this was the very moment darkness tainted her soul thirteen years ago.

"What does your nature show us, Daughter of Darkness?"

An ear-shattering scream pierced the silence, and Aya's eyes flew open to see her mother drop to her knees. Aya lurched toward her, but still her feet wouldn't move. She looked to the Vaguer, who watched calmly, his hands clasped in front of him.

"What is this?" Aya snarled, tugging against her invisible bonds. *It's not real.* Except her mother was looking at her now, her face twisted in agony. "Help her." The plea was out of her mouth before she could question the logic of it.

"Only you have the power to do that," the Vaguer replied, his obsidian eyes tracking her mother as she twisted and thrashed on the ground. Aya scanned her surroundings frantically, looking for something, anything, to help. There was nothing but that darkness, and a haze that separated them from *something*, or perhaps everything.

Gods, help me. I beg you. Help me.

She turned back to her mother, her breath coming in panicked bursts. "This isn't real," she said as Eliza twisted and contorted on the ground. Her mother let out another hair-raising wail. "Ma," Aya rasped. But whatever pain had gripped her mother had her entirely. She thrashed again, her screams doubling in volume. "Ma." The word was a sob torn from somewhere deep inside of Aya as she watched water pool beneath her mother. Eliza coughed, and water poured out of her mouth.

Drowning. Her mother was drowning.

She looked up at Aya, her blue eyes so bright they almost glowed. "See what you've done to me?" Her mother's voice was no longer blessed by the sun. It was ice and fury and hatred, and it had the hair on the back of Aya's neck rising. "This is the eternity you have damned me to," she hissed.

Because her mother's body…it had never been burned. Her soul…

Trapped. Trapped in the veil, kept from passing into the Beyond.

Aya reached for her power, for that sliver of healing that she'd plunged into her depthless, raging well to find for Will. But all she found was rage, and grief, and a violence that crackled like lightning in her veins.

Her mother couldn't be trapped within the veil. Her soul had to have gone to rest; she was at peace. Her sweet mother…

The gods wouldn't allow this. They wouldn't forsake her like this. Not after everything.

Aya tried to uproot herself, but her body wouldn't work,

wouldn't move. Eliza screamed again, and the sound cut off abruptly as she gagged on more water.

"Please," Aya sobbed. She wasn't sure who she was even pleading to—if Saudra or any of the Divine still listened to her calls. Eliza's eyes rolled back into her head, her body convulsing in violent shudders as she struggled for breath. "Please!"

Her mother's body contorted once more, her back arching as she gasped for air that wasn't there. And then she stilled, her blue eyes empty as they stared up at Aya.

Aya's breaths were panicked as she stared at her mother's broken body, the air sharp in her lungs. Dead. Her mother was dead by her hand again, and would continue dying, stuck in the veil in some sort of limbo designed straight from the hells. Aya's grief was sharp and fine as any blade, and she honed it until she could feel it crackle in the air around her.

"I see now," the Vaguer breathed. Aya whipped her head to him. Fury rose in her, so sharp, so intense, she nearly choked on it.

This was no trial. This was torture.

"Stop this," she bit out.

Her power swirled not just in her, but around her, sending the charcoal mist whirling like a bitter wind.

"Tell me, Daughter of Darkness. What would you give to right your greatest wrong?"

There was that voice again, murmuring softly in her soul as she glared at the Vaguer.

Aya gritted her teeth against the pull of her power. It was building, zinging against her skin until she could see webs of white light flickering across her arms.

The same light that had speared across the Artist Market.

Aya recoiled slightly from it, and the voice merely laughed. The darkness around her swirled, howling like a building storm. "*That's it*," the voice sang to her, a mere whisper over the raging wind. "*Embrace your rage. Embrace your essence. See what you are destined for.*" Aya raised her hand against the battering wind, air searing her lungs as she sought to steady herself. "*What would you give to gain all that you seek? To undo your greatest sin?*" The darkness swirled, faster and faster until she could feel bits of sand cutting into her face, until she could hardly see the old man mere feet from her.

Then, as quickly as it began, the wind died, and for a moment the only sound in the desert was Aya's panting breaths.

The dark mist parted like fog, revealing a kneeling figure before her. His head was bowed, his hands bound behind his back. Dread worked its way through Aya as Will met her gaze. He let out a shuddering breath.

"Aya."

She shook her head slowly, her body trembling as she took him in. His face was gaunt, his gray eyes dark and smudged with purple underneath. Horror twisted in her gut as she realized what he was kneeling before.

They weren't trenches she'd dug.

They were graves.

He was presented to her like a sacrifice.

"It's okay," Will breathed, the tenor of his voice betraying him. His eyes dropped to Aya's hand, taking note of the knife clenched in her fist—the whittling knife he'd given her. She'd slipped it into her pocket on a whim before she'd left the palace.

She hadn't remembered reaching for it now.

This is where we always end up, isn't it, Aya love?

Something wet trailed down her cheeks, and Will shook his head slowly.

"Aya, stay with me."

Her hand tightened on the knife's handle as her thoughts tripped over one another, sliding through her head like mud. The sword had done something to her, to her power. She couldn't catch her breath, couldn't steady herself against the raging of her affinity inside her, inside her very *mind*.

Aya gritted her teeth as she tried to focus.

Not real. Her mother was at peace. And Will…Will was in Rinnia and had probably yet to notice her absence.

No.

She knew him. Eventually, he would realize she was gone—and he'd come after her, the argument between them be damned.

"*What would you trade to your gods, Daughter of Darkness? Would you damn his soul for your mother's?*" The voice was coming from the Vaguer now, and she couldn't separate truth from fear as she spun back to Will.

His breaths came in deep heaves. "Aya." She shook her head, her knife hand trembling.

"No," she gritted out. She would not do this. She would not let this be her fate: a murderer, dooming those she loved to die. She would not be a bringer of death and destruction, no matter what her nature demanded she be. "No." Aya reached within herself, leashing that light that danced across her skin. Forcing it down, down where it could not hurt him.

The Vaguer started toward her, his black eyes wide.

"Aya."

She didn't understand Will's broken plea, didn't even have time to question it, because her rage pulsed, and she flung a hand toward the Vaguer, ice exploding from her palm and hitting him square in the chest. He landed hard in the sand, his rattling breaths filling the air with signs of death.

"Release me," Aya ordered, fighting against her invisible bonds. "Release me from this and I'll heal you."

A laugh erupted from the Vaguer, the sound weak and broken and so unlike his gravelly voice, she knew it didn't come from him at all. "*You don't see it, do you?*" The voice still wasn't his, but the words flowed from his lips as he struggled onto his arms, his hands reaching for his throat, his eyes bright with pain and something else, some gleam of terror that had Aya's heart stumbling. "*Your true nature always decides. You cannot escape what you were destined to be.*"

Will coughed, and Aya whirled to face him, the air leaving her lungs in a panicked rush. Because that was blood dribbling from his mouth, blood soaking his black shirt, and even though she had not moved…

Somehow her knife had. It was buried in his chest, and Will was falling just as her mother had. Aya hardly noticed her body could move as she stumbled toward him, her legs giving out entirely as she scrambled across the ground.

"No." *Not real, not real, not real.* He was an apparition, just like her mother; a hallucination brought on by the raging power inside of her.

But she could touch him—could feel the firm lines of his body as she tugged him to her, could feel the warmth of his cheeks as she cupped his face. "No no no no."

She tugged the blade from him and laid her hand on the wound, willing her healing power to rise. A dull light flared in her palm, and she pressed it to his blood-soaked skin.

"No. Please no. Will, don't leave me." Her begging was a broken sound as she clutched him to her. "Please don't leave me."

Will's mouth moved, but no sound left his lips.

He stilled, his gray eyes fixed on her face, glassy in death.

Aya screamed, her fingers digging into his arms as she clutched him tighter.

"*What would you give to right this wrong?*" the voice called to her.

Anything.

She would give anything.

She might have even said it aloud as she bowed over Will, sobs racking her body. Her grief spiked, sending the wind around her whipping as lightning flashed across the sky.

"Let go," the man wheezed, the voice his own. He thrashed on the ground, as if fighting against his next words. "*Let your power rise,*" the lilting voice said from his lips. "*Let it remove your pain.*" She could feel it doing just that: her anger, grief, and hate swirling inside of her until she could taste it, until the sweetness of vengeance consumed her. She lifted her head from Will's chest to see something shimmering before her like the desert haze. Beyond it, something moved slowly, getting closer until she could make out the outline of a body.

"*You can undo death. You can create life.*" The voice was a whisper in her very soul. Aya stood as the storm raged around her, her gaze fixed on that shimmering wall that had appeared, its essence nearly close enough to touch.

She would bring him back.

She would bring them both back.

And she would rip open the world to do it.

"*That's it,*" the voice hissed, "*Give yourself to your true nature. Step into your power. Seize all that the gods you worship refuse to give you.*"

Perhaps the voice wasn't the gods'.

Perhaps it was her own.

Another pulse of rage radiated through the air, and the veil around her thickened. She could see it more clearly now, the shimmering glow that gods created. That separated the realm from the Beyond. Aya gritted her teeth as her power built, her hand tightening on the knife she didn't realize she still held. She let her power rise until her pain was a distant memory, until her mind could remember nothing but her need for retribution. She was drawn to that shimmering *something*, intent on destroying it entirely.

Her rage was a living thing, spooling from her like fire as it crackled across the veil, searing it with heat. Aya stepped closer, her body buzzing as power emanated from her. She raised her knife, her power rallying with the motion and spreading across the blade, ready to slice through the veil.

Where were her gods when her mother drowned at sea? Where were her gods when Tova was dragged to prison, or when Will had fallen to his knees?

She'd kill them all.

Across from her, that dark outline of a figure stepped closer, their hand beckoning.

Raven hair. Pale skin. Blue eyes.

Aya raised her knife higher, the flash of its blade catching her eye. "*Revenge is waiting*," something hissed.

But she tilted her head, her gaze fixed on her blade. It tugged at something in the back of her mind, something that checked her anger, as if stuck between an inhale and an exhale.

Warm fingers trailing down the bare skin of her back.

A flash of a sly grin.

No, the voice hissed.

But that tug was there inside her, more insistent this time. Aya stepped away from the veil, her gaze locked on that whittling knife.

No matter how far the fall, he'd said.

She took another step back. Somewhere, that voice that had been calling out to her was raging at her to finish the task. But she could hardly hear it. Because it was his voice beside her now, the words like a whispered lullaby against her ear.

No matter how far the fall.

Only she could stop this, the Vaguer had said.

No matter how far the fall.

It was the last thing she heard before she plunged the blade into her own chest.

66

THE PAIN WAS BLINDING, ALMOST ENOUGH TO MAKE AYA slip back into the dark depths that held her moments before. It was easy there. Peaceful.

But then the memories started. Her mother. The veil. Will. She forced her eyes open with a grunt, the bright light of the desert searing them badly enough that she groaned. Aya pushed herself up with trembling arms, just enough to take in her surroundings.

Nothing but sand and dunes for miles.

No oasis.

No Vaguer.

She couldn't be surprised that they'd left her for dead in the desert. Not after what the relic had shown of her soul.

Your true nature always decides. You cannot escape what you were destined to be.

Aya glanced down at her chest. They hadn't bothered to remove the knife. A lucky thing. If they had, she'd be dead. She'd missed her heart—her lungs too, if her steady breath was any indication.

Amazing that in her terror, she'd still managed to be precise.

She hadn't been sure it would work. Hadn't been sure that the knife would be enough to relieve her from the visions. She didn't want to contemplate what had inspired her to do it; that the dark ritual of Evie's parents had planted a seed that she desperately grasped to try to shake herself from the thrall in which the power held her.

And if it hadn't worked…then she'd chosen her sacrifice.

She would rather die than lose herself to darkness.

Too late. I chose too late.

Aya closed her eyes against the thought. No. Those visions were not real.

But this wound was. Did that mean…?

Agony ripped through her, so sharply it stole her breath.

"Mora, please. *Please.* I beg you." The prayer to the goddess of fate was a frantic, broken gasp.

He couldn't be dead. Accepting it would mean lying back down on the desert floor, and if she did that, she wouldn't rise again.

She scanned her surroundings once more. In the distance, far enough away that she could barely make out their red hue, sat the mountains. She looked behind her to see nothing but sand.

She had no idea where they'd left her. The best she could do was head for the mountains and hope she made it there before she died of thirst.

Aya gripped the handle of the knife, her breath coming in shallow pants. She could do this. She had to get back to the palace—had to do something to stop the agony that was threatening to obliterate her.

She tugged on the handle, her gritted teeth not enough to contain her scream as the knife slid free. She had moments to act. Her palm flared with light as she seized that healing power, seized it and refused to let it falter as she laid her hand over her chest, knitting the flesh there into a red, ragged mark. The pain remained, but…healed. At least enough to keep her from bleeding to death.

Aya's palms found the sand, her body braced on all fours as she struggled to steady her breathing. A wave of nausea passed over her, whether from the pain or the early signs of dehydration, she wasn't sure. She couldn't remember the last time she'd had a sip of water.

With a grunt, Aya forced herself to her feet, her eyes fixed on the mountains.

She would get back, and Will would be there.

She refused to accept anything else.

Aya walked for a day, stopping only for short periods to rest her shaking limbs. Her mouth was dry, her throat aching as she forced herself to breathe. She longed for another freezing night, which by the high position of the sun was still hours off.

She hadn't dared to sleep. Not when she was so afraid she wouldn't wake.

Her legs trembled as she staggered another step, the world tilting, the desert haze intensifying until everything beige and blue was a blur, until the only thing she could see were those damn mountains in the distance that seemed to get further and further away.

Just a bit more. She took another step, her breath scorching her lungs. Small rocks cut into her hands as she fell.

Just a bit more.

She dragged herself forward, a frustrated sob escaping her as the sand burned her hands. She'd crawl the entire way if she had to.

But even that was too much for her sick and battered body. Aya's arms gave out, and she hit the ground with a grunt.

"Please," she rasped, tears stinging the cuts on her face as the wind kicked sand into her eyes. Her heart pounded in her chest, begging for life.

She reached to pull herself another inch, unconsciousness

beckoning her to its depths. Another gust of wind had her closing her eyes, willing herself to stay above the churning surface, because she knew, she knew if she let herself slip into that waiting darkness, she may never rise again.

Her mind reached desperately for something, anything, to keep her tethered to this world.

It found eyes the color of river stones flecked with green. The warmth of a calloused hand on her cheek. The rich tenor of a laugh so few were blessed to hear.

"Please," she whispered.

The world went black.

67

IF THIS WAS DEATH, IT WAS WARM. AYA'S HEAD FELT HEAVY, her vision blurry as her eyes peeled open. She could hear a steady crackle, almost as if fire was devouring wood near her.

Fire.

The flames had her jolting up, her hands grappling for some purchase on the rocky ground as she scrambled backward.

Away. She had to get away from the fire, from the trenches, from the *death*…

"Aya." There were hands grasping her arms, and she yanked back, her breath coming in uneven bursts. She whipped her gaze to her assailant, her heart stuttering as she registered Will on his knees before her.

No. Not again.

She had watched him die. She had held him as he bled out, had watched the life leave his eyes, and even though she'd pleaded to the gods when she'd woken in the desert that it wasn't true, she was back in the same nightmare.

Aya wrestled against whatever was pinning her to the ground, trying to free herself from the restraint of it, from these never-ending hells. She couldn't escape, couldn't escape, couldn't escape—

"Aya." Her name was a broken rasp as Will's hand found her face, his gray eyes filled with concern. He tugged on her bindings, freeing her legs. But the warm hand on her cheek had her pausing long enough to take in her surroundings again.

A cave. She was in a cave—not the desert. She glanced down.

Not bindings...a bedroll.

"You're safe," Will panted, his thumb skimming across her cheek. "You're safe."

Aya sucked in air, her chest heaving with panicked breaths. Her fingers slowly loosened from where they'd fisted in the bedroll as she looked Will over. His hair was disheveled, his eyes rimmed with red. She dragged her gaze down his chest, searching for evidence of a wound. There was nothing. His black shirt was wrinkled but otherwise unmarked.

"Is this real?" Her throat felt like sandpaper, the words rough and raw.

Will frowned, something like pain flashing across his face as he stroked her cheek again. "Of course this is real."

She wanted to believe him. Especially as he whispered her name as if he could reach into whatever terror still held her and guide her out. Aya's fingers trembled as she traced the strong line of his jaw.

No wound. No blood.

She had watched him die, and the pain of it had made her want to curl up on the ground with him and never get up again. The only thing that had made her drag herself through the godsforsaken desert was the hope that she'd find him still breathing. And here he was: skin warm, body whole.

Alive.

A small broken sound escaped her, and she threw her arms around his neck. Will rocked back with the impact, but his arms grabbed her to him, banding like steel around her waist. If he was confused, he didn't let on. He simply held her as tightly as she clung to him, his hand tracing soothing lines up and down her back.

Will leaned back, just far enough to scan her face. His eyes darkened at whatever he found there, his voice dropping low. "What happened?"

Aya pressed her lips together. She didn't know where to begin—which truth to share first. But Will brought a hand back to her face, his calluses scraping lightly against her cheek. The gentleness in the touch had her choking back another sob.

"What happened?" he repeated.

Tears welled in her eyes as she met his stare.

"I killed her."

There it was. The truth, finally laid bare.

Will blinked, his thumb stilling on her cheek as Aya's lips trembled. "I killed her." The confession continued to tumble from her like an avalanche, her whole body shaking. "I killed her. I killed her. I killed her."

And then she was sobbing, her head pressing against his chest as she spoke the words she'd never dared admit. "She left because I made her," Aya gasped, her hands fisting in Will's shirt. She couldn't bear to look at him. "I felt my affinity and I–I made her go. I persuaded her to get on that ship."

She had seen the truth in whatever apparition the relic had brought forward, had seen the moment that twisted her essence into something dark.

"My mother is dead because of me," she whispered.

"She is not dead because of you," he responded fiercely, tilting her head back as he forced her to meet his gaze.

"I saw it," she rasped. "I went to the Vaguer to learn how to survive the Decachiré. I thought that because my power reacts the same, they could help. But the practitioners survived by relinquishing their souls completely to their darkness, by letting their evil natures rule them entirely. The Vaguer have a relic of Evie's that brings forth your true nature. They urged me to meet mine to see what fuels my power and…it is dark, Will. It's so dark."

Will shook his head. "Aya, your mother was a full-grown Visya who could easily shield against your persuasion."

"Not if I controlled her the way I did you. Not if I forced her to leave the way I forced you to jump." She took a shuddering breath as she made herself hold his gaze. Made herself read what lay there.

There was nothing but gentle understanding as he pushed her hair back. "Your mother would have gotten on that ship no matter what. My father gave them no choice. If her death is on anyone's hands, it's his." She went to look away, but he stilled her head. "This guilt. It's killing you. It's convincing you that you are something that you are not."

I have always seen you.

She had no answer for him. This guilt was all she'd known, all she'd allowed herself to feel for years. It was a burden she didn't know how not to carry. And yet…

She felt something shift in her with the confession. As if shining light on the dark spot had shrunken it somehow.

"The visions…they made me believe her soul was trapped in the veil. Because her body was never burned."

Again, Will shook his head. There was agony in his voice as he said, "Her body still returned to the earth, love. The sea would have…" His voice trailed off, as if he didn't want to put words to it. But he was right: her body would've decomposed and fed the sea. Will ducked his head to meet her gaze. "If that decree still holds with the gods, then your mother's soul is at rest."

So what then was real?

Aya frowned up at him, her mind struggling to separate apparition from reality. "I thought I killed you, too."

Will's smile was weak. "Typical. Should I be offended or charmed?" His eyes twinkled in the firelight, and despite everything, Aya let out a weak laugh, even as tears slipped down her cheeks. His hand resumed its path down her back as he waited.

So she told him. Of the visions. Of how she watched her mother drown. Of how the voice—the gods or her own mind perhaps—had possessed the Vaguer. How it had asked for her choice and presented him. Of how she'd turned her power on the Vaguer instead, but it hadn't mattered.

She'd killed Will anyway.

Your true nature always decides.

"I could *feel* you," she said softly. "And I..." She shuddered as she forced the words out. "I felt you die."

There it was again: that ache that had sliced through her so viciously that she'd wanted the world to burn.

Will ran his knuckles across her jaw in the lightest of touches.

"I was so angry. At the darkness I couldn't seem to escape. At the gods, for not helping me. And there was this voice, urging me to embrace that anger, and I gave in to it."

She tore her gaze from his, too afraid to see all that would be there when she admitted what she needed to next. "They asked what I would give to right my wrongs. To save you." She swallowed, her eyes tracing the flickering flames. "I would've given anything."

She'd learned many truths in the desert, this perhaps the most terrifying of all. She would have torn the world apart to get him back.

"I saw the veil," she continued, her eyes still fixed on the fire. "As if I had summoned it somehow. And I saw someone beyond it." She paused, her lips parted as something tugged at her memory.

The healer. It had looked just like the healer in her dreams. The hallucinations the relic had called forward had truly played on all her fears.

"I felt like I could've destroyed it entirely. I would have, were it not for this." She finally looked to Will as she slid a hand in her pocket and pulled out the blood-encrusted whittling knife. His fingers skimmed the wooden handle. "It helped me block out that voice."

Will's jaw tightened as he stared at the blood. "How did you break free from the visions?" His voice was low, masked in a type of calm she knew to be dangerous.

"I turned the blade on myself."

She felt his muscles tense, his hand splaying on her back as his gaze darted to her ruined shirt. He was silent for a beat, his gray eyes growing dark as he took in the scar marring her chest.

Slowly, he met her stare. "Tell me you're lying." His voice was guttural. She searched for words, but her silence was apparently answer enough. Will swore under his breath, and in one smooth movement, he slid her off him. He stood, his hand tugging through his hair as he paced away from her.

"I know you're angry—"

"*Angry?*" He whirled back to face her. "I'm fucking furious." Aya opened her mouth to argue, but Will continued on, his fingers knotting in his hair. "I'm furious that I let you walk out of that room. That it took fucking *days* to stop being blinded by my pride and realize where you'd actually gone. I'm furious that—"

He swallowed, the words lodging in his throat.

He dragged a hand down his face as he took a steadying breath. Then another. Another.

"I was almost too late," he rasped, his hand falling to his side. "I saw you lying in the sand, and I thought I was too late."

Aya pushed herself up, her body screaming in protest. She gritted her teeth against the pain. "This is not your fault."

"Don't," he growled. "Don't do that. Don't try to assuage my guilt."

She took a step toward him, marking the way his fingers dug into his palms. The way his body trembled. "It was my choice."

"You almost died."

"It was *my* choice. If you're going to be angry with anyone, it should be me."

"Fine," Will spat out. "I'm fucking furious with you, too."

"Good. I could have done horrific things—"

Will was in front of her in an instant, his hands gripping her shoulders as he scanned her face. Rage swirled in those river-stone eyes, rage and something else that roughened his voice as he said, "I don't give a fuck what you almost did with those godsforsaken people. The only thing I care about is that I can feel the warmth of you right now."

Her eyes burned as his thumb rubbed small circles against her shoulder, as if to prove to himself that she was here. That she was real. She didn't deserve that warmth—that understanding. And yet she wanted it. She craved it, just like she craved the feeling of his rough calluses on her skin, of his arms wrapped around her the way they'd been in the king's study. It was a hunger deeper than anything she'd ever felt.

His chest rose and fell in jagged movements, his breath brushing across her lips as he tugged her closer. "You don't have to do this. You do not have to be a weapon for Gianna to wield. We can damn the prophecy to hells. We can disappear and make sure they never find us."

Aya shook her head, her throat tight with emotion. "I have power that could help in this war. I have to find a way to use it."

"Not if it's a suicide mission, Aya!"

"There must be—"

"You will not sacrifice yourself for this war!"

"I will do what is necessary to protect our kingdom!"

He released her as he took a single step back, her body going cold with the small distance. She tried to reason with him. "It is my duty. To our gods. To our queen. I took an oath—"

"*To hells with your oath!*" he roared, his arms flinging wide.

"What you speak of is *treason*," Aya shot back, hating the tremor in her voice. She didn't know why her heart ached so fiercely, but something in his words had unmoored her. Perhaps it was that he wanted to fight for her—to give her the choice when no one else had.

Will's voice was a quiet rumble, like the first thunder of an oncoming storm. "She will use you until she is through with you. She has no loyalty to you. No *love* for you."

Aya had never seen him like this, so unnerved. His breathing was uneven, his eyes wet with unshed tears. "And I won't be able to stop her. So to hells with your oath."

The confession was soft. Broken. One of those tears slipped down Will's face as he stared at her. "*Everything* I've done has been to protect you. To keep you from this. And I've failed. *Every time* I've failed. I couldn't keep you away from Gianna. I couldn't keep you from those masochists in the desert. And I can't—I can't *breathe* when I think of how many times I've almost lost you. Of how many times I've utterly failed you."

The words cracked something deep inside her as she took in the pain and the frustration and the longing in his gaze.

No one had ever failed her less.

She reached for him as if on instinct, but Will caught her wrist, giving his head a shake. "Don't," he muttered. Her own eyes burned as she swallowed, trying to get her throat to work.

"Why not?"

His eyes fluttered shut for a brief moment, as if he were in pain, and he gave her wrist a light squeeze. Silence stretched between them, so long that she was afraid he wouldn't answer, was afraid she'd somehow misunderstood. But Will's eyes darkened, his hand sliding up her wrist to curl around her hand. He brought it to his chest, where she could feel the thunderous beat of his heart.

"I don't… My control isn't…" He grappled for words, his gaze darting between her eyes and her lips. "It's too much," he breathed. "I'm feeling too much."

Aya blinked as she realized exactly what he was holding back from.

His trembling wasn't rage.

It was restraint.

Slowly she pressed her palm into his chest, against that pounding heartbeat, her nails digging into the skin beneath his shirt.

She wasn't sure which one of them moved first. She didn't particularly care. Because all there was was the feel of his lips on hers as they collided, his fingers tangling in her hair as he slanted his mouth over hers.

It wasn't gentle or tentative.

It was an unleashing. A claiming.

Will groaned, and the sound was like kindling to the fire between them. He tugged her closer, and Aya slid her arms around his neck, her fingers weaving into his silken hair.

She could die just from wanting him.

His tongue parted her lips, dragging a soft moan from her as his hands slid down her back and over her hips. Will tore his mouth away from hers to trail his lips down her neck, and she arched into him, her hips shifting against his. He nipped at the skin just above her collarbone, drawing a gasp from her as her hips moved again.

Will let out a rough laugh, his hands tightening on her hips as he buried his head in the crook of her neck. "Easy, love. You overestimate my self-control."

She didn't care. Might have even said it aloud, because Will laughed again, his lips coasting across her jaw. "As tempting as it would be to take you right here on the floor of this cave," he drawled, his lips tipping into a wicked grin as he tugged her against him again, showing her just how true his words were, "you need rest."

Aya opened her mouth to argue, but Will captured her lips again. This kiss was soft—gentle. As if they had all the time in the world to explore each other. It certainly felt that way as his hands trailed slowly up her back, over her shoulders, before finally cupping her face.

He pulled away just enough to read her, his gray eyes bright. But his brows tugged toward each other, and she returned his frown. "What?"

Will skimmed his knuckles across her cheekbone, his face contemplative. "I'm wondering how worried I need to be. You stabbed yourself less than two days ago." His eyes dropped to that scar on her chest, his fingers tracing the raised skin. Aya trembled lightly beneath his touch.

"I feel fine." Her voice was low, hardly masking the desire coursing through her. His hand floated across her chest, cupping her breast as his lips met hers again, her body arching into his touch. Slowly he backed her toward the bedroll, his tongue doing wicked things with hers.

But another tremor rocked through her, this one unprovoked.

He pulled away instantly, his breath coming in shallow pants.

"I'm fine," she assured him again. But Will merely frowned as he guided her down to the bedroll.

"I've had my fill of seeing you unconscious," he said, tucking the blankets around her. Aya let out a noise of outrage, but he was already up and making his way to the saddlebag he'd stashed against the cave wall. He returned with a waterskin and a bag of nuts and dates.

"You're intolerable," Aya mumbled as he settled next to her. But she took the waterskin, and her arm shook as she raised it to her lips and took small steady sips. Will wrapped an arm around her waist, his breath warm against her ear.

"That's a funny way to say thank you."

She let herself lean into his solid strength, her head tipping up to take in the strong lines of his jaw and the soft smile that pulled on his lips as he met her gaze.

It was one she'd never seen before. It made him look younger. More open. More free.

Aya traced that smile lightly with her fingers. "You found me."

He had come for her, just as he always had, even in the moments when she thought he couldn't deign to care. A dependable, sturdy presence. A solid wall at her back, no matter the circumstances.

After everything…he had come for her.

A smile tugged at her own mouth as she brushed her lips against his, her voice dropping low to mimic his smooth tone. "If I didn't know any better, William, I'd say you actually care."

She thought his laugh might be the most beautiful sound she'd ever heard.

68

Will monitored each of her breaths as Aya slept, her arm curled beneath her head, the other resting on top of the arm he'd draped across her waist. He savored every place she pressed against him, every movement that meant she was alive.

The fire had dwindled down to embers, and though the cold of the desert started to whisper through the cave, he hardly noticed. There was nothing but the steady rise and fall of her chest and the overwhelming emotions that threatened to swallow him whole.

In.

Out.

In.

Out.

He'd revealed more to her than he'd ever planned, even before they'd found themselves in this cave. She hadn't questioned him. She'd kissed him. And yet he knew those questions were coming. Knew there was more truth to share with her.

He tucked Aya closer and closed his eyes—as if that would be enough to steady himself and control the wave of sensations inside of him.

The moment he'd seen her limp form in the sand, his control had shattered so completely he wasn't sure there were any parts left to even piece back together.

And being near her now…with the memory of her lips against his…

It was too much.

She shifted against him, her body wriggling closer.

There had been moments when he'd thought the hope of her not hating him would kill him. That the hope of them getting through this unscathed would be the very thing that destroyed him. But now he wondered if it would be the possibility of having her—truly having her—that would be his demise.

He had never wanted anything more.

And he had never been more terrified to lose it.

Aya was hells-bent on saving the realm, no matter the cost to her soul. But he could care less about the godsdamn realm.

The only thing he cared to save was her.

Will pressed his head to the top of Aya's and let himself simply hold her as he inhaled her mint and pine scent deep into his lungs.

He would not lose her. He would make sure of that.

Even if it cost him everything.

Will wished he could drag out their journey. Their two days of travel were bliss, despite the hells they were facing. But they'd both grown quieter the closer they came to Rinnia.

"We'll be there just in time for Genemai tonight," he remarked, pulling them from their steady silence. The colorful buildings of Rinnia grew closer as they rode through the farmlands.

"They sure do love their celebrations here, don't they?" Aya settled back against his chest, and Will switched the reins to his other hand, his free arm snaking around her waist as he chuckled. He was hyperaware of each place their bodies touched, had been for their entire ride back.

And though she was teasing, he heard the strain beneath it. She was exhausted, her skin far too pale, her eyes far too dull. The relic had taken its toll. And then there was the matter of the blood she'd lost.

He wanted a healer to look at her as soon they got back, but he knew it had to wait. He had one more stop to make, one last truth to reveal.

"I'll sneak you out early," Will purred against her ear. Her laugh was like a shot of whiskey: smooth, yet burning that spot in his chest. She turned slightly, her lips brushing against his jaw. A silent thank-you.

He wondered, as they rode toward the outer stretches of the city, if she would still look at him with that fire in her eyes after whatever was about to unfold.

Aya frowned as Will steered them not toward the palace, but down a narrow street with ramshackle houses. He thanked the gods that they'd made it back early in the morning. Their visit would be far less conspicuous this way. He pulled to a stop before that rough stone cottage and slid from the saddle, giving the stallion a pat as he waited for Aya to follow.

"Where are we?" She took his outstretched hand and swung off the horse, her brow furrowing further as she scanned his face. Will merely led the horse to a small alleyway and tied him to the trough there.

"Will?"

His heart hammered as he knocked on the door. It was a monumental risk, bringing her here. She'd never helped him before. But perhaps if she sensed Aya's power and could *see*—

The door swung open, Lorna appearing in the threshold.

Aya's face paled as she took in the woman before them—as she placed the dark hair and eyes so blue they were almost gray.

"Aya," Will murmured, "you remember my mother."

69

WILL'S MOTHER WAS ALIVE, AND SHE WAS IN RINNIA. IT seemed Aya had finally learned where he'd been sneaking off to.

She tried not to stare at Lorna, who sat in a worn armchair across from the couch she and Will occupied. There was no warmth between mother and son. Will kept his body angled toward Aya, his arms braced on his knees.

"I'd love to know the reason behind your visit," Lorna finally said stiffly, her brows raised as she took a sip from her tea.

"Spare me, for once in your godsdamn life, from your lies," Will growled. "You know exactly why we're here. You know exactly who she is. You identified her power the moment you opened the door."

Aya cut her eyes to him, but Will kept his focus wholly on his mother, even as he muttered to Aya, "I sensed her shock."

If Lorna had detected her power, then that meant…

Another wave of cool surprise hit Aya.

"You're a Saj of the Maraciana," Aya breathed.

"No," Lorna said coolly. "But I have studied alongside them and have developed my affinity in the same such way."

Her chin rose as she surveyed her son. "Do you hate me so much that you'd bring death to my door?"

Will sat back, his leg pressing against Aya's as he took a shuddering breath. "Gianna won't know you're involved."

Aya's mug thunked against the worn wooden table as she set it down. "Someone better start explaining what the hells is going on." She turned to Will, her jaw aching with how hard she gritted her teeth. "Now."

His gray eyes softened as they locked on her, the warmth of his body seeping into her as he shifted. "Five years ago, I was visiting Trahir on Council business. I'd just left a tavern one night when who should appear in an alleyway but Lorna."

Aya remembered that trip. It was just before they'd begun their official training for the Dyminara. Will had been gone for weeks, and when he'd come back, he'd seemed even colder and more lethal than when he'd left.

"I thought, at best, I was drunk out of my mind. At worst, I was losing it. Ryker was there, and he managed to subdue me long enough to bring me here to speak privately, where I learned the truth: that all those years ago, she'd faked her death and fled to Trahir."

"Why?" Aya breathed, looking to Lorna.

"Enough," Lorna hissed, her blue eyes gleaming with anger. But Will continued on, his tone calm and vicious.

"Because Lorna isn't just a Saj. She's a Seer. And she's a descendent of the line who foretold the prophecy of the Second Saint."

Aya stared at Will, her frustration building.

No.

Will had proven himself to her time and time again. If he had kept Lorna from her, he had good reason. Aya's jaw shifted as she took in the Saj. The same dark fury she'd seen in Will's own features sat on her face. Aya had always assumed his quiet temper came from his father. But looking at Lorna, it was clear to see he was his mother's son.

"Are you satisfied?" Lorna hissed as she stood. "Is this your idea of punishment for my failures as a mother?"

"What punishment?" Aya demanded. "What do you know of the prophecy?"

Lorna whirled to her. "I will not risk my life for you."

Aya turned to press Will for answers, but he was on his feet, his chest heaving as he flung a finger toward her. "She almost lost her life to the Vaguer because of your selfishness, because you *refused* to help. If you think this is about Gianna, then you're a fool."

The color drained from Lorna's face as she slowly sank back into her seat. "No one survives a search for the Vaguer," she rasped.

Aya simply stared at the woman, her brow furrowed as she swallowed her questions about her queen. "I did. But not before I almost lost myself to whatever darkness their relic brought forward. I saw the veil. And had I continued to listen to the darkness's call, I would have tried to destroy it."

Lorna closed her eyes, a flicker of pain flashing across her face. "It's already happening," she breathed, more to herself than to them. "Tell me exactly what you saw."

Aya glanced at Will, noting the look of surprise that crossed his face. He hadn't expected Lorna to comply. Which meant this…this had been a visit not of calculation, but desperation.

You will not sacrifice yourself for this war.

Aya didn't trust this woman. But she trusted him. So she waited until he met her gaze, until he settled back next to her on the couch, his chin dipping in encouragement.

She told the woman everything. Lorna did not interrupt, but Aya could see the tension mounting in her body. She marked the way Lorna's hands trembled when they reached for her mug, her mouth pressed into a thinner line the further her story progressed.

A tense silence followed when Aya finished. Lorna stared at her absently, as if lost to her own thoughts.

"Unlike Visya affinities, which vary in bloodlines, the Seer ability is passed down directly, though inconsistently, through Saj bloodlines," she finally said. "It can disappear for generations, especially if the bloodline fails to produce another Saj. When it does appear, the visions are murky. Misleading. Before me, the power had been absent from my line for over a century."

"And your vision was about the prophecy?" Aya asked.

Lorna nodded. "The prophecy was foretold so long ago that it's difficult to trace exactly where it originated. It was added to the Conoscenza nearly two hundred fifty years ago."

"So the theory of a Second Saint wasn't even established until centuries after the war?" Will cut in.

Lorna shrugged. "According to our family history. The first Conoscenza was written about a century after Evie's sacrifice. It's unlikely they would've left out such a detail if it had been foretold." The Saj pressed her lips together, her brow furrowing as she looked between them. "The centuries have allowed us to live in more anonymity the further removed we've become from it. That, and very few Seers admit to having the gene."

"So why then are you worried for your safety?" Aya frowned.

Lorna sighed. "When I was fifteen, I had my first and only vision. I wasn't even sure what I was seeing." She glanced at her son. "It was with the help of your great-grandmother that we were able to piece it together." Another shuddering breath, as if she were steeling herself against whatever truth was about to unfold.

"When the rumors came that Kakos was beginning to experiment with their affinities, the late King Roderick strengthened Tala's borders and the embargo. He was certain that between the Dyminara, the trade restrictions, and our alliances, there would be no threat to Tala. But his daughter did not agree. Gianna felt her father wasn't taking the threat seriously, and that the rumors of the Diaforaté were an insult to the gods and needed to be dealt with. She became fascinated by the prophecy of the Second Saint.

"Gianna suspected what was unfolding in Kakos was an indication the prophecy was to come true; and that if she could learn as much as possible of its meaning—of its origin—then she'd hold the key to defeating the heretics."

"You were worried she was going to uncover you," Aya observed, a hint of disgust in her voice. This woman faked her death, left her son...and for what? Why flee the most devout kingdom of the realm? Why refuse to help them protect their people and the gods?

Lorna bristled under her scrutiny. "I saw a tear in the veil. It is cracked. Vulnerable."

"The gods used their own power to repair the veil after Evie opened it for them," Aya retorted. It was what kept them from interfering and what kept mortals from chasing their heavenly presence before death.

"That's not what the vision showed me. And if the veil is cracked, it throws the entire prophecy into question. We've always believed that when the prophecy speaks of the greatest wrong, it speaks of the Decachiré. But what if the greatest wrong isn't the Decachiré? What if it's that Evie opened the veil in the first place? What if it's that she weakened it, leaving us susceptible to something far worse?"

Aya frowned. "But if she hadn't, the Decachiré would've won. They would've ripped it down eventually, right? To challenge the gods?"

And if this vision was to be believed...then it meant the veil was weaker.

And Kakos still could rip it down.

Lorna shrugged. "No practitioner has ever reached that level of power. No Visya, except for Evie. Even *you* would not have been able to bring the veil down in your rage in the desert. But with training...perhaps you could have such power."

Aya rubbed her temples as she let the information soak in. "So if the Decachiré practitioners learn of this, they could summon enough power to tear it down far sooner than they could if it were whole?"

"Not just the practitioners," Will muttered, understanding lighting his gaze. Lorna nodded at her son.

"What better way for your queen to enact vengeance on those who spit on the name of her gods than to call down the wrath of the gods themselves?"

Aya stilled, her body going cold. "Gianna would never do that," she breathed. Because that would mean the destruction of their very realm. The gods had been clear: they were not to be summoned to the realm again. There would be no second chances.

"Would she not?" Lorna challenged. "Her devotion knows no bounds. The gods honored Evie's attempt to save the realm—they banished only the heretics. Perhaps Gianna thinks they will grant her the same grace as she proves her devotion."

But to take that chance…to *hope* the gods would only enact their rage on the Decachiré practitioners and no one else, despite their warnings…

"Gianna would never do that," Aya repeated.

But even as she said the words, her nails cut into her palms.

"You say that," Lorna smirked. "But I can see your doubt. And you can see why I would flee. It was too dangerous for me to stay. If she knew my connection to the prophecy, if she thought I could help her avenge her gods, well…we all know Gianna has her ways of getting what she wants."

Her eyes flicked to her son, and Will flinched. *Flinched*, as if she had hit him. Aya's body tensed, but Will laid a hand on her thigh and squeezed gently.

Not worth it. Lorna was not worth it.

"You said that with training, I may be able to garner such power," Aya began. "But the Vaguer…they said in order to survive the Decachiré, one had to yield to the darkness of one's soul. I..." Aya's voice trailed off, the words fumbling over themselves.

She didn't think she could survive such a thing.

"The Vaguer certainly have a morbid academic interest, don't they? And yet even they, like so many, fall victim to the propensity to see only one truth." Lorna looked her over, her head cocking slightly. "We are not one thing, Aya. We are who we *choose* to be. Who we tell ourselves we are. You, in your guilt and shame, told yourself you were dark. And so you fed your raw power that darkness, creating boundaries on your power that were never meant to exist in the first place and making you ill when you tried to use it. You believed in your darkness so firmly that in your rage, you were willing to sacrifice yourself to it entirely, to let it consume you, as it almost did when you called down the veil. That's what Natali sensed in you. That's what the relic brought out in you. I have no doubt that if you were to fuel yourself with something better, another truth you choose, your power would react differently."

It had, Aya realized. When it speared across the square to save Tova. When she sensed Will's anguish. When she healed him.

Will's thumb swiped across her thigh, as if he, too, were remembering.

"That voice...that voice that was urging me on..." Aya whispered.

"Your own fear, ruling you because you let it." Lorna leaned forward in her chair, her blue eyes luminous. "You faced your greatest regret in the desert. Shined light on it. And when you were lost to rage, you made a choice. You sacrificed yourself to save others. That is not a choice that yields a soul to darkness. Nor is it the choice of someone whose true nature is purely dark. Both live within you as they do in all of us. Your power does not decide—you do."

Aya's eyes burned. "But the Vaguer left me for dead in the desert."

Lorna shrugged. "Again, we can be limited by our desire to seek a single truth. I have no doubt you gave them quite the scare. Perhaps they thought you had given yourself over to darkness entirely and were seeking immortality next."

Aya wasn't sure what to believe about her essence…was still too afraid to hope. But she tucked the Saj's information away until she could have the strength to examine it fully.

"Why help us now?" Will asked.

Lorna bit her lip. "When you came here seeking answers, I believed it was on behalf of Gianna."

"And now?" he muttered.

She stared at him for a long moment, something softening in her gaze. "The prophecy is underway. It's up to you to decide what you do with what you've learned about the veil. Up to you to decide to trust."

There was more she wasn't saying. Aya could see it in the way she pursed her lips. But Lorna was turning her attention back to Aya.

"You look just like your mother," she mused. Aya raised a brow, and Lorna smiled, this time with a touch of sadness. "Stay anchored to the light. Because as you saw in the desert, darkness, with your power…it could be catastrophic." Aya felt Will stiffen next to her, but the Saj continued. "If you need a reminder…" She stood, walking to a small cabinet on the far side of the living room. She unlocked a box and lifted out a silver chain from which hung a small inverted triangle divided into four sections. Aya's heart stopped in her chest.

Her mother's necklace.

"It was found in the wreckage after the storm hit," Lorna explained as she handed it to her. "Gale sent it with my things. I suppose he believed it was mine. Let her love anchor you. Let it guard your heart. You decide your essence, Aya. No one else."

70

Aya could feel the tension radiating from Will as they rode back to the palace stables, the silence between them heavy now. It only made their arrival more jarring. Stable hands grabbed their horse while attendants ran ahead to the palace to announce their safe return. The sudden burst of activity was overwhelming.

And yet they found themselves alone on the short walk back to the palace, Will with that calculating look in his eyes as he kept his gaze locked on the path ahead. The silence continued to grow until Aya thought she'd explode.

"That's why you ultimately decided to join the Dyminara," she said as she stopped beside one of the towering trees that lined the path. Will turned back to her, his hands sliding into his pockets as he waited; as if he knew she was still putting the pieces together and was content to let her.

"Lorna told you the prophecy was why she fled. That's how you knew without a doubt it was real. And you already suspected it was me."

"I'd already been training for combat, as you well know." Will sighed as he took a step closer to her. "But yes. I had two reasons, really. I thought getting closer to Gianna might reveal why Lorna had been so desperate to flee. She never told me about her vision."

"Do you agree with her? Do you believe Gianna would do something so drastic?"

Will let out a hard breath. "I don't know," he admitted gravely. "But as for suspecting it was you…I didn't know for sure. But the day we delivered the news of your mother's death, I sensed something different about you. I was reaching out with my power, expecting to calm you. To take away your grief. But you shut me out entirely. And it wasn't just an ordinary shield. I'd never felt anything like it." He raked his fingers through his hair, letting out a soft laugh. "Until the Athatis," he added wryly. "When I returned from that trip to Trahir, I joined the Dyminara and figured I'd keep an eye on you. I didn't know what I would do if it *was* you."

His face was open and honest as he continued.

"For two years, I watched you. One day, early in our training, we were sparring, and you were strong, and beautiful, and so utterly unafraid of me it was almost laughable. And even though I knew you hated me for what my father did to your mother, even though I could feel your anger and your disgust…I could feel your intrigue, too. You didn't talk to me like Dunmeaden's Dark Prince. And for the first time since I learned my mother was alive, I found myself feeling something other than anger."

Aya's pulse thundered as he considered her. "I knew for sure you were the one the prophecy spoke of when you persuaded me to jump from the Wall. And I panicked. I was terrified of what would happen if you were discovered. I still didn't know what Gianna wanted with the Second Saint, but by then I was well aware of her ambition. And I saw how closely she watched you…as if she suspected it, too. So I tried to have you removed from the Dyminara. I figured better for you to hate me than to face whatever was coming."

And she had hated him. She had accused him of taking away everything she had ever loved. When in reality…

He had been the one to lose everything. To sacrifice everything.

"But of course, Galda didn't bite," Will muttered, "and then not only were you in the Dyminara, but you were in the Tría, and closer to Gianna than ever."

I was trying to keep you safe.

Aya swallowed hard. "You tried to pull her attention away from me," she breathed.

Will rubbed the back of his neck. "She had expressed interest in me on a few occasions. I thought that if I held that interest just enough, perhaps it would draw some of her focus off you."

Aya felt sick as Will continued. "When the Athatis attacked, I taunted you about having darkness because I was afraid you would go to the queen and admit to persuading the wolves. I never once believed that your soul was dark, Aya."

His jaw tensed as he looked away from her, as if gathering his resolve.

"After the incident in the market, I suggested to Gianna that we come here because I thought maybe the Saj here had answers. I told myself I would find a way to help you wrangle your power so that you could fight whatever was coming. And selfishly...I thought I could figure out how to keep us away from Tala after that.

"I went to Lorna so many times, desperately hoping that whatever piece of the prophecy she had could help you with your power. But I couldn't bring you. I was too afraid she would do something reckless, or harm you because she didn't want the prophecy fulfilled. But when you told me about the Vaguer, about what you had been willing to do, I knew I couldn't keep you from her anymore, even if the chance of her helping us was slim. I thought maybe if she *saw* you, if she sensed your power, she would come around."

Aya swallowed hard. All he had done, all he had been

through…to protect her. He had let her believe the worst in him, was fine to let her hate him if it meant she was safe.

"I told Tova," he confessed, his voice raw. "When I went into her cell and told her to fake her questioning, I told her what I suspected of Gianna. I told her that we needed to get you away from her. She agreed to help me. It's how I knew that letter from her was fake. I didn't tell you about Lena's or hers because I was afraid you'd run back to Tala—exactly where Gianna wants you."

Aya closed the distance between them, her hands cupping his face. There were too many words inside of her. Too many emotions welling up that she didn't know how to express. But Will closed his eyes for a beat, grasping her wrists before he pulled her hands from his face.

"Aya," he whispered. She frowned at the pain in his voice. "When we get back to the palace, Aidon will approach you about a courtship. About the alliance."

She drew back a step. "What of it?"

Will took a deep breath, his fingers flexing on her wrists, as if he were steeling himself. "I think you should agree."

Aya froze. Her mind tripped over his words, running them over and over as she tried to make sense of them.

"You can't be serious."

Will merely looked at her, the truth written in his face.

Someone had stolen her air. It was the only explanation for the crushing feeling in her chest.

"I know you have feelings for him."

Aya opened her mouth to argue, but he shook his head. "And if you think those feelings could turn into something real, then you should do this."

Aya took another step back, but Will stepped with her. He couldn't be serious. Not after everything he had just told her. "You belong with Aidon," he breathed, his face pained.

"You don't mean that."

"Did you not hear a single word Lorna said? Stay anchored

to the light. You belong with someone *good*. Not someone who has lived his life in darkness for so long."

"But...she said we are who we choose to be—"

"And as I have told you before, I have made *horrible* choices to get what I want. I always will, when it comes to you."

"Will—"

"You cannot sacrifice the fate of the world—the fate of your *soul*—for some feelings you *think* you have for me. And if this match gets us an alliance, that alliance may very well be the thing that keeps you safe."

"And yet you claim you would have run with me," she breathed.

"Exactly," Will thundered. "I would've let the entire world burn for you. And if that doesn't prove to you how wrong this is, how I would only lead you down a path you could not come back from, that *we* could not come back from—"

She shook her head. She would not hear this. But it seemed Will would make her. He stepped forward, taking her hands in his. "I have had years to come to terms with the idea that I would never have you, that you would never care for me after what I've done."

She did care, she wanted to scream. She cared more than she'd ever cared for anything. But that old instinct to lash out, to hurt him before he could hurt her further, reared its head and it was bitterness, not reason, that came out of her.

"So you would use me as a bargaining tool just as Gianna would. Me *and* Aidon would be no more than chess pieces to you."

Will dropped her hands as she let out a bitter laugh.

The vulnerability on his face only fueled the rage swirling in her. "Darkness indeed."

It was hypocritical. A low blow that hit him hard and deep. She knew it as soon as she saw the pain that filled those gray eyes. But he didn't rise to her bait. In fact, he hardly reacted at all. He simply nodded his head once, as if satisfied.

"They'll be waiting for us." He turned on his heel and started away from her.

"Will."

He didn't bother to turn around.

"Thank the gods you're okay." Josie's arms were a vise grip around Aya's neck as she hugged her. Will had disappeared inside the castle with a nod to the princess, and Josie had rushed to Aya.

Aya pushed Josie back slightly. She needed to look her friend in the eyes for what she had to say. "I'm sorry," Aya said solemnly. "For all of it. For not being there when you needed me. For running. That day in the study—"

"They found her," Josie rasped, tears lining her eyes. She grabbed Aya's hands and squeezed tight. "My uncle let me know last night. They found her."

Aya froze. Dominic had found Vi? Had she and Will been wrong?

"Is she—?"

"She's fine. Shaken, but fine. They found a rebel safe house a few towns over. She'll be back just after Genemai. They want her to see a healer first."

"That's wonderful."

Josie brought a hand to Aya's cheek, concern in her gaze as she scanned her. "You look awful," she finally said. Aya scoffed, but Josie's grin faded as she glanced to where Will had stalked off. "Do you want to talk about it?"

Aya shook her head. "Not now." She frowned as she searched the courtyard. There was no sign of Aidon.

"He's been helping Uncle with the search," Josie said knowingly. "He'll be at Genemai tonight."

"I was hoping to talk to him. To apologize for..."

Using him, she almost said. But the words froze on her tongue. Because if she did what Will advised, she'd only be using him more.

Josie gave her arm a squeeze. "Good thing we have time to practice. That was horrible," she smirked. "Annnd..." she drawled as she tugged Aya toward the palace, "good thing we have time to talk about whatever *that* was." She grinned, her chin motioning to where Will had disappeared.

Aya laughed, but the sound was tinged with heaviness.

Tired. She felt so incredibly tired. She expected it was why Josie's voice softened as she said, "But first...how about a bath and a hot meal?"

Aya leaned into her friend, her arm tightening around Josie's. "That sounds divine."

71

THE LAST PLACE WILL WANTED TO BE WAS IN THIS GODSDAMN ballroom.

The music had been going for a solid hour now, the royal court and Dominic's guests twirling on the dance floor. Will leaned against one of the towering marble columns toward the back of the ballroom, planning to stay there until it was an acceptable time to leave. Aidon had arrived, as had Dominic and Zuri. But Enzo, Josie, and Aya were nowhere to be seen.

Will straightened the collar of his white shirt before smoothing the folds of his black jacket.

"It's quite tedious, isn't it?" Aidon sighed as he appeared at Will's shoulder.

"The parties?" he asked, a hint of amusement in his voice. Aidon's eyes were trained on the dance floor, not a trace of a smile on his face. Something was bothering the general.

"Thank you," Aidon said instead. "For bringing her back. For realizing where she'd gone."

"I didn't do it for you."

"I know." Aidon shrugged. "It doesn't make me less grateful."

Will pushed off the column and rolled his shoulders, his

eyes following one of the waltzing couples. If he was going to be supportive, he supposed he could start now. "You two are good together." The words tasted bitter, but he managed to put enough lightness in them that they sounded sincere.

Aidon snorted. "That was entirely unbelievable. Care to try again?" Will glared at the prince, but Aidon simply grinned, the gesture not quite meeting his eyes. "We aren't going to get married in the name of getting an alliance, Will."

It took a moment for the words to register—for him to cycle through his disbelief and frustration that he had to convince *both* of them, godsdamn them—before hope, vicious hope, took root.

"I'm making a choice," Aidon said. There was an earnestness in his gaze that kept Will silent, even as the prince looked away. An earnestness and something more; something *pressing*. It had Will frowning as Aidon added, "And it seems she's made hers."

He followed Aidon's gaze, which was fixed on the staircase. There was Josie, looking resplendent in a gown of deep emerald-green, a silver crown on her head. But Will couldn't stop looking at the woman behind her.

"I do recall you saying you preferred Aya in black," Aidon murmured.

He had. And he hadn't seen her wearing the color since they'd arrived in Trahir. But tonight...

Tonight, she wore a gown of midnight black, the straps twined around her neck, the bodice plunging low between her breasts. The dress hugged her body, accenting every dip and hollow before pooling at her feet. Her long brown hair was pulled to one side and cascaded down her shoulder in loose curls. Kohl lined her eyes, while her lips were painted a deep, dark red.

She looked like dreams and nightmares and everything he'd ever wanted.

Will took a single step forward, his lips parted in awe. Aya scanned the ballroom, her blue eyes blazing as they found his.

She lifted her chin, and he could read the challenge there, could see it written on her proud face as she stared him down.

"For what it's worth," Aidon said as he pressed a glass of champagne into Will's hand, "I'm not fool enough to tinker with fate." Aidon clinked his glass against Will's, his smile grim. "So...to fate."

The prince walked away, not bothering to wait for Will's response. Will's eyes found Aya again, drawn to her like a magnet as he took a sip of champagne.

"To fate."

Aya wondered if this was what it felt like to burn slowly until there was nothing left. Because the way Will looked at her as she came down those stairs had set fire to her very blood, had melted away the music, the ballroom, the guests, until nothing else existed but the two of them.

And yet now she couldn't find him. Josie had been surrounded by guests as soon as they reached the bottom of the stairs, and she'd stayed with her friend, knowing that this night would be long for her; that the wait for Viviane's arrival tomorrow was slowing time for the princess.

Josie nudged her lightly. "He'll seek you out," she muttered under her breath as she greeted another visitor.

"You sure about that?" Aya was sure she'd looked far more confident on those stairs than she felt.

"I'm positive. We'll make sure of it," she added with a sly grin.

"What are you doing?"

Josie just looped her arm through her own and tugged her onto the dance floor, just as an upbeat tune started from the quartet. "We're going to make sure he sees you. And that he can't look away."

And for once, Aya didn't hesitate. She took her friend's hands, letting the music sweep her away as she started to dance. This—this was what it felt like to *feel*. To move out of the shadows and into the light. To live.

Will had made it five steps toward the throng of guests around their princess when Sion appeared at his arm, his face grave.

"Cheer up, Sion, it's a party," Will said by way of greeting. But the attendant didn't so much as crack a smile. "What's wrong?"

"The king has requested your assistance, Prince," Sion muttered. Will scanned the ballroom. Dominic had just been here, hadn't he? "He's left for his study," Sion explained. Nearby, Peter was whispering in Aidon's ear, the prince's face grave. Aidon strode out of the ballroom without a backward glance, Peter following at his heels. "It's Viviane's party..." Sion started. "They've been attacked."

"By who?"

"I don't know."

Will whipped his gaze toward Josie, the crowd surrounding her parting just enough for him to see the joy on her face. The hope.

Sion's hand was on his arm before he could take a single step toward her. "His Majesty would like to keep the princess uninformed—at least until we know more."

Will nodded at the attendant. He would find Aya afterward. Explain everything. And then...

Damn it all to hells.

He'd get on his knees and beg her forgiveness for what he'd so foolishly suggested. For what he'd considered trying to talk Aidon into mere moments ago.

"Let's go."

Aya danced until even the adrenaline and jubilation couldn't hide the soreness in her muscles. She'd visited a healer upon her return to the palace, and while they'd tended to her wounds, she still didn't feel quite like herself. So she excused herself from the dance floor, smiling as a young noble whirled Josie across the space, and went in search of Will.

She was tired of waiting; tired of hiding how she felt and what it meant to her.

She had made her choice. They would face this together.

She touched the necklace that hung at her neck—that reminder of the strength of love—and smiled softly to herself. But that smile faded the longer she wove through guests without a sight of that tall strong figure. She'd always been able to spot him in a crowd in an instant. Will demanded attention, even when he didn't want it.

Aya ducked around some councillors, her eyes finding Sion near one of the more discreet exits.

"Have you seen Will?" she asked, standing on her toes as she scanned the crowd. "I can't find him anywhere."

"He left, I'm afraid," Sion replied. "He said he tired of the celebration and that he'd rather attend the festivities at the local taverns." Disdain dripped from his words.

Aya slowly lowered her heels to the floor. "But the night just started."

Sion sniffed delicately. "The Enforcer seemed to hold the same sentiment regarding the entertainment in town."

She could feel her cheeks flush with color as she avoided Sion's stare. Perhaps she had misunderstood all that lay in his gaze earlier. Perhaps he had meant what he said yesterday.

If Will wanted to avoid her…fine. She'd let him. But he couldn't do so forever.

"Tell him…" Aya paused, choosing her words carefully. "Tell him I'd like to see him when he returns."

Sion bowed. "As you wish, madam."

Aya caught sight of Josie, still dancing, her eyes bright—brighter than they'd been in some time. She wouldn't cloud

Josie's happiness with her own somber mood. So she didn't bother to say good night as she returned to her room.

Aya closed the door to her suite with a soft click, letting her head fall back against the wood as she let out a long breath.

Perhaps she had cut Will deeply with her parting words. The wall that had been built between them was as much from her as it was from him—even more so since their arrival in Rinnia. For years, she'd never given Will a reason to think she believed anything but the worst of him.

Aya covered her face with her hands. They had been stuck in the same place for so long, she wasn't sure how to undo it. How to get him to see that she was here, that she wanted this. That perhaps a part of her always had.

She thought about the Dawning, how she'd thrown her power out without a second thought because she couldn't stand to see him hurt.

She'd turned herself off to him completely so he wouldn't feel her death.

She hadn't realized it until yesterday, when Will had mentioned that impenetrable shield she'd formed against him.

Slowly Aya lowered her hands. She wasn't sure how she knew where to find that place she'd locked so tightly—the part of her that was just for him.

But she did.

And when she found it...Aya dropped her shield.

She'd almost given in and gone to bed by the time the knock came at her door. By the way the sky had begun to lighten, she knew it was close to dawn. Her hands trembled as she tugged the door open, a teasing grin on her lips.

"You sure know how to keep someone wait—"

The words died as she took in Josie's grave face. The princess shouldered past her, glancing down the hall before snapping the door closed.

"They took him," she rumbled. Aya's heart began to pound as she scanned her friend. "They took Will. I overheard Peter talking to some guards and—"

"On what charge?" Aya was already in motion, her hands reaching for a knife she could tuck beneath her dress. Josie tensed, her eyes flicking to the blade in Aya's hand.

"Espionage," she whispered. Aya froze. Josie shook her head, tears welling in her eyes. "I'm so sorry, Aya. I had no idea they would..." Her friend's voice trailed off, her face pleading.

Aya closed her eyes for a heartbeat, willing her blood to thaw as she leashed the rage that was whirling inside her.

"Where is he?"

"The first level of the dungeons. There are rooms there for questioning."

Aya sheathed the knife at her thigh. "Can you show me?"

Josie nodded. "I'm so sorry," she whispered as Aya reached for the door.

Aya's jaw locked, her eyes fixed on the dark hall. "It's not your fault."

72

THEY'D MUTED HIS POWER. WILL HAD DISCOVERED IT AS soon as those guards seized him in the hallway—as soon as the Anima got his hands on him and slowed his heart. He'd woken up some time later in a large room that looked like one of the iron workshops back home. There were tables and tools and only two small windows that looked out over the sea. But Will was familiar with spaces like these. He knew they weren't for welding. Not iron, at least.

They must have slipped him that godsforsaken tonic at some point. Perhaps in his food, or a drink…

He could still feel sensations—like the tension in the guards standing by the door. But he couldn't manipulate them. It was as if they'd ripped apart his shield, leaving him open and vulnerable.

Will leaned his head back against the iron chair they'd chained him to and let out a shaky breath. The waiting was the worst part.

Where is she?

Surely they'd gone after Aya, too? He tried to stifle the fear that threatened to choke him. If they harmed her, if they so much as *touched* her…

He closed his eyes against the thought.

A commotion in the hallway had him lifting his head, his eyes trained on the door. There were raised voices, and footsteps, and—

His heart stopped. He'd recognize that icy tone anywhere.

Not her. Please gods, not her.

The door swung open, and a guard shoved Aya into the room, her knife glinting in his hand. She still wore her gown, and other than a few wisps of hair that had fallen around her face, nothing else seemed out of place. They hadn't even bothered to cuff her.

She was at his side in an instant, her hands skimming his face, his shoulders, his arms. "Are you hurt?"

Will tugged against the chains. "What are you doing here?"

She stepped behind him, her hands running over the thick iron. "The hells type of question is that?"

"You need to get out of here."

"Hold still. I'm going to have to freeze these off you."

"That won't be necessary," a deep voice cut in.

Will felt Aya stiffen, her hand brushing his arm as she stepped out from behind his chair. Dominic smiled from the hidden doorway he'd stepped through at the far corner of the room.

"We'll only have to chain him up again, and it's rather tedious when we have so much to do."

"An explanation, Majesty," Aya ordered, a dangerous calm in her voice. But if Dominic sensed it, he didn't seem to care. He merely slid his hands into his pockets as he strolled forward.

"All in due time," he replied smoothly. "But first, let's wait for the rest of our party to arrive."

Before Will could question him, the main door swung open again and another set of guards led Josie into the room. Will watched the color drain from Aya's face as the two friends exchanged a worried glance.

"Uncle?" Josie asked. But Dominic merely held up a hand,

his eyes fixed on whatever tunnel he had walked through to get here. Will heard footsteps echoing off the stone walls and the steady clink of a chain as it dragged across the floor.

His body screamed at him to leave—to get Aya out. Because something was wrong. Something was very, very wrong. He felt Aya shift closer to him.

The world slowed as the guards stepped through the door, a prisoner chained between them. Distantly, Will registered Josie's scream of rage as she flung herself toward them, her own guards holding her back.

Because there was Viviane, still dressed as though she was on her way to the Pysar festival. Her blue dress was torn, her face gaunt and pale. She looked anywhere but Josie as the remaining guards filed in.

And though Josie was still screaming, though Aya was demanding answers, Will's focus was on the last member of the escort.

It was Aidon who followed the guards through the door. Aidon who stared grimly at Viviane chained in the middle of the fleet of soldiers. Aidon who took his place by his uncle's side.

Will wondered if that was where Aidon had been all along.

"Now we can begin," Dominic said calmly, his hands folding in front of him—as if this was no more than a business meeting. As if he didn't have the love of his niece's life chained between six guards.

"What the hells is this?" Josie spat, still struggling against the hold her guards kept on her. Will didn't miss how many they'd assigned to her, as if they didn't underestimate her prowess in a fight. He was certain that directive hadn't come from Dominic.

I'm making my choice. The prince had told him to his fucking face. Will had been too wrapped up in his own feelings to listen.

"I do apologize you have to be involved, my dear," Dominic replied, and Will could see the regret in his eyes. "But I needed to ensure Viviane complied with our wishes."

"Which are?" Aya asked softly from his side. If she was surprised to see the prince, she didn't show it. She merely kept her face in that calm, cool mask of the Queen's Eyes, every muscle pulled taut as she stared at Dominic.

"I hear we have quite the wonder in our midst," the king mused.

Will's stomach hollowed out at the words. "You bastard," he growled to Aidon.

Dominic raised a brow and clapped his nephew on the shoulder. "This is what loyalty looks like, *Prince*," he sneered. "Something you know nothing of."

"What do you want?" Aya's tone made it clear she was done waiting.

Dominic let out a heavy sigh. "We have a problem in our kingdom," he said as he paced. "The Bellare have been gaining supporters. And now it's come to my attention that one such member was going to release knowledge of my nephew's power. Knowledge that would ensure he would never take the throne."

He paused before Viviane, his head tilting in mild curiosity. Guilt flooded Viviane's eyes as she stared at the king.

Josie paused her struggling, tears dripping down her face as she shifted her gaze to her partner. "No," she cried, her head shaking slowly. "No."

"Yes," Dominic thundered. "You were foolish to tell her. She would've used the information against your family. Against your king."

"That's why you've been framing the Bellare," Aya breathed. "They were never involved in the attacks. It was you all along."

"Two attacks," Dominic corrected. "I was responsible for two. The kidnappings. The Bellare, with their petty attacks on the Visya, merely provided the opportunity to continue to sway public opinion against them. And of course... flush you out."

Will felt Aya tense next to him. But she did not wield her power.

"We may not be as devout as Tala," the king continued, "but I am not so detached from the gods that I didn't expect talk of the prophecy to arise along with the rumors swirling about Kakos. And so I was curious when you arrived to work with the Saj of the Maraciana. We had already planned to make an example of Avis. But when someone began siphoning our tonic...I became fascinated."

Will tensed. Aidon had told Aya about that tonic.

"You were desperate, I assume," Dominic continued. "But my healers monitor every drop of the tonic that keeps my nephew safe. When we realized some was missing, I started to truly wonder... Was it possible? Did the Second Saint exist? Was she trying to hide her power? I hoped, with the right motivation, you'd show yourself and prove my suspicions correct."

Will's gaze flicked to Aidon, but the prince remained stoic, his eyes void of any emotion as his uncle spoke. Will's jaw tightened. The kidnapper in the alleyway had rushed for him first, while the other attacked Aidon. They had given Aya the perfect opportunity to unleash herself. *Aidon* had given her the perfect opportunity to unleash herself.

A trap. It had all been a trap.

Dominic sighed as he picked a piece of lint from his tan linen jacket. "But then you ran off to the Vaguer—to learn how to defeat the Decachiré, I assume—and I worried it would all be for naught. No one survives a trip to the Vaguer. But I'm nothing if not prepared for all outcomes, Aya. So I paid a visit to the Maraciana."

A nod to the door, and a guard shifted. Will's blood

went cold as Natali was dragged inside, their face battered and bruised. "With the right motivation, Natali was all too willing to assist in some research on an ancient practice."

"What do you want?" Aya growled again, her fists curling at her side.

"I want you to prove you're the saint the realm awaits."

Will tugged against his chains as one of Josie's guards approached him, standing sentinel near his shoulder.

Dominic gestured to Viviane. "Impart power to her, or I'll kill her myself."

Josie's scream ripped through the room, and the guards were on her again, holding her in place. Will dove into his well, beating against the wall blocking his power.

"And why would I ever agree to that?" Aya demanded. She was stalling. He could see her readying to attack, to spear her power across the room.

Suddenly there was a flash near Vi, and Will gasped as he felt the knife that a guard had swiped across her face.

The guard at his shoulder laid a hand on his arm, and Will's very blood was on fire.

A Sensainos.

Will couldn't contain the scream that ripped from him as his body writhed against the pain. He was burning alive, he was sure of it. The Sensainos sent another lash through him. Another. Another.

Distantly, he heard Josie sobbing. Heard Aya pleading. Heard Viviane screaming. He couldn't separate what they were doing to her and what they were doing to him. All he knew was agony.

So this was what it felt like to be a victim of his power. To be on the receiving end of the pain he had inflicted on so many. Perhaps he deserved it.

"Stop." The king's order cut through the room, and the pain relented, leaving Will gasping for air. "We could do this all day, Aya. I'll kill them both."

Aya's voice trembled as she turned her gaze to Dominic. "Why are you doing this?"

He considered her for a moment, his face pensive.

"Because," Dominic said softly, "you're going to help me build Kakos's army."

73

THIS WAS THE WORST LAYER OF THE HELLS. THE FURTHEST, darkest pit she could find.

"If you think that I will help Kakos, you're mistaken," Aya breathed. "I'd rather die."

Dominic cocked his head. "*You* won't help Kakos, my dear. My nephew will."

A chill raced up Aya's spine as Dominic grinned.

"With my connections to Kakos, I've had the pleasure of knowing the Diaforaté. Closer and closer they've come over the years to mimicking the raw power needed to break down their wells. But the power is unstable. It feeds on its host far more aggressively than the Decachiré did. But I have a theory." The king regarded her. "The power of a saint is naturally raw. And limitless. Perhaps you're the key to our conundrum, Aya. Perhaps, if one takes *your* power, there would be no adverse effects at all."

"What does that have to do with Viviane?" Aya rasped.

Dominic raised a brow. "What better way is there to prove your power is safe for Aidon?" he asked mildly. "Your power is of far more use to me in someone loyal to my cause. And once Aidon has it, he'll be the most powerful Diaforaté in the world."

Aya felt numb as she looked to Aidon, but Aidon's gaze was on the floor, his jaw tight in the growing silence.

"You were supposed to be our ally," Aya snarled to the prince.

"Ally," Dominic scoffed. "You want to know why we will never side with Tala? Ten years ago, my wife was on her deathbed. No healer could save her. But I had heard the rumors. So I sent an envoy to the south in hopes of finding a Diaforaté who wasn't bound by the gods' limitations."

His face flushed red, his anger growing with the memory.

"They almost refused to help because of your late king's embargo, because of *our* agreement to it. But Kakos was merciful. If I gave them resources and supported their cause when the time came to make their move, they would help Madelyn."

Aya's heart pounded as the king's eyes grew distant.

"There was nothing they could do, in the end. But I made a promise…as did they. They would support my nephew's claim to the throne, his affinity be damned."

His face hardened as his gaze met hers. "I vowed that day to never again be too weak to protect those I love. With your raw power, my nephew will rival the gods. And so will I, when he passes it on to me."

"You're sick," Aya breathed.

"Am I?" Dominic challenged. "Tell me…how far would *you* go, Aya, to save someone you love? To hold on to the future of which you once dreamt?"

He nodded, and Will's screams echoed through the chamber again, the sound enough to bring Aya to her knees if it weren't for her guard's grip. His body thrashed under the chains, the vein in his neck bulging as he hollered.

Dominic would kill him. She had no doubt. He would kill Will and Viviane, and it would be her fault.

Unless she did this. She had no idea if she even could. She hadn't truly mastered her power in the desert. She didn't know if she could survive it—if *Viviane* could survive power inside of her. But if she managed this…

She could buy them time.

They'd need it. They were outnumbered, not just in this room, but in the entire palace.

Aya glanced at Vi, and the woman met her gaze unflinchingly. There was fear there, but not of her. Will must have seen the shift in Aya's face because he sucked in a breath, his teeth bared as he spat out a single command: "No."

Dominic motioned to his guard, who stepped away from Will.

"I have one condition," Aya rasped. She was in no place to bargain, but Dominic rose a brow, his curiosity winning out.

"No," Will snarled again.

"Let him go, and I'll do it." Aya kept her eyes on the king, but she could see Will jerking against his bindings, his protests a steady chorus against the thundering in her chest.

"I could just kill him now."

Aya could feel her pulse hammering in her throat. But she forced her voice to remain in that lethal quiet as she said, "Then you'll never know if my power is safe to take."

Dominic considered her a moment, his green eyes calculating. "He returns to his suite under guard. Should you cooperate, we'll see to it that he goes unharmed."

Aya searched for the lie. It was too easy. But Will had a better chance at survival out of this room.

She dipped her chin.

Dominic nodded to two of the guards near Viviane, and they stalked toward Will, a set of keys in their hands.

"Aya."

She'd never heard terror in his voice, had never seen it on his face the way it was now.

"Don't do this. Please don't do this."

They unchained him, his hands still cuffed as they tugged him toward the door.

"Aya!"

Her name was a desperate command. She reached for him, her fingers brushing his arm as the guard restrained her. He was almost to the door, his gray eyes still locked on her as the guards dragged him into the hall.

The door closed behind him with a heavy and final click, the iron muffling Will's shouts as they took him away.

Aya forced herself to hold Vi's stare as the guards unshackled her, keeping just her hands and feet bound as they tugged her to the middle of the room. Natali stood at Aya's shoulder, the king having commanded them to guide Aya through the ritual.

"It's supposedly like healing," they explained, their voice a whisper. "You pour your power in the same way. But instead of keeping it tethered to you, cut it off. Release a kernel of your essence."

Aya's hands shook as she raised her palms.

"You should go," Viviane said softly, the words directed at Josie. They were the first she'd uttered. But the princess merely pressed her lips together and shook her head.

Even in betrayal, Josie would not leave her.

"Consider this a mercy," Dominic spat at Viviane. "Be thankful, my love, for my niece might spare your life."

Aya could feel Aidon's eyes boring into her, as if he could mark the power rallying under her skin. She let him see every bit of hatred she felt as she met that gaze. He was worse than his uncle, worse than this whole entire godsdamn kingdom that valued nothing but power and riches and gain.

Stay anchored in the light, Lorna had warned.

This…this was not an act of light. It was an affront to her gods.

She should kill Viviane. Should end her swiftly and painlessly and figure out the rest from there. But Vi lifted her chin in subtle defiance.

"I'm not done," was all she said.

It was confirmation enough as Aya dove into that depthless power, clinging to the memory of Josie's subtle shake of her head, of the love that anchored these two even in the midst of a betrayal that could have brought this kingdom to its knees.

She placed her hands on Viviane, her affinity lashing out as it searched for something to anchor to as it flowed into Viviane. A blinding light swirled around them, the guards shouting as it grew and pulsed throughout the room. A scream ripped from Aya, pain flaring in the cavity of her chest as she sawed against that flow of power, as she focused on separating it from herself. Her body strained against the power that bucked wildly in her.

I never want to leave you.

"Almost there," Natali breathed, their voice an anchor against the pleading of her mother in her mind.

Aya was going to die. She knew it as certainly as she knew the shade of the gray eyes she'd never see again. The pain was agonizing, but she focused on the soft encouragement coming from Natali.

You are nothing like those people, Aya.

Another hair-raising scream tore from her chest as the light gave a final searing pulse before it sucked back into Aya. Viviane collapsed, Aya falling with her. There were hands on her, dragging her away from Vi's body, followed by a pinch in her arm as they injected her with something. But Aya was reaching for Viviane, desperately searching for something that showed the woman was unharmed.

Josie broke free of her hold and was on the floor in an instant, pulling Viviane's head into her lap. Her fingers found her neck, searching, searching…

Aya's breath caught as her friend met her gaze, relief flickering through those brown eyes as she nodded.

Natali stared at Viviane for a moment in concentration before they said, "It was successful. Her power is raw. And it is limitless." Those amber eyes found Aya's, and they were colder, far colder, than Aya had ever seen. "Once Aidon has her power, there will be no need to keep the saint, your Majesty. You could even use the human for the prince's siphoning should you wish to dispose of the saint sooner," they said with a nod toward Viviane's limp figure.

Aya doubled over and emptied the contents of her stomach on the floor. The guard holding her swore as she released her, and Aya gasped, forcing air into her lungs as she looked toward the king.

She would kill him. She reached for her power, only to hit a solid wall inside her.

The injection.

No matter. She'd use her bare hands. She lunged for Dominic, but Aidon was there, his arm catching her chest as he forced her back. Aya hit the iron table with a deafening sound, the impact reverberating down her spine and knocking the wind out of her.

"You disgust me," she wheezed as he towered over her. She hated him. Hated how he'd fooled her, hated how she'd let herself be deceived. She opened her mouth to curse him from here to the deepest layers of the hells, but he was already walking away, his steps slow and steady.

A pair of guards seized her, pinning her arms to her side as Dominic strolled forward. His hand was cold as he grasped her chin, forcing her gaze to meet his.

"I *could* keep you, you know," he said, his voice soft with contemplation. "The Visya the Diaforaté take power from typically become shells of themselves. Nearly soulless beings, left to wander in their misery. But with your limitless power, we could take it again. And again. And again. Would you ever start to feel emptiness, Aya? How long could I pull from you until your soul begins to break?"

The king reared back as Aya spit in his face, his grip tightening to the point where she swore her bones would snap.

"And this is exactly why I won't bother to spare your miserable life," he snarled. "I'll use you tomorrow. I admit, there's something poetic about taking something from Gianna after what her father's actions nearly took from me. And with your limitless power, Aidon will fuel our army for me. Perhaps Viviane will be willing to donate to our cause as well. Either way…I won't have to be bothered with the sight of you." He shoved her head back roughly as he released her. "Take her to the dungeons," he muttered to the guards. His green eyes were cold as they found hers. "Consider this a parting gift, my dear."

She couldn't find the meaning in his words. But she didn't have any fight left as the guards grabbed her and shackled her hands before tugging her from the room.

They marched her further underground, the stone passageway dark and damp, their grip on her arms tight enough to bruise.

She didn't care.

Safe. Viviane. Will. They were safe.

Will would find some way to seek retribution. She only hoped he would wait until the time was right. That he wouldn't do anything reckless. That he would find a way to use the time she had bought him to get as far away as possible.

Aya didn't struggle against their hold. She didn't ask questions about where they were taking her. She should feel something, she realized. Fear. Anger. Anguish. But there was a hollowness in her chest, and it echoed through every inch of her as they walked her further into the dungeons, the echo of their footsteps the only sound.

Perhaps this was for the best. If that was what her power was capable of, then she'd rather die than have to wield it again.

Safe. They were safe.

She would face whatever came next. Even death.

The guard turned her roughly around the corner, leading her toward a solid wooden door. There was no window—just a large lock. Her stomach turned as they unshackled her hands and unlocked the door.

It took a moment for her eyes to adjust to the low Incend flame that sat in bowls high on the cell walls. Took a moment for her to take in the rough bed, the small bathroom chamber, and the chains that hung unused on the wall.

Her heart stuttered.

Because there, beneath the chains, his head resting against the wall and eyes closed, sat Will. A broken sound left Aya's lips, and Will's eyes snapped to hers, her name a mere rasp as he scrambled to his feet.

The guards pushed Aya into the room, her legs trembling beneath her as she stumbled into his waiting arms.

Consider this a parting gift, my dear.

He was not safe.

He was as good as dead.

They both were.

74

Aya."

Her name was a prayer to the gods—of thanksgiving, of desperation, of anger—as Will caught her in his arms.

She was alive. She survived the hells they'd put her through, and she was here, in his arms, and…

She was staring at the guards, the color draining from her face. "No," she whispered, and his heart clenched at the brokenness in that one word.

She lunged for them, her movements so fast he hardly had time to tighten his hold on her waist. She fought, her body thrashing as she lunged again and again toward those guards, who merely chuckled as they backed out of the cell.

"No!" The word was torn from her throat, her scream echoing off the walls. Will could hardly hear the lock click as she bucked in his arms like a wild animal, screaming promises of death, promises of pain, promises from every dark place she swore she had inside her.

Her feet left the floor as Will dragged her deeper into the chamber. His body screamed in protest as echoes of pain still lanced through him, but he forced it down as he tugged her against him, his arms a vise grip around her waist.

"Aya." His voice was a soft, calm command. She doubled over, and the sound of her sobs filled the chamber. He bowed with her, his lips pressed against her ear. "Aya." Broken. She was broken. Her hands found his forearms, her nails digging into the muscle as if she could keep him there.

"They can't have you." Her body trembled as the words spilled from her in a rush. "They can't have you."

He wanted to reassure her. To tell her that he would get them out of here—would get *her* out of here, even if it killed him. But he could not lie to her. Not anymore.

She had gambled her life for his. After all he had done. After what he had asked her to do just yesterday. He shuddered as he thought of whose arms he'd tried to push her into, of how wrong he'd been.

Will had spent years trying to convince himself that keeping Aya at a distance was better for her. For both of them. He had spent years locked in an internal battle of what he wanted and what he thought was right.

He had pushed her away. And yet Dominic still knew how to hurt her. He had used Will to do it.

Will buried his head in her neck, letting his lips find her pulse. He breathed her in deep, as if he could take her intoxicating scent with him into whatever came after this life.

The seven hells, most likely, if the gods were judging his actions.

"Aya," he whispered again, the truth he'd kept buried for years rising to his lips. Another broken sound escaped her as she dug her nails into his skin, as if she knew what he was about to confess.

As if she knew what it meant if he did.

"No." She shook her head, tears dripping down her face as she turned in his hold and gripped the front of his shirt. Her eyes searched his as she shook him slightly. "Don't do that," she rasped. "Don't give up."

Will slid a hand to her cheek, a sad smile tugging at his

lips. As if his confession was anything but a surrender to her—to a truth he had kept inside for too long.

She had chosen him. After he'd been a complete and utter fool, she had still chosen him. He dragged his eyes down her dress, the fabric ripped and torn.

She was beautiful. Always so godsdamn beautiful.

"I saw you walk down those stairs…and I wanted you so badly that I thought I might set this whole godsforsaken world on fire just to have you," he breathed as he brushed a tear off her cheek.

She released another muffled sob and tugged him closer, her fingers twisting in the fabric of his shirt. "Read me," was her only response.

Will's hand stilled on her cheek, his eyes darting across her face. "I can't. Ever since the Dawning—"

"I shielded against you." The confession was soft, her face open. "I didn't want you to feel me die, so I closed myself off to you entirely. I didn't realize it until last night." Aya slid her hands to his arms, squeezing once. "Read me."

Will frowned and searched her face again, his thumb stroking her cheek just once. She closed her eyes at the touch, a soft whisper falling from her lips. "Please."

He could not deny her. So he cupped her face more fully, his heart pounding as he closed his eyes and tried to concentrate on the sensations overwhelming him.

Will focused on Aya. So Aya focused on Will.

She took in the stubble on his jaw, the muscles that were clenched tight just moments before loosening as he tried to read her. She memorized the way his hands felt on her cheeks, the roughness of his skin at such odds with the gentle way he held her. Her eyes traced the planes of his face, marking every line, every scar, every inch of him. She let every other feeling disappear as warmth filled her chest, as that surge paced through her blood and threatened to undo her completely.

Galda always told her nothing was more powerful than control. But Aya was beginning to wonder if perhaps the trainer had been wrong.

Because the burning she felt inside—that rush as his hands cupped her face—was strong enough to rattle the veil.

Perhaps even obliterate the Beyond.

Will's lips parted, his breath leaving him in a rush as his eyes flew open to meet hers. The heat in them was enough to burn down the entire world. He stared at her for a moment, his chest heaving, his eyes wet.

Aya slid a hand to the base of his neck, her fingers curling in his hair as she brought his forehead to hers. "No matter how far the fall," she whispered.

It was the only confirmation Will needed before his lips crashed against hers. Aya slid her hands over his arms, his muscles pulling taut under her touch as he pulled her closer, his lips gentle and yet demanding at the same time. A sound escaped her—a mix between a sob and a moan, those emotions still rising, still threatening to overwhelm her entirely.

She let them.

Her back hit the wall as he pinned her to the stone, his hands settling on her hips, his leg pushed between hers. Will groaned as Aya's hands tugged through his hair, and the sound had her doing it again as he trailed kisses and nips down her neck. She let her head fall back against the wall, blinking away the searing in her eyes.

Will's lips left her neck, his eyes meeting hers as his hand cupped her cheek. "Did I hurt you?" he panted. Aya gave a small shake of her head, her lips pressing together.

It was too much—to have him only to lose him. To know that it could've been different. The agony of it was like an unending weight on her chest.

He tucked a piece of hair behind her ear, his breathing

uneven as he pressed a soft kiss to her lips. "It would never have been long enough," he murmured against her skin. His fingers trailed down her neck, his palm coming to rest over that scar on her chest. "But even still. If you think for one second that we're not going to fight our way out tomorrow, then you forget who we are."

They would be outnumbered. And with no power and no weapons, they would surely die. But…

Who we are.

Aya pulled him closer, her body sinking into his as she kissed him once. Twice. A third time.

"Fight with me," he whispered against her lips as he pulled her off the wall. He followed the command with a sweep of his tongue against hers. With his hands tangling in her hair, he slowly moved her across the cell and pinned her to the flimsy mattress.

She didn't know if he was trying to distract her or convince her. It didn't matter. Because her mind went blank as he rolled his hips against hers, drawing a sharp gasp from her as their centers connected.

He trailed blazing kisses down her neck. "Fight with me," he rumbled against her throat.

His hand trailed across her ribs, his fingers tracing the exposed skin there as his lips found hers again. She arched into his touch, urging his hand higher. Will chuckled against her mouth just before he slid under her dress and cupped her breast, swallowing her moan with another searing kiss. His fingers taunted and teased her, pulling another gasp from her as she melted into his touch.

Her hand reached for her belt, but he grabbed her wrist and pinned it to the bed. Aya shifted her hips, desperate for friction against the ache that was building. Will groaned as she pressed against him, a muscle in his jaw twitching as he gritted his teeth. "Behave," he all but growled as he nipped at her neck.

"I want you," Aya breathed, reaching for him with her other hand, only for him to pin that one, too. She gazed up at him, taking in the heat in his stare.

"And you'll have me," he promised, his fingers loosening against the wrist he'd just pinned. "But not here." She opened her mouth to object, but his hand slid down her arms, her sides, her legs…stopping only to gather the fabric of her dress. She arched as he pulled it off her.

He sat back, his eyes dragging slowly down her body. "So fucking beautiful," he rasped. Aya could feel her thighs press together, her body desperate for his touch. But Will merely leaned forward, pressing a kiss over the scar on her chest.

"You'll have me," he repeated, "but not like this." But he moved his mouth to her breast anyway. Aya groaned as he sucked on her and waited until she was writhing beneath him before moving to the other. "Not when you seem so content to let tomorrow happen as it will," he murmured as he kissed his way up her neck. She made a noise of protest and felt him grin against her as his hand slid down her side, her skin pebbling in its wake.

His fingers coasted across her thigh, tracing small circles on her skin.

"But I'm not above giving you some motivation." He tugged on her lip with his teeth, and she arched into him again.

She thought she may have cursed at him. She wasn't entirely sure, because all she could focus on was that damn hand as it skated across her thigh, closer to where she might have been begging him to touch her. Will chuckled again, and then his fingers were on her, and she was gasping, her breath stretching across her lungs as if she couldn't get enough air.

"Fight with me," he murmured against her lips as he lightly circled that small bundle of nerves, wringing a gasp from her. He slid a finger inside her with a groan. "Fuck, Aya."

She arched into his hand, her hips writhing as he curled that finger inside of her. "Fight with me," he murmured again, his gray eyes bright as he watched her squirm. He added another finger, and a moan escaped her.

Every thrust of his fingers was an echo of the word.

Fight.

She rocked into him, her hips echoing his movements. Will groaned, his mouth pressing to hers in another searing kiss.

Fight.

He held her there, right on that ledge, until her body was shaking, and his name was a desperate plea she breathed again and again.

Fight.

"Say it," he ordered softly, his thumb flicking the bundle of nerves between her thighs.

She cried out as her body tensed, her muscles quivering. She was on the brink of coming apart entirely.

"Will," she breathed. "Please."

"Say it," he growled.

Aya tilted her head back against the oncoming wave. "I'll fight with you," she gasped.

Will let out a noise of approval, his thumb flicking her again as his teeth nipped that space on her collarbone. Aya shattered completely.

He continued to stroke her until her trembling ceased and she was limp in his arms. But that fire in her still burned, and she went to sit up, her hand reaching for him again. Will caught her wrist, pressing a kiss to the inside of it.

"Motivation, remember?" His eyes sparked with mischief as he grinned at her.

"You can't be serious." She wanted him. Her whole body trembled with the force of it. But Will tugged her down next to him, tucking her back against his front. The heat in her blood surged as she felt just how badly he wanted her, too.

"Get through tomorrow," he murmured against her ear.

He was serious.

Aya thought she might still hate him after all. Told him as

much, too. But Will just laughed, the sound so out of place with the hells they were about to face. His arm tightened on her, locking her closer.

"Sometimes it amazes me that you're a spy," he whispered. "Because you're a horrible liar, my love."

75

"SONNOIRA, MI COUERA."

Sleep, my heart.

The words were a soft hum in her ear as Aya floated in the place between wakefulness and sleep. She wasn't sure where she was, or what was real and what was the haze of a dream as she floated deeper into a memory.

She was standing outside the Athatis compound, her hip braced against the outer wall of the barn. A deep, melodic voice sang in the Old Language—a somber song, sung only when he thought no one was listening.

And even though it had terrified her at the time, she thought she might be content to listen to him forever.

Without windows in the cell, it was impossible to tell when morning had come. But Aya could feel her body starting to tense as time continued to pass, her mind no longer letting her slip in and out of that restless slumber. That wall still sat between her and her magic, despite the number of times she'd thrown herself at it.

She turned in Will's hold to find him watching her, his

gray eyes calculating. She traced his jaw with her fingers, the stubble pricking her. "I've seen that look before," she said. Will raised a brow, a smirk tugging on his lips as he nipped at her finger. "I always knew you couldn't resist watching me." Aya nudged him as she settled her head on his chest.

His fingers dragged through her hair, his voice vibrating against her cheek as he said, "Our best chance is waiting until we get to wherever they take us. This prison is a labyrinth, and Aidon will have his men at every turn."

The mere thought of the prince made her want to scream. She hadn't given herself time to think about his betrayal—hadn't been able to fully explore the depth of that wound. He had done his job thoroughly. He'd gotten close to her, made her feel understood…hells, even pretended that he too had nerves and hesitation about a match in the name of duty, all to garner her trust.

She'd thought they were friends, and that was the lie that hurt worst of all.

"It would be foolish for Dominic to move us anywhere together," Aya said, frowning as she propped herself up on her elbows. "Even with the tonic in our systems." They'd given Will an injection as well when they'd dragged him to the dungeons.

"Ah, but you and I both know the king loves a spectacle." She stiffened, and Will's fingers paused in her hair, his hand moving to cup the back of her head. "I'm sorry, that was—"

"Tactless," she finished with a small smirk. "Good to know you're your usual self. If you weren't, I'd truly know these were our last moments."

His fingers slid to the base of her neck, his gray eyes devouring her in the flickering firelight. "If these are our last moments, then know I will climb out of the hells and take on the gods if it means finding you again in the Beyond."

Aya blinked away the burning in her eyes as she leaned down and brushed her lips against his. He held her there, his heart hammering in time to the footsteps that had begun echoing down the hall.

"Fight with me," Will whispered one more time.

Aya pressed her forehead against his, letting his woodsmoke and spiced-honey scent settle her raging pulse.

"Always."

76

IT WAS SICK, AYA THOUGHT, THAT DOMINIC HAD CHOSEN THE throne room for their execution.

The king sat on his golden throne, looking the picture of ease. Zuri stood to his left, her jaw tense as she gazed unseeingly at the door, her hands clasped tight.

And Aidon stood on his uncle's right, his hand resting on the pommel of his sword, Peter just behind him.

Enzo was nowhere to be seen.

Perhaps he'd argued with the king one too many times. Or perhaps it was simply that the pecking order had changed; or would, when the prince took Aya's power.

Tala will seek retribution for this. It should have brought Aya some comfort. But war was coming whether they died or not. The king had chosen Kakos. Conflict between their kingdoms was inevitable.

The guards left Aya and Will in the center of the room, anchoring their shackles to the floor before stationing themselves at each exit. Aya glanced at Will, her heart sinking as he met her stare. There was no way out.

"Josie refuses to join us," Aidon said to the king. "I suggest we begin."

Dominic let out a contemplative noise. "Perhaps, like her father, she'll come around."

Aya watched Zuri's face for some sort of reaction, but the woman's gaze was stony as she kept her eyes fixed on the throne room doors.

"Very well." Dominic sighed. "Bring the Saj."

Natali did not struggle, not as the guard dragged them in by their shackles, leading them directly to the king. They dipped their head in acknowledgment to Dominic, and Aya couldn't help the sting of betrayal that ripped through her.

"Start with the Enforcer," Dominic commanded.

But Aidon didn't move. His eyes remained fixed on Aya, none of the usual warmth in his stare. "No," he said slowly. "Let him watch. I can't think of anything more fitting for Gianna's Second, can you?"

Aya's hands curled into fists as her stomach turned.

"By all means." Dominic waved his hand. "Start with the saint."

Slowly, as if he were counting every step, Aidon approached her, Natali trailing behind him. Will wrestled against his chains, the rattling filling the room, the sounds of his threats a distant rumble under the pounding of Aya's pulse in her ears.

"It's as your uncle instructed, Your Highness," Natali was saying. "It will work better if she's indisposed. There's less chance of retaliation. Once she is, push your affinity into her, the same way you pull your flame to the surface. Latch on to her power..."

Aya tried to listen, tried to make sense of what the Saj was saying. But the words were a distant hum as she stared at the prince—her *friend*—his knuckles tightening on the hilt of the knife he drew from the sheath at his side while Natali continued on.

"Do you remember what you said to me about inner wounds?" he murmured, his brown eyes boring into hers.

She blinked, her mind trying to process the question over the screaming inside her.

Fight. Fight. Fight.

In one smooth motion, he rammed the knife into her chest—right over the scar that marked home.

Will was dying. He was on his knees, and his chest was on fire, a mirror to Aya's pain, and he was screaming because his heart hurt more than the phantom wound on his chest that he could not shield against, tonic or no.

He would kill him. He would kill him and this entire godsdamn court.

Aya wheezed as she sagged in Aidon's hold, her breath coming in wet rasps. Blood soaked her chest, the black fabric of her dress unable to hide the rich crimson as it spilled from her. He was still screaming, still straining against those godsforsaken chains.

He had felt this before—the cold that crept across him now.

Aya was dying, and the pain of it would kill him before Aidon's knife ever could.

Aya hardly registered Aidon's arm around her as she panted for breath. The blood was leaking from her at an alarming rate, despite the knife embedded in her chest.

Dominic was shouting something. Will was screaming. Natali was murmuring instructions under their breath. And beneath it all was Aidon's smooth baritone, repeating something she couldn't quite make out over the agony coursing through her.

And even with that knife there...

A gaping outside wound.

It's the inside wounds I struggle with more.

Aidon's image blurred before her as she tried to focus.

It's the inside wounds I struggle with more.

Her heart was slowing—she could feel her pulse weakening as she turned inward and faced that essence she'd buried deep, now locked beneath that block on her power.

It's the inside wounds I struggle with more.

"You're being reckless," Dominic thundered from his throne. "Do it now, Aidon!"

Aya needed more time. She met the king's gaze, her breath rattling as she tried to bring his face into focus. "Gianna was willing to give you me," she wheezed. "You could have kept me prisoner."

"Your queen would never part with such an asset," Dominic bit out. "When I pressed you at Pysar and you had no idea of her plans, I suspected she had no true intentions of such a marriage. I know your queen and the mask she presents. Just as I know she would offer you up and reclaim you as soon as we agreed to join you in war." His hands flexed on the arms of his throne. "Allies, indeed." He spat the words as if they were poison. "And even if she stayed true to her word...why keep a saint when I can become a god?"

Aya's lungs seared as she took another breath, throwing herself against that wall inside of her. Her power trickled through, but it was too small to close the wound.

"Finish it, Aidon," Dominic commanded as he pushed off his throne, his long stride gobbling up the space between them. But Aidon didn't move. His gaze stayed fixed on her face, his eyes tracking her every breath.

Aya reached down and ripped the knife from her chest.

Will's screams reverberated throughout the throne room, mixing with Aidon's and the king's as he roared his fury. Aya fell to the floor, and banged against the wall inside her, begging as blood seeped out of her chest. She had mere seconds.

She slumped to the side, her eyes finding Will's as her head rested against the cool marble floor. He was on his knees, his body folded over on itself as he bellowed her name.

Fight, he had told her.

Aya sobbed as she pushed and pushed against that wall. As she focused on closing that hole in her chest.

Fight.

Aidon was yelling, his arm wrapped around his uncle, hauling him away from her, but Aya kept her eyes trained on Will. On the way his lips moved as he begged her to stay.

Fight.

She had made him a promise.

And it was that promise she clung to as she threw herself against the wall one last time.

A resounding crack echoed through the throne room as her shackles snapped.

And Aya exploded into light.

Aidon dove to the floor as light pulsed through the room, so bright that he could *feel* the heat of it crackling across the space. There was a shout and a thud, and through his searing eyes, he saw Will slump to the floor, Peter's knife embedded in his stomach. Aidon hadn't even seen his friend move. But Peter held Aidon's gaze, a grim look on his face as he tugged the blade out of Will's gut with a vicious twist.

Aya's scream of agony was unlike anything Aidon had ever heard. Her very skin was alight with power as she flung out a hand toward Peter. He dropped like a stone. The guards advanced, but she sent another pulse of light, and they crumpled like puppets whose strings had been cut.

Aya ran to Will, his name falling from her lips as she dropped to her knees, her hands flaring with healing light as she begged him to stay, stay, stay. She had eyes for nothing else—would let nothing distract her from trying to save him. Aidon knew it as his uncle advanced on her, the knife that was still coated with her blood raised, ready to plunge it into her back as she bowed over Will.

Aidon lunged toward his uncle, a flash of silver catching his eye. He looked up just in time to catch the knife his mother flung to him.

And to plunge it into Dominic's heart.

77

AYA REGISTERED THE SOUND OF A BLADE CUTTING THROUGH flesh. The gurgling of death. There was a thud behind her, and she turned in time to see the king fall, the knife Aidon had embedded in his chest flashing in the sunlight streaming into the throne room.

She expected someone to scream. But there was nothing but silence as Dominic took his last breath. Aidon's face was cold and distant as he stared down at him. "I hope you rot in hells," he breathed.

Aya opened her mouth to say something—but Aidon's eyes flicked to Will, and she was pulled back to his shuddering breath.

Light flared in her palms again as she laid her shaking hands over his wound. "It's going to be fine. You're going to be fine." His eyes closed as Aidon kneeled next to her, his hands pressing against where the blood continued to soak Will's shirt.

"Open your eyes," Aya ordered, her voice cracking. He didn't. Aya tugged on that healing light with every ounce of strength she had. "Fight with me," she said through her teeth. Will's breath was thinning. Aidon was saying something, but she couldn't hear him over the roaring in her ears. She dove into her power with reckless abandon, dragging up every last drop she could find, not caring if she emptied herself too quickly, if it destroyed her entirely. "Fight with me." Her head pressed against his as she kept that healing light pouring into him, as Aidon kept his hands pressed to the wound as it knitted together too slowly.

So much blood. He'd lost so much blood.

"Please," she begged.

The wound finally closed, but Will did not open his eyes.

Aya pressed her lips together, choking on a sob as Aidon sat back on his heels to give them space. To give her time to say goodbye as Will's chest stilled.

But he'd made her a promise.

No matter how far the fall.

"Don't you dare leave me," she spat as she sent a pulse of healing power into him.

"I will never forgive you."

Another.

"I will drag you back from the hells myself and kill you for it."

Another.

"I mean it."

Will gasped at that last pulse of power, his eyes fluttering open as he sucked in air. His breaths deepened as he stared at her, his gray eyes focusing on her face.

"With threats like that, I wouldn't dream of it," he wheezed, his voice raspy and weak and nothing like him at all. It was still the most beautiful sound she'd ever heard. Aya pressed her lips together, a sob racking her as she leaned her head against his chest.

Will's fingers tangled in her hair as he slowly sat up, keeping her head against him. She felt him tense, and she followed his gaze to where the king lay. Aidon was still kneeling beside her, his eyes glazed as he stared at his uncle, at the blood that pooled beneath him.

Zuri's footsteps were steady as she walked to her son's side. Carefully, she removed his jacket, which she laid over Dominic's body. Aidon continued to stare at the figure, his hands clenched at his sides.

"Aidon," Aya said, her voice gentle as she reached for him. He jumped as she touched his arm.

"You knew," he rasped. It took her a moment to realize he wasn't addressing her; that his eyes were wet as he looked up at Zuri. "You knew."

78

YOU KNEW, AND YOU DID NOTHING.

They were the words Josie had screamed at Aidon when he snuck into her room and faced her rage. He had taken every blow she'd given him until he could finally explain. Then he'd left her to deal with the guards while he smuggled Viviane into a carriage. They'd be in the mountains by now.

It was the first step in his repentance.

You knew, and you did nothing.

No. It was worse, so much worse than that.

He had known…but he hadn't known enough, hadn't solved this puzzle fast enough to ensure no harm came to any of them.

Aidon stood, his hands trembling as he met his mother's gaze.

"You knew," he breathed. "You knew he sought out a Diaforaté to save Madelyn."

Zuri's brown eyes were grave as she took a step toward him and placed a hand on his arm. "I did," she said quietly.

"And so you condoned his actions," Aidon hissed as he stepped out of her grasp. Too much. This was too much.

He had to get out of this room. Perhaps even out of this godsdamn city.

His mother was not swayed. "I did not know of the bargain he made. When she died, he led us to believe he was enraged with Kakos; that they were untrustworthy, and the rumors of their dark-affinity work were lies. He blamed them for her death."

"But you suspected, didn't you?"

Her gaze softened. "I have long feared what your uncle was capable of. But yes. When the tradesmen were caught in Tala, your father and I began to suspect perhaps his loyalties were not as he said they were." His mother cupped his chin, forcing him to meet her gaze. "And I waited until we had a chance to act."

Because Dominic made an agreement with the most dangerous kingdom in the realm—one she did not expect them to escape. Not without allies.

She had been lying in wait.

It had been his mother who had taught him the value of patience, after all. His mother who had emphasized that the power behind a blade was not nearly as important as the timing of the strike.

A move he understood intimately.

Five weeks, he'd known Aya'd been stealing the tonic. In small amounts, hardly noticeable with the size of their stores, but he'd known exactly what he was looking for. He'd let the knowledge slip on purpose to see what Aya would do—to see if his uncle was right in his doubts of Tala.

Dominic had accused them of wanting to further their own interests; perhaps even framing the tradesmen to gain leverage in their trade agreements. And while Aidon couldn't prove it, he *did* have a way to see if they were truly here to deepen Tala's pockets.

A gamble, he could admit, but Aya would never have suspected what the tonic was truly for; that Aidon had been taking it every day since his power had been discovered.

He told her Dominic had been hoping to leverage it in trade. But even then, Aya and Will hadn't *done* anything with it. With their missives to Tala being watched, he would've known if they'd sent a sample to their kingdom so that they might create their own, or even share word of it. He'd had their rooms searched, and there had been no sign of it there.

And so he waited…

Because something was nagging at him, that familiar battle sense urging him to pay attention, to *look* for the threats he could not see.

Helene's kidnapping. The attack on Aya and Will. The Bellare's lack of revelations during questioning. Viviane's disappearance. Avis's rage. The implication of a match between him and Aya that his uncle had never shared with him. Each was a piece he couldn't quite grasp as he circled closer and closer to some truth, some *thing* he was missing but couldn't put his finger on.

But his uncle…his uncle had been the common thread in it all.

Aidon ran a hand over his face, his pulse thudding in his throat as he looked at Aya and Will. "I told him of your power to garner his trust, to get in on whatever he was planning so I could uncover who was involved and put an end to it. I had no idea he'd already suspected you, or that *this* was what he intended."

He hadn't realized his uncle was monitoring the tonic so closely—or that he'd suspected a saint in their midst. And he'd given Dominic the confirmation he'd been waiting for to make his next move.

Aidon had set this very plan in motion and endangered them all.

"Dominic told me he suspected your power…and that he'd uncovered the Bellare's plan to reveal my power to the kingdom, to render me ineligible to rule." He fixed his gaze on Will. "He said you were a part of it, and that, should you return, you'd need to be questioned. I agreed, thinking I'd be the one to do it, and that once you were back, we could figure out a plan."

He had shown his uncle exactly what he wanted to see:

Duty.

Responsibility.

Loyalty.

"But then you returned, and he brought me to the dungeons, where he revealed Viviane and my father." *A necessity*, Dominic had explained to Aidon when he asked after his father as they strolled through the dungeons. *He won't agree with my methods.* His mother remained free, and Aidon knew it was to make sure he'd behave.

"I needed time," he rasped. He jerked his chin toward the Enforcer. "I slipped you the tonic, hoping it was just to subdue you for a short time for questioning. I let him believe I was on board with it so he'd keep me involved. So that when I saw an opportunity, I could get us out. All of us."

Duty, to his kingdom.

Responsibility, to his family.

Loyalty, to his friends.

It had driven him to walk the razor's edge, close enough to learn each step while his uncle remained two ahead.

Aidon shook his head as he moved his gaze to Aya. "I had no idea that he was going to use Vi like that, or that he wanted to steal your power, until we were in that room. I thought he was bringing Vi in for questioning. I didn't even know you'd both be there."

It had been nearly impossible to keep a straight face, to keep playing this part he needed to play.

Patience, Aidon.

That patience had nearly been the death of them all. But then they had been outnumbered. His friends were in danger, as was his family. He would have done anything to protect them, and he suspected Dominic knew it.

"Where is Josie, Aidon?" There was an undercurrent of worry to his mother's voice as she glanced at the throne room doors.

"Gone," he muttered. "I got her and Viviane out of the palace. I would've gotten Father out, too, but…"

"But he came to see me last night in the prison," Natali said for him. "He was looking for a way to counteract the effects of the tonic so you could access your power. I told him that it would either need to pass through the system, or a healer would need to use their affinity to remove it."

Time. Aidon hadn't had time, and he didn't know which healers he could trust.

Our affinities are not boundless, Natali had said. *We have limits.*

He had them—he certainly knew that. But Aya…

Aidon gazed at the rough red mark marring her chest, the blood coating her skin. His voice lodged in his throat. "I wondered if your raw power might work differently," Aidon finally managed.

Aya turned her gaze to Natali, and the Saj shrugged. "I suggested motivation," they said. "Lots of it. There's a balance to power. It's interesting, isn't it? How we try so desperately to fix what's on the outside and leave the inside unattended. And yet sometimes, one does improve the other."

"'It's the inside wounds I struggle with more,'" Aya whispered.

He'd remembered it, too. And so Aidon had driven that blade into Aya's chest—right over the scar she'd returned from the desert with—and gave her a single pleading command.

Heal.

Heal, so they could fight this fight together.

Heal, so they could make it out alive.

Aya frowned at the Saj. "You told the king to kill me."

Natali clasped their hands in front of them. "I did. Because your power is limitless only in *you*. I lied when I sensed Viviane, knowing that if the source was eliminated, the king could not complete his work for Kakos. Besides," they added wryly, "I was hopeful the prince would have a change of heart."

Will swore quietly. "That's quite a fucking risk you both took." The words lacked any real heat, and Aidon wondered if it was the Enforcer's reluctant thank-you. Or at the very least an acknowledgment of all that had been done.

"You have no idea." Careful…he'd tried to be so damn careful as he walked that line with Dominic, as he stayed close enough to let it unfold to the point where he could stop it. And even still, it had happened too fast. His uncle had hidden too much.

His mother's hand was warm as it rested against his cheek. Perhaps she saw the agony he was trying to bury. "You did all you could to keep us safe. And we are. Now the rightful ruler can ascend the throne," she said softly.

Aidon didn't know what to make of that. What to make of any of it. But his uncle was dead. The *king* was dead. Which meant…

He thought he might be ill. His eyes flicked to the dead guards. His soldiers. None of whom were loyal to him. Would any of the rest be?

A squeeze on his arm drew him out of his thoughts. His mother's gaze was level, steady. "We will figure this all out together. But first…" She glanced at Aya, who was helping Will stand, her power having broken through his shackles. "We need a plan," she murmured.

A plan. Because his uncle was dead, and though they were the only witnesses to it, this news would spread. And who would believe them when they shared the truth? Who could Aidon truly count on, besides the people in this room?

The Saj who had aided him, despite the sure death awaiting them should he fail.

The allies who had become friends.

The mother who had helped save them all.

And Josie, of course. His sister who loved fiercely, even in betrayal.

"They won't accept this," Aidon murmured, his brow furrowed as he stepped toward the throne. The sun shone through the windows behind it, the brightness of the day so at odds with what had unfolded. "Our people weren't here to witness his treason, and despite the rumors of war brewing, he's never given them reason to take it seriously."

"Tell them." Aya's voice was a mere rasp behind him. He glanced over his shoulder to see her brow furrowed, that look of determination that was uniquely hers settling on her features.

Aidon blinked at her. "You can't mean…"

"Tell them."

Aidon faced his friend fully. "If Tala confesses to meddling in my uncle's treason, my armies will fight this alliance," he said. He wasn't sure why he was arguing. Wasn't this exactly what he had asked of Aya? But… "This is bigger than telling my uncle, or even my troops. This is the kingdom, the realm. We would lose the advantage in the coming war."

Aya shook her head, ever stubborn as she stepped toward him. "We need you on the throne, and we need your armies and your kingdom following you. If this is the proof you think they need, then tell them."

He was surprised to see the calmness on her face as she shrugged. "Besides, Tala wasn't the one meddling," she said simply. "I was."

Aidon glanced to Will to find his eyes trained on Aya with a burning intensity. Perhaps he could see it, too—the subtle shift that was starting to happen in her, that was unfolding before their very eyes.

"Tell them the Second Saint is real." Aya's eyes moved to Zuri, who was watching her intently. Then back to Aidon, the blue in them like ice. "Tell them the Second War is here, and it's time they chose a side. They either stand against the Decachiré, or they stand against the gods."

Natali stepped up to Aidon's shoulder, their amber eyes fixed on Aya. "And so the Second Saint rises."

79

Aya didn't breathe easily until they'd been at open sea for three days, until the only thing they'd seen for miles was the dark blue of the Anath's waters.

Zuri had secured them immediate passage from Rinnia. She'd written a letter herself to Gianna to alert her of their return, as well as Trahir's commitment to upholding their alliance. She remained advisor to the king—the new king—and would be taking on correspondence with other kingdoms.

Aya was worried about Aidon—about the weight of his uncle's actions and his death at Aidon's hands. And while Aidon assured her that he was fine…

She knew how anger and guilt, even when it was undeserved, could fester.

Will took up a spot next to her, his arms folded on the balustrade as he stared out at the sea. Quiet. Calculating.

"You're worried," Aya remarked, her eyes passing over him. Zuri had brought a healer to them before they left. And though they had claimed Will would make a full recovery, she still found herself watching him carefully, as if she could monitor every breath he took, every wince that he thought he could hide from her.

"I don't like walking into a situation with so many unknowns," he conceded.

Because Gianna...she was still an unknown. She desperately wanted Aya to use her power, but *why* and *how*? Aya wanted to believe Gianna would not ask her to tear down the veil, but she couldn't be sure. That doubt had been planted by none other than Gianna herself.

"I don't trust her either," Aya murmured.

Will frowned at the water. "Lately I've been wondering if it's foolish to trust anyone." His hands tightened on the rail. "I know you forgive Aidon for what he did, but you'll forgive me if I cannot."

She knew his anger would pass. She knew in time he would understand, as she did. They both understood what it was to serve someone you didn't truly know, and to take desperate actions to save those you loved.

"He saved our lives," Aya said quietly.

He cut her a glance. "It was too great a gamble. He could've killed us all."

She rolled her eyes. "I'm well aware, thank you."

Will turned to face her, his arms folding across his chest as he smirked. "I *am* curious, though. After such an impressive display of healing..." He held out his left hand, his palm up, the scar of his Dyminara oath exposed. "Do you think you could heal this?"

Aya blinked at him. Healers couldn't heal blood oaths. She said as much, and Will's lips twisted into a devilish grin.

"Well, thank the gods no one would call *you* a healer. You hardly have the disposition." He dodged her punch, his hand latching onto her wrist and tugging her closer. "Humor me," he murmured, his breath brushing across her lips. "Unless you think your delicate healing powers aren't up to the task. I know how you struggle with *patience*." A wicked light gleamed in his eyes, as if he, too, were remembering how he'd had her begging for release the night before. They still hadn't crossed that final line together. Not with the terrors that pulled them both from sleep.

Besides, Will had insisted he wanted to be *fully* healed lest he taint the "life-changing" experience.

She'd almost stabbed him again.

But it didn't mean they hadn't spent the last two nights at sea getting to know each other's bodies in the ways that they could.

Aya shut down the memory of his lips trailing down her chest, her stomach, *lower*, and snatched his hand, muttering something about payback as her cheeks heated.

"Oh, I look forward to it," Will purred.

"Let me focus," she snapped, pressing her lips together to fight off her smile. She ran her thumb over the scar, tracing the thin ridge slowly. She paused, biting her lip as she looked up at him. "You're sure?"

Will simply squeezed her hand. "Undoubtedly."

She didn't ask him why. He had given her space to sort through her own mess, and she would give him the same. Especially when it came to Gianna. He owed her no explanations.

Aya closed her eyes and focused on the warmth of his skin beneath her fingertips. She reached for that healing light, coaxing it until it grew, until she could feel the light flaring from her as she focused on that scar—on removing the pain of that vow.

The vow he had made for her.

To protect her.

To be near her.

Even if he had to make her hate him in the process.

She'd fallen for him anyway. For his cunning and his loyalty. For his confidence and his courage. For his willingness to *feel*. To live. To be. He had chipped away at the ice she had kept wrapped around herself for years. Had blown heat into her very soul.

Aya opened her eyes, her thumb tracing the smooth skin of his palm.

Will gave her hand a gentle squeeze, his gray eyes bright as he pulled her toward him. "Thank you," he murmured, his lips coasting across her jaw. His hands moved to her hips, and Aya bit back a small sound as he kissed the space beneath her ear. "I have one more request." His voice was low, and it heated her blood as he nipped at her skin.

"Someone's feeling greedy," Aya breathed. She felt Will grin against her neck, his hand trailing from her hip to her leg.

"When it comes to you? Always." Air rushed in as he stepped back, the knife she'd strapped to her thigh now in his hand. She blinked. She hadn't even felt him take it.

"Ass," Aya muttered.

Will flipped the blade, handing the handle to Aya. "Let me take a new oath."

She glanced to the outstretched blade, then back to his face, her eyes widening as his request sank in. She shook her head as she took a step back.

"I can't ask that of you—"

"You didn't." He dropped the blade and reached forward to tuck a strand of hair behind her ear, his thumb skimming her cheek as he cocked his head. Considering her. Reading her. "Of course, if *you* have objections—"

"I don't," Aya interrupted. But he had hated the oath to the Dyminara.

Perhaps because it hadn't been to the Dyminara. Not really. It had been to Gianna.

"I don't have objections," Aya said. "I just have a condition."

"A condition," he repeated.

"Yes."

"By all means," Will drawled, his arms folding across his chest. "Negotiate away, Aya love." She slid her hands up his arms, letting them meet at the base of his neck as she stepped closer.

"Together," was all she said. Will's eyes flared as he registered her meaning. He scanned her face, as if searching for the proof there.

"You're sure?" he breathed.

Her mouth twisted into a grin. "Undoubtedly."

She stepped back and held out her hand for the blade. Will handed it over and extended his left hand, his other curling around her waist. He didn't flinch as she ran the knife across his palm. He merely kept his gaze locked on her, his gray eyes blazing as he said, "By my blood and before the gods, I pledge my life to protect you. To fight beside you." The corner of his lips tipped into a soft smile as he added, "No matter how far the fall."

He leaned in, his lips warm against her skin as he kissed away the tears that had slipped down her cheeks. She handed him the knife, and he ran his thumb over the bare skin of her palm, giving her one final chance—one last out. She answered by capturing his lips with her own, the sting of the blade hardly noticeable beneath the tempest of desire surging inside her as his lips moved against hers. She managed to pull away just far enough to press her forehead to his, her voice steady as she made her oath.

"By my blood and before the gods, I pledge my life to protect you. To fight beside you. No matter how far the fall."

The green flecks in Will's eyes sparkled like stars as he brushed his lips against hers once. Twice. And then he was deepening the kiss as he moved their hands over the rail, letting drops of their blood fall into the ocean below.

The final seal of the oath. Bound by nature itself.

There was so much left to sort through. Gianna. The veil. The pending war.

But Aya felt anchored as she stared into the water, Will a warm and steady presence at her back.

Together. They would get through it together.

No matter how far the fall.

Epilogue

THE PAIN HAD RETURNED. OR PERHAPS IT HAD NEVER LEFT. She hardly remembered which moments were real and which were part of her nightmares, so it was difficult to tell where the fake pain started and the real began.

Perhaps it was all one big nightmare.

Perhaps it was all real pain.

She screamed as it lashed through her, her throat raw. When was the last time they'd given her water?

She'd long since stopped trying to keep track of time. The moments all blurred together anyway.

She was going to die here. She was sure of it.

The pain disappeared, and she was left gasping.

"This doesn't have to go this way," the voice chided. She hated that voice. Its softness had once been warm and kind. Now it just meant more pain, more visions, more terror.

She's after her, and I am trying to help her.

She clung to that memory. The one where he had held back as much as he could; where he cried with her as they both realized they would do unspeakable things to protect those they loved.

She was safe. They were safe.

It was the only reason this woman could not break her.

They had gotten her out. She was safe. They were safe.

Soft footsteps scuffed against the stone floor, almost in time with the *drip, drip, drip* of the blood from her nose as it splattered onto the ground. The footsteps stopped just before where she lay, her body broken.

She dragged her eyes across the swirling stone pattern to those silver shoes, up that white dress, to the face that was all softness and light and wicked deception. Her light brown hair glinted in the soft firelight that lit the cell. She crouched down, her brown eyes solemn as they met her own.

"Would you really prefer to wait for my Enforcer?"

A laugh ripped from her, the sound merely a wheeze as her lungs clenched. Blood splattered onto those silver shoes, but she didn't stop—*couldn't* stop the hysteria that rose from that threat.

A perfectly arched brow rose. "Is something funny?"

"You think he's yours," she rasped.

"You doubt my Second's loyalty?"

Another bout of hysteria gripped her, and it took her several moments to calm herself. Perhaps she was going insane.

She was going to die here. She was sure of it.

"Only to you," she finally was able to say.

I am trying to help her.

She was safe. They were safe.

"Thank you, Tova," that calm voice purred. Tova sucked in a breath as Gianna stood, her brow furrowed. "You have been most helpful today. Let's continue our progress tomorrow, shall we? Perhaps we'll write a letter."

Tova blinked, her thoughts muddled. Had she been helpful? She hadn't given her anything. Had she?

Tova curled in on herself as Gianna left the cell, her words circling like vultures in her mind.

You have been most helpful today.

She was safe. They were safe. Tova and Will had ensured

it. He would not let anything happen to Aya. And he would be with her.

She was safe. They were safe.

She was safe. They were safe.

She was safe. They were safe.

She wondered if she might break anyway.

COMING SOON

The exciting second book in the Curse of Saints trilogy!

The Curse of Sins

Bonus features:

A scene from Will's POV

Character art of Aya and Will

Character profiles

A glossary of key terms

1

WILL WAS WELL-ACCUSTOMED TO SCREAMS OF AGONY. After three years in Gianna's Tría, he knew exactly how to pull them out of those he questioned, so intimately familiar with the sound that he could match the variance of pitch to the depth of their pain.

He'd thought he'd heard the worst of such sounds in those godforsaken dungeons. But nothing had prepared him for the sickening crack as Aya's head hit the cobbles, the sound cutting through the freezing winter air like a blade, or the scream that wrenched itself from somewhere deep in his chest, her name searing through his throat as he crashed to his knees.

He had no time to prepare as pain, vicious pain, lanced through his head, his chest, his ribs, sharp enough to blur his vision.

He should've braced for this, should have known it would overwhelm him entirely, but he'd been desperate to get to her, he still *needed* to get to her—

Will grunted, his head spinning as the pain vanished so quickly, it sent him careening forward, his palms smacking the icy ground he knelt upon. He forced his vision to focus, his gaze cutting to Aya as he sucked in a breath through gritted teeth.

Brien had stopped his pursuit, his paws still on Aya's chest, his head cocked as he looked down at her limp form.

No.

Will threw out his affinity, not to manipulate, but to feel—because he should be able to feel her, even unconscious he should be able to feel *something*, some part of her that would prove…

Will cut off the thought as her name ripped from him again, and again, his affinity searching, swirling, tearing through the space between them.

It found nothing.

The essence of her, cold and smooth like midnight, which had brushed against his affinity for years, was gone, and in its place was a vicious emptiness that left him gasping for air.

No.

There was only one thing emptiness like this could mean.

Aya was dead.

No.

The word was a resounding echo in his head, a plea to the gods that hadn't bothered to listen to him for years.

She was dead. That stubborn, lethal, godsdamn *beautiful* light that had wrecked his life was gone, and the pain of it would destroy him.

"No!"

It took him a moment to realize he was screaming the word over and over, her named mixed into his denials, his throat burning in the bitter, cold air as he unleashed his fury.

Brien and the rest of the Athatis scattered—all except one. Aya's runt shook his head rapidly before he approached his bonded, his gray body rigid as he peered down at her. In the moonlight, Will could just make out the blood that framed her head like a gruesome sort of halo.

Tyr nudged Aya's cheek, a low whine escaping the wolf.

Will's breath was ragged as he pushed himself up, his legs trembling beneath him, his body unsure of how to move without the feeling of her woven throughout it.

He'd never realized how constant her presence was; how much it sank into his very being, even when she shielded against him.

As if there had been a single moment he hadn't been aware of the very breaths she took.

But now…

Pointless. It was pointless to breathe when she wasn't, pointless to exist when she didn't.

I won't survive this.

The thought was wild and desperate and coated in an agony worse than any pain he'd felt in any interrogation.

Tyr whined again, his snout butting her shoulder this time, but still Aya remained lifeless. The wolf lowered himself to the ground with no regard for the blood he lay in.

Will wiped at the wetness on his cheeks. There was such silence in his head. Perhaps the whole godsdamn world had gone quiet at this…this *failure* of his.

Slowly, as if his body moved on its own accord, he reached down and picked up his discarded knife, his eyes fixed on the wolf that lay helplessly by his bonded's side.

Aya would demand mercy.

It's what she wanted, wasn't it? It was the very fucking reason they'd found themselves here—because she'd wanted Tyr to live.

She'd wanted me to live.

He shut out the thought immediately, unable to let his mind focus on what she had done to save him. It didn't fucking matter now anyways.

He tightened his grip on the handle of the blade.

Aya… Aya would hate him for taking her bonded from this world.

But she wasn't here to beg Will to spare Tyr.

And for that…Will was going to kill him.

Will kept his eyes on Tyr's gray fur as he stalked forward. He couldn't stand to look too closely at Aya, to see her broken and bloody and *gone*. Tyr met his gaze, but the wolf didn't bother to move into a defensive position. He merely whined again, and the noise was the kindling to the fire of Will's rage.

He raised the blade, his fingers tightening on the smooth metal of the handle as Tyr laid his head on her chest and—

Will froze, his arm still raised as he stared down at Tyr. Everything about the wolf was still. Except his head.

It moved with the small rise and fall of Aya's chest.

Will let out a strangled noise as he dropped to his knees, the knife clattering to the cobbles. He shouldered Tyr out of the way, and for once in his life, the stubborn runt listened. Aya's skin was warm as Will pressed his fingers to her neck, another broken sound wrenching from him as he found a pulse.

The rush of relief that coursed through him was enough to make him dizzy. Will bowed over, his forehead pressing against Aya's as his other hand found her cheek.

"Thank Mora," he breathed, voice trembling. "You're alive."

He whispered the words again. Again. Again.

Perhaps if he said it enough, his shaking limbs would steady. Perhaps the agony that had ripped his heart in two would ease.

Will focused on the warmth of Aya's skin beneath his fingers, the soft curve of her jaw against the palm of his hand.

Just feeling her was enough to—

Will paused, his breath coming in uneven pants as he raised his head, his eyes scanning her face. Her dark brown hair was fanned out around her head, the strands thick with blood.

He still couldn't feel her.

His affinity had reached for her instinctively, no better

than a moth to a flame. And it still met that nothingness that had his gut clenching. He'd never *not* been able to feel the essence of someone. Even when a person shielded, a Sensainos could sense *them* beneath it. Everyone, from humans to Visya, had an essence woven in them. Some believed it was their very being—their life force.

And Will could sense Aya's better than anyone's.

"Aya." Her name was a command as he moved his hand from her neck to her shoulder and squeezed gently. "Wake up, Aya." Tyr keened, and Will grit his teeth at the sound. "I know something's wrong," he spat at the wolf, his temper flaring with the panic coursing through him.

Calm. He needed to be calm. He forced a breath through his nose as he gazed at Aya again. He hadn't imagined the power he felt rippling around him when Brien had been seconds away from tearing out his throat. Aya had persuaded them; Will was sure of it.

She had committed an act the gods deemed forbidden.

Was that why he couldn't feel her?

It didn't make sense. Will knew just how capable Aya was of the impossible—even when she'd sent him careening off that wall, he'd still been able to feel her afterwards.

His thumb swiped her cheek once, just one moment of tenderness, one moment to show what he never could when she was awake, and then he was moving.

He tugged off his shirt and gently lifted her head, tying the garment into a makeshift bandage and sending a silent plea to Mora that it would be enough to staunch the bleeding when he moved her.

He'd need someone discreet—someone who could heal her without asking too many questions.

Will slid a hand beneath Aya's shoulders, readying to lift her, but Tyr moved suddenly, a snarl loosening from deep in his chest as he whipped around toward the alleyway they'd run down. Will followed his gaze.

Someone was running toward them, their pace desperate. The wolf's hackles fell moments before Will recognized Tova's moon-white hair.

"What the hells happened?" Tova demanded, her hazel eyes blazing with that internal fire as she skidded to a halt beside them. The color drained from her face as she took in Aya. "Hepha help me," she breathed. "Is she…is she…"

"No."

Aya would stay on this side of life, even if Will had to hold her here himself.

She would not leave them. He wouldn't allow it.

"What happened?" Tova pressed again as Will lifted Aya gently, an arm beneath her knees, the other banding around her shoulders. His fingers found her pulse again as he held her head against his chest, and every beat cleared his mind further until the outlines of a plan began to take shape.

"Not now," Will muttered, his brow furrowed as he looked toward the route that would take them to the Quarter.

It would be the longer option, especially with the pace he'd have to keep to not jostle her too mch. But she would be safest with Suja, and he knew the healer was likely awaiting any injured Dyminara from tonight's attack.

He tried his affinity again, sending a wave of peace over Aya, but it met nothing. Yet he could sense Tova when he tried; could even feel the panic she didn't bother to hide behind that iron-locked shield so many Visya kept in place without a second thought.

Godsdamit.

It wasn't his affinity, then.

Will cut a glance to Tova. "Get Suja. Bring her straight to Aya's room." He had barely made it a step before the general was in his path.

"She looks a breath away from death," she snarled. "Bring her to nearest healing quarters."

"Suja is the best healer—"

"She won't survive the trip!"

Will's anger flared as he wrestled against the sensations threatening to overwhelm him. He felt rubbed raw, his terror at thinking Aya dead shattering that careful control he often kept over his emotions.

"Get out of my way," he ordered, his voice soft and dangerous. Tova lifted her chin, but Will took a step forward. "The longer you wait, the longer she suffers."

Tova shot him a murderous glare, but remained blessedly silent. She spun on her heel and took off toward the Quarter without a backwards glance.

Will could feel Tyr's gaze fixed on him as he started off with Aya. "Go back to Akeeta," he called over his shoulder. His bonded would look after Tyr. Will pushed away the guilt that began to curl in his stomach as he thought of what he'd almost done.

He didn't have time for such regret. Not when Aya's breath was so shallow. Not when he was walking into the heart of the lion's den after she'd just committed an impossible act.

One step at a time, he reminded himself.

First, he'd ensure she was healed. Perhaps Suja's findings would help him understand why he couldn't feel her anymore. He trusted the healer's discretion, but he certainly wasn't going to provide that information himself.

Will glanced down at the woman in his arms. He could already make out the blood darkening his black shirt.

"Why didn't you just end them," he whispered.

It was a foolish question, he realized as he quickened his pace, his arms holding her tighter against his chest.

He knew why.

Despite the poison that dripped from her words, despite the steel in her gaze and the ice in her disposition, there was nothing Aya wouldn't do to protect those she loved.

Besides…how many unforgivable things had Will done to achieve the same?

Too many.

And yet he knew as he started up the path with Aya in his arms that this was only the beginning.

Yes, he'd done unforgiveable things. And he would do so much more.

Aya

Character Profiles

Will

Pronunciation: *Will*
Alias: The Dark Prince of Dunmeaden
Role: The Queen of Tala's Second-in-Command, overseer of the Tala Merchant Council, Enforcer
Description: Tall, firm build with black hair and pale skin tinged with olive. Gray eyes with green flecks and a mouth that favors a smirk.
Zodiac Sign: Scorpio
Scent: Woodsmoke and spiced-honey
Favorite Color: Black
Favorite Food: Whisky (swears it counts)
Favorite Leisurely Activity: Reading (prefers historical fiction) and annoying Aya

Aya

Pronunciation: *Eye-Uh*
Alias: The Queen's Eyes

Role: The Queen of Tala's Third-in-Command, Spymaster of the Dyminara
Description: Short with subtle curves, pale skin and pale blue eyes that Will says matches her icy disposition perfectly. Long, dark brown hair that she favors tying in a braid to keep it out of her face.
Zodiac Sign: Capricorn
Scent: Mint and evergreen
Favorite Color: Light gray
Favorite Food: Pa's meat pie
Favorite Leisurely Activity: Whittling or training with Tyr

Aidon

Pronunciation: *Ay-din*
Alias: None
Role: The Crown Prince of Trahir and General of His Majesty's armies
Description: Tall, lean build with brown skin and dark brown curly hair worn cropped close to his head. Warm brown eyes that seem to always have a hint of mischief in them.
Zodiac Sign: Leo
Scent: Burnt Embers
Favorite Color: Blue
Favorite Food: Fried fish found on the docks of Rinnia
Favorite Leisurely Activity: Archery, sailing, or attempting to paint with Josie and Vi (and failing miserably)

Will

Glossary

Anima: Visya with life and death affinity
Aquine: God of water
the Athatis: The sacred wolves who protect the Dyminara and the Kingdom of Tala
Auqin: Visya with water affinity
the Bellare: Rebel group in Trahir that resists the modernization of the kingdom
Caeli: Visya with air affinity
Cero: God of earth
the Conoscenza: The book of the gods, used by Visya to worship the Nine Divine
Decachiré: The dark-affinity work that strives for limitless power
the Dawning: Celebration of Saint Evie and her sacrifice that rid the realm of the Decachiré
Diaforaté: Visya who siphon power to create the raw power they had before the War
Dyminara: The Crown's elite force of Visya warriors, scholars, and spies who serve the Kingdom of Tala
Genemai: Birth of Magic festival
Hepha: Goddess of flame
Incend: Visya with fire affinity
Maraciana: Libraries of the Saj that study affinities
***mi couera*:** Term of endearment in the Old Language, "my heart"
Mora: Goddess of fate
Nikatos: God of war
Order of the Corpsoma: Visya with physical affinities
Order of the Dultra: Visya with elemental affinities
Order of the Espri: Visya with mind, emotion, and sensation affinities

Pathos: God of sensation
Persi: Visya with persuasion affinity
***Phanmata*:** In the Old Language, "the lingering ghosts of nightmares"
Pysar: Trahir celebration of the coming spring and the delicacies that established the kingdom's place in trade
Sage: Goddess of wisdom
Saj: Visya with advanced knowledge affinity
Saudra: Goddess of persuasion
Sensainos: Visya with sensation and emotion affinity
Terra: Visya with earth affinity
the Tría: The Crown's three most trusted Dyminara
the Vaguer: Devout worshippers of Saint Evie who were excommunicated from the Maraciana
Velos: God of wind
the Ventaleh: Bitter winter wind of the north; said to be a reminder from the gods that they hold the power to cleanse the world
Visya: Mortal with a kernel of godlike power
Zeluus: Visya with strength affinity

While you wait for your copy of
The Curse of Sins, check out another exciting
fantasy world introduced in
Maxym M. Martineau's

KINGDOM of EXILES

**My heart wasn't part of the deal when
I bargained for my life,
But assassins so rarely keep their word.**

Exiled Charmer Leena Edenfrell is running out of time. Empty pockets forced her to sell her beloved magical beasts—an offense punishable by death—and now there's a price on her head. With the realm's most talented murderer-for-hire nipping at her heels, Leena makes Noc an offer he can't refuse: powerful mythical creatures in exchange for her life.

Plagued by a curse that kills everyone he loves, Noc agrees to Leena's terms in hopes of finding a cure. Never mind that the dark magic binding the assassin's oath will eventually force him to choose between Leena's continued survival…and his own.

1

leena

BY THE TIME EVENING FELL, THREE THINGS WERE CERTAIN: the gelatinous chunks of lamb were absolute shit, my beady-eyed client was hankering for more than the beasts in my possession, and someone was watching me.

Two out of the three were perfectly normal.

I slid the meat to the side and propped my elbows against the heavy plank table. My client lasted two seconds before his gaze roved to the book-shaped locket dangling in my cleavage. Wedging his thick fingers between the collar of his dress tunic and his neck, he tugged gently on the fabric.

"You have what I came for?" His heavy gold ring glinted in the candlelight. It bore the intricate etching of a scale: Wilheim's symbol for the capital bank. A businessman. A rare visitor in Midnight Jester, my preferred black-market tavern. My pocket hummed with the possibility of money, and I fingered the bronze key hidden there.

"Maybe." I nudged the metal dinner plate farther away. "How did you find me?" Dez, the bartender, sourced most of my clients, but brocade tunics and Midnight Jester didn't mingle.

I shifted in the booth, the unseen pair of eyes burrowing

farther into the back of my head. Faint movement from the shadows flickered into my awareness. Movement that should have gone unnoticed, but I'd learned to be prepared for such things.

"Dez brought a liquor shipment to a bar I frequent in Wilheim. He said you could acquire things." He extracted his sausage fingers from the folds of his neck and placed his hands flat on the table.

Believable. Dez made a mean spiced liquor that he sold on the side—a cheap yet tasty alternative to the overpriced alcohol brewed within the safe confines of Wilheim. But that didn't explain the lurker.

Hidden eyes followed me as I scanned the tables. Cobweb-laden rafters held wrought-iron, candlelit chandeliers. Every rickety chair was occupied with regulars in grubby tunics, their shifty gazes accompanying hurried whispers of outlawed bargains. Who here cared about me? A Council member? A potential client?

My temple throbbed, and I forced myself to return my client's gaze. "Like a Gyss."

The man sat upright. Yellow teeth peeked around chapped lips in an eager smile. "Yes. I was told you have one available."

"They don't come cheap."

He grimaced. "I know. Dez said it would cost me one hundred bits."

One hundred? I tossed a sidelong glance to Dez. Elbow-deep in conversation with a patron at the bar, he didn't notice. One hundred was high for a Gyss. He'd done me a solid. I could've handed over the key right then and there, but I had a rare opportunity on my hands: a senseless businessman in a dry spell looking for luck. Why else would he want a Gyss?

"One-fifty."

He launched to his feet, nearly upending the table, and his outburst grabbed the attention of every delinquent in the place. Dez raised a careful eyebrow, flexing his hands for effect, and the businessman sheepishly returned to his seat. He cleared his throat, and his fingers retreated to the thick folds of his neck. "One-fifty is high."

Crossing my arms behind my head in an indolent lean, I shrugged. "Take it or leave it."

"I'll find someone else. I don't need to be swindled."

"Be my guest." I nodded to the quiet tables around us. "Though none of them will have it for you now, if ever. They're not like me."

He hissed a breath. "Are all Charmers this conniving?"

I leaned forward, offering him my best grin and a slow wink. "The ones you'll deal with? Hell yes."

"Shit." He pinched his nose. "All right. One-fifty. But this Gyss better work. Otherwise, you'll have to find a way to make it up to me." With obvious slowness, he moved his fingers to his chin, tracing the length of his rounded jaw with his thumb. A faint gleam coursed through his gaze, and I crossed my ankles to keep myself from kicking him under the table. I needed the money, and I didn't want to dirty my new boots with his groin.

I barely kept the growl from my voice. "I can assure you the Gyss will grant your wish. One every six months."

"Excellent." He extended his hand, waiting for the shake to seal the deal.

"You know Gyss need payment for every wish, correct?"

His hand twitched. "Yeah, yeah. Fulfill a request, get a wish."

"And I'm not responsible for what the Gyss requests. That's on the beast, not on me."

"Fine. Get on with it already before Sentinels ransack this shithole."

Sentinels? He wished. The capital's muscle-bound soldiers wouldn't come near this scourge. The festering dark woods of the Kitska Forest were crammed flush against the west side of Midnight Jester. The errant, bone-shattering calls of monsters scraping through the air were enough to deter even the bravest of men.

No, Sentinels would never come here.

I clasped the businessman's outstretched hand. Clammy skin slicked along my palm, and a chill crawled up my arm. He moved away, reaching into his pocket for a velvet coin purse. As he pulled at the leather strings, a handful of silver chips and gold autrics clanked against the table.

One hundred and fifty bits. Funny how pebble-size pieces of flat metal carried such weight. Those of us living outside of Wilheim's protection had to fight for our coin. Ration our supplies. My last bits had gone to a much-needed new pair of leather boots. This man probably had fine silk slippers for every occasion.

With this kind of money, I'd have the chance to get something much more important than footwear. I slid my hand into my pocket and extracted a bronze key. Power vibrated from the metal into my palm, and I shot the businessman another glance. "Are you familiar with the Charmer's Law?"

His eyes skewered the key. "Buying and selling beasts is strictly forbidden—I know."

I rolled the key between my forefinger and thumb. "Not that. The Charmer's Law is meant to protect the beasts. If I find out you're mistreating this Gyss, I have the right to kill you. In any way I deem fit."

The man's face blanched, sweat dampening the collar of his tunic. "You're joking."

"I don't joke about beasts." I dropped the key on the table. Offering him a wolfish smile, I cocked my head to the side. "Still interested?"

He wavered for only a breath, then made a mad dash for the key. Thick hands pressed it flush to his breast pocket. "That won't be necessary. I'll treat the Gyss right."

As he pushed away from the table, he offered a parting nod. I jutted my chin out and kept my expression tight.

"Think twice before wishing. The consequences can be extreme." A familiar sliver of unease threaded through me. I hated dealing in Gyss, but his needs seemed straightforward enough. Money. Power. He'd never be able to fulfill the boon the Gyss would require for more.

This Gyss wouldn't be used against me. Not like before. The breadth of their ability was dependent on their master, and this man didn't have the aptitude for true chaos. No, my exiled existence would be safe a couple hundred years yet. There were Charmers who lived well into their late two hundreds. At the ripe age of twenty-nine, I had plenty of time.

The invisible daggers, courtesy of my mystery lurker, dug deeper into my back. Maybe I was overestimating my life span.

Tracking the businessman's escape, I settled into the booth's cushions to count my coins. No need to rush with the stalker's eyes on me. A thief, maybe? Bits were hard to come by, and I had enough to get me to the south coast and back with room to spare. The Myad, and the opportunity to prove my worth to my people, was within my reach.

I just needed to acquire the blood of a murderer—given freely, with no strings attached. It was a necessary ingredient for the Myad's taming, and something that wouldn't happen in Midnight Jester where bartering patrons couldn't distinguish favor from paycheck. I'd deal with it in Ortega Key. For now, I needed to get there before the beast disappeared.

"You taking off?" Dez sidled into the opposite side of the booth, a toothy grin pulling the jagged scar running from his earlobe to his chin tight. With a square jaw and a nose broken one too many times, he had a rugged charm about him. "It's nice having you around."

I toyed with one of the silver chips. Living above the tavern had its perks. Giving Dez a quick appraisal, my mind flashed back to the night before when we'd been tangled in the sheets. A carnal release with none of the attachments, at least for me. We'd never broached that discussion, but I often caught his gaze lingering when it shouldn't have. I'd have to deal with that eventually. There was only so much of myself I was willing to give.

"I'll only be gone for a short while. There's been a rare beast sighting in the south, and if I hang around here, I'll miss it." I reached for my coin purse and slid my earnings off the table.

"You know you don't have to prove anything to anyone here." Voice low, he let his gaze wander from head to head. "Hell, you're easily the best person in this establishment."

"In your eyes." My people would rather welcome a flesh-eating Tormalac into their homes than allow me back into our sacred grounds. "Charmers are only as strong as the beasts they keep. I have to be prepared."

"Prepared for what?" Dez asked. I knew what he wanted. A little bit of honesty. An ounce of trust. I just couldn't cave. There was a reason I was the only Charmer for miles around, and telling him the truth meant he could be used to find me. The Charmers Council had worse rulings than exile.

"I'll come back. You know I love this place."

"You know you love me." Another glimmer of hope.

"And you know I don't do love." I leaned in, a slow smile claiming my face. "But that doesn't mean I don't enjoy your company."

His eyes shone. "I'll take that. For now."

Heat ignited in my stomach. Maybe a few more hours wouldn't hurt. "Can Belinda watch the bar?" All thumbs with her head in the clouds, the bar maiden skipped across the floor, sloshing frothy beers and ales as she went. She couldn't handle a serving tray to save her life, but her tits raked in money Dez couldn't ignore.

He didn't bother to look away and check. "She'll manage."

"Good." As I made a move to stand, a high-pitched whine

sliced through my mind, and my feet cemented to the floor. Iky—my camouflaged beast I kept on hand during all black-market dealings. With senses sharper than a Sentinel's blade, he would've been able to discern any shift in the tavern's close quarters. We'd had a few brushes with two-bit murderers and thieves before. Nothing he couldn't handle. It looked like my unseen stalker was going to make his move after all. "Actually, we'll have to revisit that idea."

I scoured the tables. By all appearances, everything was fine. No one jumped. No one made a move to block the bar's only door. The regulars I'd grown to know over the years were neck-deep in their own worlds and not the least bit interested in my dealings. But with the weighted stare abruptly gone and the body count the same, something was definitely off.

"What? Why?" Dez shifted uncomfortably in the booth.

"Any shady characters in recently?"

He raised a brow. "Seriously?"

"Shadier than usual."

All humor wiped from his voice. "What's going on?"

"I'm being watched. Or I was. Iky noticed a shift."

Dez's hardened gaze spied the lopsided coatrack tucked against the wall. Forgotten threadbare coats clung to the hooks like leaves that wouldn't die. It was Iky's favorite place to lurk. Dez discovered Iky once when he most unceremoniously tossed another left-behind cloak and missed. A floating red garment gave even the regulars a scare.

"All right. Promise me you'll take care?"

"Of course." I rested my hand on his shoulder. "I'll be back before you know it."

"Sure." Dez stood, spreading his hands wide and gesturing to the crowd. "I just came up with a new special, folks! Cured pig with red flakes." A signal only local outlaws would truly understand: danger, potential spy.

For a moment, everyone stiffened. Eyes darted in

erratic patterns before the slow murmuring of mundane conversation—weather, the royal family's upcoming ball, anything other than what we were all here for—flitted through the air. With his coded warning in effect, Dez took up his place behind the counter, polishing glasses with one eye on the door and the other on his patrons.

Always assume they're snitches. Dez's previous warning rattled through my brain as I reached for the busted iron doorknob, a still-invisible Iky right on my heels. How long had my deal with the businessman taken? I'd stationed Iky behind me before that, which meant his hours in our plane were waning. I'd have to send him back to the beast sanctuary soon. With no time for delay, I pushed through the door and met the evening air with guarded eyes.

Staying in the tavern wasn't an option. What if the Charmers Council had finally caught on to my crimes? I couldn't jeopardize Dez or his establishment. This place was a haven for those who had nowhere else to go. Myself included.

I glanced east in the direction of Wilheim, our capital city. I'd never had the opportunity to pass through those gleaming white walls of marble and diamond. Stretching tall to kiss the underside of the clouds, the concentric, impenetrable towers guarded an impressive mountain where the royal family lived. Where the fortunate lived. Most of us scavenging on the outskirts were banned for one reason or another from passing through the magic-clad ivory gates.

Shaking my head, I quickened my pace. Though the royal family's jurisdiction technically covered the continent of Lendria, everyone knew that law didn't apply past those glistening stones. Out here, magic and darkness and questionable dealings reigned supreme. Iky let out another private whine, and my gaze jumped to the forest line. My stalker was back. Invisible to me, but not hidden from my beast's senses. My destination was the train station, but if this lurker was from the Council, I didn't want them getting a whiff of the Myad and stealing my beast. I needed to deal with the threat first.

I know you're there, creep.

Flipping the collar of my jacket up, I picked my way down the winding dirt path away from Wilheim and the train depot. Lure them out, trap them, free and clear. Easy enough. The descending sun crept toward the riotous treetops of the Kitska Forest. Steeped in shadows, the dark leaves shivered in the dusk air, and a small whistling met my ears. The sheer density of the woods invited a certain level of hysteria to the unfamiliar—out here, one couldn't tell the difference between a pair of eyes and oversize pinesco pods.

Needles and mulch crunched beneath my knee-high boots, and my feet screamed at the ache of unbroken leather pressing against my joints. Soon enough, I'd wear the boots in and be wishing for more bits to replace the holes.

A twig snapped in the distance, and I splayed out my right hand. One of the forest's many monsters, or my stalker?

The Charmer's symbol, a barren rosewood tree on the back of my right hand, exploded to life. A crisscross network of roots inked down my knuckles and wrapped around my fingertips in gnarled directions. Iky responded to the flux of power and distanced himself from me. Searching. Pursuing. The lack of his watery scent left me unnerved, but I needed to give my lurker a chance to strike. Then Iky would snare him.

A frigid breath skated along the back of my neck.

I whirled, thrusting my hand forward and focusing on the well of power humming beneath the surface. But Iky had done his job without fault. Just beyond my reach stood a tall, slender man dressed entirely in black. With a voluminous pompadour, thin-rimmed silver specs, and freshly polished dress shoes, he looked suited for a night in Wilheim—not a stroll in the Kitska Forest. His arms pressed flush to his sides, he was rendered immobile, and an unused, glittering black knife limply dangled from his gloved fingertips.

I dropped my hand, and the ink work along my skin receded. "Iky, be a dear."

Iky materialized at last. Tall and amorphous with see-through skin, he adjusted his body constitution, color, and shape to suit my needs. With elongated arms, Iky had wrapped the man in a bundle, pressing him so tightly his chest struggled to inflate.

"Give him a bit more breathing room."

Iky loosened his arms, and the man let out a sharp gasp. The shadows clinging to the forest's limbs seemed to darken.

"Who are you?"

No response. Harsh ice-green eyes speared me. The high planes of his face sharpened, and a small vein throbbed along his temple.

"Why were you trying to kill me?" I glanced pointedly at the knife. He dropped it to the ground, and Iky nudged it toward me with a newly formed extremity. It receded as quickly as it appeared, folding back into his body mass with a quiet splash.

The man pursed thin lips, and a rattling breeze ushered in more thin shadows. It was no secret that these woods were cursed, but this darkness was thicker. Unfamiliar. Something else was going on here.

Deal with the threat, and get the hell out.

"Iky?" I nodded toward my beast. Iky's arms tightened, and the man sputtered. "If you don't tell me something, this is only going to get worse."

The sharp snap of a splintering rib broke the silence. He wheezed, words I couldn't make out intermingling with pained gasps. I glanced at Iky, and he stopped.

Murder dripped from my would-be killer's glare. "I'd never dream of telling you a damn thing."

My brows furrowed. "That so? Iky, you know what to do." A new extremity formed, wrapping its way around the man's pinky finger. With a sharp and fluid motion, Iky snapped it.

The man swallowed a cry, face gone parchment-pale as I studied him. He wasn't a familiar presence in Midnight Jester. Most of the men and women who stumbled through the tavern were scarred, reeking of bad choices and worse fates, but this man? From his immaculately trimmed hair to the smooth glow of his clean skin, everything about him screamed privileged.

I resisted the urge to glance back toward Wilheim. "Who are you?" Taking a few steps forward, I studied his black garb. Long-sleeved, button-up tunic. Satin, no less. Slim-cut trousers hemmed just about his shoes. Not nearly ethereal enough to be a Charmer. Certainly not brilliant enough to be a Sentinel. Their armor threatened to outshine even the brightest diamond.

He glowered. "I don't see the need to repeat myself." In my peripheral vision, onyx tendrils slithered across the forest floor and edged toward me. A heartbeat pulsed from their swirling depths. Whatever monster watched us from the forest, we were clearly running out of time.

"You're too scrawny to be a Sentinel, though you certainly have the arrogance of one." I inched away from the cursed wood. "You don't have the emblem of a Charmer, so you're not one of my kind." Thank the gods for that.

"Are you done fishing?"

"No." I flicked my wrist, and Iky broke another finger. The man's scream rattled pinesco pods, sending misshapen dead leaves to the ground. Shadows devoured them whole. "You were trying to kill me, which means you're likely a murderer for hire."

A slow smile dared to grace his lips. "You won't make it out of this alive."

Oh, but I would. And a new idea was brewing in the back of my brain. One that had to do with favors and blood and the golden opportunity standing right in front of me.

I started to circle him, assessing his potential. The

problem was, offering freedom in exchange for his blood didn't exactly mean the blood was "freely given." Semantics, but in the game of taming beasts, semantics were everything. "And why is that?"

"Because I'm a member of Cruor."

The world slipped out from beneath my feet. Heavy ringing filled my ears, and the treetops spun together. I'd assumed assassin from the get-go, but *Cruor*? Who would go to such lengths as to hire the undead?

Realization struck hard and fast, and my gaze jerked to the pooling mass of darkness near his feet. He leached shadows from the corners and hidden crevices of the forest. Even the once-solid blade had dispersed, joining the curling tendrils around my captive. They licked his skin and gathered in his aura, waiting to do his bidding. That wasn't some Kitska monster gathering the darkness—it was *him*.

He'd been toying with me all this time, and I had seconds to react.

"Iky, serrated. *Now*." Iky shifted, coating his arms with thousands of miniscule barbs that punctured the man's clothing and skin, and locked him in place. Blood trickled from a multitude of pinprick holes. Gleaming red droplets that wormed their way out and oozed down his ink-black coat like veining through marble. Blood I couldn't use. The first wasted rivulets dripped from his fingers and splattered against the gravel path. He watched them with fierce eyes, and the dark wisps receded. Good. At least he had enough sense to realize when he was beaten. "If you try to dissipate on me, you'll end up as mincemeat. Why am I on Cruor's shit list?"

Irritation tightened his face as my beast and I so deftly turned the tables. "I'm not going to dignify that with a response. As if I'd tell a *job* the details of my work."

Egotism, even in the face of death. The Charmers Council had to be behind this. If they'd somehow caught on to my underhanded dealings, they'd sooner hire someone to kill me than leave the sanctity of Hireath. But Cruor? I chewed on the inside of my cheek. Charmers valued all life. Execution was rare. Hiring someone who walked with the shadows all but guaranteed my death. With me already sentenced to a lifelong exile for a crime I most certainly did *not* commit, they must have felt a more extreme response was appropriate. No chance to plea my case. No chance to return to my people.

Gripping my hands into fists, I glared at the assassin. "Gods be damned. Killing was not on my agenda today."

A brittle laugh devoid of humor scraped through the air. "If you kill me, another will be sent."

He was right, of course, and I prayed my next words wouldn't be my death sentence. I needed this bounty gone. I had business in the south I couldn't postpone. The Myad was my only hope of ever going *home*. "Then take me to Cruor."

His green eyes widened a fraction. "Your logic escapes me."

"Good thing it's not your job to understand how I think. Take me to Cruor, or Iky will end you. Plain and simple."

"As if you could kill me."

Iky snapped another finger without my prompting, and the man hissed.

"What were you saying?" I asked.

"Fine." He rotated his head, peering around trees before jutting his chin to the left. "You won't like this."

Tendrils exploded in a swirling vortex that blanketed out the Kitska Forest. Rivers of black surged beneath our feet, and my stomach turned itself inside out. We were thrust forward, and yet we hadn't moved a muscle. Intertwining shadows sped through us, around us, careening us toward a destination I couldn't even begin to pinpoint. Tears pricked the corners of my eyes, and I sucked in a breath.

And then we came to a screeching halt, the outside world slamming back into us as the darkness abruptly receded. I white-knuckled a fist against my stomach and glared at the assassin in Iky's arms. His smirk was maddening.

The comfort of Midnight Jester was now what felt like a world away.

Slowly, I unfurled my hand and caught sight of my Charmer's symbol, weighing Iky's branch and my apparent insanity against his time. Every beast had a weakness, and his was a shelf life. Two hours of strength for every twenty-two hours of sleep. With every minute that passed, Iky's limb retreated to the base until it would fade from existence, forcibly returning him to the beast realm to regain his stamina.

I had fifteen minutes, give or take.

Stepping to the side, I gestured to the woods. "Let's get this over with. Iky, pick him up." His hooks retracted a fraction, and Iky cradled the man to his chest like an overgrown child.

The assassin scoffed, unintelligible curses dropping from his lips.

The void had transported us close, but I still couldn't see the hidden death grotto known as Cruor. Yet I could feel it. The weight of eyes and shadows. My hairs stood on end as we made our way through the suffocating foliage, darkness dripping from limbs like tacky sap. Above us, birds squawked and feathers scraped together as they took flight, swirling upward and chasing the setting sun into the horizon. A heavy branch creaked. A shadow more human than night rocketed from one tree to the next. The assassin stared after the figure without saying a word, but smugness laced his expression. One of his brethren, then, going to alert the others.

Icy hands wrenched my heart, and I gripped the book-shaped locket hanging about my neck—the miniature bestiary all Charmers carried—and begged the gods for favorable odds. I could have waited. Could have called forth another beast, but Iky's strength took a serious toll on my power, and my arsenal that could fight off the legendary might of Cruor was small. Besides, summoning another could be the difference between a peaceful negotiation and a declaration of war.

The latter I would surely lose. I needed every chance to run I could get, in case negotiations went south.

Mangled iron fencing battled against the overgrowth of the cursed forest, marking the edge of Cruor's property, and I paused at the gates. In the distance, the evening sky birthed a manor shrouded in darkness. Alone on a hill and two stories tall, with more windows than my eyes could count, the guild was just shy of a castle.

Slate black and covered in vibrant red gems, a rycrim core glittered from between neatly trimmed hedges and the side of the house. Magic energy pulsed from it in an invisible dome over the mansion.

I'd begged Dez to invest in a rycrim core for months. Changing every candle by hand, warming the bathwater over a fire—I wanted the simplicity of self-lighting fixtures, a faucet that immediately poured scalding water. But convenience cost more bits than we could afford to spare. Murder apparently paid well.

Iky whined aloud, a low vibration thrumming through the air. Less than ten minutes left.

With a heavy breath, I pushed the gate open and tried to shake the eerie grating of hinges as I stared down the winding path leading me straight to death's door.

Acknowledgments

I HAVE DREAMT OF BEING AN AUTHOR SINCE I WAS ELEVEN years old. Seeing this dream come true with *The Curse of Saints* has truly been the most incredible, surreal experience, and absolutely would not be possible without the help of so many wonderful people!

First and foremost, thank you to Jessica Killingley, the best agent and friend any person could ask for. Jessica, there are not enough words in the universe to capture the essence that is you. You are my biggest champion, my fiercest defender, and the net that appears when I jump. Thank you for encouraging me to pursue this story, for pushing me whenever I wanted to stare at the cursor and cry, and for agreeing to go on this incredible journey with me. You make dreams come true.

Thank you also to Jason, James, Joanna, and the entire bks Agency team for your ongoing support in making this dream a reality, and for the warmest welcome a new author could possibly have into this world.

There is no way this version of TCOS would exist without Rebecca, my incredible editor! Becs, thank you for believing in this story, for loving Aya as much as I do, and for helping me transform TCOS into the best story it could possibly be. I still cannot believe you canceled your entire birthday to ensure you got to work on *The Curse of Saints*, and that you willingly walked through the grocery store talking about knives and stab wounds with me on the phone! You are undeniably incredible.

Thank you to the entire Penguin Michael Joseph team, whose passion for TCOS is overwhelming and infectious. Jorgie, Steph, Sophie, Eugenie, Clio, Nick, and Jane…you have made my debut author experience a fairy tale. I cannot thank you enough.

A huge thank you also to Mary and the entire Casablanca team at Sourcebooks for your enthusiasm for sharing Aya and Will's story with the U.S. and Canada, and your willingness to jump right in!

This book also wouldn't be possible without the incredible team of sensitivity readers at Writing Diversely. Thank you for your resources, feedback, and time in helping me make TCOS representative of the diverse world we live in a respectful and accurate way. And thank you to Anna, who gave my first developmental edit report. Your feedback was crucial in transforming this story, and while I *did* take a day to cry about it, it was exactly what I needed to hear to turn this into the book it is today!

I am eternally grateful to the authors who drew me in to fantasy and inspire me daily. Thank you Sabaa Tahir, Victoria Aveyard, Ayana Gray, Leigh Bardugo, and Mary Pearson for your brilliant work.

I am constantly amazed by the community of readers who flocked to *The Curse of Saints* long before the book was even finished. Thank *you*, reader, for picking up this book.

Thank you, Yousr, for being my first beta reader and biggest encourager. I am so glad TikTok brought us together! Thank you, Kendall, for your instant friendship and your pep talks! And thank you to the BookTok and Bookstagram communities, who helped put *The Curse of Saints* on the map, and who encouraged me to "finish the dang book already!" Your support, passion, and excitement changed my life, and I cannot imagine a better community to share Aya and her friends with.

And speaking of friends…I would be incredibly lost without mine.

Thank you, Ellie, for answering every single call, text, and email. Your advice throughout this journey has kept me going in my lowest moments, and I will be forever grateful for you telling me to remember to tell the story that was on my heart to tell.

Evan, you have been by my side through every major milestone over the last nine years. From hiring me for my first writing job, to coworking on our businesses down by the river, to reflecting on life at the Battery, to writing books and agonizing over plot holes, I cannot express how grateful I am to have you in my life. Thank you for being an incredible friend today and always. You are simply the best.

Thank you, Rhonda and Jonnice, for celebrating every single part of this journey with me, and for loving me as I am. I am blessed to do life with you two.

Shaylene, I cannot have dreamt of a better way to celebrate this book than with you. Thank you for the FaceTime calls, the belly laughs, and for being a shining example of what a soul sister is.

Jensen, thank you for loving me for twenty-eight years, and for being my rock always. You are my foundation, boogie.

Thank you, Liz and Remy, for, your constant support, and always understanding when I say I have to stay in and write! I'm lucky to have friends like you.

Laura, thank you for your years of friendship, for my lavender goodie bag, and for always being willing to dream with me.

Brad, you talked me off the ledge when I got my editorial report (and fifty other ledges before that), and I'm incredibly grateful. Thank you for always believing in me, especially in the times when I don't believe in myself.

To my mentor, Cheryl, thank you for your incredible advice and reminders that it's okay if it's a tequila instead of champagne day!

And thank you to every single one of my friends who had a hand in this journey… Tiffany, for always encouraging me to go after my biggest, boldest dreams; Jenn, for being my first ever "online" friend; Topsie, for every single hype-up you've ever given me; Tomasha, for helping me see myself outside of work; Jamar, for reminding me to be brave out there on social; Emily, for introducing me to fan fiction and Scrivener; Amanda and Sam, for ignoring my request to force me to focus on another book instead of start this one; Sierra, for your thoughtful beta feedback; Alexandria, for every reminder that God is with me; Alec, for championing me always; and Tyler, David, Brooke, Shelby, and Sirmantha, for being incredible friends and encouraging me to keep on going and dreaming.

I absolutely would not be here without the incredible support of my family, who is my everything. Thank you, Mom and Dad, for always encouraging me to chase my dreams and to never settle, and for pretending you didn't know I was staying up until 3 a.m. reading when I had school the next day.

Billy, you have always had my back and been my role model. Thank you for sending me funny Reels, always answering the phone, feeding me, expanding my cocktail knowledge, staying up until 3 a.m. to try to catch Santa, and for reminding me to say in touch with our childlike wonderment. When life is at its hardest, you are my safe place to run to. You always were and always will be my hero. I love you so much.

Thank you, Courtney, for helping me navigate this new career, butter noodles, half workdays and half pool days, dress shopping and baking shows, and years and years of friendship that I could never capture on a single page. I love you more than I love falling asleep on your couch while trying to stay up and watch TV, and we all know how much I love that.

Thank you, Morgan, for your excitement about this book, your hugs, your deep conversations and friendship, and for always feeding me when I come over! I love you and am so glad you joined our family!

Mollie, words can't capture our bond. Thank you for being my best friend; for our daily FaceTimes, for helping with every part of this journey, for Ormsby's and tapas and birthday parties and trivia. And thank you most of all for being a shining example of how to be true to yourself in a world that asks us to be anything but. I love you, peanut.

To Bubbie and Squish, thank you for giving me the role I love most. Being an author is incredible, but being your Auntie Kate is the greatest honor of my life, and I love you both more than words will ever be able to explain.

Thank you to my fur babies, Porter, Tilly, Duke, and Clara, for your constant snuggles and kisses.

And last but not least, thank you to my other half, my soulmate, my best friend. Cassie, this story would not exist without you, but far more importantly, *I* would not be who I am without you. There is no one else I'd rather drive through the Scottish Highlands, gamble in Vegas, trudge through New York, gallivant through London, sleep in the airport, float in muddy lake water, or sit on the couch with. You are the Tova to my Aya. I would follow you anywhere—no matter how far the fall. I love you to the moon and back. Thank you for being the best friend a person could ask for.

About the Author

KATE DRAMIS is an Atlanta-based writer whose obsession with fantasy worlds and escaping into a good love story eventually drove her to chase her dreams of being an author.

Inspired by a dream about a woman calling down lightning to save a friend, *The Curse of Saints* is Kate's debut fantasy novel and the first in the trilogy.

When she's not busy writing banter that makes her laugh in an embarrassingly loud fashion, you can find her impulse-booking her latest travel adventure, snuggling with her three dogs and cat, or tormenting her growing legion of readers on katelyndramis.com, TikTok, and Instagram with vague book teasers.